By: Aya Walksfar

Published by Wild Haven Press

Copyright 2014

This book is a work of fiction. With the exception of recognized historical figures, the characters in this novel are fictional. Any resemblance to actual persons, living or dead, is purely coincidental.

Copyright 2014 by Aya Walksfar
1st Edition

All rights reserved. In accordance with the U.S. Copyright Act of 1976, the scanning, uploading, and electronic sharing of any part of this book without the permission of the publisher constitute unlawful piracy and theft of the author's intellectual property. Thank you for your support of the author's rights.

Cover Art: Tamara Sands
Editing: Lee Porche
Print Formatter: Stevan Ray Richards Jr.
EBook Formatting: Stevan Ray Richards Jr.

This book is licensed for your personal enjoyment only. This book may not be re-sold or given away to other people. If you would like to share this book with another person, please purchase an additional copy for each recipient. If you're reading this book and did not purchase it, or it was not purchased for your use only, then please purchase your own copy. Thank you for respecting the hard work of this author.

ISBN: 978-0-9904602-7-5

PRAISE FOR THE NOVELS OF AYA WALKSFAR

SPECIAL CRIMES TEAM SERIES:
SKETCH OF A MURDER, BOOK 1

▪Detective in Special Assault Unit: "Loving the book! Especially the killer talking in first person...great!"

▪JesterDev, Amazon Reviewer: "Grab yourself a comfortable seat because once you pick up this book you'll find yourself unwilling to put it down."

▪Debbie, Amazon Reviewer: "A strong plot and well developed characters makes for a very good read. If you like murder, suspense and intrigue this book is for you."

▪Gunnar Angel Lawrence: "A great story involving characters you come to care about, in a struggle against an adversary who seems to be two steps ahead of them the whole way. It's an all-round good read for those who enjoy the thrill of the chase and the twists and turns of a murder mystery."

STREET HARVEST, Book 2, Special Crimes Team

▪Anonymous (March 6, 2014): "Her best yet!"

▪Booklover: "I have been a fan of Aya Walksfar since I read "Dead Men and Cats." Since then I've read all her books. Every one of them is good, but this is the best. I've never read a book about crime solving that was so full of appropriately-related and meaningful "other things." She brings in Native American spirituality, a young but wise-beyond-her-years seer, and strong children, to name a few of those "other things." And The Sisterhood--my favorite!"

OTHER MYSTERIES: DEAD MEN AND CATS, a novella

- Cate Agosta: "It is fast paced and laced with twists and turns that make you think."

- K. Ree: "I loved the characters; they were so very real."

AWARD WINNING LITERARY NOVEL: GOOD INTENTIONS, Second Edition

- Jeb and Kathy Harris: "This is an intriguing coming of age book with an element of mystery. The protagonist's struggle is very relatable, whatever your background or age."

- Mohadoha "mohadoha" (Qatar): "Really strong female characters and real struggles. Love, loss, family and secrets: a complex tale for complex characters. Don't want to say too much more to avoid spoilers! "I look forward to more books by this author."

- Booklover: "Great book on many levels. I enjoyed the writing style used for this novel. It was brilliant to write in the first person from many different points of view. I felt as though I knew and understood each character."

Dedication

No book is written alone.

My mother and my grandmother first saw the value of my work. Their encouragement laid the groundwork for what I accomplish today. Their Spirits still guide me from the Other Side.

My sister, Lois Dodson, continues what my mother and grandmother began: she gives me constant encouragement and has an unwavering belief in the value of my work.

I would be a ship with no rudder without my wife, Deva. She is the whisper in the night when everything seems so dark; she is the laughter that lifts me above the difficult times; she is my heart.

Beta Readers are an author's BEST FRIEND! I am truly fortunate to have access to the invaluable feedback from:

My wife, Deva, my first line—and frequently also a second line—Beta Reader. She is the one who catches timeline and other glaring breaks in logic.

My second line of Beta Readers give the final 'okay'; because of them, my work is more powerful, more real. Thank you, Brenda Nettleship, a wonderful author in her own right; Ruby Standing Deer, best-selling author of a series about ancient Native Americans (Book 1: Circles, Book 2: Spirals, and Book 3: Stones); and my good friend, Barb Keogan.

Not every author is blessed with a fantastic editor who is also easy to work with; I am. Thank you, Lee Porche, for all of your hard work, for sharing your expertise, for not getting exasperated when I make the same mistake for the five thousandth time, and for encouraging me to become even better!

A cover is the first thing a reader will see. I want to thank my fantastic cover design artist, Tamara Sands, for making my book's cover outstanding.

Chapter 1

Two weeks ago, on July 15th, I turned eighteen. The child welfare system no longer had any interest in me, nor would they continue to financially support me. The last check from them arrived yesterday. George Hellerson, my foster father, drank it up last night. His hangover had kept him prostrate in bed until an hour ago.

Now, he cussed and slammed things around downstairs. I imagined that the kitchen resembled a disaster area—busted dishes, dented pots and pans. It usually appeared like a localized hurricane hit it after one of his rampages. Just so long as he didn't slam or bust up Miriam, my foster mother and his wife, I really didn't care. I felt sorry that Miriam had to clean up after the bastard, and that the things she had scrounged money to buy would have to be replaced, but there wasn't much I could do about it. And, Miriam wouldn't do anything about it.

At six-foot-two, George epitomized the word bully. I, Jazmine Wheeler, hated him. That was saying something. I didn't usually waste my time and energy on hating anyone. Never changed a thing, so why bother?

George, though, had hate down pat and hated me back with more energy than I put into even thinking about him. Fact is I think George hated everyone and everything. He perpetually scowled, snarled, and generally made himself unlovable—unlovable hell! It was difficult to stand the sight of him. Might have been why he hadn't held down a job for more than a few months since I'd moved in four years ago.

Well-muscled due to hours of jogging and working out, I only stood five-foot-six, but he feared me. Probably had a lot to do with the knife I carried, and slept with it under my pillow. George had gotten well acquainted with my little pig sticker a week after I first moved in. He had decided to pay me a middle-of-the-night visit.

His move on me hadn't been any different from the previous foster father I'd had. This time, though, I wasn't simply tucking tail and running off to avoid being raped. Sick of being on the short end of the stick, I figured if I had to leave I'd make someone pay.

To tell the truth, I couldn't see why either of them would bother trying to warm my bed. I certainly didn't consider myself good-looking. It wasn't like I was ugly, just that I had rather smallish breasts, and average legs. After hours of being outside, my face had tanned to a toasty brown. My best feature was my chestnut hair. Even with that, winning a beauty contest wasn't going to happen. Every morning the bathroom mirror confirmed what I already knew: dark brows heavy enough that I took ribbing from other girls for not thinning them, a nose that was mostly straight, maybe a little sharper than some but not greatly so, and lips that could've been a little fuller and more inviting. There were times I thought my lips got on the thin side from all the times I had to clamp them together to keep my mouth shut, and myself out of trouble.

Though I dislike violence, and am more prone to try to talk people down from their anger, my mom had taught me how to fight, and how to defend myself with a knife—B.M, before the meth got to her. That night when George snuck into my bedroom, he would've kicked me out for not putting out, except I threatened to make him sing soprano. Desperation must've shouted from my tense body and flared nostrils, the kind of desperation that causes bloodshed. Seattle, December is no time to live on the streets. Been there; done that. Ever since that night, four years ago, the man wanted me out of his house.

A week earlier, I'd rented a basement room complete with a miniscule bath that had a tiny, elbow-banging shower, a mini-sink, and a toilet. I'd bought a small microwave and a camper-size refrigerator that the store would deliver once I moved in. The big draw to the place was the private outside entrance. Unfortunately, my apartment wouldn't be ready for occupancy until tomorrow. I had hoped to stay one more night at my foster home.

George wanted me out. He stumbled into my room last night and demanded that I leave right then. "Like hell I'm going anywhere tonight, asshole," I told him as I cleaned under my

Run or Die!

fingernails with my knife. He glanced at the blade then staggered down the hall.

Now, the early afternoon sun shone through the window as the sound of Miriam's voice drifted up the stairs. She'd gone downstairs to plead with George to show some compassion. I could've told her to save her breath, except I didn't want to hurt her feelings. George did a great job of that all by himself. How such a nice woman wound up with such a self-centered, downright mean...no sense in completing that thought!

I'd never told Miriam about the attempted rape. At the time, I still smarted from having told my last foster mother about her husband only to be accused of lying. Mom had always said, "Best to tend to your own troubles, girl." Good advice I became determined to follow after that incident.

Pulling out another cardboard box, I shrugged to myself. Not much to pack, though I'd lived here since age fourteen. One of my earliest lessons after mom died dealt with material possessions. To accumulate material stuff—not that I'd ever owned much even when I lived with Mom—simply gave me more to lose as I bounced from one foster home to another; more I'd have to fight to keep. I chose my battles carefully, and most possessions didn't rate fighting over.

The dearth of possessions was fortuitous since I could fit it all in a couple of large locker. at the Greyhound Bus Station. Hated wasting money for a taxi, but I couldn't lug my backpack and three cardboard boxes that far.

My Word-A-Day journal went into my backpack. Loved that thing. Pages smudged and the hard cloth cover stained, I studied a word a day from it. When I reached the end, I started over again. I'd never written on the pages.

Miriam gave it to me a few months after I moved in. She said I didn't have to sound illiterate if I didn't want to. After that I tried hard to sound more like I thought she wanted me to and less like the streets. I loved the shock value: my looks (silver ring in my eyebrow; tattoo of a labrys—a double-headed axe—on my left upper arm, which stood out clearly during short sleeve weather; scruffy jeans; t-shirts with rude sayings; and worn hiking boots), and a vocabulary worthy of a school teacher.

Aya Walksfar

I pushed my hand into the slit in the bottom side of my mattress and retrieved the flat tin box. A picture of a German Shepherd dog embossed the top. Miriam and I had been out shopping for school clothes on a welfare budget the week before the first Christmas I'd spent with the Hellersons when we'd seen a cop with a beautiful black-and-tan German Shepherd. Like some little kid staring into the candy store window, I stood there on the sidewalk gaping after the dog.

I'd only ever had one dog: a stray I'd dragged home when I was eight, during a snowstorm with temperatures in the teens, an unusual occurrence in Seattle. After the weather turned decent, Mom and I walked the dog that I'd named Clarice to a vet clinic a few blocks away. Though Clarice had a gray muzzle, the vet pronounced her healthy. She said she had a German Shepherd, too, and had scratched under Clarice's chin while she'd given me tips on training.

I loved Clarice as passionately as she loved me. Six months before Mom died, Clarice—old when I'd found her—went to sleep and never woke up.

That first Christmas morning with Miriam, she fixed breakfast for the two of us while George slept off his drunk. After breakfast she handed me a tin box filled with homemade fudge. I hadn't expected any gifts. Who gives foster kids gifts? None of my other foster families had. Besides, George yelled at her all the time about spending money, so I knew she didn't have two cents more than what she absolutely needed to buy groceries. Still, she'd found a way to buy the box and acquire a pretty blue ribbon she tied in a bow around it. The last time I'd cried I was nine; Mom had nearly died from an overdose. That Christmas with Miriam, I clenched my jaw tight and blinked hard to keep the tears from spilling.

Those memories, like so many others, got shoved into the back of my mind as I popped the lid of the tin box open and removed the money I'd saved from odd jobs. Toward the last of her life, the meth beat down on Mom hard, but somehow she'd still found odd jobs, or a john willing to pay, to keep us going. I could still hear her voice: "We don't take charity. We work for what we get."

Run or Die!

This little stash, along with my current job at Micky D's, would hold me for a while. Before it ran out, I'd have a plan. Always thinking and planning, because when it came right down to it, I'd realized years ago I couldn't count on anyone out there to take care of me. Not even my mom.

I brushed a stray lock of my long, thick chestnut hair out of my eyes and made a mental note to get the split ends trimmed as soon as I got my next paycheck. Reddish-brown hair and gray eyes, real mixed up genetics there. Weird, too, since Mom's hair had been white-blonde and wispy; and her eyes had been a watery blue. When I was a little kid, I'd asked Mom what my father had looked like. She'd gotten all teary and ran into her bedroom and closed the door. That had been the last time I asked about my father.

I stuffed the bills into my wallet and stuck it back in the hip pocket of my skinny jeans. Carefully wrapping the tin box in a ragged hand towel, I put it in my backpack. In spite of the little glitch, like where I would spend the night, it had been a great day. Officially free of the System and glad of it. Even the squirrelly, too-hot-for-Seattle, July weather couldn't burn away my giddiness. Crazy weather for Seattle. I'd grown up expecting moderate temperatures even in the middle of summer. Global climate change undoubtedly. There were times I got down thinking about shit like that, so I stuffed it in the can't-do-a-damn-thing-about-it box and promptly forgot it. Can't fix it, forget it.

A tentative knock on the half-open door to my bedroom pulled my head around. Two strides across the small room and I swung the door completely open then ushered Miriam in. "Hey, I told you, you don't have to knock if the door's kinda open." She brushed past me and I softly closed the door. Miriam stood in the middle of the floor, the cracked linoleum looking as worn out as she did, her hands clasped in front of her.

The old housedress, shapeless and faded, hung off her bony shoulders and the hem touched below her knees. Iron gray had just about overwhelmed her shoulder-length, ash-blonde hair. A shorter cut would've looked nicer on her, framing a gently rounded face with interesting blue eyes and laugh wrinkles bracketing her mouth, in spite of the hell she lived in every day. But *he* wouldn't allow her to have it cut. The jerk.

The bare mattress sank into a familiar dip as I plopped on the edge of it and patted a spot next to me.

Miriam shuffled over and sighed as she sank down. I threw an arm around her shoulders, felt the protrusion of her collarbone, and gave her a little squeeze. "Hey, it's all right." I kissed her forehead and let go so I could rub circles on her back. *Damn it! She's lost more weight!* I could clearly feel her vertebrae.

She dabbed sad eyes with the corner of a paper towel she held wadded in her hand. "He's just gotten...unpredictable—these rages and him never wanting me to go anywhere—before the accident..."

A gentle breeze stirred the curtains at the only window in the room. Miriam had found a swathe of cloth at a Goodwill Store and had hand-sewn them. She was like that: always trying to find something to make my life a little bit better. Sometimes, I daydreamed that in a parallel universe somewhere, George didn't exist and Miriam was my mother.

Defeat sat like a lead weight in my chest. I tried to push it out with a sigh. "He is what he is, Miriam." I shoved to my feet and restlessly paced over to the window. I kept my back to her, unwilling to let her see the anger in my eyes. I hated feeling helpless. *Why can't she see that lumbering brute for what he is? Why does she stay with him? Once I'm gone, I know it's going to get worse for her. He already tested me the other night when he shoved her into the couch. Wonder if the idiot knows how close I came to showing him just what I thought of wife-beaters? What's going to happen to her?*

The heaviness in my chest kept my breaths shallow as I turned around to face her. It almost hurt me to look at her she seemed so fragile. The bones of her hands showed prominently through her dry, reddened skin. She twisted her thin fingers together in her lap.

Staring down at them, she declared softly, "You think he's always been like this." Her voice echoed the hopelessness apparent in her slumped shoulders and bent back.

Run or Die!

It hadn't exactly been a question, but I felt like I had to answer it anyway. I snatched the roll of shipping tape from the pressed-board dresser, and slapped a strip across the top of the last box. Rage churned in my gut, but she got enough of that from him. Deliberately I slowed my movements, pried open the grip of my anger and softened my shoulders. Deep breaths in, exhale slowly and evenly. Feeling more in control, I quietly said, "People's personalities don't change unless they've had a brain injury, Miriam. It wasn't his head that got crushed when he drunk himself into a stupor and hit that van full of kids; it was his leg."

I'd been at the Hellers for three weeks the first time Miriam and I had this discussion. The sounds of flesh hitting flesh had awakened me. The bottom half of the open staircase overlooked the living room. I crept down in time to witness George snatching Miriam up off the floor and backhanding her. She'd reeled across the room and bounced off the couch.

I'd never interfered with my mom's "dates" unless they got physical, and then I couldn't help but interfere. I blame it on the Before-Meth-Mom. She'd been like that, too. Couldn't stand by and watch a woman get slapped around.

That night I jumped the last three steps and grabbed his wrist as he reached for her again. A quick twist and a hip roll and good old George slammed to the floor on his back. My boot pressed against his throat. "Coward. I'm going to let you up then you can decide whether to get your ass kicked by me or to leave. Your choice." When I backed away, he scrambled to his feet and stormed from the house, not returning until late the following day.

I helped Miriam onto the couch then hurried to the bathroom and grabbed a washcloth. In the kitchen I popped the ice cube tray out of the freezer and loaded a Ziploc baggy with ice. Being careful, I wiped the blood from her face and handed her the ice pack. I left her on the couch while I made coffee and brought it in. In spite of her swollen lip and black eye, we talked for hours.

That's when she told me that eight months before I'd shown up, George had drunk a bit too much and had broadsided a van, smashing his leg. He hadn't sustained any other injuries. The gray light of dawn seeped in past the living room curtains before she finally admitted that even before the accident, George had had "quite the temper."

When he slunk home the following day, I met him out in the front yard. After our little "talk," he stopped hitting Miriam, just yelled and threw plates and destroyed some of her favorite knick-knacks. I despised the way he acted, but as long as he didn't use her for a punching bag I kept my nose out of their business.

How many times have we had this conversation since that night? I finished taping and set the box on top of the other two. Briefly, I wished I had enough meanness in me to tell her the absolute truth about George, about that midnight visit when I'd come to live with them, and about those women at the bar he frequented. It scared me that someday he'd bring home AIDS, or some other sexually-transmitted disease. If she ended up sick with something he dragged home, he'd blame her and accuse her of fooling around.

He never accepted the blame for anything that went wrong in his life, whether he ran out of gas because he didn't fill the tank or lost a job for too many days of arriving hung over and useless. Miriam's fault, everything that went wrong was Miriam's fault. A quick scan of the room helped me push those memories away.

Miriam believed the best of people. Sometimes, I wanted to somehow open her eyes and force her to see the ugly truth. In spite of my record in schools and with social services for having a knack for attracting trouble, Miriam had believed in me, had believed I could make something of myself. Would I have stayed and finished high school if she hadn't believed the best of me? Probably not.

"You'll stay in touch, won't you, Jaz?" The waver in her voice tugged at my heart.

I slanted a look at her. She blinked, but tears slipped down her creased cheeks anyhow. In three strides, I crossed to her side and cradled both of her hands between my palms. Her light blue eyes stared up at me from beneath a forehead prematurely lined with furrows. Only in her late thirties, her face looked as tired as the faces of some of the prostitutes who lounged on the corner down from my new apartment. "Come with me, Miriam. It's not the greatest apartment, but we'll get a better one in no time. As

Run or Die!

much as you like kids, I'm sure you can find some childcare work to do, and until then I have my job and a little bit in the bank."

A smile tugged the corners of her mouth, yet it only made her appear sadder. "I love you for that generous heart of yours." She gently disengaged one hand from mine and placed it against my cheek. "But my place is here. For better or for worse, he is my husband."

With one finger, I touched her bruised cheekbone. A couple of nights ago when I was at work, George had hit her. When I got home, she refused to let me retaliate. "Once I'm gone, I'm afraid he's going to really hurt you."

She grabbed both of my hands, brought them to her cracked lips, and kissed them. More tears flooded her eyes and wended their way down her face. "Maybe he will. Don't think I don't know how much he holds back because of you." She cocked her head. "Did I ever thank you for that night when you stopped him?"

I ducked my eyes away from her. "You did."

She sighed, a sound filled with loss and pain. "You've been a joy to me, Jazmine. Your smile has made these years more than I could've hoped for."

In silence, we held hands, each of us preoccupied with her thoughts. I couldn't leave it, though. One last time, I had to ask, "Why do you stay, Miriam? He isn't going to change. You have to know that."

Another long inhale and exhale as she turned eyes full of broken dreams to me. "I...I don't know exactly, Jaz. I grew up thinking marriage was forever. That's part of it, I guess. And, I keep thinking if I could just find some way to help him... He was so different when we first met."

Her eyes took on a faraway look. "He brought me flowers, and told me he couldn't live without me." She blinked and from wherever she'd gone in her memories, she returned. Her eyes met mine, begging me to find some way to understand something that I couldn't. "There are times that he cries, Jaz. He cries and says he doesn't know why he does these things, and I know in my heart that he is truly sorry. And...maybe, I'm just too tired to start over again."

I wanted to scream, "He's a lying snake! The only things that matter to him come from a bottle, and how many women he can fuck. He doesn't care about you. He doesn't care about what you need." My hands itched to shake her, wake her up, make her see the good years she could have if not for him. I bit my lip and dropped my gaze to the floor.

She put a finger under my chin and lifted my face. "Jaz, if he does hurt me, it isn't your fault. You've done your best to convince me to leave. To tell the truth, honey, as much as I'll miss you, I'm glad you're going."

Chapter 2

Mickey D's had been a good interim job while I'd been in school. Between what I made there and the other odd jobs that I'd found, I had enough to pay a couple of months' rent on my apartment, purchase a new laptop complete with a multi-talented printer, and still have a small stash of cash. Once I settled into the 'hood, however, I fired up my computer and started researching.

I'd had enough of flipping burgers, and I sure didn't want to put my feet into my mom's tracks. There's nothing wrong with selling your body to the highest bidder if that's what cranks it for you, except the life expectancy for a woman in the Trade is pretty short. And violent.

What other ways exist for a fresh high school graduate with mediocre grades to haul her own freight? My last school counselor wanted me to apply for grant money and go to college. With no inclination toward further education, I'd scratched that idea off my list. That pretty much left only drugs. Selling drugs for dealers in the 'hood would have been every bit as bad, if not worse, than standing on a street corner. Simply a different way to sell my life and my soul. Not going to happen.

Before the meth took mom, she'd bordered on being a technophile. She'd bought me my first laptop when I hit second grade. That old laptop had been the first thing stolen from me when I entered foster care. Still, having grown up with the wonders of the internet, I convinced myself that the answer to my dilemma floated in cyber space. I only needed to cruise the web to discover how I could make a living. The third night of surfing the net, I rubbed my itchy eyes. One more click then I would give up and go to bed. That last click hit pay dirt, literally.

The next day I drained my savings account as low as I dared and bought a quiet generator. Being handy at building simple things, I built shelves and set up banks of grow lights. My landlady didn't care what I did as long as I paid my rent on time, didn't have parties—like I could in that closet of an apartment—and didn't run up her electric bill. Erring on the side of caution, I hauled in the plant pots and bags of soil after she went to bed.

Run or Die

My basement apartment boasted a tiny window that opened out against the ground behind a bunch of overgrown bushes. After taping a flex hose onto the generator's exhaust pipe, I ran it out of the window. A piece of plywood cut to fit around the exhaust hose and to close off the rest of the window completed that part of my project.

A guy I knew from high school introduced me to a woman who cloned marijuana plants. She explained that seeds took too long to mature and as many as half of them could be males. Males would cause my female plants to seed and destroy some of the potency of my product. Several days of two-hour classes and some hands-on experience cost a chunk of change, but she demonstrated how to sex the plants and the cloning technique. I nearly ruptured myself laughing when she said the males had two to three balls and the females only had one. At the end of our sessions, I bought a bunch of clones to get started. Pot plants loved my environment. My green babies shot up, became leggy adolescents, and within three months matured into bushy females. Six months later my business was as large as I wanted to grow it—pun intended.

Though pretty satisfied with my life, I knew things would have to change sooner or later. Eventually the law—legal or not, I had zero intention of jumping through hoops—or bigger dealers, would come down on my head for my growing and selling operation, no matter how small. I'd deal with it when it happened. Till then, I kicked back and prepared to cruise for a while. I didn't realize the changes in my life would arrive soon, and radically.

Seattle isn't a bad place to live, believe me, I'm a native here. Most people don't hassle you if you stay low key. I knew how to do low key, so that mild January day the physical attack caught me totally unprepared.

Seattle Central Community College was a great place to hang whether meeting customers or simply kicking back and watching people. I could see everything from the normies, easily spotted in their color-coordinated clothes accessorized with nifty purses and briefcases, to a guy with a purple Mohawk hair-do and so many tattoos that the only un-inked skin I could see circled his eyes.

Aya Walksfar

The bright sun warmed my back as I bent over and dug through my backpack for the next to the last baggie. From the corner of my eye, I watched my eighteen-year-old customer. Not a wannabe gangsta, the young black man wore faded jeans that rode his lean hips—but didn't display the crack of his butt—a t-shirt, and New Balance walking shoes. Normally laid back and friendly, he chatted about what classes he took at Seattle Central and what girl he liked. This day he jittered in place like he'd taken one hit too many off a crack pipe. He shot nervous glances down the block toward the intersection where a crowd of people waited for the light to change. As the light changed, he snatched the baggie from my hand, and took off weaving and dodging around the people drifting along the sidewalk.

A leggy girl hustled up the sidewalk, arms swinging, head jutted forward. The woman clearly had an agenda. A quick scan and I could tell I didn't know her, and she wasn't the type to be a customer. Pot heads don't tend to hurry much. Since it was no business of mine, I turned away to pick up my pack from the little square of grass.

"Hey, you!" Even breathy from hurrying, she had a melodious voice.

I started to straighten up and pivot to face the young black woman when I spotted her fist coming. I yanked my head back just in time, or she would've decked me right there. I took the hit on my shoulder and staggered back a couple of steps with her boring in on me, a windmill of flailing fists.

In my experience, girls do a lot of screaming, crying, slapping, and hair pulling. Not her. Silent, she kept coming at me. Not wanting to wind up with a couple of black eyes or a fat lip, I dropped the backpack. Even then I struggled to block the worst of her blows. I kept yelling at her to stop, let's talk, but it made as much impression as a teaspoon of fresh water poured into the ocean.

I hate violence. Avoid it whenever I can, and keep it to a minimum if I can't completely sidestep it. I needed to stop her before she landed a lucky punch and ticked me off big time.

Finally, I snagged her arm, ducked down, and came up behind her, tucking her hand up between her shoulder blades. My

Run or Die

one hand dug into her shoulder muscle right on the sweet spot. She buckled to the grass and I followed her down. A knee planted firmly on her side helped to stabilize the awkward position. "I don't know what you're on, but you need to chill."

Black-brown eyes blazed up at me. "I'm not on anything. It's my little brother! You got him hooked on that crap."

With a firm shake of my head, I let my voice drop low because now she really had started to piss me off. "You got the wrong woman. I don't sell to kids."

"You may not see him as a kid, but he's my baby brother! And, I'm gonna kick your ass." She surged against my hold.

I shoved down harder and cranked her arm up a tiny bit. She stopped struggling. "Girl, you need to *chill out.*"

Catching my breath, I gauged the gathering crowd. I shifted my weight and bent close to her ear. "Look, I'll buy you a cup of coffee and you tell me how to recognize your brother and I'll tell you if he's a consumer. From there maybe we can discuss this like reasonable people. What do you say? Think quick or we'll both be getting a free ride in the back of a squad car. By now someone's bound to have gone for the college's security guard."

"All right," she growled.

I let go of her arm and leapt back. While she sat up and rubbed her shoulder, I did a fast survey of the crowd. College kids, street kids, transients. A few business people cutting their eyes away, pretending not to notice. No cell phones out and not a lot of interest in two females wrestling. No blood except for my cut lip, and even that barely trickled. I turned my back and ignored them, reaching a hand out to help her to her feet. "Come on. You don't want to get hassled for assault, and I don't want to get hassled for selling a bit of smoke."

She glanced at my hand like I'd picked my nose and the boogers were still there then scrambled to her feet without my help.

After a double check that I had tied the top flap of my faded blue backpack, I swung it onto my shoulders. With a quick motion, I spun around and darted through the milling people. Within a few feet, she caught up and matched me stride for stride.

Aya Walksfar

Two blocks away, Magic Murphy's, a hole-in-the-wall coffee shop a block off of Broadway in the Capitol Hill neighborhood, squatted between its dingy neighbors, a bead store on the north side, and a tobacco shop on the south side. Magic's plate glass window sparkled in the afternoon sun. Red lettering spelled out the name in crisp script. Bells jingled a merry tune as I pushed the door open. I lifted a hand to the little black woman hustling behind the counter of the crowded room, her long dreadlocks swinging around her face. "Hey, Mama, how's it holdin'?" I called to her from the back of the short line.

She grinned a broad gap-toothed grin at me and held up a large, heavy white mug. Though strong and black, Mama's coffee always slid over my tongue as smooth as melted chocolate.

I answered with two fingers held up. She grabbed a second mug. Steam rose from the filled mugs by the time we shuffled our way to the counter. I tossed a ten next to the cash register. While waiting for change, I jerked my chin toward the condiment island in the center of the room. "Sugar, cream, and napkins are over there." Change scooped up, I dropped a dollar bill into the tip jar. "I'll be right over there, in that corner by the window."

"I take my coffee black," she snapped like I'd asked her some kind of obnoxious question.

With a shrug, I headed for my favorite spot. Her Nike running shoes squeaked behind me as she forcefully placed her feet. I guessed it was her version of stomping.

After dumping my backpack on an empty chair, I slumped down on the chair next to it, across the gouged and scarred wood table from where she sat. Her chair scraped against the hardwood floor as she scooted closer to the table. I eyed her as I sipped my coffee.

Tired of her silent glaring, I asked, "So, what's the deal?"

Her light caramel skin flushed dark as she leaned over the table, eyes locked on mine. "That boy that left before I got there, he's my baby brother, Ellison."

Deliberately, I slouched lower in the chair and stretched my legs out parallel to the table. "Hell, woman, he's just a bit over a year younger than me. I may not be legit, but if a kid looks too young, I insist on ID or no sale. I don't want no babies on my brain." When I saw her open her lips like she might go on a rampage, I held up my hand. "Whoa! Don't blow a cork. Doesn't matter to me. If it bothers you that much, I'll cut him off. Just don't think that's gonna keep him from smoking. He'll find someone else to buy from." I sipped the hot brew, studying her over the rim of the cup.

Her lips twisted into a sneer, and exposed the edge of slightly crooked, white teeth. Her elegant, long fingers clenched around her cup. For a moment, I thought she might throw her coffee at me. "Now you're going to tell me that it's better for him to buy from you. Let me see," she tapped a rose-pink fingernail against her full upper lip as she stared above my head. She dropped her eyes back to my face. "Oh, yeah, you'll say he's safer to buy from you because you don't cut your shit with toxic plants or sprinkle it with hallucinogens. You're going to tell me those other dealers are more violent, and more willing to get him hooked on something worse than pot." With a triumphant look in her eye, she sat up straight. "Well? Am I right?"

Her crossed arms emphasized the jut of her nicely rounded breasts. I sucked in a deep breath and forced my eyes up higher. One brow raised, I stared at her as I set my cup down. Got to say, the girl had a brass set of tits. She never lowered her gaze. Finally, I crossed my arms, making certain that they covered my tits rather than pushed them up. "I'm not going to tell you anything. I said I'd cut him off, and I will. But people can't get clean for someone else. It has to be for themselves. So, yeah, he'll find another dealer. And, yeah, I'm better than the others for the exact reasons you said. I don't cut my shit and I don't sell anything except pot. I don't want meth heads or any of those other druggies around me."

Arms dropped, a puzzled look settled over her face, drew her beautifully-shaped brows together. "Why do you do this?'

"Sell pot?" I unfolded my arms, leaned forward, and cradled my cup between my hands, determined to keep my eyes up where they belonged. I could feel the creep of hot embarrassment climbing the back of my neck. Here I was, doing the exact thing I despised men doing to me, honing in on a woman's breasts. Briefly, I tried to recall the last time I'd gotten laid, but it didn't readily come to mind. Must've been *real* memorable. I snorted to myself then hoped she hadn't heard.

"Yes, why do you sell pot?" For the first time no acid dripped from her words, and only curiosity lit her eyes, like someone seeing a wolf, or some other dangerous creature, up close for the first time, but behind a barrier, like at the zoo. Nothing to fear. Stare all you want.

My eyes tripped away from hers as I gave a short shake of my head at myself, wondered why I willingly defended my choices to this woman. The woman obviously out-classed me even in her skinny, designer jeans, her dirtied silk blouse, and cute, two-inch heeled, leather boots. "It pays the bills." When I looked back, she had settled comfortably against her chair, the perfect picture of a friend enjoying a chat.

Running a finger around the rim of her cup, in a reasonable voice she said, "There are other jobs." She took a drink of her coffee, and I couldn't take my eyes off of her slender throat. I didn't know anyone could make coffee drinking look sexy.

Reel in your tongue, girl. She's not from your 'hood. What is it about her that makes my hormones zip around like they're on cocaine?

I pulled my eyes from her and let a smile stretch my lips. I knew how it must look: grim and foreboding. That's what I'd been told more than once. A sharp bark of laughter escaped. "Yeah, seriously. Flipping burgers, salesgirl, or maybe a barista in one of these little carts that are all over the place, *if* I'm willing to flounce my tits in some guy's face. That's the kind of jobs women like me can get: low-paying, servant jobs. No thanks."

She pursed her lips, watching me with those bottomless, almond-shaped eyes. "What if I told you I could get you a job, a real job that paid decent money?"

"What are you, independently wealthy?" My eyes skipped around the room. Bright sun poured in the windows, spilled into the dip of the worn plank floor. Two girls with textbooks cradled in their arms bopped in, giggled, and looked down their noses as they checked the place out, like they were slumming. Outside a drunk stumbled past the plate glass window clutching a brown paper bag.

With one hand she grabbed hold of a shank of her long, black, wavy hair and flipped it behind her shoulder. My eyes followed the movement and I missed part of what she said. "...owns a painting business. She needs another painter."

It took an effort, but I tuned back in, shifted forward on my chair, and braced my forearms on the table. "Sorry. Space-cadeting. You know some woman who owns a painting business. Like painting houses, right?"

"Yes."

A wash of disappointment broke over me. Too bad. I wouldn't have minded making legit money. Sooner or later, this illegal shit would catch up to me. Maybe it had started to already. "I'm sure she's looking for some guy." The bitter memory of the last house painting job I had applied for flooded my mouth. I took a deep gulp of coffee to wash the nasty taste of discrimination away.

The owner hadn't wanted a woman, especially a lesbian woman. Oh, he'd come up with a different reason, but the lie shouted from his eyes. Before that, I'd applied for an apprentice mechanic position at a two-man shop. The owner listened for all of five minutes then hustled me out the door. In the real world, women still scraped to get a foothold.

Her chuckle sounded like ice cream on a hot day. Made me hungry for more. "Not Aunt Sylvia. She only hires women."

My eyebrows shot up. "Isn't someone going to yell reverse discrimination?"

She swiveled sideways and crossed one leg over the other one, all lady-like. A slender arm rested on the small square table. "It's rehab for abused women; that's how she can do it. Men would compromise the feeling of safety in the workplace for them."

I snorted. "I'd probably scare them senseless."

Face firming in disapproval, she locked onto my eyes. "Any other excuses? Let's get them all out of the way. Or, do you just not *want* to make an honest living?"

Aya Walksfar

With a sneer, I crossed my arms and lifted my chin. "Am I allowed to ask if there's any work in the middle of winter?"

She waved a dismissive hand. "Of course, there is. Why else would I offer to help you get on?"

All levity vanished from my face. "When and where?"

The smile that blossomed on her lips had me wanting to run my tongue across her mouth, to see if she tasted as sweet as she looked. I'd never believed in love at first sight; lust, maybe, but not love. I wondered if I might have to revise my belief.

"My name's Alicia Anderson. What's yours?" She held her hand across the table.

I enfolded her fingers with mine. A goofy grin tugged the corners of my mouth upward. "Jazmine Wheeler. Call me Jaz."

***

I prided myself on staying in shape, being able to lift weights that some of the guys in the gym where I worked out couldn't lift. The first day on the job, I scoped out the crew. Thin-armed, skinny women, mostly; and a few overweight women who huffed and puffed while standing still.

If these gals could do it, then house painting had to be a pretty cushy job, especially interior painting. By the end of the day, after setting up and taking down scaffolding and horsing around antique furniture that weighed about as much as a Mini Cooper car, I had muscles aching that I didn't even know existed, and a whole new respect for those women.

February came in blustery with cold rains slashing Seattle. I felt grateful to be slapping paint on the inside walls of houses rather than standing on a corner waiting for my customers, or a cop, whoever got there first. Sylvia dropped me off at my apartment, saying it was too cold and too dark to catch a bus that would dump me blocks from my place.

I walked into my dingy basement room, draped my jacket over my only chair—a hard-seated wood thing that wobbled and squealed if I sat on it—then plopped onto the landlady-provided, springless-wonder couch. A broken spring promptly poked me in the butt. Too tired to move, I flopped my head against the back, the worn upholstery bristly against my cheek.

My cell phone rang. I eyeballed it lying on the rickety occasional table at the far end of the couch. Sprawled out, for a moment I considered letting it go to voice mail, but lately Alicia had started calling in the evening. I groaned, slid across the couch, and snagged it. Trying to sound more upbeat than beat up, I said, "Hey."

A crisp, official voice asked, "Is this Jazmine Wheeler?"

My heart started to pound. I shot up straight. "Yeah, who's this?"

"This is Nurse Anne Jenkins here at Harborview Medical Center. Do you know Mrs. Miriam Hellerson?"

I was on my feet with no memory of how I'd gotten there. My fingers gripped the slender phone and it took all I could do to push out words. "Yeah, is she all right?"

"You need to come to Harborview ICU. Everything will be explained when you arrive." She hung up before I could ask anything else.

Harborview Hospital hulked on a hill a couple of miles from my apartment. I flagged a cab on Broadway, a few blocks from my place. Within minutes, the cabbie stopped in front of the emergency entrance. I jumped out, threw a twenty at the guy, and jogged down the long, squeaky hospital corridors to ICU. A nurse in pale blue pants and matching baggy shirt stood behind a half-circle counter lined with monitors. She glanced up as I approached and held up one finger.

I shifted from foot to foot as I waited. I know it was only five minutes, since I looked at my watch, yet the wait felt like it would never end. When she finally stood up, I noticed the white, rectangular nametag: Nurse A. Jenkins.

"I'm Jazmine Wheeler. You phoned about Miriam Hellerson. Is she all right?" She took so long to answer that I jammed my hands in my paint-spattered jeans pockets, battling the temptation to choke the information out of her.

At last, in a voice that sounded so even and neutral that it felt unreal, she said, "Mrs. Hellerson was brought in two hours ago by ambulance. She'd been severely beaten." She went on explaining the horrendous injuries, the life-threatening injuries administered by good old George. None of the medical-speak made any sense to me. I wanted to cry; I wanted to rage; I wanted to kill George. Fortunately, the police already had him. And, Miriam was conscious now and asking for me.

Glass-fronted rooms made a three-quarter circle around the nurse's station. A few steps took me into Miriam's room. I walked to her white-sheeted bed in rhythm to the hiss and the beeps of the machines surrounding her.

She must have sensed me there. It had always made me feel wanted, connected, that she could do that. No other foster parent had ever done that. My real mother hadn't done that, or if she had it was lost under the jitters of the meth before I could remember it.

She cracked open the eye not hidden by the white gauze head wrap. "Jaz," she croaked.

I folded her bony, cold hand between both of my paint-speckled ones and leaned close. In an attempt to warm her fingers, I cradled her hand against my chest. "Hey, don't try to talk. You need to get well then we'll talk. I'm gonna be right here until you're well." I blinked hard, hearing the lie in my voice.

She tried to smile, the corners of her lips tried to turn up, but they wavered and fell. "Know better." She sucked in a raspy breath. "Wanted...to tell you...love you, hon." She closed her eyes, too exhausted to hold them open any longer. Her chest heaved as she fought to swallow one more lungful of air.

I kissed her gently on the forehead and, never releasing her hand, toed a chair closer to her bed and sat on the edge of the molded plastic. I shrugged out of my jacket. Lavender and sky-blue paint flecked my t-shirt. My leather construction boots sported more paint splatters. I didn't care. Nothing mattered, except Miriam.

Miriam never regained consciousness. It was like she had waited for me to come. The ICU doctors and nurses let me sit next to her, except when they had to do embarrassing things. I knew she'd want me to step out then. She'd always been shy about her body.

Run or Die

The first day I missed work, Alicia called. With my ringer off, I didn't hear it and her call went to voice mail. The evening of the second day that I missed work, she walked into Miriam's room carrying a cup of black coffee and some new jeans and a new t-shirt. A size too big, the jeans bagged. The t-shirt, a size too small, stretched tight across my shoulders. Tears burned my eyes that she would do such a thing. She never said how she tracked me down. Probably some of those "community connections" her aunt appeared to have.

I drank the coffee, but waited until she left to change. Alicia didn't attempt to intrude on my silence with worse-than-useless platitudes or inane conversation. It seemed as if she understood that I couldn't talk to her. I couldn't talk to anyone, except Miriam. She kept her stay short.

The next day, she arrived with coffee, two burgers, and a large fries. I wouldn't have eaten, but she poked me until I caved simply to please her. When I finished, she crumpled up the wrappings and carried them out with her.

Every day she arrived. Every day she brought food and coffee and mostly silent company.

The nurses offered me a cot next to Miriam. I shook my head, afraid to lie down, afraid that the quiet hush of the corridors, the incessant beeps of the machines would lull me asleep and Miriam would slip away.

So, I talked. I told her about my apartment, about my job as a house painter, about Alicia, about her brother Ellison, her Grandma Pearl, and her Aunt Sylvia. I told her about the new exhibits I'd seen at the Seattle Art Museum and how Alicia had dragged me up James Street to see the Saint James Cathedral.

I wanted to tell her how many times I'd phoned only to have George slam the receiver in my ear. How I'd stopped by a few times and he refused to let me in, refused to ask her to come to the door. How I stopped trying, afraid he'd hurt her because he kept saying, "the only thing ya doin' comin' here is hurtin' her." I interpreted that as threats to her and I stayed away though it broke my heart. I wanted to tell her about the loneliness that had eaten away at me until I met Alicia.

Aya Walksfar

I didn't tell her any of those things. When time is short, you don't waste it on things that don't matter anymore. Instead, you say those things you'll never have another chance to say. Busy trying to keep her alive, I hadn't been able to do that with my mom.

Mostly I told Miriam how much I loved her; how she'd made my life feel important simply by being there for me. How I had always wanted to make her proud of me.

As the days slid into the fourth evening, I ran out of things to say. So, I said what had to be said. "I love you, Miriam. I really do. You've been the only real family I've ever had, the only real mother for a very long time. Oh, I know my mother tried, but like you told me, she was sick, real sick. You helped me to see past the beatings, past the yelling; helped me to see the troubled woman inside. Because of you, I don't hate her as much anymore. Not even for dying and leaving me." I sniffled and used the heel of my hand to wipe away errant tears. "I don't know what I'm going to do when you leave, but I have to let you go."

I sucked in an unsteady breath and let it wobble out. "I love you, Mom Miriam. I love you, but you can leave whenever you're ready. You have someplace more important to be. Maybe I'll see you again someday." I stroked her arm, over and over.

I don't know how long it was before her body jerked and trembled. As her body settled to the bed, the heart monitor screamed its humming alarm. I kissed her forehead as the nurses and the white-coated doctor burst through the door. Letting go of her hand, I walked out.

Miriam had taken me at my word. She had left.

***

Somehow, having my biological mother die while I tried to walk her through a bad run of drugs allowed Miriam and me to talk about the hard things, like death and dying and what did I want to be when I grew up. We never found an answer to the last thing, but we knew what each of us wanted once our bodies became deserted houses.

Run or Die

The only decent thing George ever did: not contest the handwritten paper in Miriam's purse that gave me the right to take care of her body. I had enough in my savings account to buy a beautiful, biodegradable wood urn for her ashes. The second summer with Miriam, I'd taken her to visit the Grandma Cedar at the Washington Park Arboretum. Like Mom and me, Miriam had loved the old cedar tree. It was the only place I knew that had a chance of never becoming a subdivision. At least, not any time soon, I hoped.

On the fourth night after Miriam's death, a full moon rose and gave me enough light to do what I needed to do. Alicia, Ellison, Aunt Sylvia, and Grandma Pearl snuck into the arboretum with me. I brought a camp shovel along. Once the hole under the cedar reached thigh deep on me, I lay on my stomach and gently lowered the urn. Pushing back up on my feet, I brushed the mud from the front of my damp jacket then the five of us stood there in silence, saying whatever prayers we had to say within our own hearts. After a few minutes, we each dropped a clump of sweet-smelling earth into the black hole. I finished filling it in, and everyone helped scatter cedar needles over the space so no one would find the final resting place of Miriam's ashes.

After that day, I spent most of my off hours with Alicia and her family. Many nights Alicia threw me a pillow and blankets so I could flop out on the old curved-arm couch. Grandma Pearl's home, a rambling clapboard house with a canary-yellow body and lime green trim, gave me a sense of belonging. No television set in any room, yet each room held a wealth of overstuffed bookshelves. I felt welcomed in a way that no foster home, and certainly not my tiny apartment with its concrete walls and cold floor, had ever welcomed me.

Alicia's entire family devoured books, talked at mealtimes about books, and could usually be found with their noses in books. I could read well enough, but had never had much interest in books. Figured doer rather than thinker summed up my personality.

I think I could plead self-defense. I'd read or be left out. Not that they would ostracize me; I would simply have nothing to contribute. One night after everyone hit the blankets, I cruised the bookshelves in the living room. The dark-gloved hand on the cover of Kay Hooper's *Whisper of Evil* snagged my attention. The back cover blurb about a killer stalking a small town called Silence completed the capture.

That book hooked me and after that I shared Alicia's book addiction. Armed with the words from Leon Uris' *Exodus,* Alice Walker's *The Color Purple,* and even the werecoyote from Patricia Brigg's *Mercy Thompson* series, I belonged.

When I did finally drag myself home to my basement apartment, oftentimes I'd look up from where I sprawled on my single bed. Moonlight shivered through the branches of the bush outside my tiny window. Shelves gone, plants given away, generator sold; a different room than B.A., before Alicia. A room that held hope, and tiny, emerging dreams.

July 15th, six months after I met Alicia, I turned nineteen. Alicia read Robert Frost's *The Road Less Traveled* to me then handed me the slender volume: *101 Best Loved Poems of the American People.*

"My ninth grade teacher gave me that book."

I tried to hand it back to her. "I can't take something that means that much to you."

She reached over and put her hands over mine, gently forced my fingers around the paperback book with its creased cover. "I want you to have it. That book has given me hours of enjoyment just reading it aloud and listening to how the words make their own music." Her eyes shone.

I swallowed a lump in my throat and croaked, "Thanks."

Grandma Pearl gave me *The Prophet* by Kahlil Gibran. I held the thin, hard-cover book in my hands. "What're you guys trying to do? Gang up on me?" My smile wavered as I reverently turned to page 29 and read aloud. "Your joy is your sorrow unmasked. And the selfsame well from which your laughter rises was oftentimes filled with your tears."

One night shortly after Miriam's death, Grandma Pearl found me sitting in her kitchen, hunched over a cup of cold coffee. I don't know what she read in my face, but she left and returned with Gibran's book. In a melodious, soft voice so like Alicia's she read Gibran's thoughts on joy and sorrow aloud. Afterwards, she closed the book and left it lying on the table and went back to bed. Daylight crept across the kitchen floor by the time I closed the covers of *The Prophet*.

After I laid Gibran's book aside, Ellison shot me a big grin as he handed me a narrow package. "This isn't a book."

I rolled my eyes, eliciting laughter from everyone at the kitchen table. "Thank God!" In seconds I'd ripped open the box and stared down at the most beautiful Buck knife I had ever seen. My jaw dropped as I lifted my eyes to the young man across the table.

"Do you like it?" He squirmed and jiggled in his chair.

"I love it," I said so fervently that he blushed and glanced away.

Sylvia's laughter broke the awkward moment. "I hope you like my gift as much as you do Ellison's."

I think I liked Sylvia's gift most of all: a four-day weekend with pay. Nearly every moment of that weekend I spent with Alicia. During that long weekend of lazy days and city adventures, I fell irrevocably in love with Alicia.

On Thanksgiving Day, the year I turned twenty, Alicia became another cancer stat. She died from an aggressive form of cancer, pancreatic cancer. When Alicia died, I died, too. I may have still been walking and talking, but I was a dead woman walking and talking. I quit going to work because I couldn't stand to see her family. When the rent came due, it felt right to go back to my old ways, and a bit beyond. Why not? Nothing mattered, nothing at all.

Though I had never drank nor did drugs before I copped the "tude," no time like the present time. Drunk and stoned one night, I built a fire in the trash can behind my basement apartment and fed that fire almost every book in my apartment. The old bitch I paid for the moldy basement space poked her nose out her kitchen door, but one look at my face sent her slamming back into her house. I stared down at my hands, at the three books not yet part of the conflagration: the *Word-A-Day Journal* Miriam had given to me, Alicia's book of poems, and Grandma Pearl's *The Prophet*. Three times I walked over to the trash can and held those bound pages above the greedy fire; and, three times I moved away from the flames. The fourth time, I flipped open the cover of the poem book, prepared to rip the pages out and feed my memories to the heat. I glanced down. "Two roads diverged in a yellow road/And sorry I could not travel both…" I slapped the cover shut, stooped and picked up the other two books then marched into my apartment.

From the corner of the closet shelf I took down a small box. Packing tape ripped off, I wrapped paper towels around the books and laid them with Ellison's Buck knife and Miriam's tin box. I dug out the partial roll of tape that I'd flung in my junk box and used all of it to secure the flaps of that box, almost like I feared the objects escaping some night and attacking me with memories. The box returned to the closet shelf, out of sight and, hopefully, out of mind.

Mid-January whirled into Seattle on a cape of icy rain. I staggered out of The Leather and Stud Bar on Capitol Hill, not nearly numb enough to avoid the constant ache inside.

"Hey, Joe, bet this is one of them queer bitches." A hard shove followed the rough words.

I bounced off the brick wall of the bar, but managed to stay on my feet. "Fuck off, asshole," I slurred.

A flurry of hard fists and booted feet beat me to the ground. From some distant world, Ellison's voice called my name. Through the slit of one swollen eye, I thought I saw him bent over me, his lips moving, but I couldn't hear a word he said. A dream, or a nightmare, I didn't know which, so I welcomed the blackness that wrapped warm arms around my cold body.

When I next opened my eyes, the red demon eyes of a clock glared at me: 1:00. I groaned and shifted, stilled. The bed I lay in did not belong to me. Too soft and it smelled like a rain-washed morning. Head pounding, I rolled over until I could drop my feet to the floor and sit up. Squinty-eyed, I peered around. Heavy, dark blue drapes blocked any light from entering the sole window in the small, neat bedroom. I stumbled across the room and yanked them open. Darkness. The darkness of a city street at night.

Shuffling over to the light switch on the wall, I flicked on the overhead light. My head spun and, for a moment, my stomach heaved. I clenched my teeth and swallowed down the bitter bile. *Alicia's bedroom. What the hell am I doing in Alicia's bedroom at one o'clock in the morning?*

From down the hall the distinct shush-thump-shush of Grandma Pearl's footsteps accompanied by her walker moved along the hallway carpet. I swung around to face the door as it opened. The quick movement swamped me with vertigo. I caught myself by slapping a palm against the pale blue wall. My legs shook. My hands trembled. Cold sweat beaded on my forehead. A sour odor drifted up from my body.

Grandma Pearl stepped across the threshold and stared at me from fathomless black eyes. "'Bout time you woke up."

"Why...?" I licked cracked, dry lips and tried again. "Why am I here?" I rasped.

"It's where you belong. This is your bedroom now." She let go of the walker, folded her arms under her generous breasts—the exact same stance that Alicia had taken whenever she was irritated by me—and steadily met my gaze.

I crept along the wall. When I reached the dresser, I fell back against it, pressed the heels of my hands against my throbbing eyes. "No." My arms fell to my sides and I dragged my face up to meet her eyes.

Soft, yellow light from the hallway ceiling fixture outlined her short, round figure. "Yes." She gave a brusque nod. "Get showered and get dressed and get yourself down to the kitchen." Though reliant on the walker, she marched out. She never doubted that I'd fall into line the way her daughter and grandchildren always did.

As her footsteps faded, I made my slow way over to the window. I didn't want to be here. Not here in this house full of Alicia, or in this life devoid of Alicia. Through the rain's tears running down the window glass, I watched as an old woman shuffled and staggered her way up the cracked and littered sidewalk. A baggy long coat swayed with every uneven step. She stopped and lifted the brown paper bag that she clutched in her hand. The sick light of the nearby street lamp threw the hidden bottle she lifted to her lips, most likely full of cheap wine, into sharp relief against the gray-dark of the city. She took a long swallow then wiped her mouth on the back of her hand.

I felt dirty, like I'd watched a pornographic movie.

Alicia's voice whispered in my mind. "Promise me that you'll do something good with your life. I want you to grow beyond where we live right now."

At that moment, I would have promised her anything. And so I did. "I promise." I think I even meant that promise when I made it.

She'd taken my hand then and smiled at me. Her smile: the last thing the cancer stole. "Just remember, Jaz, love and the memories of love are meant to strengthen us. No matter what happens, my love will always be with you."

Here in this room, Alicia's room, where we had so often laughed, her voice wouldn't let me go. I wasn't sure I wanted to run away from her, again.

With the fingers of my right hand, I scrubbed at my forehead. My left hand grasped the window frame, propping me up. *That's what I've been doing: propping myself up on booze and drugs. How ashamed of me Alicia would be. And Miriam...what would she think?* I wanted to cry, but no amount of tears would make any part of this right. I had to do that.

After a quick shower, I found a folded pair of jeans and a t-shirt on the bed. I dressed quickly then made my way downstairs.

Eggs, bacon, hash browns, and toast waited for me at the place where I had sat so often, Alicia beside me. I swallowed hard then forced myself to sit down and eat. Though the food tried to clog my throat, I chewed and swallowed another bite of toast. "I can't stay here. Besides, I have my own apartment."

Ellison slouched against the kitchen door jamb, hair tousled from interrupted sleep, and snorted. "Not hardly."

My head jerked up and I stared at him. The fork in my hand, laden with egg, hung in mid-air. "What does that mean?"

He straightened up and glowered at me. In that moment I could see Alicia in his face, in his eyes, in that stubborn jaw. My mouth became as dry as dust. A deep gulp of cold milk finally washed the feeling away.

Run or Die

Not speaking, he stood there as if he waited for me to get myself together enough to hear. "You drank and drugged yourself out of your apartment, Jaz. Aunt Sylvia has been dropping by your place, just to keep an eye on you, and she saw that old woman coming out of the house with cardboard boxes. She went over and lifted a flap and saw the book *Alicia* gave you."

His words thrust into the wound my heart already bore and ripped it wider. I surged to my feet. "That old bitch!"

"Jazmine!" Grandma Pearl snapped, her voice slashing through my anger.

I sank down on the chair. "Gone. Everything I owned, gone." Elbows propped on the table, I dropped my head to my hands.

"Hey, it's okay." Ellison hastened to assure me, his anger quickly vanquished beneath my obvious distress. Like Alicia, Ellison had a soft heart and couldn't stand to see any person, or any creature, suffer. "You know Auntie ain't gonna let your stuff sit out on the sidewalk. She brought it home for you. Grandma put it in Alicia's old room, your room now. It's all in the closet." He walked over behind my chair and awkwardly patted my shoulder. "Hey, don't cry, that's so...that's so girly."

A watery laugh bubbled up. I raised my head. With a paper napkin, I wiped my eyes and finished my breakfast.

Chapter 3

Early April: On the Road

Mapquest said from Seattle to the small town of Elmsworth, California, was exactly 846.5 miles. It claimed I would arrive at my destination in fourteen point three hours. Where in creation did they pull that number from? Obviously, whoever came up with it did not factor in the Portland cloverleaf. Between homicidal drivers who despised motorcyclists, a rain squall that pretty much blinded me by obscuring the face plate of my helmet, and exit signs that I missed, I wandered around for well over an hour, taking the wrong exits in a panic and then finding myself miles away from where I should have been.

Whoever came up with those travel times didn't believe that the blind curves along Highway 101, where the road dove for what appeared to be a hundred feet straight down to the gravelly beaches, warranted any less speed than the open, flat lanes of Interstate 5. Luckily, the sun shone in a bleached-out blue sky once I crossed the Oregon-California border.

Nothing could have prepared me for the wild beauty of the Smith River racing beside the road. I camped on a beach in a little town called Crescent City then meandered toward the bigger city of Eureka. I didn't quite make it there before I found a camping spot among the towering redwood trees. For three days I wandered in the quiet and solitude among those giants. My heart ached. Alicia would have loved the redwoods.

My final destination lay south of Eureka. I still didn't know how Grandma Pearl had talked me into going to the farm her daughter, Aretha Hopewell, owned.

In spite of enjoying the redwoods, I'm a city woman. I love trees as long as they are close to stores and restaurants, museums, and all those other conveniences. What was I doing heading down the coast highway to a town that didn't even rate a dot on the regular print maps?

Once I made it to Elmsworth, I followed the directions Aretha sent via letter. According to the letter, I would travel

Run or Die

versus needs. She believed that dreams trumped needs, and finally convinced me.

Unwilling to let me keep procrastinating, she dragged me to every motorcycle dealer around the Puget Sound area. I vacillated over which bike to choose until Alicia fell in love with a hot-red Suzuki. The V-Strom 650, I'd argued, was a dual-purpose bike. Why would I want a dual-purpose bike?

Alicia had grinned. "Dirt roads. All around this area are tons of dirt roads." Her eyes shone so brightly that I didn't have the heart to tell her I liked city streets.

She got her motorcycle endorsement two weeks before I passed the test on the second try.

I squinted my eyes against the waning afternoon sun, shoved the memories into their treasure chest, and slapped the lock on it. Forcefully, I snatched my tattered covering of numbness and wrapped it tight around myself. Even the chill breeze streaming past couldn't touch me.

I rounded a sharp curve and from that high point, glanced out over the now-rolling flanks of the hillside. There, just like Aretha had written, squatted a weathered wood structure built close to a stack of gray-blue boulders. The sparkling glass-front windows zipped sun-balls into my eyes. The road split into a Y. I leaned the bike left and continued on.

What had been a narrow, one-lane road with a few turnouts squeezed down even further until it became little more than a mucky trail. It wove between the bony shoulders of the land rising above the road on one side and what had morphed from steep drop-offs to gentle swells of land on the other side.

Sure that I'd missed the final turnoff, I sat up straighter, slowed the bike, and gazed around. The hillside had shrunken into humps of fields sporting patches of snow and undulating to the distant horizon. She'd written that a blizzard had hit the hill in late February. I'd nearly decided to turn around when I finally spotted the line of drunken wood posts, wire bagging between them, weaving down the hill. A couple of miles further along, I eased through the dappled shade of the first copse of trees that I'd seen along this road. The chill dropped to downright cold, so I didn't linger. Besides, a glance at my watch said it was edging towards two-thirty. I certainly didn't want to be lost on this hillside in the night. Scattered across the flatter land, deciduous trees lifted barren arms to the weakening sun. The road stretched out its sharp angles and began curving gently. At last, relief from the dangerous switchbacks.

Though it felt later, my watch read three o'clock when at last I arrived at a sturdy gate of logs built from small trees. To either side of the gate, shiny barbed wire marched in a ruler-straight line tightly hugging the consistently spaced, split cedar posts. Exactly as Aretha had described. *Damn, the woman's precise.* I wondered if that boded good, or ill.

I kicked the bike stand down and dismounted. The gate swung easily aside and I rode in, then got off and shut it again. Like the letter had instructed.

Across the open, rocky field and up on a slight rise, the blank eyes of the windows peered from under the straight brow of a narrow porch. I idled along the mud-slick, two-tire track, toward the house. A small herd of goats lifted their heads to watch me pass within a few feet of them. Their golden eyes showed curiosity, but no fear, or maybe that was simply my interpretation since their ears hung long and low like a hound dog's ears.

Close to the porch steps I shut down my bike. A caramel-skinned woman stepped out of the dark wood door and walked to the edge of the porch. My heart caught in my chest. Long, wavy hair hung past her shoulders, touching her slender waist. Full, kissable lips graced the heart-shaped face. Deep, dark eyes stared unblinkingly at me.

"You going to sit there all day, or do you think you might come in?" The melodious voice wrenched my heart.

My heart stuttered then pounded. I wanted to howl in pain. *Alicia!*

Aretha...Alicia's aunt. No one warned me. *How could Grandma Pearl be so cruel?* They could've been twin sisters, except for the decade of difference in their ages.

Run! Get the hell out! Go! Instead, I sat there, staring. In a trance, I dismounted and walked toward her. "Are..." I gulped and tried again. "Are you Aretha?"

Run or Die

She sketched a stiff nod at me. At the foot of the two steps up to the porch, I pulled my gloves off. I stuffed them in my helmet then extended my hand. "I'm Jazmine Wheeler."

Her hands never twitched from her sides as she stared at mine. Feeling foolish, I let my hand drop.

In a voice between soprano and tenor, leaning a bit toward tenor, Aretha said, "Just because I told my mother you could come here, does not mean we are best friends. She thought the work and the air could help heal you, but I'll tell you right now, if I didn't need the farm help, I would never have hired you." She spit her speech out in one long spiel then spun on her work boot heel and stamped inside.

Alicia's voice had been maybe a hair lighter than Aretha's. Still in that moment, I hated Aretha, and I loved Aretha. Looking at her, I saw Alicia alive again. Even her voice thrilled through me, so closely resembling Alicia's.

Dazed, I followed her into the cabin. Inside was nothing more than one large room with a rough log interior. Built of wide, golden oak planks, the floor sported old scars and gouges, but glistened in the sunlight that snuck beneath the porch roof and streamed in the windows. Obviously salvaged, the windows—old multi-paned things with peeling white paint—stretched across the front of the cabin. Though they wouldn't do much to keep the winter's cold at bay, I liked the looks of them better than any of the more modern windows.

"Put your helmet on the chair by the door then hang your jacket on the peg on the other side." She waved a long-fingered hand in the general direction without looking away from the plain wood kitchen cupboard. At least her blunt nails bore no pink polish, Alicia's favorite.

I set the helmet on the chair then slipped out of the heavy motorcycle jacket and peeled the black nylon outer-pants off, hanging both on the same peg. The cabin bordered on being too cool, but my jeans and flannel shirt made it comfortable enough. I drifted into the center of the room and surveyed my surroundings.

A brown canvas, camp cot stood against one wall, a pillow lying on top of a handmade, patchwork quilt. Alicia had loved handmade quilts, and had dragged me to several street fairs to look at different ones. This one appeared to be high quality. I stepped closer, inspecting the tight stitching, and noted from the corner of my eye how Aretha glared at me, like she thought I might tuck the quilt under my shirt and make off with it.

"Alicia's mother made that before a drunk white man killed her in a collision that spun her compact car underneath an eighteen-wheeler." Aretha snarled as she stomped over to a black iron, wood cook stove.

From bits and pieces, I'd discovered that Alicia's mom had died in a wreck. Other than that, I didn't know anything about her. I'd never asked Alicia about her mom, maybe because I feared she would ask about mine. But now I understood her love of quilts, and pain laced with regret lanced through me. It was a piece of Alicia that my fear had stolen the opportunity to share. I despised myself in that moment.

Nearly gasping, I sucked in a deep breath then swiveled to look at Aretha. All I saw was her back. Being here was painful enough without her 'tude. I wanted to slap some manners into her, except I knew I'd never be able to lift a hand to someone who so closely resembled Alicia, even if Grandma Pearl wouldn't have "whupped up" on me when she found out.

She lifted a battered, blue-enameled tea kettle, pivoted partway toward me, and wagged it slightly. "Tea?" She asked in a voice that clearly wished me gone.

Not knowing what to do with my hands, I crammed them into the front pockets of my jeans and scuffed closer. "Do you have coffee?"

Her upper lip curled like I'd cursed at her. "No." The clipped word held none of Alicia's warmth.

I narrowed my eyes then chided myself for letting her get to me. I knew better than to let someone burrow under my skin, so I shrugged. "Tea sounds good."

"Sit." She jerked her chin at the nearby table.

I ran my hand along the silky surface of the obviously old and well-cared-for table as I lowered myself onto a sturdy wood chair. Table and four chairs. A quick scan of the room and I corrected myself: table and six-chairs.

Run or Die

Aretha set a chipped saucer and a stained heavy china mug that looked like a restaurant reject in front of me. Grudgingly, she said, "Table and chairs belonged to our Grandma. Mama's mother."

"I didn't know Alicia had another aunt until Grandma Pearl told me about you." Of course, there had really been no reason for me to know. Just another part of Alicia's life B.J., Before Jaz, that had slipped through my hands. Abruptly, I shoved the thought away and sipped the hot brew, watching Aretha.

Lightning flashed across her face, a sharp emotion—not quite rage, but hotter than anger. "Wasn't none of your business. I don't like my business discussed with strangers—especially white strangers—and my family knows that. You may have slept with my niece, but that didn't make you part of our family. And, *my* mother is *not* your Grandma."

With a hand flung up in the classic stop gesture, I leaned against the chair. "Whoa! Never said I was part of your family. What I said was: I didn't know Alicia had another aunt until recently. Your mother, Pearl, is the one who told me to call her Grandma Pearl. Now take that however you want to, but back off! I don't need this crap."

She scowled at me, eyes slitted, lips flattened against her straight, white teeth. Even as I grasped onto the straightness of her teeth—two of Alicia's front teeth were a hair crooked—I kept my eyes locked on hers. Her face held my mother's look. My mother's look on Alicia's face. It was obscene, and felt as dangerous as my mother's fits of violence toward the end of her life.

At last, Aretha inhaled deeply through her mouth and exhaled slowly through her nose. Her shoulders slumped. "The less we talk, the better we'll get along. There's a cot, like that one over there, in the shed out back. Blankets on the shelves over there." She pointed with one finger. "Food in the refrigerator. It's propane, so don't worry about food poisoning. Personal hygiene products and whatnot—towels, washcloths, soap, whatever you need—are in that dresser over there."

In a neutral tone that I'd perfected when I needed to deal with my mother during her more volatile moods, I said, "I have my own soap and shampoo."

She started to shake her head before all the words had left my mouth. "No. Do not use anything *except* what I provide. You'll contaminate the creek. It's warmed up enough to bathe in the creek. When the weather gets too cold, around December, then I heat water and bathe in a galvanized tub. I don't expect that you'll still be here by the time cold weather arrives." She pushed up from the table, left her tea sitting there. "I have chores to do. Look around and pick a corner for yourself. Get set up. I'll be back before full dark."

She returned to the cabin as the sun painted the horizon a fiery red. I stood up from where I'd been squatting against the outside wall. As her boots clumped up on the porch, she flicked a look at me then stepped inside. A few minutes later she walked out with a flashlight in hand, and without a glance in my direction, headed for the creek. I listened to the mutterings of the chickens in the coop not far from the house until the birds drifted into silence then I slowly stretched and ambled inside.

Droplets of water clung to her hair when she walked into the cabin. They glistened in the soft glow of the kerosene lanterns that I'd lit. As she passed me, my hand reached out, my fingers yearned to brush away the droplets, like I'd done so many times with Alicia. I fisted my hands and forced my eyes away.

She brushed out her hair, walked over to the stove, opened the door, and stirred the fire. "Dinner's cornbread and reheated white beans. Be ready in about fifteen minutes. You can get the plates out."

***

When I'd lowered my bike's kickstand, I'd had every intention of leaving that wretched hillside within the hour. Somehow, I let dark fall without remounting my bike and idling off. The next day, as the sky shouted out good morning, it simply felt easier to stay than to go.

Run or Die

The days folded into each other, seamless, physically exhausting. Aretha shoved several books into my hands and ordered me to learn about indigenous plant life. I studied sketches and photographs of invasive weeds, read about changing the soil's pH to battle some of them. Some nights I fell asleep on my cot, squinting up at poor-quality photographs in the dim lantern light. Other nights, Aretha quizzed me with the gentleness of a natural born sadist, opening books and pointing to illustrations of leaves and stems, buds and flowers.

I hoed until she deemed me competent to plant seeds. It took a while longer to earn the right to mound dirt around seedlings. The spring rains came, sometimes pounding the tender seedlings into the ground and at other times the rain felt as light as a wisp of cloud brushing a motherly hand along the tiny leaves.

If neither hoeing nor planting needed to be done, I chopped wood for the stove and herded the goats to their pen down the hill from the cabin. Somewhere in those days, I learned to like the quiet, to enjoy the way the bleating of the goats echoed in the evenings, and how the scree of the Red-tailed Hawk pulled my eyes upward during the day. I learned to savor the sharp taste of goat cheese and goat milk.

I'd been there a bit more than a month when one morning, instead of pulling on overalls, Aretha shimmied into tight jeans. "What's up?" I yanked on clean jeans and a t-shirt.

"Going to town." She finished dressing.

I quickly tied my Avia running shoes, glad to be out of my heavy bike riding boots Aretha insisted I wear to protect my ankles against rattlesnakes. "I'm going with you."

The lines of her face hardened and, for a moment, I thought she might deny me. Then she turned away with a shrug. "Suit yourself."

The classic Volkswagen Bug, parked next to the cabin, gleamed beneath the early morning sun as I started toward it.

"Where you going?" Aretha called as she strode toward a lean-to behind the house.

I jogged to catch up with her. "Aren't we taking your car?"

"How would I carry goat feed in that little thing?" She shook her head like she couldn't believe my stupidity, and rounded the side of the larger of the two sheds behind the house. The unpainted, plywood door swung open easily.

Kept busy planting, hoeing, and repairing fence, I hadn't had time to explore much, including this particular shed. An older black truck squatted in the shadows. Not a speck of dust lay on its faded hood. I walked to the passenger door. It opened without a squeak. Inside the truck, not so much as a paper lay on the floorboards. Not the tiniest tear marred the tuck-and-roll leather seat.

My mother had a boyfriend who drove a truck that looked exactly like this one, even down to the faded paint. He'd called it a classic. Classic or not, this engine hummed like a new truck.

I closed my eyes on the way down the hill—the only way I could stand Aretha's nonchalant speed as she slithered and slid around mucky curves.

A few scattered, puffball clouds spotted the achingly blue sky. Off the hill, the valley's warmth allowed me to roll down the window and lay an arm on the opening. Along the road, boxy-looking black cattle grazed in a pasture that rolled beyond sight. Aretha called them Black Angus. Some fields had been plowed and planted, the brown dirt dotted by tender green. Houses, mostly older farm homes, popped up from the flat valley land at irregular intervals.

My eyes darted everywhere, checking out the town I'd only idled through once. Aretha drove straight to the hamburger joint and hopped out. "Hamburger Haven," declared a painted sign above the door, the H in Haven chipped and faded nearly beyond recognition. I followed, detoured around a few puddles from the rain the night before, and wondered how the food tasted. The dingy gray, linoleum tiles made me think of wonderful things like E. Coli. The kid behind the counter, dressed in stained t-shirt and baggy jeans, didn't help my confidence about the food.

While things like food poisoning and E.Coli screeched in my mind, Aretha ordered two double-cheeseburgers, two large fries, and two diet Pepsis, and slapped down a twenty. Change stuffed in her pocket, she said, "Come on. They'll bring our food to us." Her voice made the simple statement into an abrasive command.

Run or Die

I followed her to the cramped booth by the fly-specked window, silently fuming. *This is just like her. Can't say two civil words hardly, but arrogantly orders my food.* By the time the food arrived, my stomach rumbled and complained. I shoved aside my irritation at Aretha as well as my doubts about sanitation, and ate. In spite of the grungy appearance of the hamburger shack, juice dripped from the burger and the hand-cut fries had been browned to perfection.

After eating, I trailed behind her around the grocery store as she did the regal queen thing, telling me to go get this and to go grab that. I'd just about had it when she finally got into a checkout line longer than I believed possible. Had the entire town decided they had to shop right at that moment? I gazed around, trying to blank out my mind. I wanted to be anywhere but here.

At the truck, I angrily shoved the plastic bags of groceries into the bed while Aretha loaded the various flats of diet Pepsi and bottled water. I suppose that's why I didn't hear them approach.

A rough male voice said, "Hey, nigger, what kinda pervert is that with you?"

I spun around. Except for a flicker of her eyes, Aretha kept loading the truck like she hadn't heard. Two parking stalls from us, a thickset man that I judged to be in his early twenties leaned against the tailgate of a new Jeep four-by-four, painted in camouflage colors. Two other young white men flanked him. Muscled arms crossed over the thick chest of the man who'd spoken. What I could see of his bull neck was sunburned. Dark stubble fuzzed his cheeks. A scar gouged a wide gnarly line from one corner of his mouth. It looked like someone with a seriously bad setting in a ring had hit him. The buzz-cut, pale hair looked nearly white, and a sneer completed the picture of someone only a half-step up the evolutionary chain from Cro-Magnon man.

Adrenaline kicked my heart into overdrive. This dude was not the talking kind.

On his right stood a tall, thin man, greasy blond hair hanging in his acne-pitted face. For a moment, I felt sorry for him. He must have had a gruesome case of pimples as a teenager.

When he opened his mouth, however, all of my sympathy took wings and flew north.

"We've been nice enough to put up with your nigger ass 'cause niggers ain't smart enough to know when they ain't wanted. I knew we shoulda chased your black ass out. You're just a magnet for perverts." The way he ran his eyes up and down me had me wishing for a shower, with lots of very hot water and a ton of soap, but even then I suspected I wouldn't feel entirely clean for a while.

The third guy with lank, dull brown hair, an average build, and a nondescript face, dressed neatly in jeans and a mended short sleeve, button-up shirt, shuffled his feet and studied the ground. A wild card. I hated wild cards in confrontations.

I edged along the dropped tailgate toward the side of the truck where the jack and the tire iron lay against the inside of the bed. Where I grew up, only those who had to work up their courage to attack jacked their jaws like he did. Scared spitless, but strung out on hate too much to let others be. No sense trying to talk to people like that. They couldn't hear.

I held my tongue and observed. From the corner of my eye, I noted that Aretha had finished loading. She turned around calmly and faced the men. Like me, she waited and watched and stayed silent.

The guys crept closer, some of their cockiness gone. I guess they didn't know how to take women who didn't beg or plead or try to reason with them. The dirty-blond-haired guy licked his lips and peered nervously around long strings of lifeless hair, looking to Cro-Magnon to give the signal, maybe trying to suck up some courage from his leader. The other guy hung back a couple of steps, as if he wanted nothing more than to dissociate.

Cro-Magnon's eyes flicked to either side, checking out his backup. With a nasty leer in his voice, he said, "Hey, lezzie, whatcha hangin' with a nigger for? She a pervert, too?" He glanced at his homies standing on either side. "What do you guys say that we go ahead and stomp the nigger right here and now; then we'll haul the lezzie up to Peak Road 'n teach 'er what women are made for."

Run or Die

Without taking my eyes from them, I reached behind and picked up the tire iron. Focused on Aretha I hoped they didn't notice it hanging from my hand, next to my thigh. That would make the surprise so much more...stunning. I felt my lips stretch into an evil grimace. It had been a long time since I'd last fought and, as much as I hated violence, I found myself looking forward to busting heads. Hopefully, it wouldn't land me in some podunk jail.

In my peripheral vision, I noticed a man hurrying toward us. When he got closer, I found myself praying he was on our side and not reinforcements for our tormenters. A baseball bat swung easily from his ham-sized fist. A tight-sleeved tee showed off developed shoulder muscles that rippled with every swing of the bat. A big man; not fat, simply big. He moved quickly, light on his feet, agile for a man his size. He'd checked us out at the store, bagging our groceries with a minimum of talk. Had he resented waiting on us? Or was he naturally a taciturn man? I couldn't recall if he spoke much with anyone who'd checked out ahead of us.

He stopped a few feet from the confrontation, but equidistant between the men and us. With a strong, baritone voice, he said, "You men need to go on home."

At that moment, being a lesbian notwithstanding, I could have joyously kissed him.

Cro-Magnon swiveled his head, his beady eyes glowering at the intruder. "We jus' gonna teach this here nigger 'n this here queer they don' belong here, messin' up our town."

The store clerk held his voice to a low monotone. "You don't know enough to teach anyone anything, William."

Cro-Magnon bristled. "Bill, you know my name's Bill."

The big guy shrugged. "Your mother named you William, and William you are to me."

William tensed, like he thought about jumping the man. I could see when he decided against it. The tightness in his shoulders drained away and his eyes momentarily dipped. "You ain' no nigger lover, are you, Mr. Russell?"

Aya Walksfar

The store clerk stared from creepy blank eyes, silent. A shiver ran up my spine. I didn't know where that man had been, but it had to have been some place really bad.

William must have felt the same unease that trickled up my neck. He kicked a pebble. "Hey, no harm done." His fisted hands belied his words. "Me and the guys was jus' havin' a li'l fun."

Greasy Hair's face twisted like he'd smelled something bad. "My folks ain't gonna like tradin' at no store that lets niggers and queers mess up the place." He thrust his chest out.

Russell shook his head, like he couldn't believe anyone would say that. "I don't think that needs to be dignified with an answer." His voice took on a dangerous edge. "Get on home before I tell your parents your idea of fun is harassing women."

Upper lip curled, William sneered. "Them two ain't women. My daddy's not gonna care 'bout me chasin' off niggers and queers."

"Yeah, William, your father's a big man. A *real* man." The way he said it left no doubt that he meant the opposite.

William squinted his whole face in confusion, but didn't reply. Either too dense to catch the sarcasm, or too afraid to confront the speaker.

Russell shifted his eyes to Greasy Hair. "Ralph, your dad and I fish together. I can't imagine that he actually feels that way, and I can't imagine that he's going to be pleased about your behavior."

Greasy Hair dropped his eyes and his head drooped.

Eyes shifted to the last man, Russell said, "Jimmy, what, in all that is good, are you doing here? And with these troublemakers?"

The young man never lifted his eyes from the asphalt of the parking lot.

Russell waved the bat like he was trying to backhand a baseball with it. "Get! Go on, get! Before you three really tick me off."

The men hesitated until Russell took a decisive step toward them. Slowly, they backed up and climbed into William's Jeep. He squealed out of the parking lot.

Run or Die

The store clerk watched until the Jeep went around a curve in the road before he turned back to us. "I'm sorry that happened." He tipped the end of the bat in the direction that the truck had roared off. "Ralph and Jimmy aren't bad guys, not really. Just got mixed up in bad company and I think they don't know how to get out. William, though," he shifted his eyes, looking first at one of us and then at the other one. "William's been bad since grade school. Don't get caught out alone with him."

"I'm sure the Klan is all good old boys, too! That they're all just caught up with a bad man or two." Aretha snarled then stomped to the driver's side then got in, slamming the door.

I shot a look her way, but she wasn't paying any attention, so I pivoted toward Mr. Russell. "Thanks for helping out. I wasn't sure which jail the sheriff would throw me under if I had to break some heads."

He sighed, moved his feet in place. "The sheriff's a good man. If you want to report this, he'd take your statements."

I grabbed the empty grocery cart as Aretha called out the open truck window, "What good would it do?"

Russell didn't answer as he walked back toward the store with me. I pushed the cart into the rack with the others then glanced at him. He rubbed his hand on the back of his neck, a movement I did when tension tied my neck muscles into knots. "She's right, you know. Sheriff Daly wouldn't be able to do much. He'd go talk to them, but with only me as a witness..." He held his hands out to the sides, the one not holding the bat lay palm up, vulnerable, helpless.

***

Aretha stopped at the little feed store on the far end of town. We loaded fifty bags of grain and a couple of bags of drought-resistant, pasture grass seed.

The trip up the hill nearly suffocated me with unspoken words. She drove up close to the porch. I jumped out before she shifted into first and shut the truck off. She met me around the rear of the truck. I snatched a grocery bag from the truck bed so hard the plastic split, spilling cans all over the ground. Frustration exploded from me. I whirled and slapped my hand against the lowered tailgate. The sting dampened my anger, but I still wanted to stomp those cans. Instead, I forced myself to load them in the ruined bag.

She squatted to help. "Whatever it is, get over it!" she snapped.

I slammed a can on the tailgate then stooped to round up some more of the loose ones. "You could've at least said thanks. It wasn't like he was obligated to come out and help us."

She rose stiffly to her five-foot-nine height. "Do you think that little set-to was the first time those young men have accosted me in *that* parking lot?"

Some of my anger drained away, replaced with bewilderment. I stood there holding a can, forgotten in my hand. "What are you saying?"

Fists propped on her hips, she glared at me. "What I am *saying* is that those men have hassled me for the past two years, starting right after I moved up here. Why do you think Russell came out to stop them this time? One guess, White Girl, and I'll even give you a hint. It wasn't because of me."

Mouth gaped, I stared at her.

"Ahh, now you're getting a clue." She bent over and retrieved the last can, tossing it into the bag. "Besides, if you had ignored them, the way *I've* been doing all this time, they would've gotten tired and left."

"Hey!" I yelled toward her back.

She twisted her head to look over her shoulder. "What?"

"Maybe those other times he didn't see it happening. Maybe Russell isn't guilty of anything more than not paying attention. You ever think of that?"

"Excuses, White Girl. We both know the real reason he came out today and not those other times." She marched down the hill.

"Ever imagine that you could be wrong?" I shouted. "The whole world's not out to get you, you know."

She halted then slowly swiveled around to face me. In a voice just loud enough for me to hear, she said, "You're right." Every word dripped acid. "The whole world isn't out to get black people. Only the white part of that world." She spun and stomped down the hill.

    I finished unpacking and putting the groceries away. As I prepared a meal of macaroni and cheese with hamburger mixed in, I heard the truck drive to the back. I washed my dishes in the dishpan and dumped the water on the tomatoes planted on the east side of the house to catch the sun. She still hadn't come into the cabin when I stretched out on my cot. Coyotes singing down near the creek serenaded me to sleep.

    The next morning the smell of frying bacon teased me awake. An uneasy truce had taken effect.

Chapter 4

A couple of weeks after the town incident, my shoulders ached from pounding nails all morning, attaching board siding to the frame of a small barn. The calves of my legs wanted to tie themselves into knots from running up and down the aluminum ladder. It reminded me a lot of my first days working for Alicia's Aunt Sylvia. After it drizzled rain all morning, the sun finally broke through the overcast sky. The clouds cleared out. Humidity rose, draining my energy in proportion to its increase.

When the sun hit mid-sky, I tossed the hammer to the ground. With the tail of my t-shirt, I wiped rivulets of sweat from my face then picked up my lunch sack, a recycled plastic grocery bag. Early that morning, Aretha had packed our lunches, figuring it would save time and energy to eat down here instead of tramping up the hill to the house. Achy tired, I definitely appreciated her foresight.

A jumble of large and small rocks stood a few feet from the new barn area. One boulder loomed over a bunch of the others, creating an inviting pool of shade. Seated on a rock with a smooshed top, my feet dangling a short ways above the ground, I pulled an apple from the bag. The pocketknife Ellison had given me so long ago neatly cut the apple into quarters. With a napkin spread over the warm stone at my elbow, I laid the apple pieces next to my sandwich. Not paying attention to the slope of the rock, I laid the knife on the stone next to the napkin, wanting to rinse the juice from it before I put it away. When I turned to pick up my water bottle, my arm bumped the knife and the darn thing slid into a crack between the tall boulder and the shorter rock.

I peered into the crack, but the cool blackness hid the knife. Poking a stick in the gap, I felt some spongy resistance, but shifting slightly to one side, I located the hard shape of my knife. No way to fish it out with the stick. The space wasn't that deep, so I turned sideways and thrust my arm into the opening. My fingertips brushed the knife then something pierced my hand like twin, red-hot nails.

Run or Die

"Sonofabitch!" I yelled as I yanked my arm out and jumped away from the stack of rocks. Two round holes glimmered with beads of blood in the meaty part of my hand, between my thumb and forefinger.

Aretha squirreled down her ladder, tossed her hammer to the ground, and ran over.

"I think a snake bit me!" I squeezed the flesh and two more drops of blood oozed out.

She swept a look around. "How'd you get bit?"

I jerked my head toward the rock crevice. "My knife fell in there."

She grabbed my hand. "Idiot, city-bred people! No common sense. Rattlers hide in rocks during the day to keep cool. The only way they can do it." She stepped back. "What'd you do? Just haul off and stick your hand in there?"

Defensive, I momentarily forgot the bite wound. "No, I stuck a stick in there first, but I couldn't fish my knife out." I pointed toward the stick on the ground.

She snatched up the stick, strode to the crevice, and poked in it. The faint rustle of dry leaves drifted up from the dark. "Sounds like a smaller one. Didn't you hear that?" Mouth twisted with disgust, she tossed the stick to the side.

I shrugged as heat crept up my neck. "I thought I was just stirring up some dry leaves, or maybe a chipmunk or something was messing around in there."

"Or something is right. That something was a rattlesnake. We need to get you to the hospital in Willits."

By the time I reached Aretha's Volkswagen parked next to the cabin, my hand throbbed with laser flashes of pain. She ordered me into the backseat then demanded that I recline as much as possible with my elbow propped on the front passenger seat back and my hand held straight up in the air.

Fatigued to the point of collapse, I fought to stay awake enough to keep my hand elevated. The car faded in and out. Chilled, so cold. Burning up. Pain, throbbing to the beat of my racing heart. Alicia's cooling voice, telling me to hang on. The squeal of gurney wheels. The sharp prick of a needle.

The next morning, a golden haze seeped through the slatted blinds of the hospital room. A backless hospital gown tangled around my body. A pulley setup held my hand above my heart. In a recliner next to the bed, Aretha sat asleep.

The next time I woke, a chubby black nurse with lively eyes sung out in a cheerful tone, "Good morning. Breakfast is coming." She poked a thermometer in my mouth and took my good wrist in her cool fingers. Scribbling on the chart hanging at the foot of my bed, she slanted a sideways look at Aretha, who rubbed her eyes as she pulled herself up from the chair. "Dr. Randal will be in around ten."

Without glancing my way, Aretha gave a brusque nod at the nurse then headed for the door. "I'll be back before then."

The nurse smiled as the door closed on Aretha's vanishing form. "Such a sweet lady," she murmured then turned to me. "You are very fortunate to work for a lady like her."

I wanted to snipe at her and ask if she was talking about the same woman I knew, but I kept my mouth shut for a change. I deserved Aretha's cold shoulder. She'd warned me about the rattlesnakes.

The orderly had just removed the breakfast tray when Dr. Randal, a rotund white man, ambled into the room with Aretha close behind. "You're a lucky girl," he said as he checked my chart then peered up at me from behind round-rimmed glasses. "From what Ms. Hopewell tells me it was apparently a small snake that struck and the bite was probably close to being a dry bite." He unhooked the traction device and unwrapped the gauze. "Your hand was twice its normal size when you were admitted yesterday. This morning it's barely swollen. That, young lady, is an excellent sign."

He scribbled in the chart. "I'll write release orders and a prescription for a few pain killers. Your hand may continue hurting for another day or so. Let me know if swelling or pain increases, or if there's tingling or numbness, or a metallic taste in your mouth." Within a few minutes he was gone and a nurse arrived with a wheelchair.

I slept all the way to Aretha's cabin. And, continued to sleep until the next morning, except for an urgent call of nature.

Run or Die

Aretha had provided a slop jar, but I'd be damned if I used one. The moon gave enough light that I didn't need a flashlight. I managed to stand and stagger out the door without waking Aretha. By the time I reached the latrine behind the house, I had to sit for a while after I was done to get ready for the return journey. My legs trembled as I sank onto the cot and fell quickly asleep.

My clothes stunk when I woke up. Sweat and illness stiffened the jeans and denim shirt I'd slept in. "God, I need a bath."

"Yes, you do." She said without looking away from the stove where frying bacon popped. The mouthwatering smell drifted over to me. "After we eat, I'll fix you a tub of water."

With the slow movements of a long-term convalescent, I made my way over to a chair and slumped on it. "I've caused you enough extra work. I'll get down to the creek later today. I think I'm just a little weak from sleeping too much and from whatever painkillers the doctor gave me."

"I'll fix you a tub of water." The finality in her voice brooked no arguments.

In spite of my pride, I had to admit I didn't honestly think I could make it to the creek and back. I changed the subject. "Sometime later this week, I'll need to go into Willits and set up some kind of payment plan with the hospital and that doctor."

She poured tea for both of us and carried the cups to the table. "It's taken care of."

My eyes flashed up. "I don't do charity."

She returned to the stove and dished up scrambled eggs and crisp bacon, and pulled fresh biscuits from the oven. "Not charity. Dr. Randal owes me some money, and we have an arrangement with the hospital in case I ever need it."

I puffed up as she set the plate in front of me. "Well, Dr. Randal doesn't owe *me* anything and *I don't* have an arrangement with the hospital." Angrily, I stabbed a bite of egg and stuffed it in my mouth.

Aretha settled gracefully on the chair across from me. "You're my employee, so the arrangements apply to you as well as to me."

Aya Walksfar

"I can haul my own freight." I frowned at her.

She took a sip of tea and set the cup carefully on the table. "You will haul your own freight, as you so colloquially put it. You'll work off the bill. Now let's eat."

Whenever she put "closed" to a subject, Alicia had given me a certain stern look. Aretha shot the look at me now. It would be futile to argue. Some way I'd repay her.

The following morning all the swelling had gone from my hand. For the first time in days, I felt ready to work. Aretha tossed the Buck knife Ellison had given me on the table then served up breakfast. "Thanks." Tears burned my eyes, so I refused to look up from the knife.

"You're welcome. Think you can work on the barn? I still want to hustle and rebuild the goats' shed by the end of the month. I need a better place for the nannies to give birth." She slipped into her chair and began eating.

Trying for the same nonchalance she exhibited, I picked up my fork. "Yeah, all rested up."

It's funny how some turning points in life zip right past. Never recognized until much later, if ever, for the portentous moments that they are. Then again, maybe it wouldn't have been such a pivotal point if Sarah Lee hadn't given birth.

I knew zilch about pregnant animals, less about goats, and even less about goats that were two weeks overdue. Since the other nannies had birthed in the field, one even had twins, I couldn't figure out what troubling bee buzzed around in Aretha's bonnet.

Sarah Lee didn't appear to be in any distress. Animals had babies all the time without a lot of hoopla. I shook my head, but wisely refrained from commenting when Aretha woke me up every hour as she clomped in and out visiting the goat shed. I wasn't surprised the night she rudely shook me awake.

"Jaz, get up! Sarah Lee's in trouble."

My feet hit the floor. I had shoved them into my boots before the sleep webs cleared from my brain. "What...?" I didn't even know the questions to ask. I shut up and finished lacing up my boots.

Run or Die

Aretha scurried around the cabin, snatching up rags and checking out the contents of a leather satchel. "Come on."

I scrambled down the hill right behind her. The three-quarter moon shone a pale silver light on the young green of the early June grass. Plaintive baas worked their way out of the shed and wandered up the hill like lost ghosts.

We stepped inside, and pushed our way through the clot of milling goats to the far wall where Sarah Lee lay panting. As we drew close, she moaned, the sound so human that my heart clenched in sympathy. Aretha hung the lantern on a head-high, wooden peg then quickly knelt close to the rear of the goat. "Pet her and talk to her, but don't let her get up and don't let her fight me," she ordered.

Kneeling beside the distressed animal, I finally understood Aretha's concern. I stroked the coarse neck fur, trying to believe the words I murmured to Sarah Lee. I risked a glance at Aretha. Sweat slicked her face. Grunting, she shoved her hand further into the goat. I looked away. Time had no place, no meaning, there in those dim confines as the other goats shuffled nervously close by.

"Hallelujah," her whispered word more a prayer than a victory shout.

She jumped to her feet and carried the tiny, bloody body a couple of feet away, where she knelt on a clean bed of straw and vigorously rubbed the baby. I leaned closer to Sarah Lee, stroked her face, kissed the side of it. "You did it, girl. Your baby's born."

For a moment, her golden eye focused on me then slowly the lid settled at half-mast. A soft sigh escaped into the sudden quiet. Even the other goats were still as if they held their collective breath. The shushing of the rag on the newborn's coat seemed to take up the whole space. The hand I stroked down Sarah Lee's neck stalled out. I stared hard at her unmoving side. Unbelieving, I placed a hand across her nostrils. Tentatively, I scooted around until I could place my ear against her side. I jerked up and called to Aretha.

"What?"

"Sarah Lee's not breathing." I licked lips gone dry and tried to swallow.

"Of course, she's breathing. She's just tired and her breathing's shallow. Hard to see in this light."

"No," I replied carefully as if saying it would make it real. "She isn't breathing and I can't find a heartbeat."

"Get over here and take care of drying this baby."

Later that night as we scooped the last of the dirt onto Sarah Lee's grave, Aretha stared across the fresh mound and down the hill to Boulder Creek. "She got too tired. Just too tired to keep on living." She drifted away, not toward the cabin, but down the hill.

I walked back to the cabin. The baby goat mewled from the nest of blankets next to my cot. I walked over and picked him up. Cradled in my arms, he settled. "I'm going to call you Little Kid." He was an orphan, now, just like me. "I know I'm not as good as having your mom, but...hey, I'll do my best by you."

Little Kid was charcoal gray with black legs and a black stripe down the middle of his back. A white diamond dominated the center of his forehead, the only white on him. At eleven pounds he resembled a leggy pup. I couldn't see how something so tiny could kill a full grown nanny. Aretha said breach births could do that, exhaust the momma plumb to death.

Even after Aretha returned to the cabin the next morning she refused to look at Little Kid. Sarah Lee had been her first goat and her favorite. Too smart for her own good, she'd figured out how to open the screen door, get into the cabin, and put her front hooves on the table to eat the butter, if we forgot to put it away. She loved butter. I often thought Aretha left it out just so Sarah Lee could have a treat.

Little Kid's care fell to me. The way the tiny goat sighed and settled his head against my chest made the every-two-hour feedings feel tolerable, and sometimes even pleasant. Gradually, he gained weight and the feedings went to every four hours. Slowly, he gained more weight until he arrived at twenty-four pounds, a very active twenty-four pounds. I cut down to morning and night feedings and left a bowl of softened mash for him in-between meals. At night he slept next to my cot, my hand dangling down, touching him.

Run or Die

My twenty-first birthday came with barely a nod from me, except I gave Little Kid an extra handful of sweet feed. I whispered to him, "You need to get growing or you're going to be one of them pigmy goats like in that goat book of Aretha's."

But the only thing that grew during those hot, dry days of summer was the connection between Aretha and me. Maybe when I took care of Little Kid I forced her to see me as a person. Whatever caused it, her air of martyrdom faded and she started treating me like I'd joined the human race.

Still whenever a supply run had to be made, she went alone, leaving me to care for the animals and do whatever other work that needed to be done. I wondered why, yet didn't dare ask for fear of shattering our tentative truce.

A few days after Little Kid's second-month birthday, the crash of the cheap metal shelves against the rear wall of the cabin and the thump of canisters jerked me awake. I leaped off the cot, eyes darting everywhere in the graying light of dawn seeping in through the window. Powdered white and speckled with black tea leaves, Little Kid bounced around the cabin, boinging off my cot then leaping and skidding in the gritty salt and sugar spilled in a wave across the floor. The little monster must've leaped for the top shelf and unbalanced the three-shelf unit.

He raced over to me and playfully butted my stomach, leaving behind an oval head print on my dark blue tank top. Aretha swung her feet to the floor. "He goes out to the goat shed, today." She yanked on her jeans, tee, and boots then stomped out of the cabin.

I rubbed Little Kid's head. "Oops! Now you've done it." He followed me out of the cabin, gamboling in the early morning light. That evening when he started out of the goat shed behind me, I had to shove his tiny face back through the gate as I shut it. He stood in the deepening evening, face pressed against the bars of the gate, mewling as he watched me walk away.

I wanted to race back and carry him to the cabin. But, it was Aretha's cabin, and Aretha's goat, I told myself. It didn't help. For the first week, I'd wake up and sneak down to check on Little Kid. The first two nights, he'd bedded down by the gate, undoubtedly waiting for me to return and take him with me. An older nanny, ClaraBelle, lay with her side against him. By the third night, ClaraBelle had talked him into sleeping in the shed with all the other goats.

He continued to follow me during the day as I worked, sometimes dozing among the fast growing corn stalks while I hoed, both of us giving Aretha the cold shoulder. After the second week, it got to be too much work to stay mad at Aretha, especially since Little Kid had settled and no longer cried to follow me to the cabin at night.

August blasted us like an out-of-control furnace. At almost three months old, Little Kid hadn't grown much bigger than he'd been at two months. Aretha said since he never received the colostrum from his mother's milk, he'd never catch up to a normal kid. It didn't matter. He'd butt his little head against my stomach and I had to stop work to scratch behind his floppy ears.

It'd been a while since I'd gone to town, so that late summer afternoon when Aretha invited me to run down to Willits with her, I jumped at the chance. I changed clothes then quickly shut Little Kid into the yard with the other goats. She'd already started the truck by the time I scrambled into the passenger seat. She threw it into gear and I grabbed the "oh-Jesus" handle above my head and tried to dissociate.

An hour south of Elmsworth, Willits sprawled across Highway 101. The only time I'd been there I'd been too sick to care about the small city or much of anything else. The first thing I noticed was the huge archway over the two lane highway that bisected the city. "Doesn't look very big." I commented softly, not sure if Aretha wanted conversation.

"It's not. Last census was five thousand people, but my contention is that they counted the dogs." She glanced over as one side of her mouth quirked upward.

"Must be a lot to do then," I said dryly as I gazed around. It looked like all the other small cities and towns I'd passed through on my way to Elmsworth. To tell the truth, I'd been surprised so many existed. Maybe I'd thought they'd all went the way of steam engine trains.

She didn't reply to my comment, just swung a right off the highway and up a quiet side street. Leafy trees lined the street,

Run or Die

draping a welcome shade over the heat of the day. The tiny square of asphalt parking lot Aretha pulled into held three other vehicles: a newer Volvo, a beat-up pickup truck, and an aged Chevy sedan. A small white sign that marked the parking spot closest to the boxy building's entrance read "Dr. Phillip Randal." By the time I got around to the back end of the truck, Aretha had hauled a large cardboard box out of the bed. She nodded at the second one. "Bring that along...please."

I recognized the smells seeping from the folded flaps as the same smells that permeated the cabin where bunches of weedy-looking plants hung upside down from the rafters and sometimes witch's brews bubbled on the cast iron cook stove. Why would we be carting this stuff into a doctor's office?

"Hey, Aretha." The pasty-white girl behind the receptionist's desk smiled and waved.

I braced myself for a scathing reply from Aretha. Instead I heard her ask civilly, "How's the rash?"

The girl hurried around the desk, beaming. She hiked her mid-calf skirt above a knobby knee and proudly held out a skinny leg for Aretha's inspection. "Gone!" She announced as if some miracle had occurred.

She gave the woman a slight nod. "Looks good. Keep the salve handy in case you have another outbreak."

Dr. Randal, a rotund man with wobbly chins and bristles of gray hair sticking out like a wiry halo that had fallen over his hairy ears, steamed around a corner of the hall. He barreled over to Aretha, grasped her shoulders in his pudgy white hands, and kissed her right cheek with an audible smack. Briefly, I wondered why he'd acted so coolly at the hospital. Professionalism, or something else? I shook the thoughts out of my head. Not my business.

Aretha stiffened slightly, but then relaxed so quickly it left me wondering if I'd actually seen the tension. I followed along as she walked behind the doctor to his cluttered office. She set her box on the corner of a jumbled desk and motioned for me to set mine on a nearby chair.

"Well, am I ever glad you came today, and not only because I'm out of supplies." He plopped into a creaky desk chair then fell silent, shooting significant looks at me then looking back at Aretha.

She stood at ease in front of the desk, one hand resting on the cardboard box, plainly ignoring his darting eyes.

I hiked a hip on the chair arm where I had deposited the second box. *What's with the cloak and dagger looks from the doc? Wonder what's going on?* With a smile to myself, I added, *Just what are those plants?*

He finally huffed a noisy breath and shifted in his chair, effectively cutting me out of his sight line. Talk about see no evil!

"I have a woman I want you to see," he announced in an important voice.

Before he could continue, Aretha gave a firm shake of her head. "I make poultices and potions, Phillip. I don't doctor people. Remember? I don't have the fancy license and I could go to jail if I doctored people." Her words held a sharpness that reminded me of the proverbial two-edged sword.

Wearily, he sank against his desk chair, causing it to squeal like a door hinge in need of lubrication. "Come on, Aretha. I hustled over when you needed me at the hospital." He ran a hand over the bald spot on top of his head. "I can't help her. She cries all the time. Has night sweats so bad that, in her words, she sweats like a laborer at high noon. Just this once, won't you see her, talk to her?"

Eyes narrowed, she leaned forward and hissed, "*Just this once*. Once is all it would take to wind up prosecuted for practicing medicine without a license, isn't that right, Phillip?"

He held his hands out in an open, appeasing gesture. "Can't you ever forget and forgive? I thought you were some kind of quack peddling God knows what to gullible people in my town."

She stood up, rigidly straight, with her arms locked over her breasts.

"Please, Aretha. I can't use any stronger antidepressant. It would either be those prohibitively expensive ones, or it would have to be one of the others that would make her a zombie. They can't afford the former, and the latter would be unacceptable to her husband."

Run or Die

"Not acceptable. What you really mean is that he beats her." Her jaw tightened, the muscle clenching and releasing.

"She claims he only slaps her sometimes to try to snap her out of her depression." His voice reflected his skepticism.

"I can make a special trip in again tomorrow, bring you some tea, some herbs..." She frowned. "Don't go shaking your head at me, Phillip."

He threw up his hands in a helpless gesture. "Her husband won't allow her to come here anymore. Says it's a waste of time and money."

As ungracious as a sullen teenager, Aretha let her arms drop to her sides. "What do you want me to do?"

***

A few days later, as we ran plastic tubing from a metal water tank that resembled a Goodyear blimp down to the house, Dr. Randal's patient arrived.

Her print dress, faded from too many washings, held as much life as her short, brittle auburn hair. She wrung red, roughened hands and kept wringing them together as she mumbled to her feet.

Exasperated, Aretha finally snapped. "For God's ever-loving sake, woman, look up here and tell me your name."

The pale face turned up toward the taller, darker woman. Washed out blue eyes squinted against the noonday sun. "I'm Helen Dooley. Me 'n my man live over yonder on Bell Road."

Aretha propped her hands on her slender hips and gave a brisk nod. "What can I do for you?"

"Dr. Randal, he said you might have somethin' to take care of my...my female troubles." Red crept up the woman's neck as her eyes darted away from Aretha.

I stood as still and quiet as I could, hoping they'd forget my presence next to that monster water tank.

Aretha's lips set into a tight line. If I had been a betting person, I would have bet that she wanted to tell that woman to take her troubles on down the road. She said, "Where does your man think you are?"

Aya Walksfar

The woman glanced up then dropped her eyes to her dusty feet. "Tol' him I was goin' berry pickin'. Won't 'spect me back till dark."

"You have any berries?" Aretha cocked her head and studied the woman.

For the first time since she'd climbed out of her rust bucket car, her head lifted and she looked at Aretha with something close to pride shining in her eyes. "Oh, yes, ma'am. Got plenty berries. I'm a fast picker 'n I know the bes' spots. 'Specially for the early berries. Figgered maybe you'd like some fresh berries."

"I could use some. Bring what you can spare and come on down to the cabin."

Less than fifteen minutes later the woman walked out of the cabin and drove away. The herb tea and the women's potion laid hidden in a canvas tote bag that she used like a purse.

"Aretha, why'd you take care of that woman?" I stared at her. "You didn't want to."

She tucked away the large bottle of potion and wiped the table where a couple of drops had spilled. "When I first came here, I thought it would be a win-win situation. I knew about herbal medicine and people who wanted to try that route could come to me. We'd barter. Like in the old days." Rag hung up, she made her way out of the cabin and up the hill to the water tank.

I matched her step for step through the browning grass. "What happened?"

A bitter smile ghosted across her lips. "Dr. Randal happened."

Face scrunched in puzzlement, I slanted a look at her. "I don't get it. He buys your potions and teas."

"Now he does." She said in that tone Grandma Pearl used when she closed a subject to further discussion.

Late that night as the moon rose, a thin crescent in the sky, I called from my cot, "Aretha?"

"Hmm?"

"Why didn't you tell that woman to go away?"

She heaved a sigh. "You aren't going to let it be, are you?"

"Just curious," I muttered, but loud enough for her to clearly hear across the room.

"My aunt, Mom's sister, was a doctoring woman in Alabama." Her voice drifted quietly across the small space.

Even after these months, I still heard Alicia in Aretha's voice. Somewhere along the way the dreadful pain had settled mostly into a dull ache.

"I stayed with her in the summers and she taught me about herb lore. Sometimes, late at night white people would come to the back door, wanting potions and salves. Some of these were the same white devils who covered up in sheets and harassed black people. I wanted to poison those devils."

I heard a dark chuckle before she continued. "Auntie told me that there were two curses that could be brought down upon doctoring women. The first curse occurs if we use the guise of healing to bring harm to another. That harm will return to us threefold. She called it the Threefold Law."

"Sounds like something a Wiccan girl I once knew told me."

"Wiccan followers have a history of female healers." She fell silent.

A lone coyote yipped. It sounded lost, lonesome. I shivered. When I couldn't bear the silence any longer, I asked, "What's the second curse?"

"Any healer who refuses help to one in need, forever after their life will be tainted by need."

I heard her turn over on her cot. "Good night, Aretha."

Early September with the heat unrelenting, it seemed insane to be chopping and splitting firewood. Sweat slicked my naked back and slithered its way under the waistband of my jeans. Somewhere over the summer, I'd lost a lot of my self-consciousness. And, I'd quit blushing every time Aretha stripped her shirt off—sans bra—while she worked, exposing her milk-chocolate nipples to the sun.

I swung the double-bladed axe. It thunked into the tree round then the wood split and fell to the ground. I picked up the next round, placed it on the chopping block, but before I could swing the axe, Aretha shut off the chainsaw and looked over at me.

"How's a milkshake sound?" She ran the back of her hand across her forehead, gathering a river, or maybe only a creek, worth of sweat that ran down her arm, leaving trails in the sawdust.

Glad for any excuse to be out of the hot sun, I put the axe in the tool shed. Within minutes, I'd donned my t-shirt, put the goats up, and beat her to the truck.

Cro-Magnon William had parked his Jeep under the maple tree behind the burger joint. I didn't see the vehicle, or them, until I stepped in the door. He and his buds looked up from a table in the back corner, the only table occupied.

Aretha never broke stride on her way to the counter. Following close behind, I hoped she didn't stir up a deadly hornet's nest. I breathed a silent sigh of relief when William and his posse did nothing more than shoot nasty looks our way.

A thin boy waited on us, speaking only enough to take our orders for burgers, fries, and shakes, flicking nervous glances over at William and his crowd. The gum-smacking girl behind the counter ran her eyes over us like we were dog turds on two legs then sauntered over to William's table. From the corner of my eye, I watched her lean against William's shoulder.

I took the two white bags when the young man handed them over without a word. Aretha scooped up the cardboard holder with our shakes and we headed out the door. The thud of the pulse in my throat started slowing down once we cleared the door and headed across the parking lot.

A dozen steps from the burger joint, I heard the tattle tale jingle of the bells on the door. I didn't bother turning around. I could hear the slap of their feet against the asphalt a few strides behind us. They split around us and stopped when they got positioned between us and Aretha's truck. Not to be paranoid or anything, but I didn't think the boy or the girl behind the burger joint's counter meant to help us. That might have had something to do with the girl turning the sign to "closed."

Cro-Magnon William grinned, showing off yellow teeth. "Mr. Russell ain't around today, bitches."

The only weapons in my hands were two bags with burgers and fries. Too bad my mom hadn't cooked them. They would've been lethal. I must have smiled at the thought because Cro-Magnon did his best imitation of being a dog.

Run or Die

He growled. "Whatcha smilin' at, lesbo?" He grabbed the crotch of his pants. "Thinkin' 'bout the good time I'm gonna give you?"

Mom used to tell me I didn't have a lick of sense when I got riled. She also told me that whenever I reached that crazy-mad point, I would jut my jaw, slit my eyes, and then smile this cold smile that could frost the Devil's ass. Until Mom said that, I had never noticed. One of the things my mother gave me: insights into myself. Right now, my insight said I would probably get my butt kicked. I didn't care.

I locked eyes with Cro-Magnon. "What I'm smiling about is you. You're real brave when you've got your two homies there to take the beating for you, but you're too much of a coward to fight me by yourself."

Face contorted in a snarl, he spread his arms like he meant to give me a great, big, old hug—or crush my ribs—and rushed me.

I dropped the burger bags and held my ground. He swung, his arm looping wide. I ducked the wild throw and dodged away. He stood, spraddle-legged, shoulders hunched, doing a good imitation of a dummy. Wait! Not an imitation; it's the real William.

I waited. He rushed, again; got close. I swung my foot up and out. A solid hit between the thighs. Doubled over, he grabbed his crotch and began folding to the ground. I grabbed a handful of dirty hair and yanked his head back then down into my oncoming knee. Blood spurted. When I let go, he dropped. A maniacal smile stretched my lips as I turned toward the other two guys. "Pick up your rubbish, *boys,* and get out of my face."

I watched while they looped William's limp arms around their shoulders and dragged him to his Jeep.

Aretha's voice swung me around. She peered into the bags. "Burgers and fries are fine. Let's eat."

All the way back to the cabin, she shot speculative looks at me, like I was the freak sideshow at a carnival. When I gave her the "what's-your-problem" look she turned her attention to the hard baked road for the rest of the ride home.

That evening darkness drifted down as soft as a feather. The half-moon cast a surreal, silvery light over the land. Little Kid butted my thigh as I walked to the goat shed gate. It had become his nightly habit. I bent over and kissed the velvet softness of his muzzle then stepped out and latched the gate. Standing there I couldn't recall why I'd ever thought that rural nights would be silent. Chirring and hooting and rustling whispered from every point on the farm. I grinned and strolled up to the cabin.

Aretha sat on the edge of the porch, her bare toes drawing lines in the dry, loose dirt. "Hey, made us some iced sun tea."

With a sigh, I eased down close to her and accepted the sweaty, cool glass. I pressed it to my forehead before taking a long gulp of the sweet liquid. "When I first got here you used to have a glass of homemade wine every now and then. How come you don't anymore?"

She peered over the rim of her glass. "Where'd that come from?"

"I don't know. Just wondering, I guess."

"My husband was a recovering alcoholic. He told me it was helpful if I didn't drink around him."

"I'm not in recovery, Aretha. That's not why I refused a taste of the wine. I just never liked the taste of alcohol."

"And, I do like the taste of sun tea." A companionable quiet rested between us as we finished our tea. "Where did you learn to fight like that?"

I smiled and turned my head slightly so I could see her. The corners of my lips tipped upward. "You've wanted to ask that all day, haven't you?"

She shrugged and resumed staring out across the land bathed in silver light.

I let my head fall back and stared up at the stars. The Big Dipper tilted above the trees. In my mind I could almost see sparkling water pouring over the earth. My eyes roamed across the black sky, drifted into the swathe of stars called the Milky Way. The name finally made sense. At home, I'd never seen the sash of gauzy white spread across the heavens before I arrived at Aretha's. City lights had blinded me to a lot of things. "My mom."

"Some mother." Admiration sounded in her voice.

Run or Die

I dropped my eyes to her face, clear in the moon's brilliance. "Don't sound so awe-stricken. She had to know how to fight. Prostitution's a rough profession."

"Ouch." After a moment, she asked, "What happened?"

"Got hooked on meth. Same old song. Got some bad shit. Died." I shrugged, but my throat closed up. After a while, I cleared my throat. "Wish I hadn't lost it in town. Cro-Magnon isn't likely to let that kind of humiliation go."

She sighed and tilted her head toward the night sky. "You didn't have a choice."

"Still..."

"I know." She climbed to her feet. "I think I want something a bit stronger than tea. I know it's hot, but what do you say to a cup of coffee and some of that apple pie Mrs. Edison bartered for that jar of burn salve?" She headed into the cabin.

"When did you get coffee?" I shot to my feet and hustled behind her.

Her laugh tinkled like wind chimes. "Picked up a couple of pounds on one of my runs to town. Was saving it for a special occasion." She stopped in the doorway and faced me. "Jaz, no matter what happens I want you to know it *really* wasn't your fault. I saw his Jeep parked over on the side. I could've driven on by, went down to Willits for burgers and shakes. I even briefly considered doing that, but I'm tired. Tired of having to go out of my way because of someone else's prejudice."

"Me, too." The night wrapped around us. An owl hooted. Trouble would surely come, but for now I drank in the soft breeze that wandered up from Boulder Creek.

Chapter 5

October came and still the flawless azure sky stretched over us. The hills slid from golden brown to parched dead tan. Night temperatures dropped radically, sometimes close to freezing, yet the daytime temperatures hovered in the seventies.

I no longer allowed Aretha to go to town alone. Each time we went, dust billowed in rooster tails behind us. By the time we arrived, the fine grit coated us.

On our mid-October grocery run, Russell caught up with us as we wheeled our cart toward the truck. "Of course, I'll help you out with these groceries." He spoke overly loud, overly hardy, like he was trying to convince someone that he wasn't being nice; just business-like.

It didn't set right with me, that kind of pretending. Still, there was something so strange, so insistent in his tea-brown eyes that I let the cart go.

He pushed the cart up to the lowered tailgate and began unloading the groceries. Not looking at either of us, he spoke softly, "There's a rumor that William and his friends might be thinking about paying your place a visit. There was some talk about burning you out."

A bolt of anger crashed across Aretha's face. "Why the subterfuge? Why not tell us in the store? Why all that..." She waved a hand to indicate the nonsense about helping us with our groceries.

Russell had the good grace to blush. "Last time I helped you, I lost business." In a bitter voice, he said, "Apparently, there were more folks in town that didn't want trouble with William's people than I figured on. I have a family—a wife and three little kids—and bills." He set the last bag of groceries in the bed of the truck, wheeled the cart around and called with patently false cheer, "Have a nice day, ladies."

Headed up the hill, I said, "Macho posturing, that's all that is. Burning someone out takes more balls than William has."

She slanted me a look, but didn't reply.

Run or Die
***

  That very evening as soon as full dark fell, she haltered Hershey, the lead nanny. "Make yourself useful and get a halter on Hemingway."

  I drew in air to argue, but one look at the tension around her mouth and I haltered the billy goat.

  Instead of heading straight downhill, Aretha led the way into the woods. The flashlight prevented me from smashing into trees. She waded across Boulder Creek, still running low from a dry summer. On the other side, she meandered through more woods until we arrived at a ravine, really more like a sizeable gully. The vertical slopes and boxed end created three sides for a corral of sorts.

  "Tie Hemingway to this tree, next to Hershey, then start debelling the others."

  Working efficiently, we finished our tasks in minutes and headed back the way we came. "Why didn't we tie any of the others? Aren't you afraid they'll wander off?"

  "Goats are herd animals. They need to be with their herd. With the leaders tied, the others will stay close."

  "What about that cougar I spotted last month? Seems like those goats are dinner on the hoof." I didn't want to admit it, but I worried about Little Kid.

  Aretha stopped and let me catch up. "Don't worry about her. She's been here since before I arrived. Even before I had a chicken coop or goat shed, she wandered around, but she's never taken any of my animals." In the dim glow of the flashlights, I saw Aretha smile, the same gentle smile I'd seen so often on Alicia's lips. "It was like she was giving me permission to share the hill with her."

  The rest of the climb up to the cabin area I locked down my questions. She knew more about the animals and this hill than I did, yet I couldn't understand why she let those punks spook her.

  With the chickens half asleep, Aretha figured they would stay put once we placed them on the lower tree branches far enough in the woods for them to be hidden. Other than a bit of fluttering, none of the chickens objected to our invasion of the chicken house.

She hauled Albert, the Ameraucana rooster, while I carried Cinders, the White Leghorn hen, out of the chicken house and stuck them side by side on a branch in a tree. We'd walked four steps when with a whoosh of wings they flew past us and landed in the chicken yard before we got there. They strutted back through the open chicken house door and hopped up on their roost.

Hoping we could get some of the less independent chickens to stay put, we hauled more of them out to the trees in the woods. Every chicken we placed in a tree flew back to the coop. After a while, Aretha gave up. "Let them sleep where they feel comfortable. Those idiots are after us; I can't imagine them wanting to fool with chickens."

The first night sleeping on the ground chilled me so badly that it required four cups of coffee to warm up the next morning. Unfortunately, it went from cold to progressively colder, sometimes dipping close to freezing. I turned up the control on my heated motorcycle gear, grateful that I'd paid the extra money to get jacket, gloves, and pants that worked on a lithium battery as well as off the bike plug in. Even at that, I shivered. Aretha had to be suffering more than I was. "Oh come on, Aretha. Those guys were just blowing hot air. I haven't had any decent sleep in days."

Lips compressed, she shook her head. "I have a bad feeling, Jaz."

The jumble of boulders we slept behind afforded a view of most of the farm without exposing us. Every night we unrolled our sleeping bags in its deepest shadows. Aretha split sentry duty into two shifts. Now every time we made a town run she purchased five pounds of my favorite French Roast coffee, almost like an apology for making me freeze.

The day before Halloween the dove gray sky unfolded empty of clouds. The crisp coldness of the night diluted the sun's warmth. We cooked up the last batch of applesauce and jarred it before mid-morning. The root cellar I'd helped to hand-dig lay under a plain wood trapdoor in the ground. The door blended with its surroundings, difficult to see during the day and nearly impossible to see after dark. Half as big as the cabin, shelves lined the rough board walls. Proudly, I handed the last jars of applesauce down to Aretha. Much of our winter's groceries I'd helped to preserve.

Over an early dinner, I questioned Aretha. "What do we accomplish by hiding?"

She chewed and swallowed. "I expect them to bust into the cabin. If we're there, there'll be a fight. Since we won't be there, I expect they'll bust up some stuff, maybe break the windows, vandalize the cabin, then leave." She picked up her cup and took a long drink. "Best case scenario: we'll see their faces clear enough that we can confidently identify them for the sheriff. I'm hoping the worst case scenario will be that the cabin gets busted up and a big mess made, but we can't clearly identify anyone."

Something in her wording and in her voice made me study her face closer. *Hoping the worst case scenario is a mess? What does she really think the worst case scenario might be?* My stomach plummeted.

Aretha doesn't even have a nodding acquaintance with hysterical. What does she think is going to happen, and why does she think it might be worse than the cabin being vandalized?

Growing up in a rough part of the city, I had an intimate acquaintance with violence. All the possible scenarios that came to mind sent a shudder racing up my spine with skittering, icy claws. A fog of foreboding settled around me that no amount of self-talk dissipated.

That weekend, William and his posse invaded Aretha's land. They came in the darkest hour before dawn on a Sunday morning, still staggering from Saturday night's excesses. Aretha poked me in the side when she spotted the headlights topping the rise. I jerked awake soundlessly and rolled out of the warmth of the down sleeping bag. She pointed up the hill. Two sets of headlights eased over the top of the rise. Keeping low and silent, I scooted closer to the boulders, hunkered in the blackness cast there.

Their headlights blinked out. The two distinct engine sounds—one the well-known sound of William's Jeep and the other rumbling like a diesel truck—shut off, one after the other.

Aya Walksfar

The weak light from the sliver of crescent moon failed to do more than silhouette the vehicles. The pop and crunch of tires announced their coasting descent. Knowing every stone and rut of the road, the inevitable sounds of vehicles moving then stopping told us when they arrived at the bottom of the hill just a few steps from the padlocked gate. The night magnified the sounds of doors opening. Snatches of conversation rode the cold air.

"Idiots," I whispered. "Didn't even think to unscrew the inside lights."

For a moment, we could count the number of intruders. Six, and three of them appeared to be as big as William.

Six flashlights clicked on, the beams jiggling as they clambered over the gate. The spots of light jerked and wandered up the dirt track.

One light dipped toward the ground then rose again like someone had tripped. "Damn!"

"Shut up." William's voice hissed loud enough for a deaf man to hear.

Partway up the slope from the gate, three of the flashlights drew ahead. The beams behind them silhouetted familiar figures: Cro-Magnon William, Greasy Hair Ralph, and Mute Jimmy. As they drew closer, I could make out hulking black shadows bringing up the rear, but not much else.

They arrived in front of the porch and milled about. The beams of their lights wavered over them then bounced in different directions. The quick flashes revealed long objects swinging from the hands of William and two of the strangers. *Baseball bats? Did they intend to beat us with baseball bats?*

Fear strangled me. I'd seen what a baseball bat in an angry person's hand could do to the human body. I swallowed hard. *It doesn't matter. They don't know where we are.* The words became a chant in my mind, loosening fear's hold ever so slightly.

The idea of taking them on with our sawed-off tree branch clubs now seemed ludicrous, although I felt somewhat safer with one lying on the ground next to me.

"Hey, nigger! Come out here!" William yelled. When no one responded, he yelled again. "Hey, bitches, I said get out here now!"

"Maybe they ain't there." I recognized Ralph's whiny voice.

Run or Die

"Jimmy, you and Sam kick that door in 'n let's drag their sorry asses out here. Show 'em what real men can do," William ordered.

Boots thudded against the solid plank door. "Fuck! That hurt!" Someone yelled.

Idiots didn't even check to see if it was locked. A grimace twisted my lips. Aretha had left the door unlocked hoping to circumvent this kind of damage.

Wood cracked and the door banged open.

Flashlights from behind them lit up the two figures crowded in the doorway. "They ain't here." If I didn't know better, I would have sworn that Jimmy's voice sounded almost relieved, but I shrugged away the notion. "Ya know, I didn't see that Volkswagen anywhere. Maybe they stayed in town."

William crossed in front of the flashlights that shone on the open door. The other men backed away as he stepped across the threshold. "Goddamn it! Bitches did a runner." He disappeared into the cabin. No one followed him in.

Sounds of breaking wood and shattering glass ripped jagged holes into the lightening hour. By the time he stepped out onto the porch, gray edged the horizon.

For a moment, it appeared as if he stared right at our spot next to the boulders. A shudder rippled through me.

He moved off the porch. "Fuckin' bitches! They can't hide forever! I'll get 'em, sooner or later."

He whirled around and raised the stick he held. Gunfire erupted! My heart kicked up and ran off like a spooked horse. The shooting stopped as abruptly as it had begun.

I felt Aretha tremble as she hunkered against my side.

Whoosh! Red and orange flames shot up the face of the cabin.

Aretha lunged to her feet. "Auntie!" The crackling of the fire and the raucous cheers of the men swallowed her cry.

I tackled her and dragged her further behind the boulders, clamped my hand across her mouth. Arms wrapped tight around her, I rocked her and whispered, "Shh...shh. It's going to be all right." The lie tasted like soured milk in my mouth.

Another barrage of gunfire. *God, what is this? A war zone?*

Aretha's entire body shook. My heart pounded against my chest and an iron band of fear squeezed my lungs until I could only pull in shallow, panting breaths.

William gave a rebel yell. The others took it up. More gunfire ricocheted through the early morning gray.

I shut my eyes. *Assholes, just go! Leave!* More shots tore through the still air as I held Aretha tighter, pressed her head against my chest, and kept rocking her. Her fingers dug into the back of my jacket.

It felt like forever before I heard their vehicles rev up. William's glass packs thundered across the hills. More gunfire and rebel yells splintered the coming dawn as they roared away.

By the time we stood and edged around the boulders, fiery orange-red streaks slashed the eastern sky. We staggered down the hill and untied the goats. They immediately started grazing as they followed us.

The cabin's small size and the dryness of the season had conspired. The odor of gasoline stung my eyes. With the roof already caved in, we stood back from the blaze, watching as the walls crumbled. The sun had clambered above the treetops by the time we could hear anything except the hunger of the fire.

A few timbers stubbornly stood, swaying like dying soldiers before they tumbled to the ground. The barren dirt around the immediate area of the cabin had kept the fire contained. Something to be grateful for amid the wreckage: we didn't have to fight a grass fire with nothing more than a hose with gravity-fed water from the water tank.

The charred wood of the cabin had compacted down to the size of a large slash burn. Not much bigger than the pile of brush we'd burned earlier in the spring before dry weather arrived.

Their attempt to burn the woodshed on the east side of the cabin partially failed. Green, sap-wet wood requires determination, and a lot of gasoline, to get it started. They must've run out of gas. Fire had chewed up the board walls. Flames had obviously scorched and charred some of the stacked split wood, but most of it remained useable. Anger ran through me. Hours of my hard labor gone!

Run or Die

The truck shed/toolshed on the west side of the cabin had not fared as well as the woodshed. It had burned down way before the cabin flames died out. I kicked through the gray ashes and small chunks of blackened wood. The head of a Maddox clunked against my boot, and I nudged it off to the side. Once it got a new handle on it, it'd be useable again. The shovels, made of lighter metal, were no longer worth the price of a new handle. Total losses, like most of the tools. I stared at my feet, nudging pieces of unrecognizable objects aside as I shuffled through the destruction, avoiding most of the lingering hot spots.

Further down the hill the new barn still stood. I heaved a silent sigh of relief. The goat house stood to the right of the barn. The chicken coop squatted a bit closer to the house. From up by the cabin, all three buildings appeared unmolested. Too far for drunks to stagger, or maybe they simply hadn't noticed it?

Fate teases us with such hopes of small good fortunes.

Aretha turned from the blackened pile of rubble that had been her home. The periodic baaing of the goats broke the quiet of the hillside. "The chickens..."

I shifted my eyes to her. She frowned. "The chickens," she repeated. "The chickens aren't out." Despair clung like the odor of something dead in her voice.

I blinked. A hollow feeling opened up inside of me, the same kind of feeling I'd had the day Mom died even as I desperately walked her and prayed to a God I didn't believe in for the ambulance to hurry. I licked dry lips. My voice came out a croak. "Let them out."

Tears pooled in her eyes, spilled over and wound silently down warm brown cheeks. "They aren't locked in."

Eyes closed, I shook my head. Cotton brain, my mother used to call it, the feeling that your brain is suffocated beneath a mound of cotton. Everything sounds far away. Every move is like swimming in cold molasses. My feet felt like lumps of rock, slowing my every step, making it difficult to even shuffle to where Aretha stood staring down the hill. We started down the slope. I stumbled. Aretha caught my arm, saving me from a face plant on the dirt. She never let go of my arm, and linked awkwardly together we groped our way through the changed world.

Aya Walksfar

Shotgun blasts. I had been so certain that they were shooting up the cabin. My stomach churned as my eyes lit on red shell casings strewn along the outside of the chicken yard fence. Red blots on the thin brown grass, like scattered droplets of blood.

Pellets had blown through the thin plywood sides, giving the chicken house the appearance of a flat, wooden sieve. I walked around to the partially open door at the front. Now I remembered. Since we'd started hiding, Aretha had left it open enough so the chickens could get into the yard, that way we could sleep during the more restful hours of early morning. Neither of us slept well at night. Reluctantly, I nudged aside the stone that propped it open and though my arm ached from pulling against the sadness, I pulled until the door stood wide.

The sun chose that moment to reach the gap in the trees and the hills. Golden streams poured over the silent chicken yard, spilled across the threshold, and illuminated the carnage.

Bloody, sometimes headless, bodies lay in tiny grotesque heaps. Blood splatters, like macabre ink blot images of the Rorschach Test I'd once been forced to take, smeared the plywood. Shotgun blasts had flung clumps of colorful feathers around like confetti, some stuck in dried puddles of blood, across the narrow dirt floor.

My stomach heaved. Cold sweat sprung out on my body. I spun and crashed into Aretha's frozen form standing as still as death behind me. Staggering, I darted around her and away from the heart-wrenching sight. A few feet from the chicken house door, I bent over with my hands braced against my knees, and retched. Thin drool hung from the corner of my mouth. I wanted to wipe it away, but the dry heaves kept me bent over. A miniscule pool of watery fluid formed at my feet. I sank to my knees, barely missing the gross puddle, beaten to the ground by this horror.

I don't know how long I knelt on the hard dirt before I braced my hand on the ground and shoved to my feet with a grunt. With the stiff steps of an old woman, I made my way over to the chicken house door and halted next to Aretha. The heavy feeling of crippling age rode my back. I could hardly stand upright, arm clasped around my stomach, hunched over like a crone. I

Run or Die

clutched the edge of the rough wood doorframe. A large splinter punctured the heel of my hand. The needle-like pain grounded me, and I stood up straight.

Aretha, dry eyes focused somewhere beyond the bloody walls of the chicken house, spoke in a faraway voice. "Albert and Cinders. They were the first ones here. For a long time, it was just me and them. There wasn't any house for them, or for me. Not yet. At night, they roosted on the lowest branch of whichever tree I slept under. I told them that if they stuck around," she swallowed, blinked then went on. "If they stuck around and, kept a sharp eye out for hawks and coyotes, that they could live here until they died of old age. I promised them that together we'd watch this place grow." She sighed, a deep melancholy sound, then turned and walked away.

My gaze fixed on the headless body of the Ameraucana rooster. He'd obviously been flung from his perch by a shotgun blast. The peppering of holes behind his special spot shouted in mute testimony. Cinders, a White Leghorn hen with black speckles on the crown of her head, lay in a crumpled heap of feathers against the far wall, Albert's flowing black tail feathers lay limp across her shattered wing.

They had been inseparable, pecking the dirt side-by-side, roosting every night wing-to-wing. The same blast had most likely killed them both. Bile scalded the back of my throat. I hoped it had been quick. That they had died never knowing the panic I could see in the stretched wings of some of the dead chickens.

Arms wrapped around her stomach, Aretha stood next to the chicken yard gate, staring down the hill. As I walked up next to her, she said, "We have to bury them, Jaz. I can't...I can't stand the thought of...of coyotes..." Her words died away, killed by her pain. The muscles in her jaw clenched and released; clenched and released. Finally she turned to face me, lifted tortured eyes. "I can't stand the thought of coyotes ripping into them. They've suffered enough."

Wordlessly, I nodded.

With a handle-less piece of shovel, the edges of its metal surface pitted and rotted by heat, I dug the grave in the chicken yard. We buried them in a flock, laid wing-against-wing, the way many of them often roosted. "It's the place, ironically, where they felt the safest." Aretha's flat voice scared me in a way that the attack hadn't.

Afterwards we walked the additional several yards to the goat house. Aretha had locked the swinging door just as if the goats had been put to bed. We approached the front of the small shelter standing in the meadow. Shotgun and rifle fire had blown away chunks of wood out of the plywood walls. Several different types of shell casings peppered the ground.

Did they think the goats were trapped in there, too scared to make a noise? Or didn't they care one way or the other, as long as they wreaked destruction? Jaw clenched I shook my head hard to rid myself of those thoughts.

Staring at the riddled structure, it became real in a gut-level way that it hadn't before: they had come here with the intent to kill every living thing that called this farm home. A chill emptiness spread under my breastbone. "William won't stop. He won't stop until we're both dead." I cleared my throat, but still could hardly speak around the lump of fear. I'd never been hunted with such viciousness. "We have to go to the police."

"Do you truly think they give a care about a queer and a nigger?" Aretha's voice sounded so reasonable, so normal. "What makes you think the police weren't a part of this? It wouldn't be the first time the white establishment joined with other racists."

Anger swirled and wove its strands around the fear in my gut. The raging emotions became a fireball burning me up from inside. I whirled around, all that heat blazing from my eyes. I shouted, waving my hands. "What the hell do you intend to do then? Keep hiding until they find us and kill us, too?"

She rubbed her hands down her face. Eyes red-rimmed and hollow with sadness, her gaze hooked my eyes and held them. "What *you're* going to do is to get on your bike and get out of here. I want you hours away from here, from Elmsworth, before nightfall."

Brows drawn tight over my eyes, I stared at her. "What?"

She spun around and strode off up the hill, calling over her shoulder as she moved further away. "You heard me. Get on your bike and get gone."

Run or Die

"Like hell I will!" I yelled as I ran up the hill after her. My hand shot out, snagged her shoulder, and yanked her around. Breath heaving in and out as much from anger as from exertion, I demanded, "What do you think I am? Some kind of cur dog that runs off with its tail tucked between its legs when trouble shows up?"

Her eyes met mine, calm, steady, like some kind of suicide bomber. Goose bumps paraded down my arms.

In that eerily reasonable voice, she said, "No, Jaz. Quite the opposite really. I think you are a brave and loyal friend, but I refuse to be responsible for your death. Go back to Seattle. This isn't your fight."

Mom used to tell me my willingness to listen was just a thin veneer over my stubbornness. My chin jutted forward. "I'm the queer William meant to kill."

She turned and faced down the hillside. Near the bottom of the hill a herd of four does with a couple of leggy fawns and a buck grazed. I remembered when the fawns still wore their spotted coats.

"William *didn't* kill you, Jaz. All you've lost so far is a few clothes. You haven't even lost those three books or that tin box you showed me once. They're in the saddlebags on your bike. The only other things of value are your Buck knife that you carry everywhere and your motorcycle gear. What you're not wearing of that, you put down by your bike." Her focus shifted back to me. "Don't place yourself in the position to lose anything else, possibly even your life."

A breeze slipped past. I shivered then yanked my hands from her shoulders and planted my fists on my hips. "You think I'm going to slink off like some whipped dog? Woman, you don't know me very well."

"Listen, pride isn't worth dying for, especially when it won't change a single thing." She continued in a tone that suggested she dealt with a person of compromised mental ability. "You've saved some money, and if you need me to, I can go into town and get the rest of what I owe you out of my account this afternoon; otherwise I can mail you a check when I get some checks ordered since all of mine got turned to ash." A pleading note entered her voice. "You were going to leave, sooner or later. It's simply a bit sooner than you thought. Call this..." Aretha waved her hand to include the entire hill, "an unusual life experience then get on your bike and haul your butt out of here."

Hands spread, I asked, "Why are you trying to get rid of me?"

She threw her hands in the air and shouted, "I'm not trying to get rid of you!" When I cocked my head and raised my brows at her, she conceded, "Okay. I am trying to convince you to leave. That is not exactly the same as trying to get rid of you. Momma would never forgive me if I got you killed."

"Like I could stand Grandma Pearl's disappointment if I left you here to face this alone? To be honest, if I did that I wouldn't be able to stand myself either." My hands dropped to my sides. I shoved them into the front pockets of my jacket. Feet spread a bit wider apart as if I balanced in expectation of a physical attack, I hunched my shoulders. Truth be told, emotions held more power to hurt me than any physical attack ever had. If I walked away now, I'd have to face the fact that I'd run from fear; I'd run when someone needed me.

She glanced away and whispered, "I don't want to be responsible for getting you hurt."

A stray sunbeam glinted off her raven hair.

"You aren't responsible, Aretha. I am. My decision." I pulled a hand out of my pocket and raked it through the tangled mess of my hair, pulled a dead leaf free of its strands. "If I can't stay here, I'll camp out in the hills, but I *am not* leaving."

She threw her hands skyward and her head back, shouting at the blue expanse. "Girl, you are so stubborn!" She leveled her best I'm-so-mad look at me. "Why is it that my momma gets involved with nothing but pigheaded fools?"

I raised one eyebrow, something I'd perfected to use in good-natured arguments with Alicia. "Because Grandma Pearl loves us?"

For a long moment, she stood there, her face empty of anything, except grief, then the corners of her lips tipped upwards. A brief smile, a sad smile, yet I knew she'd let me stay.

Run or Die
***

Andersville lay ten miles south of Elmsworth. A hotbed of activity, compared to Elmsworth. *Two* grocery stores, a hamburger stand, *and* Betty's Café. The two small towns shared a sheriff and two deputies. Aretha had once informed me that according to local lore, when the towns decided to share a sheriff they held a fishing tournament to determine which town got the sheriff's office building. Apparently, Andersville had better fishermen.

They may have had better fishermen, but judging by the sheriff's office their architectural skills sucked. Unless you happen to like square, beige boxes. The inside vied with the outside for the 'ugliest building' award. The miniscule square lobby would be crowded with more than four, average size people. Bad architecture on the outside; horrible odor on the inside.

Against the far wall stood a dented, gray metal desk, the kind found in any low-budget government office. My social worker had an identical one. A telephone with a few buttons sat on one side of the desk. In the middle of the desk the sports section of the local paper laid spread out. A deputy presided over this grandeur with the face of an English bulldog: all loose flaps of skin and bristly hair.

He barely lifted his eyes from the sports page as Aretha gave a *Reader's Digest* version of what happened. When she finished, he heaved a put-upon sigh, his heavy lips in a pout. "Only me an' one other deputy an' the sheriff here in this office. Shirley's off today, an' besides I don't see the sheriff sendin' her out by herself, an' me an' the sheriff we don't hardly ever git out ya'lls way."

Aretha's nostrils flared as her voice climbed an octave higher. "What do you mean you hardly ever get out our way? This is not a social event to which we are inviting you and the sheriff!" She inhaled a deep breath and visibly fought to control her anger. "Those men burned my cabin, shot up my goat house, and killed every single one of my chickens. They meant to kill us, too, but we weren't in the house."

Aya Walksfar

With a sneer, he ran his eyes over us in much the same manner as a person evaluating a side of beef, and finding it unacceptable. "Now, ma'am, how can ya'll be sure of that? Some of the boys hereabouts can git to drinkin' an' one thing leads to 'nother. They might git a bit rowdy, no doubt. Mostly they don' mean no harm." His big belly pressed against the edge of the desk. Yellowed teeth shone between his lips in a smile that never reached his piggy eyes.

Tired of hanging back, I stepped up next to Aretha. I placed my fists dead center of his newspaper, leaned close, and dropped my voice low. "We *demand* to see the sheriff..." I glanced at his name tag, "Deputy Jones."

Something in my eyes must've warned him that I held onto my temper by a gossamer strand.

The desk chair squealed as he hefted himself to his feet. "The sheriff ain't gonna be pleased bein' bothered when he's busy. Ya'll go sit." A fat finger pointed at the four plastic and chrome chairs against the front wall. Without waiting to see if we complied, he hitched up his equipment belt and exited through the door in the far corner.

A round-face clock with large digits hung across from the reception desk. Five minutes after noon. The coffee and donuts we'd picked up from Betty's Café had tasted wonderful going down, but now threatened to reappear. Cop shops made me nervous. The only times I'd ever entered one, I'd gone to bail my mother out of jail.

The empty lobby/reception area stank of stale cigarettes and old vomit. There wasn't even a crumpled magazine to read. I paced the confining space. For fifteen minutes each stride elevated my temper until, ready to storm through the building and yank the sheriff out of his office myself, I halted in front of Aretha. My mouth opened just as the sheriff hurried through the door, clapping a hat on his thick, auburn hair.

He stopped a foot or so to the side of where we stood. A glance at me then he focused on her. "I'm Sheriff Abe Daly. You're Aretha Hopewell?"

She jerked her chin down in acknowledgment.

Run or Die

"Sorry I took so long. Had to do some delegating. Heard you had some midnight riders." He hustled to the heavy glass-front door and held it open for us. Outside he pointed to a well-used, but well-loved, Chevy three-quarter-ton truck with four-wheel drive parked next to the curb. "That's my rig. Where are you ladies parked?"

Aretha pointed out her V-dub directly in front of his truck.

"Great. I'll follow you on out to your place. Get a good look at what happened."

He stayed close until we hit the dirt road going up then wisely dropped back. We hadn't shut the gate, so Aretha drove up and parked next to the cabin's ruins. A wisp of smoke drifted skyward as we got out.

Sheriff Daly walked up behind us so quietly that we both startled when he spoke. "Place must've burned relatively quick. I'd wager they used gas. Easy accelerant to get. A bit risky, but drunks don't usually think about that. If you'd both stay right here, I'd like to take a look-see then we'll talk." The Nikon swinging from his neck looked well used. He walked around the rubble, snapping pictures. When he returned to where we stood, he said, "I assume that was the house. Give me a guided tour of the rest of it."

Aretha went to the goat house first, like she couldn't yet bear to see the chicken coop. Daly took several photos then stooped, hands encased in latex, picking up shells, dropping them in paper bags, and writing out labels for each bag. "I'd leave them lay if I thought having a crime scene unit out would yield any evidence, but the chances of that are slim to none. I'll send these shells into the lab to see what they can tell us, though."

He stared at the empty goat house. "Where are your animals?"

I tilted my head down the hill and toward the tree-line across Boulder Creek. "Other side of the creek."

"Where were they last night?"

"We had them tied out in the woods," Aretha said.

"Now I know why they say you shouldn't let anyone know where your goat's tied." He ducked his head. "I'm sorry. That must have sounded callous. However, I do need to know why you and your goats were hiding last night."

Aretha's words erupted in staccato bursts. "Russell at One Stop Grocery in Elmsworth. A couple of weeks ago he walked us out to my truck. Warned us of rumors that William and his friends threatened to burn me out."

"Did Russell say where he heard the rumor?"

Aretha shook her head. "He almost didn't tell us that much. Said the last time he helped us, he lost business and he had a wife and children."

"The last time he helped?" Daly waited.

Aretha drew a full breath and let it ease out as she told about William, Ralph, and Jimmy confronting us in the parking lot twice.

Sheriff Daly gave a slow shake of his head. "Beats me why Russell would want that kind of business. Now, show me where the chickens were."

Aretha stopped outside of the chicken yard, panic clear in her dark eyes. I put a hand on her shoulder. "Go on up to the car. I can take care of this."

Jerkily she nodded, and arms tight around her waist, she walked old-lady slow toward the burned down cabin.

The sheriff watched until she got to the car and leaned against the rear fender, her back to us. He stepped through the narrow chicken wire gate and around the mounded area where the chickens were buried. Moments later he ducked back out of the chicken house. "They made a mess of them poor things."

I tightened my lips while the anger surged. God! I wanted to pound on those men!

He stopped and scuffed the toe of one boot on the edge of the burial mound. "Buried all of them right here?"

"Yes," I choked out as a horrid possibility occurred to me. My face must have telegraphed my thoughts.

Quickly, Daly reassured me. "No reason to dig them up. Pretty obvious how they died. I'll take some photos of everything for my report."

I watched as he finished his photography then trailed him up the hill. He walked with the weary tread of a man burdened by his own knowledge. He stopped in front of Aretha and lifted his head. "I'm going to give it to you straight. The guns used are common to this area. Maybe if we find the rifles, we can match them. Lot of families own one or more."

Glancing at the small, spiral bound notebook in his hand, he said, "Cabin was torched, no doubt. I think I can assume that the red gas can over by that boulder was theirs." When Aretha silently nodded, he continued. "I'll take the can and the shells to the lab for fingerprinting. Even if we get good prints, they're only useful if we have prints on file to match them or if we have a suspect." He hesitated a moment then said, "Don't expect any answers too soon. We use the county's facilities and they aren't going to see this as a priority case."

"Define 'too soon.' Are you talking about a few weeks, or a few months? Or maybe never; maybe the shells and the gas can will mysteriously disappear," Aretha said in a flat voice.

For a moment, his face hardened at the implications then shifted back into a neutral mask. "The county has never lost evidence that I'm aware of." He gave that some time to sink in then grimaced. "As for the time frame: I'm afraid a few months is the more realistic estimate."

Aretha locked eyes with him, but didn't say a word.

"I've taken photos from every angle I can think of, but I don't expect to gain much from them. The important thing is that this attack has been recorded. If I find a way to link those men to this attack, everything is documented."

"What do you mean *if* you can link William and his posse to this attack? We told you: we recognized three of them and we recognized the sound of William's Jeep." My voice rose so high I squeaked.

An uncomfortable look crossed his face. "I'll be talking to all three of them, but for the time being that's all I can do. Unfortunately, it was dark when they arrived and barely daylight when they left and, according to what you said, the only times they were illuminated was when they stepped in front of their own flashlights and when they stood in front of the fire. The flashlights would've backlit them and hidden their faces. The fire would have compromised your eyesight and they were a distance away..."

"Just spit it out, Whitey." Aretha's voice dripped venom as she interrupted him. "What you're saying is tough luck. It's our word against theirs, and who's going to believe a nigger and a queer? Too bad I got burned out. Too bad we would've been dead had we slept in my cabin, but there's nothing you can do. Your hands are tied. Just like with the Klan: no one knows anything, no one can stop them. No one really tries."

Helplessly he raised and spread his hands then let them drop to his sides. "There is clear evidence of a crime. However, there is no clear evidence of who committed that crime and..."

Again, Aretha's angry voice interrupted him. "What are you going to do? Wait till they kill us? Even then, what? You'll wring your hands and cry that you don't have enough evidence to prosecute the murderers!"

"Believe me, Ms. Hopewell, I will question the men you named. I will pursue any information these shells and that gas can give me." He dropped his head, gave it a tired shake. When he lifted his eyes to Aretha's I was jarred by the pain I saw in their depths. Then he blinked, and I was left wondering what I *had* seen. "Sometimes, as much as I hate it, the law is inadequate."

Words sweetly coated in honeyed sarcasm, Aretha said, "Thank you. Thank you so much for that incredibly astute insight, Sheriff Daly. Can you elucidate our alternatives for us, please?"

He clasped his hands in front of himself. "If you were any other women, Ms. Hopewell," he gave a brief nod at me, "Ms. Wheeler, I would suggest you leave. Move somewhere, temporarily, that is less isolated, until this blows over or I get a break on the case. But," he held up a hand when I opened my mouth to protest, "but, it's obvious neither one of you is that type of woman.

"My next suggestion is that you purchase a rifle. You won't need a concealed permit for a rifle. A twenty-two can stop a man. Just remember that self-defense can only occur when someone is actively attacking you or your family. And, *only* the amount of force necessary to halt the attack is deemed reasonable. In other words, if you shoot someone in the back, or when they have their hands in the air and are standing still, that is not self-defense." He looked from me to Aretha then back again.

"You might consider getting a dog. A trained protection dog is expensive. Be careful, though. A poorly trained protection dog is a dangerous animal. You need to realize that a protection dog is a weapon. Everything I said about guns applies to the use of dogs. Besides, a gun or a knife trumps teeth and claws every time. A dog could give you some time to run, but that may be all the dog can do regardless of how well trained it might be." He gave us time to digest that then continued.

"Post your land with 'no trespassing' signs. Get a camera with a zoom lens. Keep it with you. If you see anyone, take their picture. Give it to me and we'll start proceedings for the misdemeanor of trespassing. Might give them something to think about, like your willingness to prosecute."

Hands fisted at her sides, I wondered for a moment if she'd take a swing at the cop, but she abruptly spun and marched off.

Daly watched her leave then turned to me. "I'll do the best I can." He started for his truck, detouring long enough to pick up the gas can.

I walked along with him. "When will you talk to William and his posse?"

He glanced up at the sun sliding into evening. "Tomorrow morning. I'll let them know they are all under investigation, and they are. If, and when, I get enough evidence, I will make an arrest. I wish I knew who the other three men were. It would give me three more to ride herd on, three more who might have one beer too many and brag." He shook his head, pulled the truck door open, and slid behind the wheel.

Before he shut the door, he glanced over where Aretha stood next to the remains of her cabin then settled his eyes back on me. "Watch out for her. I've heard a lot of good things about her down in town and in Willits. Watch your backs, don't go anywhere alone, not even on this hill."

After Daly's truck rounded the bend, I returned to Aretha. "What do you want to do?"

She inhaled deeply, bent her head back, and stared up at the cloudless sky as she exhaled softly. A Red-tailed Hawk soared in circles above us. Once, twice, three times, then a fourth time before it straightened its flight pattern and flew down-slope towards the creek. She brought her head down and regarded me. "We're going to Willits. First thing we'll do is eat a real dinner then rent a motel room in town. On the way to the motel, we'll stop at a grocery store and pick up snacks, diet Pepsis, and a big bottle of wonderful smelling bath oil. I intend to take the longest, hottest bath in the history of womankind."

I frowned. "We're running away? What about the goats?"

"Not running away. Taking a night off. I am certain that even Amazon warriors got a night off to rest. As for the goats, we'll feed, water, and lock them in the goat yard. They'll have access to their shed that way."

"What if those guys come back?"

Aretha peered across the hill at the shot-up shed. "We'll clean up around it so the goats don't wind up getting hurt from a sharp corner or a piece of wood sticking out. That's the best we can do." She turned her gaze to me. "Even if we were here, there wouldn't be much we could do to stop them. I don't own a gun of any kind, *yet*. As much as I love each one of them, I don't intend to throw our lives away in a futile attempt to protect them."

I blinked and cast my gaze down the hill. I didn't want to think about Hershey and Hemingway and Little Kid dying, but at this moment in time, there was pitifully little we could do to protect them, or ourselves.

***

Dusky dark draped over the city of Willits as Aretha's truck idled through. Clots of children in witch's hats, Batman capes, and sheets with holes for eyes ran from house to house, their joyous screams echoing in the cold rain. With everything that had happened, I'd forgotten about it being Halloween.

Fortunately, Sleepy Hollow Motel had few residences around it so the young goblins and ghouls mostly stayed away. The motel sat four blocks off of Highway 101. As quiet as it was, it might as well have been in the middle of a deserted town. Exactly what I wanted; I'd had my fill of excitement for a while. Once

Run or Die

Aretha rented the room and we grabbed two keys, we headed upstairs.

Not a big motel, but its rooms felt homey and large. What passed for single beds in our room more closely resembled a lot of queen-size beds. The bathtub, an older model that you could practically swim in, drew my eye.

"Don't even consider bathing right now," Aretha said. "We have to go buy some clean clothes."

The outdoor store boasted everything we needed: jeans, warm socks, warm underwear, and flannel shirts. With clean clothes in hand, we buzzed back to the motel and took turns soaking up the hot water.

When I stepped out of the bathroom still toweling my hair, she said, "Ready to eat?"

"Yeah, I could do with some food."

"I know just the place."

The restaurant sat on the other side of town. Aretha parked in the pristine lot on one side of the building and we walked in.

Alicia had loved small, funky, organic restaurants. I think she made me go to every one of them that existed in Seattle. Compared to Mother Earth's Bounty, though, those restaurants would rate as poseurs. Every item on the menu boasted organic in front of its ingredients and the restaurant had elevated recycling to a fine, and beautiful, art form.

The hostess led us to a table with a view into an attached greenhouse. Inside, laid out in artistic patterns, grew a garden bright with every shade of green possible, punctuated by a variety of reds and golds and blues. Aretha looked at it a minute then said, "It's an herb garden. A good one. One of the reasons I love coming to this restaurant, especially if I can sit here."

The waiter arrived promptly with two cups of hot, black, and smooth-as-good-silk coffee.

I'd barely had time to sip the brew when in my peripheral vision I noticed an ebony woman of generous proportions, sailing through the crowded restaurant. Sailing pretty much described her graceful movement, her long skirt swishing around her ankles. I turned and watched as she bore down upon our table. The closer she drew, the more imposing and regal she appeared.

She arrived at our table—she didn't stop, or halt. She arrived!—and held a be-ringed hand out to Aretha. "I'm Folami Winters, the owner of Mother Earth's Bounty. I want to personally convey my outrage at what happened to you."

Aretha set her cup down and eyed Ms. Winters quizzically, but took the proffered hand. "How do you know what happened to me?"

Ms. Winters lifted her eyebrows, a smile teasing at her full lips. "This whole area is very much a small town. If there is any way I can help..." She flipped a hand to encompass the unknowable before continuing. "Late this afternoon, as soon as I was apprised of your situation, I drove to Andersville and registered my written protest with Sheriff Daly."

"Thank you," Aretha said quietly.

They exchanged a few more pleasantries then Ms. Winters left as majestically as she had arrived. "Wow! Some lady," I remarked, finally bringing my attention back to the table.

"Yes," Aretha agreed as she picked up her menu. "In all the times I've come here, I've never personally met her."

Glancing over the top of the menu I held in front of me, I tried hard for nonchalance. "Say, was I like invisible or something?"

Aretha shut her menu and laid it aside as she thoughtfully studied me. "Yes, in a way, I suppose you were invisible. I doubt, however, that she was trying to be rude." She shrugged, obviously searching for words to explain the phenomena. "Whites do it to Blacks. Rich people do it to poor people. Employers do it to their household help. It's like we aren't important enough to be noticed."

"Because I have white skin, I'm not important?" Nostrils flared, my jaw clamped together.

Aretha picked her menu up again and opened it. "That isn't what I said." She leveled her eyes at me over the top of the menu. "A white person endures a type of treatment that many black people have suffered all of their lives, and suddenly it's a federal case."

Run or Die

Shoulders tense, stomach a hard knot, I said, "I don't do that to other people. I don't think I have ever done it. I don't deserve to have anyone treat me that way, no matter how many blacks have suffered that treatment from whites. I am not responsible for the actions of an entire race."

She scowled across the polished plank table. "Let's drop it, okay? As much as possible, I'd like to enjoy a stress-free meal."

We ordered and finished the meal mostly in silence, but the good food did a lot to relieve some of the tension thrumming between us. The tightness drained from Aretha's shoulders and I felt my own shoulders relax. Back at the motel, I claimed the bed closest to the window since I hated being blocked in by walls. We watched a DVD that neither of us had seen before, a comedy that I couldn't recall five minutes after we turned off the television.

By the time I shut off my light, Aretha's light snores already vibrated gently on the still air of the room. I punched my pillow and tossed around, getting tangled in my sheet and blankets until I finally got up and remade the bed. After a while, exhaustion overwhelmed my consciousness and I fell into a restless sleep. Every hour or so, I jerked up, wide-eyed and with my heart pounding. I couldn't recall the dreams, just that they left me feeling shaky and ready to bolt. Deep breathing got my heart slowed enough so that I could hear Aretha's breathing. Somehow, that seemed to calm me and I lay back down only to repeat the performance time and again.

The next morning I slumped in an overstuffed chair upholstered in some kind of slick flowered material, as tired as if I'd been running all night. Dawn crept over the tops of the buildings, casting a rosy glow on an ugly world. When I heard Aretha rustle the bedding as she got up, I stood and stretched."Hey, city girl, you beat me awake."

I shoved hard on the feeling of dread in the pit of my stomach, flicked a smile at her, and ran a comb through my hair. "Yeah, and I've been sitting here starving for hours, waiting for you to get done with your beauty rest, but I guess some of us need it more than others." The grin felt false on my lips, but Aretha didn't comment, so maybe I slipped that one past her.

Aya Walksfar

At ten-thirty Mother Earth's Bounty appeared to be between rush hours. People occupied three tables. Aretha headed for the table next to the greenhouse. We'd barely sat down when Ms. Winters followed our waitress over. She waited until the young woman took our orders and left before she greeted Aretha. "How are you this morning?"

"I'm doing as well as can be expected." Aretha reached across the table and laid a hand lightly on my forearm. "In all the confusion yesterday, I forgot to introduce you to a friend of mine, Jaz Wheeler. My mother sent her down from Seattle to help me on the farm this past summer. Poor woman lost everything she had with her, except what was on her back or in the saddlebags on her motorcycle."

Ms. Winters settled dark eyes on me. She didn't offer to shake hands, but she gave me a brisk nod. A waitress called Ms. Winters away and the food arrived shortly afterwards. Aretha and I both shoveled in eggs, bacon, gravy, hash browns, and pancakes.

On the way out of town, we stopped at a feed store and stocked up on enough goat food and hay for a month. The second stop was Rainbow Grocery. Fortunately, the cold cellar had been away from the cabin and not easily seen, so Aretha only needed to purchase some of the staples, like sugar and flour.

We hit the outdoor supplies and clothing store last. Maybe I'd been too exhausted the evening before for it to register: I had to buy all new clothes because William burned the cabin. For a moment, a private pity party clamored in my mind. My clothes, my Avia running shoes, even a couple of novels, gone, just like that. At least, things I needed or cherished the most had been in the saddlebags on my bike.

Then the truth slapped me upside my head. Aretha had lost everything except the clothes she wore and the sleeping bag she'd been sitting on. The quilt her dead sister made, her Grandma's table. Only a box of photos and some important papers that she'd had the foresight to store in the cold cellar had survived the assault. Everything else, gone.

Aretha laid a rifle and two boxes of shells on top of the clothes at the checkout counter.

Run or Die

I stared down at the cold metal. *We could have lost our lives.* For a moment, breakfast threatened to crawl up my throat. I swallowed it back down.

Once Aretha turned onto Washboard Road and started up the hill to the farm, her hands tightened on the wheel until her knuckles stood out nearly-white against her caramel skin. Attention focused out the side window, I tried to quiet the worries shouting in my mind. *What if...* Fear prevented me from finishing that thought.

At the gate, I hopped out and opened the padlocked barrier. Baaing and squalling fretted down the slope. Hershey and Hemingway must've recognized the sound of the pickup truck. I took a breath and realized it was the first deep breath I'd taken since we started up the hill.

Aretha parked next to the mound of black ashes and I jumped out then ran down to the goat house. Closer to the goat yard, I could see the others and make out the quieter baas. Frantic, my gaze skipped around until I located Little Kid at the rear of the crowd. Relief made my hands tremble as I unlatched the gate.

The goats shoved through, immediately putting their heads down to graze. I gave a shaky laugh. "If you guys think you can guilt-trip me for taking a night off, think again," I told them as I moved through the crowd, stopping and scratching behind their floppy ears with Little Kid close on my heels. "It's just fortunate for you guys that those idiots didn't get around to burning down the goat house and what feed we had stored in the feed room. At least, I had enough hay and grain to leave so that you didn't starve. Don't worry, though. Aretha bought some more."

When I turned to go back up the hill, Aretha stood nearby. A hint of a smile softened her lips. For the first time since the fire, standing there as the goats pushed and shoved against my legs, the tension drained from my achy shoulders.

I stood there and marveled at the woman who looked so much like Alicia. What is there about people like Aretha, who can find something good, something to smile about in the midst of adversity? Alicia had been the same way after the cancer diagnosis. My mother had been like that, too, even during those last horrible weeks of her life.

I recalled a time Mom had been two months behind on the rent, and the gas had been shut off in the middle of winter for nonpayment. Dressed in our warmest clothes, coats zipped to our chins, gloves on, Mom started telling one of her outrageous, funny stories. Before I realized it, I was laughing so hard that tears ran from my eyes. I examined the memory then folded it and filed it away to study later. After we resolved this thing with these guys. If there was an "after."

"I'll take the truck back down to the ravine. We can leave the hay and feed on it once we tie the tarp I bought over the top of the truck bed. We'll unpack our stuff once we get the goats settled for the night." Aretha drove slowly through the meadow, skillfully dodging a couple of boulders. Only the lightest of tire impressions on the brown grass marked the passage of the vehicle. The goats followed the truck, eradicating even that.

She parked on the opposite side of her Volkswagen from my bike. After tarping the load of hay and bags of feed, we stuffed our new green duffel bags with our crisp, new clothes and shouldered them. With a couple of buckets of feed, we led the goats along the narrow gully and up into the woods. If the men spotted the vehicles somehow, we didn't want them finding the goats.

A little stream broke away from Boulder Creek and meandered through a thicket of conifers and bare-branched deciduous trees. It didn't take long to craft a makeshift corral with small logs and rope. The stream chuckled pleasantly through the middle.

Duffel bag slung on my shoulder, I followed Aretha up the slope. She rounded a jumble of steel-gray boulders. I clambered along the same path, rounded the boulders, and blinked. Where had she vanished? A copse of alder trees with some heavy underbrush stood a few feet from the boulders. The wiry limbs of the underbrush created a visual and nearly impenetrable barrier. I figured a rabbit would do okay getting through them, but where had she disappeared?

Run or Die

Stumped, I stood there, feeling stupid, when a few feet away she popped up from behind several tall, leafless bushes that grew thick along the base of the boulders. "In here." She waved to indicate the least dense brush growth.

Squeezing between the boulder and the scratchy bushes, I watched her stoop and disappear. When I got closer, I spotted the dark line that indicated a crevice in the boulder. Duffel bag dragged along, stomach sucked in, I squeezed through the rough-walled opening.

A couple of feet in, the crack widened so I could walk normally. Another three feet and it bent to the left and I stepped into a small room lit by Aretha's flashlight. I dropped my duffel bag next to hers against one rough wall and gazed around. Rock and dirt formed the ceiling and the sides. Packed dirt made the floor. With a low whistle, I scanned the natural room. "This is really something."

She played the flashlight beam around the cave. "The boulders are stacked against the hillside, so other than maybe getting a glimpse of part of them, the trees and the slope of the hill blocks anyone up near the cabin from really seeing this. We'll grab some of the canned foods in the cold room and haul them down here. There's enough room in here, and air flow, for the camp stove and a few kerosene lanterns. We'll need to be careful at night. Flashlight beams can be spotted even when there are trees around. During the day, we'll need to be cautious about unwelcome visitors spying on us. This place and the route to it are difficult to spot."

"I like having a wall at my back, but tell me there's an escape route."

Aretha chuckled and pointed to the farthest corner, the beam of light picked up what looked like the entrance to a burrow of some sort. "Come on, I'll show you the escape route once we have everything set up. It's a little claustrophobic, but plenty big enough for us. Those men would have a hard time getting through it, though."

Holding the bag of burgers and fries aloft, she said, "Grab that new coffeepot and coffee makings out of the truck and meet me up by the campfire." She retrieved the rifle and a box of shells from against the wall behind her.

Flames dipped and flared as I set the pot of coffee to one side of them on a bed of red coals. I snagged my burgers and fries, set a short, round section of log vertical, and settled on it. "What's the plan? Hide until they finally catch us and pick us off?" I unwrapped a burger and stuffed my mouth full of the juicy sandwich.

She glanced up from where she sat on the log across the fire from me. For a moment, her hands stilled then she went back to feeding shells into the rifle's magazine. Brows knitted over her dark eyes. "Setting up a secure place to sleep is not hiding." She shoved another shell into the magazine.

"Sorry," I muttered, not feeling all that sorry, though. The coffee started perking. I pulled it off of its bed of hot embers. That close to the heat, it would finish perking without boiling over.

She gave an unladylike snort. "Yeah, I can tell how sorry you are from the way you said that."

My eyes snapped up at her. "Look, I'm not used to letting jerks push me around. That's not how it works where I come from."

"I've reported the crime." Aretha lifted her face and peered across the dancing flames at me. "Legally, that's all I can do. I have some money put away. If I'm careful, and use some salvaged materials, I can rebuild. That's the only way I know to keep those men from winning."

I broke eye contact, and gazed past her toward the rubble heap that had once been a cabin. "I know. I'm the one who said to get the cops involved, and I'm glad we did. Still it doesn't seem right to simply roll over and accept that we can't fight back."

With a huff of exasperation, she tossed the extra shells back in the box that sat on the ground next to her feet. She snatched up the burger bag and rooted around in it before extracting the fries and a burger. "What should I do?" She asked as she unwrapped her dinner. "Hunt them down and kill them? That's what I want to do! But then I spend the rest of my life in prison and they still win!"

Run or Die

My eyes flashed at her. I knew I was being unfair, but I couldn't stop myself. I despised being helpless, and I felt as helpless as the day I held Miriam's hand at the ER. "Forget I said anything! We'll build another cabin and then we'll go to town and tell them so they can come and burn it down, too. Maybe we should have a can of gas handy, in case they forget theirs!" Burger and fries papers crumpled into a ball, I threw them on the fire then grabbed the coffeepot bare-handed. "Shit! That hurt!" Hurriedly setting the pot on the ground, I waved my hand in the air.

Aretha glanced up then returned to eating. "You best go put some salve on that burn. It's in the First Aid Kit behind the truck seat."

I stomped down the hill. A while later, when I returned to the fire pit she'd poured two cups of coffee and set one by the log round where I sat. So tired that my legs trembled, I sank down, took a tentative sip of the coffee, and unwrapped my second burger.

Not speaking, we ate, but without the chickens muttering in the near-distance and the goats milling around, the silence disturbed me. The sun had eased below the line of undulating hills by the time we finished eating. The deepening twilight swallowed us as we ambled down the hill.

That night I tossed on the hard, cold floor of the cave. Several times I woke to the dense blackness, certain that I heard them coming for us. When I did sleep, I ran through endless corridors with nameless, faceless men chasing me. Right before I jerked to consciousness, I slammed into a dead end. Their mean-edged laughter echoed in my head as they drew nearer.

At daylight, Aretha nudged me awake with the toe of her boot. My body screamed for rest, but I rose out of my sleeping bag glad to be released from the nightmares.

A cold rain beat on us as we walked up the hill. Aretha immediately began sifting through the ashes and chunks of burned material that had once been her home. I built a campfire and set a kettle on the edge of it to heat water for washing.

By the time I'd cooked the eggs, bacon, and coffee, wet ashes streaked Aretha's face and covered her hands in gray goo. I pretended I didn't see the tracks her tears had carved through the dirt on her face. I poured the heated water into the small galvanized bucket she'd bought at the hardware store. Without a word, she went over to the bucket. While she washed, I dished up breakfast.

As we ate, a terrible ache settled around my heart. Like Alicia, Aretha never gave up. No matter the odds, she never gave up. That kind of tenacity could end badly, real badly.

After breakfast, we tossed our paper plates in the fire. Aretha refilled our coffee then settled on her log. Everything about her actions shouted that she had something to say. I sipped coffee and waited.

She glanced at me then down the hill. "What did you think about our Rabbit Escape Hatch?"

The non-topic gave me whiplash. I'd expected a lot of things, but that one hadn't made the list. "One word: claustrophobic." A shiver ran down my back as I thought about the emergency exit from the cave. Boulders leaned drunkenly against each other, forming a tight crawl space that felt like it extended all the way to Mars. When I finally wiggled out of the tunnel, heart pounding, I'd surveyed the surroundings. The tunnel dumped out into a brushy area of the woods.

Aretha had grinned like a madwoman. "We could follow this ravine almost to the main road, if we needed to, or you can bear left when it bends around and it's a shortcut to Washboard Road. I did a bit of exploring when I first moved up here. My paranoia was leaking out."

Now she sighed and sadness ghosted over her features. "I think you need to know why I knew where there was a cave and that it had an emergency exit."

I wagged my head in easy negation. "You don't owe me any explanations. If I had lived up here alone I would've been looking for a rabbit hole, too. One of those just-in-case things."

She turned speculative eyes on me. "Thanks, but the reason behind my 'rabbit hole' is the reason I could've gotten us both killed the other night."

"You mean because of what happened to your aunt?" I asked in the most offhand voice I could manage.

Run or Die

She closed her eyes and when she opened them she said, "I'm not going into the gory details, but the Klan burned my aunt's house...with her in it."

I grimaced, recalling the time I'd burned my hand and how badly that had hurt. What an awful way to die.

Lost in her memory, Aretha talked on. "She saw them coming and got me out through the cellar and told me to run. I got to the edge of the woods and hunkered down. I couldn't leave. Not when she might still get out."

She took a deep breath and let it seep out. Her next words rushed out, as if that would deny them the power to hurt. "I identified four of the men who threw torches into Aunt Betsy's house. But it wasn't the fire that really killed her."

She blinked, but tears wound down her face anyhow. "One man tossed in a gas can that blew up. The explosion must have been real close to where my aunt was. I knew that man. He'd come one night when I was in bed. I'd snuck down and hidden in the stairwell. He'd told Aunt Betsy that she'd better quit putting ideas into his wife's head." In a voice so quiet I nearly didn't hear the words, she said, "As a young girl, I wondered what ideas he was talking about."

Lips compressed into a straight, angry line, teeth grinding together, I could hear George's voice. *"You need to quit putting ideas in Miriam's head. It ain't never gonna do her no good, and just might get her hurt."* I didn't realize I'd zoned out until Aretha's sharp voice shook me loose from the past.

"Are you all right? All of a sudden you looked like you were in really bad pain."

I lifted my head and cleared my throat. "I'm sorry. Go on with what you were saying."

She studied me for a moment longer then gave a nearly-imperceptible movement of her shoulders. "The sheriff said it was my word against the words of upstanding, God-fearing members of the community. None of the men were ever arrested. A nigger girl's word against white folks simply didn't carry any weight. Besides, what's one less nigger?"

"Damn! No wonder you don't trust cops, and don't like whites."

"Just guessing, but I don't think you trust cops much, either." She didn't comment on the second part of my sentence.

Birds chirped in the woods to the east of me. I lost myself in the cheerful sound until Aretha reeled me back to reality.

"I've been thinking about what you said. You're right. Not every white person is responsible for the crimes some members of the race have perpetrated against black people. Sometimes, it's difficult to remember that." She climbed to her feet, tossed the dregs of her coffee on the fire, and headed toward the rubble pile. "We'd best get busy."

That night, seated on our sleeping bags, lantern light dancing along the sloping, scratchy rock walls, she handed me a cold Pepsi then popped the top of her own can of soda. She lifted her can and tapped it against mine in a toast. "Here's to us: the ones who don't run."

I nodded. "To us. Given the choice to run or die, we don't run and we don't quit."

Chapter 6

Exactly one week after we returned to the farm as it was lightly snaining, a mixture of snow and rain that reached past the down, waterproof jacket I'd bought, Sheriff Abe Daly drove up. He climbed out of his truck and hitched up his equipment belt.

I straightened up, put a hand against the small of my back, and stretched as I watched him make his ponderous way over. I dropped the handful of bent nails that I'd salvaged into the empty, restaurant veggie can we used. Moving out of the ash and gray goo, I bent and wiped my cowhide gloves on a tuft of grass while I waited for Daly.

Aretha tossed another chunk of charred board on a pile that we used for our campfires. The boards burned like charcoal and made a good fire for cooking. She walked through the center of the soggy ashes and stood next to me.

The sheriff stopped a polite distance away. "Looks like you ladies have been hard at it. About ready for a break?" He held up three brown paper sacks that were getting rain speckled. "I brought some burgers and fries. A big thermos of coffee and fixings are in my rig. Since I got two full-size seats, we could sit in the truck. It's warmer and drier in there."

Aretha removed her gloves one finger at a time, staring at him. "Why?"

He didn't pretend not to understand her question. "I was coming up to give you my report, like I said I'd do. I got to thinking how it was when my family got burned out when I was a boy. Nothing like this." He nodded toward the cabin area. "A chimney fire. What I remember most, though, was how the neighbors brought us food. There's something about that, bringing food that is. It's always more than food, you know?"

She gripped her wet leather gloves in one hand and took so long before she said anything that I wondered if she'd answer. "Give us a minute to wash up, so we don't get the inside of your truck too nasty."

Earlier I'd set a bucket of water on a flat rock close to the embers of the campfire because I hated washing up in cold water.

Daly put the bags back in his truck then joined us to wash his hands in the tepid water. Clean enough, we trooped to his truck.

He opened the passenger side door for Aretha and while she slid in, I opened the back door and hopped into the warmth. I squirmed out of my jacket while Aretha settled herself. Daly waited for her to shed her jacket and lay it on the console before he shut the door then rounded the hood of his truck and climbed in. He handed her a bag of food then twisted around and handed me one. Meanwhile, Aretha filled a Styrofoam cup and handed it over the seat to me before filling two more for Daly and herself.

We ate in silence. I watched the snow-rain mixture splat against the windshield then melt and chase other droplets down the glass. Daly started the truck and switched on the heater. The diesel chugged in a friendly manner.

Not el cheapos, the cheeseburgers had double meat patties, fat juicy ones smothered in lettuce, tomatoes, onions, green bell pepper slices, and pickles. The fries were extra-large orders of plump, deep-fried potatoes. Not a hint of bitterness tainted the strong, hot coffee.

After I ate, I handed my crumpled wastepaper to Aretha. She stuffed it into one of the bags to toss on the fire. Daly jerked his head towards the rear of his truck. "There's a big Coleman cooler, one I take when I go hunting, in the rear. You can keep it for a bit. I put some ice in it, a pound of bacon, some eggs. It keeps things cold a real long time if you don't fan the lid." He gave a little chuckle. "'Course the way the weather's turning you might not need a cooler for long."

"What gives with you?" I demanded as I slit my eyes and scooted to the edge of the backseat. "You come up here doing a Santa gig, but I haven't believed in Santa since I was four."

He skooshed around on the driver's seat, rested one arm on the steering wheel, his big hand dangling, and met my eyes. "Maybe I'm embarrassed to be part of a place that looks the other way when this kind of thing happens."

He waited like he expected me to say something or maybe applaud, but I kept staring at him until he glanced away. "I spoke to Russell." He shifted his focus to Aretha. "He's not talking. In fact, he denied saying anything about any rumors. He even denied helping you that day in the parking lot."

Face toward the sloped meadow, anger sparked like a live wire in his voice. "Like I expected, the three of them clammed up so tight it'd take a jack hammer to get them open. I talked till I was darn near blue in the face to everyone I could catch up to in town." Disgust seeped through his words like cold seeping around an old window. "In a town where everyone knows everyone else's business, no one knows anything about what happened here." He took off his cop hat and twirled it around and around in his big hands then shifted on the soft leather seat until I could clearly see his face.

Not that he had eyes for anyone other than Aretha. *A good thing or a bad thing?* I rolled my shoulders and shed the question like water off a tin roof. Not my business as long as he did his job.

Seriously good looking, his startling ocean-blue eyes stared out from beneath a mop of unruly auburn waves. Darkly tanned skin that only comes from hours in the sun covered a square, strong jaw. Full, inviting lips drew my eyes even though I didn't pick from that particular tree.

"Did you expect anything different? She's queer and I'm a nigger." Aretha waved a hand at me then placed a palm on her chest.

Daly flinched at her words like he'd been struck. "I expected more of Russell. Maybe because he was..." He broke off, cleared his throat. "Maybe I was a fool and actually expected some of the people around here to act like good people. That's why I wanted to be sheriff: I wanted to protect the goodness in the people in my area."

"Nice daydream," I sarcastically remarked as I moved against the back of the soft leather seat and took a hefty gulp of my still-warm coffee.

His head whipped around, eyes wide with indignation. "Maybe, but you know what? I still believe. I believe that beneath all that fear that's got them gagged, there is a whole lot of goodness. Good people who will eventually do the right thing. I don't think I'd want to live in a world where I couldn't hang onto that belief."

He locked his gaze on Aretha. "I won't quit investigating until I find the evidence I need, or get booted out of office. I promise you that."

That night the snain stopped and the clouds cleared from the sky. The stars felt close enough to reach up and snatch from their blanket of black velvet. The next morning heralded the serious onset of fall.

Nippy fall mornings laid out a priceless carpet of crystalline frost. The sunrise scattered diamonds across it. I'd always disliked the fall, seeing it as the time when everything died, the beginning of the long cold winter when winds sliced through the coat you hid within and you couldn't get truly warm again until spring. But that year, fall tugged at my heart. Some days felt as crisp as newly-minted dollar bills.

Autumn deepened. A wild wind tore away what few gold and orange and red leaves clung tenaciously to the alders and maples. The deep winter-green of the conifers became green candles glowing in the increasingly barren landscape.

Cold rains morphed into icy pellets then into snow. Nighttime temperatures kept dropping. With the cabin unfinished and the cave's rock-walled room difficult to keep even a little bit warm, bathing came close to inhumane treatment. My teeth chattered so hard I bit my tongue more than once. Hair washing bordered on torture. We built a lean-to with tarps and saplings for the goats.

Neither of us ventured far from the other one. Once a week we took the truck from the ravine, careful to drive out at a rocky spot that wouldn't hold telltale signs, and went to Willits to replenish supplies. We ate supper at Mother Earth's Bounty frequently enough that Ms. Winters had begun nodding and saying hello to me. The staff had always been kind to me, making me feel at home. Though I must admit, at home the food hadn't been near so good. Mom's idea of a home-cooked meal usually included a chicken burnt to charcoal on the outside and bloody raw in the middle.

November marched onward, and the nightmares took hold again. Always the same ones. Two of them. Like a one-two punch. Alicia trapped in a black sinkhole, being sucked under, but I couldn't reach her. I awoke shaking and knowing I'd failed to save her. In the second nightmare, Alicia ran while a man chased her. I could see them ahead of me, but no matter how hard I tried, I couldn't catch up. I always woke up screaming her name as he lifted a knife and it plunged toward her back.

Aretha woke me a number of times when I started thrashing too hard. She never asked questions, just turned on the Coleman, two-burner camp stove and made a pot of coffee. Gone were the days of tea. Seemed like we both needed the stronger fortification of the black brew.

The week of Thanksgiving, a thick cloud of gray doom swallowed me whole. Food regurgitated more easily than it stayed down. Coffee, lots of coffee, the only thing that stayed put consistently. Maybe on some level I hoped it would keep me from falling asleep and dreaming.

On Thanksgiving Day, Aretha poured us a refill on our coffee and shut off the propane camp stove. "I feel like I have bugs crawling in my hair. What do you say that we head to town and stay overnight? Get a real meal and a real bath? We'll put the goats in the corral down in the woods and give them plenty of food."

"Fine by me." With my heart rent by nightmares and memories, the location of my body didn't matter to me.

The truck slithered around Buzzard Peak, the highest point before we headed down the hill. The dirt track had churned into a slick, mucky mess. I stared out the passenger side of the truck, over the sharp drop-off, not caring if we stayed on the road or slid and tumbled down the hillside.

At the restaurant, I dragged over to what Aretha and I had begun calling "our table." Aretha stopped and chatted with Ms. Winters then came over. Ms. Winters brought over two steaming bowls of homemade chicken soup. I wanted to get mad at Aretha for talking about my business with the restaurant owner, but I couldn't summon the energy.

The chicken soup and homemade bread stayed down better than anything I'd eaten recently. At the hotel, I fell asleep listening to an old Bill Cosby video where he did a monologue. I actually slept through the entire night without dreams. The anniversary of Alicia's death passed. I thought the hardest time in my life was past, at least for another year.

Since that night, I've wondered, what would we have done had we stayed on the farm instead of indulging ourselves in Willits? Killed, or been killed?

The sun shouldered the early morning clouds aside as we headed up the hill. When Aretha topped the last rise to the farm, a breeze coming into the partially open car window carried a hint of smoke. My heart accelerated. I reached down on the floorboard for the rifle. As soon as we rounded the last curve where we could see the gate and the partially-built cabin, the sour smell of something burned hung thick in the air.

"Damn it!" I swore as I stared at the damp, charred corner posts that hadn't burned.

Aretha didn't speak. Just drove up and parked as close to the destroyed unfinished cabin as she could.

Frantic, I leapt from the car. The cold air, tainted with smoke, held a different smell, a sweet-sour stench, a stomach-churning smell.

They had laid into the goat house with sledge hammers and axes. Boards had splintered, some hung from the studs, pieces knocked several feet away from the structure. The crossbeam in the front had been left intact.

Somehow, they'd found the goats. Maybe one had baaed. Hershey led the gruesome line up with Hemingway's corpse dangling so close that they touched even in death. Clarabelle, the oldest nanny, saved from starving out in a field when Aretha noticed her last summer, hung close by with her amber eyes half-open and glazed. All of them, strung upside down from the crossbeam. Sliced and stabbed multiple times, they'd been alive as they bled out. Blood had sprayed onto the savaged parts of the shed left standing.

My breath rasped in and out as I made my slow way to the end of the beam. Little Kid hung head down. Dozens of knife wounds bled red on his blue-gray fur. His eyes blinked when he saw me. "He's alive!" I screamed as I yanked out the sheath knife on my belt and hacked at the rope.

Run or Die

Aretha caught him and sank to the wet ground, cradling him in her lap. My legs unhinged and I fell to my knees beside her.

"Get the first aid kit," she barked.

I cleaned and she stitched. "We'll have to get massive doses of antibiotics into him. I can get him started with the ones I have on hand, but if he lives through the night, we'll need to get more tomorrow." She caught the corner of her lower lip between her teeth.

All night, Little Kid lay across our laps in the cave. Candlelight flickered over his yellow eyes whenever he opened them and looked up at me. Swaddled in our sleeping bags, I held him. For a while it looked like he might make it, yet as dawn neared his breathing took on a labored quality. I held him until his last breath rattled into silence.

I wiped the heel of my hands across my eyes. "I...I need to bury him."

"Not yet." Aretha's voice held the cold edge of steel. "There's a joint town meeting tonight at the Valley Christian Church. Happens third Saturday of every month. Little Kid's attending that meeting then we'll give him a proper burial."

Every citizen in Elmsworth, Andersville, and their adjacent areas must have attended that meeting. The church's huge parking lot overflowed into the dead grass of the neighboring yard. The big room in the back of the church, where people gathered for banquets and special social occasions, held wall-to-wall folding metal chairs. People milled about, chatting quietly.

We walked into the stuffy room and silence rippled along with us, querulous voices raised again once we passed. People standing in the aisles parted like the Red Sea.

A hush fell as we made our way to the dais at the front. Our clothes smelled of smoke, soot still blackened our faces, blood stained our hands. We marched up the three steps. I cradled Little Kid's bloody form in my arms like the baby he had been.

Stepping behind the podium, I rested his little body on the wood stand and tapped a finger on the microphone. The taps echoed through the PA speakers that hung in the corners of the long room. I cleared my throat, and barked out the command. "Find a chair and sit. This meeting is called to order."

People automatically responded, drifting to chairs. Someone close to the front asked a woman next to him, "Who's that?"

"Don't you know?" Her voice sounded scandalized. "That's the queer from up on the hill. The one tryin' to stir up trouble for Bill Radley."

A heavyset man on the other side of the aisle bellowed. "Whaddya think ya doin' callin' this meetin' to order? Where's Gary?"

I stared down at him. He must have realized how thin an edge I walked because he sputtered into silence.

"I'm right here, Lloyd." A Pillsbury Doughboy-type man waddled down the aisle, his florid face flushed red. Sheriff Abe Daly walked close behind him. The man, who'd identified himself as Gary, squeezed into a chair in the front row. The sheriff continued up onto the dais and stood directly behind us.

I glanced at Aretha. She shrugged her eyebrows. Apparently, she had no more clue than I did as to whether the sheriff stood on the dais to control us or to support us. Didn't matter. I focused all my pain, all my anger on the crowd. "Be quiet." The words cracked across the space.

A grudging silence descended. All eyes turned to us, some curious, some hate-filled, some dropped away in shame.

"My name is Jazmine Wheeler. This woman," I tilted my head in Aretha's direction, "is Aretha Hopewell. She owns a farm on the hill up Washboard Road. There's been some trouble up there."

A low buzzing started to build.

"Listen up!" The whip crack of words sliced their voices in two and silenced them.

I stepped out from behind the podium, holding Little Kid, exposing his wounds for all to see.

A gasp sounded from a woman in the front row. A man further back asked, "What is that she's holdin'?"

Another man answered. "A dead goat. What in tarnation did they bring a dead goat in here for?"

I swiveled my head to look over my shoulder at Aretha. "Tell them about Little Kid."

Run or Die

She stepped behind the podium. Her soft voice blended with the screech from the PA system and she adjusted the microphone. "The little goat that Jaz is holding is Little Kid. Little Kid was a breach birth. His momma died. He would've died, too, but Jaz fostered him, getting up every two hours to feed and clean him. He slept on her cot for a while then as he grew he slept on the floor next to her. Little Kid was part of a dream."

A hush fell as Aretha's melodic voice wove its spell. "When I was fifteen, the Ku Klux Klan burned my auntie's house." She let the words drip down on them, acid rain on their indifference. "With my auntie in it."

Restless shifting caused chairs to squeak and rattle. She waited until they settled again. "Five years ago, I drove up here from my job in Los Angeles. I was sick of the hate and the violence of the big city. I loved the peacefulness of this area, the rural feel. Two years ago, I had saved enough to buy forty acres and to get started on my dream. I bought land as far up in the hill as I could find. I bought two chickens, the start of my flock. Albert, an Ameraucana rooster, and Cinders, a White Leghorn hen. I built my cabin then bought a few goats. I was well on my way to my dream."

She gazed out over the crowd. Some glared back, more venom in their faces than a rattlesnake has in its fangs. Here and there among the audience, I noticed a veil of what looked like sympathy shadowing a few faces.

Aretha told the story in a quiet voice. "There have always been folks who turned a cold shoulder to me in town. Didn't matter. I just shined them on and went my way. Figured everyone had a right to their own feelings. Some young men verbally harassed me. Again, I shined them on, hoped they would tire if I didn't respond. In August of this year those incidents took a violent turn.

"Three young men—William Radley, Ralph Henley, and Jimmy Donaldson—men who had always kept their harassment verbal, cornered Jaz and me in town, in Elmsworth at the Hamburger Haven. The first time they backed off because Mr. Russell came out from the grocery store and told them to leave. The second time when William attacked Jaz, she beat him in a fair fight, if you can call a man as large as William fighting a woman as small as Jaz fair.

"A few weeks later, Mr. Russell warned us that there was talk of burning me out. But he didn't want to get involved, afraid that his business would suffer losses. He scurried away as soon as he had whispered the warning. We started sleeping outside, hidden by a clump of boulders. "They came in the middle of the night, sure that they would catch us sleeping. They brought three other young men with them. They burned my cabin and my woodshed, my tool and equipment shed. They shot up my goat house, and my partially finished barn. They shot into the plywood walls of my chicken house."

She paused, and I imagined how she fought to control her emotions, just like I did. "A shotgun blast into the chicken house blew off Albert's head. Roosting next to him, Cinders was blown apart, as well. No chickens survived that assault. As they torched my cabin, I heard William yell, 'Fuckin' bitches! They can't hide forever! I'll get 'em, sooner or later.'"

She bowed her head. No one stirred. She raised her face, not trying to wipe away the tears that tracked down her cheeks. "On Thanksgiving Day, Jaz and I went to Willits for the night. We wanted to enjoy hot showers, eat a real meal, and sleep in an actual bed. Since William and his friends burned the cabin we haven't had any of those normal comforts.

"That very night, they returned. They returned. They found the goats this time. They didn't kill my goats."

I shifted so I could see her from the corners of my eyes. Tears poured from her eyes. Her hands trembled. My heart ached for her. I hoped she could hold it together for just a little while longer then we could walk out of here.

She gripped the edges of the podium then she continued. "They tortured those poor animals." Several people gasped; a buzzing washed through the crowd.

In the back, a harsh male voice rumbled. A different lighter voice loudly shushed him.

Aretha waited until silence rippled through the room. "William Radley and his friends found those poor goats where we had built a hidden corral. It was way down in the woods. Those men caught those helpless animals and those men tortured them to death."

She stopped and drew a shaky breath. "We arrived home Friday morning. Found the beginning we'd made on building a new cabin burned. We found Hershey, the lead nanny, and Hemingway, the young billy, and Clarabelle, sweet Clarabelle who nurtured any creature that came close to her, and all of the other goats hanging from the front crossbeam of the goat house.

I bit the inside of my cheek to force the tears away from my eyes. They would not witness my pain!

"Little Kid..." I heard the arrested sob in Aretha's voice. "Little Kid hung from the far end of the crossbeam. Little Kid was a baby...just a baby, but somehow he was still alive, blood streaking his beautiful charcoal gray fur. We carefully cleaned his wounds and I stitched him up and Jaz cradled him. We wrapped him in our sleeping bags and covered him with our coats and rocked him. He died in Jaz's arms as the sun rose this morning."

She swung her gaze around the room, pinning the people where they sat on the metal folding chairs. "What kind of people *are you* to stand silent in the face of such atrocities?"

I cradled Little Kid in my arms as I walked up the aisle. Aretha strode close behind. Some people stood and turned, watched our progress. An old white man with weathered skin, standing near the doors at the rear of the church, removed his hat and bowed his head as we passed.

Chapter 7

Winter chased behind Fall like a man racing for home base. During the first week, December dumped a half inch of snow on the hill. Within a couple of days the snow melted beneath the weak sun only to freeze into globs of dirty ice overnight.

The canary-yellow car looked like a chunk of butter as it slid down the dark strip of road and stopped at the closed gate. The driver stepped out and opened the gate, drove through then got back out and closed the gate.

I stopped shoveling and glanced over toward Aretha. She, too, had quit digging in the ashes to watch the car's progress up the dirt track to where we worked.

The nearly-new Lexus parked in the flat area a few yards from where the front porch of the cabin used to be. A willowy blonde unfolded from behind the wheel. "Hey!" She lifted her hand in a wave as she started toward us.

I couldn't help thinking that her car cost more than Aretha's original cabin. With a quick downward motion, I stabbed the shovel into the ashy slush and waited as she minced over the muddy ground. From the corner of my eye, I noticed Aretha prop her shovel against a boulder and walk slowly toward the visitor.

Part of me wanted the young woman to fall on her dainty backside, smearing mud on those tight designer jeans, that lovely beige jacket, and those made-for-show-not-for-work boots. *What's Ms. Runway Model doing here?*

Annoyed at the interruption, I straightened up and made my way over to stand next to where Aretha had halted just outside of the burned area. She fidgeted with her gloves as Blondie tiptoed over the ruts until she got within arm's reach. I figured she was only a few years younger than me, but that was where any similarity ended. The girl flashed a big, white, orthodontia-advertisement smile and stuck out a dainty hand with long, manicured nails painted a delicate lavender.

Aretha pointedly glanced at the proffered hand, but didn't move to raise her own. "What do you want?" The chill of her words hung in the brisk air.

Run or Die

I folded my arms and glared at the stranger. Once I would have bristled at Aretha's manner, but since Little Kid had been killed a frozen core took up the inside of my chest. I didn't think it would ever thaw; nor did I want it to.

Her smile slowly faded as the young woman let her arm fall. A blush flashed onto creamy white cheeks. "I'm...I'm Cynthia McKenna." She waited like the name should mean something to us.

When we continued to stare silently back at her, she went on. "Fergus McKenna's my granddad." She tilted her head, her eyes skipping from one to the other of us. "You know," she continued in an unsure voice, "Fergus McKenna? He and I live about five miles that way?" She swung her arm toward her shoulder, index finger pointing behind her.

"Why should I know Mr. McKenna?" Aretha asked in a voice filled with sharp ice shards of anger.

"Um, well um..." Cynthia ducked her gaze and scuffed the toe of one boot. "Well, um, I guess there's no reason. I, um, I just thought you might know who he is since we live pretty close to you."

Aretha raised her chin a notch, body rigidly straight. "I have been too busy trying to run my farm, and here recently trying to stay alive, to worry about who my neighbors might be."

Cynthia's azure eyes darted up to meet Aretha's dark gaze. "Ah, well...the reason I'm here...uh, Granddad and I heard about...well, about your troubles..."

"Troubles?" Aretha's brows lowered as she narrowed her eyes. "Is that what you and your grandfather call it when people come onto a person's land, kill every living creature and try to murder the owner? You call it 'troubles'?"

Cheeks flushed bright rouge-red, Cynthia's eyes widened and I could see a glint of tears. She blinked rapidly then closed her eyes. Her chest rose as she drew in slow breaths through her nostrils, and held them a moment before letting them out.

When she opened her eyes, the stumbling, stuttering girl had vanished. In her place stood a young woman who knew what she meant to say. "Ms. Hopewell, Granddad and I are very sorry for what has been done here. We don't go to town often, so we were unaware of the drastically increased level of harassment you experienced." Her eyes swept past us to the lingering evidence of violence. "When we heard about your cabin being burned...well, Granddad was pretty upset. We in no way condone that sort of behavior. That's why I'm here. We are well aware that there isn't much we can do about what's already occurred, but we'd like to help..."

Nostrils flared wide, Aretha leaned aggressively forward. "I don't want your help. I don't want your sympathy. I don't want anything you have. All I want is for people to Leave. Me. Alone. Now, climb your skinny butt back into your fancy car and get off my land." Aretha whirled and stomped away.

Tears glistened in the young woman's eyes then slowly spilled over and tracked down her cheeks. "I...I just wanted to help." She stared after Aretha then shifted her wide-eyed gaze to me. "Is it so wrong to want to help someone?"

Before I could think of an answer, she turned and with slumped shoulders, walked away. I watched as she carefully backed her vehicle then pointed it toward the gate. I kept watching as her car idled up the hill and around the curve.

Once her vehicle disappeared from sight, I sighed and headed back to work. For the rest of the day, her words kept pinging in my brain: is it so wrong to want to help someone? Hard behind those words rang another question: *where were you when those men burned Aretha's cabin? Where were you when they tortured Little Kid?*

Something my mom used to say came to mind: all the best of intentions are pretty useless when you're a day late and a dollar short. Cynthia McKenna and her granddad were way beyond a day late and a dollar short. Still, is kindness ever too little, too late? I shook my head hard to dislodge the thought. It didn't matter. Aretha and I didn't need their pity, or their charity.

Chapter 8

A couple of days later, a shiver chased goose bumps up my arms as I crawled into my sleeping bag. The wind howled around the boulders, sounding like a demented ghost wailing. Occasionally, it found a crack and whipped through the cave. Lantern flames danced and flared, tossing shadow monsters on the damp, cold rock walls.

Wrapped up in her sleeping bag with her back braced against the opposite wall, Aretha waited for the lantern light to cease flickering before she returned to perusing her newspaper. After a while she folded the *Willits Herald,* leaving the ad section exposed, then tucked it under a small rock next to her bedroll. A hint of a smile crept shyly across her lips as she blew out the lantern.

In darkness so black that I literally couldn't see my hand in front of my face, her voice floated across to me. "After tomorrow, we'll have a decent bed to sleep in."

"I don't think a bed's going to fit through the entrance to this cave," I shot back.

"You just wait. Tomorrow night we are going to curl up under real sheets and blankets on a real mattress." She refused to elaborate further no matter how much I coaxed.

The next morning dawned clear with the vibrant blue sky that stretched on forever. The cold seared my lungs as I scrunched out from between the rocks then stretched, inhaling deeply.

Up the hill, Aretha stirred the ashes of last night's campfire. A tendril of gray smoke hung motionless in the still air. I started up the slope hoping to find some coffee in the thermos from the night before, even though it would be cold by now.

Aretha had done me one better. She'd left my cup of coffee tucked against a warm rock. Using the sleeve of my jacket as a pot holder, I picked up the blue enameled camp cup and sipped the strong black coffee while waiting for the fresh pot to perk. Settled on my log, legs stretched out, I watched her flip the bacon onto a waiting paper plate then expertly crack a half dozen eggs one-handed into the hot bacon grease. The eggs scrambled up quickly. When she handed me a paper plate with my share of the bacon and eggs, she said, "Eat up. We have places to go."

I cocked an eyebrow at her as I forked up a big bite of egg. "And people to see?"

She grinned momentarily. "Yes, and people to see." Her grin faltered then quickly faded as she glanced around the farm. "Only good thing about the animals being gone is we don't have to worry about feeding and putting them up before we leave."

Tears burned my eyes as I bent over my plate.

After breakfast we covered the fire with ashes then walked briskly down to the ravine. Aretha swerved to the truck and had already started it by the time I climbed in and buckled up. In my best nonchalant voice, I asked, "Why are we taking the truck? We going on a supply run?"

"Nice try, Slick." She flashed a devilish look at me then dodged around a boulder and kept driving along the dry creek bed to our exit point onto the road.

"Come on, Aretha. Why all the cloak-and-dagger stuff?" I knew I sounded like some little kid, but I didn't care.

"Don't you like surprises? After all it's only a couple of weeks or so until Christmas," she teased.

"I think I've had all the surprises I want for a while," I muttered.

Her smile faded a bit and I immediately felt bad for my depressing comment. Who was I to piss on her parade? I picked up the folded newspaper on the seat and shook it at her. "Does this surprise have anything to do with this week-old paper?" I lightened my voice and sure enough, Aretha's grin reappeared.

"All will be revealed...in good time."

I poked my lips way out in a comical pout and sent my voice into a nasal whine. "I wanna knooooowwww! Noooowwww!"

"Spoiled brat." She chuckled.

Her warm molasses chuckle tasted nearly as sweet as a cinnamon roll. "All right," I groaned theatrically. "I'll wait, but at least I should get a Danish and a cup of coffee from Mother Earth's for being good and waiting."

Run or Die

Good-naturedly, she conceded. "Okay, if you promise to stop whining, we'll go there first."

With the truck warmed up, I squirmed out of my jacket and settled against the seat to watch the frosted countryside slide past. Aretha barely slowed to the speed limit as we passed through Elmsworth. As soon as we hit the town's boundary, she mashed the accelerator to the floorboard.

We hit Mother Earth's Bounty between the breakfast and lunch crowds. The evergreen wreaths adorned with red ribbons and the living White Pine tree in its huge tub nearly made me want to turn right around and leave. Christmas came in a close second to Thanksgiving for being the worst day of the year.

The smells of baking pastries overwhelmed my distaste for the coming holiday. Five minutes into our Danish and coffee, Aretha's fingers tapped restlessly on her cup. I grinned, leaned back, and deliberately sipped my coffee more slowly.

Finally, she shot me a mock glare. "You'd better finish up or I'm going without you."

Back on the road, and ten minutes south of Willits, we turned onto a muddy track with a drunken street sign proclaiming that this was Harney Road. Naked tree branches scraped the side of the truck and caught on the side mirror, slapped against the rolled-up passenger window. We bounced on the rutted road for another ten minutes or so before Harney Road snaked to the left. A smaller and more rutted track branched to the right. Of course, we followed the track to the right.

Leafless trees crowded both sides and edged in until the track narrowed to a rut hardly wide enough to accommodate the truck. Certain that we'd taken a wrong turn onto an old, dead end logging road, I heaved a relieved sigh when we finally broke out into a large clearing. Not much of a clearing, though trees and bushes had been chased back to the woods. Car hulls and crumpled trucks bunched together like a herd of cattle. To one side, a pyramid of freezers and refrigerators with gaping doors listed dangerously. A partially burned heap of garbage sat in a sodden pile within throwing distance of the house. A log, its end jammed into the ground, propped up one wall of the shack. The porch floor undulated along the front of the one-story place. The building's swayback roofline completed the scene from a cheaply made movie about white trash.

The house door banged open as Aretha shut off the truck and we piled out. A burly white man in a grease-stained t-shirt clumped out and ambled across the churned mud. Iron gray hair tumbled loose down his broad back to his belt. A face so scarred and battered that it appeared to have argued with a Mack truck, and lost, sat atop a massive torso. He drew closer and I could plainly see an old gash slashed across his crooked nose. Hairy arms bulged and rippled with muscles that could never be acquired in a gym.

When he halted in front of us, he reached a work-roughened hand out to Aretha. His fingers engulfed hers as they shook. "Everyone calls me Big Al."

After Aretha introduced herself, he swung toward me. His blunt, thick fingers, as grease-stained as his shirt, wrapped around my hand in a firm, but not challenging, grip. The calluses and cracked skin rasped against my palm.

Introductions completed, he yanked up on his jeans that had ridden low on his hips, though I couldn't tell that it made any difference. "Jenny run up from down below and told me ya'll might be coming to see the trailer today. It's around back there." He jerked his head to one side to indicate the rear of the house.

A sturdy, log lean-to stood behind the ramshackle house. Parked inside the lean-to was the cleanest little travel trailer I'd ever seen. Its brush-painted, green sides gleamed. A tiny window sparkled as a stray beam of sunlight found it. Though not new, a lot of tread remained on the tires. The door opened with a gentle twist on the brass knob, then snapped shut as soon as I released it.

"I put that there spring on it. Hate having doors what don't shut on their own." Big Al pounded an unfiltered cigarette on a crumpled pack as he spoke. Cigarette stuck in one corner of his mouth, he stuffed the pack in the pocket of his flannel shirt. He lit up, took a long drag, then, as smoke drifted from his flattened nostrils, he waved toward the trailer. "Go on in and take a look. I think ya'll be surprised."

Run or Die

The lemony scent of Pledge and the fresh smell of a hint of Clorox met me as soon as I stepped inside. The trailer had been gutted. In place of a useless toilet area, a shiny white, apartment-size, propane refrigerator sat against the blond, oak board wall. A full size, double-basin sink with oak finished cabinets below and above it occupied the space next to the refrigerator. The stove had a full-size oven with a grease hood over it. More cabinets bracketed the stove, sided with some type of shiny fireboard. Propane lights made out of some kind of metal and shaped like an open tulip graced the walls on either side of the kitchen area. At the other end, two beds with thin mattresses hung from fancy wall chains.

Big Al stuck his head in the door. A narrow, folded up table occupied the wall between the beds. "Go ahead and pull that table down. It's made of cherry wood. Built her myself."

The beds became benches. With the table hooked back up, he urged us to hook the beds up, too. "See." He proudly waved one hand around. "Lots more room to get dressed." With a light pat against the side of the closest floor-to-ceiling cabinet, he added, "These here are for ya'lls clothes. Go ahead. Open one of them."

Grasping the handle of one, I swung it open. Right above the door, a thick round bar ran from back to front. The clothes would hang facing the door instead of in the conventional sideways manner.

Aretha shook her head admiringly. "I don't know about Jaz, but I'm sold."

I grinned at her. "Looks like home to me."

"Well then, we'll just go on in and I'll fix you ladies some coffee while we do business."

As we made our way around the house, I decided that I'd temporarily become a non-coffee drinker. If the inside was anywhere near as bad as the outside of the building, I didn't want to put anything in my mouth that I couldn't scald first.

Like the trailer, the inside of Big Al's shack shocked me. Jam-packed like a packrat's nest, everything appeared to have a place and everything appeared to be in its place. Cups hung from pegs on the wall. Cabinet doors were closed. The white enamel of the sink gleamed. Not a crumb littered the table. Al served coffee so black that a quarter of a cup of canned milk barely whitened it. He set a crock of crumbly cheese beside a plain white restaurant platter with bread and sausage arranged in neat rows.

My stomach growled. Gratefully disregarding my earlier resolution, I reached for the cheese. The soft stuff spread on my bread like thick, dry butter. I took a tentative bite as I reached for a round from the sausage stick. "This is really good. Thanks," I mumbled around a mouthful of food.

The big smile he flashed over his shoulder framed crooked teeth. "Not everybody likes goat cheese and goat sausage. Made them myself."

I washed the food down with a hefty drink of coffee. "Aretha has...had goats. Guess I got used to her cheese. Never had the sausage, though. Really good."

"Ya'll don't have goats, now?" He stopped pawing through a file drawer and regarded us as if not having goats made us somehow strange.

Aretha carefully set her cup on the table. "Some folks in Elmsworth don't like blacks and they don't like lesbians. They burned me out twice. Killed all of my chickens the first time. The last time they found and slaughtered my goats."

"Damn...excuse my French, ladies, but that ain't right." His black brows crunched together. "Ya'll report it to the sheriff?"

Aretha nodded. "Reported the first attack. For what little good it did. The sheriff knows about the second attack, too."

He resumed digging in his files. "Did ya'll have any idea who it was?"

"We know three of the men." She daintily nibbled a sausage round.

"Sheriff arrested them, yet?"

"No."

Big Al triumphantly waved a paper, and ambled over to the table. He took a gulp of his coffee. "Ain't right." He shook his head mournfully before he brightened up. "Well, this here," he tapped the title to the trailer with a blunt fingertip then signed it and shoved it over to Aretha. "She ain't no cabin nor nothing, but she'll keep ya'll dry and warm till ya'll rebuild." He stared into Aretha's face. "When ya'll ready in the spring, I'll be having some young'uns. They's all registered Nubians, great little milkers and downright friendly."

Aretha fished her wallet from her hip pocket. She counted out eight one-hundred-dollar bills on the table in front of Big Al. He scribbled a receipt then handed the receipt and four of the bills back to her.

A dark look flashed across her face. "I don't need, nor do I accept, charity."

He wagged his head. "Ain't charity, Missy. I'm just paying it forward. Giving back what was give to me one time." He stood up and handed her a small key ring then stepped around the table to lead the way to the door. "When spring comes, don't ya'll forget about my goats."

Night had settled softly over the hill by the time we got back to Aretha's land. Without even unhitching the trailer, we piled out of the truck and into our new home. After a dinner of cold cuts and coffee, we turned in. I slept soundly knowing our visitors wouldn't return yet. Best to get a good night's sleep while we could. Once William and his posse learned about our new house, they would return.

During the second week of December the snow arrived in earnest. Winds shoved and ploughed it into drifts then skimmed across it, piling it even deeper wherever the land dipped. The road in would've been impossible, except four-wheel drive vehicles had compacted travel ruts along most of it. The snow on the road into Aretha's lay pristine and white.

Accepting the risk of discovery, Aretha continued to park in the ravine. Fortunately, the ravine acted as a snow break and the white stuff failed to pile deep along the path we drove the truck. The ravine path led to a private road that the owner kept religiously plowed.

Temperatures dropped into the low double-digits. Snow crusted over, crunching and squeaking when I walked on it. Foolishly, we allowed the weather to lull us into a feeling of safety.

When they came for us again, the temperatures had dropped to twenty-three degrees, but the bitter winds had died out early that evening. Sound travels easily on such nights. "Come on, Bill," Ralph whined. "It's freezing out here."

"Shut up!" William's deeper voice rolled heavily through the dark.

Silently, I swung my legs from the bunk. Already dressed, I slid my feet into my boots and quickly laced and tied them. By the time I stood up, the camera hung around Aretha's neck and she cradled the rifle in the crook of one arm. She loaded her jacket pockets with shells.

Pulling on my jacket, I stepped past her, shoved the door open on well-oiled hinges, and held it. She slipped outside. I eased the door shut, seriously glad that she'd thought to position the trailer with the door facing out toward the woods.

Though no moon shone, the snow lit the place nearly as good as those sickly street lamps lit the sidewalks back home. Aretha darted into the shadows of the trees. Dressed in black, the midnight beneath the trees swallowed her shape. I followed so close behind that I almost stepped on her heels. Beneath the thick canopy of interlaced branches, some of them conifers, the dark ground aided our invisibility. Soggy leaves muffled the sounds of our passing.

She handed me the rifle and aimed the zoom lens of her newly-purchased camera. Equipped with the latest technology in digital, she set it for night-action photography.

The trailer door whispered open. The white glow of a flashlight shone from the window over the sink. "Goddamn it!" William's voice exploded.

"They're hiding, like before. I told you they wouldn't be here. Let's leave, okay?" Ralph pleaded.

"They were here." William's voice fell silent for a few moments. "Damn you, Ralph, I told you to shut up! Their beds are still warm. They heard your whiny mouth. That's why they ain't here." A crash shattered the silence of the cold night.

"Stop...*please*, stop....Bill, please..." Ralph's voice rose in a shrill plea.

"I told you to shut the fuck up!" William raged.

"Don't! Please, don't!" Ralph's voice soared higher, fear infusing it.

"I. Told. You. To. Shut. The. Fuck. Up!" A grunt emphasized each word.

Run or Die

My guts churned and adrenaline dried my mouth.

Aretha pulled her face away from the camera. My eyes had adjusted enough to see how wide and round her eyes were. "We've got to do something," she hissed into my ear. "He'll beat that boy to death!"

"Yeah, okay." I whispered back then licked dry lips. My heart jigged up my throat. I swallowed. "But let's stay hidden until the last minute."

We'd crept to within shouting distance of the trailer when the door slammed back against the side. Aretha yanked the camera up, snapping off shots as William leaped out, and sprinted toward the gate. The bulky shape of one of his football player buds raced after him. Briefly, I wondered why Jimmy hadn't accompanied the posse.

William's Jeep roared awake as Aretha dashed for the trailer. Rifle gripped in my hands, I ran close behind her. She yanked open the trailer door and froze. "Oh, dear God," she breathed out.

The young man lying in the middle of the tiny floor space with frothy red blood leaking from the corner of his mouth barely appeared human. If I hadn't heard William call him by name, I would never have recognized the ruined face.

Aretha whispered, "Oh, God," then leaped into the trailer. As she reached Ralph's side, a wet sigh burbled out. His thin chest went still. She flipped his jacket open and shoved her ear against the plaid flannel of his shirt.

She yanked the camera from around her neck, set it on the floor, and began CPR. Push-push-push, pinch nostrils, breathe, push-push-push, pinch nostrils, breathe. "Breathe! Come on, boy, breathe!" She grunted as she tried to force his heart to beat.

I stepped the rest of the way into the trailer, squeezed against the door to stay out of her way. Rifle dangling loose in my hand, I watched as she fought a lost cause. I'd heard that wet burble sound once before when a drunk beat another drunk to death for sucking up the last of the wine. Ralph died seconds after we'd entered the trailer.

My eyes wandered up to the round face of the clock on the wall. The minute hand swept past the black numbers once, twice, three times, four times, five times. No response from the body on the floor. I edged carefully to her side, avoiding the blood splatters as much as possible. I reached down and put my hands beneath her arms and lifted her away from the dead man. "He's gone, Aretha."

She turned her face to me, tears running down her cheeks. "No...oh God, no."

I wrapped my arms around her shaking body and held her close. When her sobs subsided, I said, "We have to go to town. Get Sheriff Daly."

She shoved away from me, stepped sideways, and reached for a blanket from the closest bunk.

I snatched it from her hands. She stood looking like a deer caught in the headlights. "It'd be better if we don't bother anything more."

Waving at the body lying at our feet, she spoke slowly, trancelike. "We've got to cover him. It's the only decent thing..."

I shook my head and spoke as gently and concisely as I would to a frightened child. "No, it's better to just leave him. He'll be all right. When the sheriff gets here, he'll take good care of him." I bent over and picked up the camera, slung it over my shoulder.

"It's so cold..." A shiver wracked her. She wrapped her arms around herself.

"The door will be closed and it really isn't that cold in here. That little propane heater does a good job." Firmly, I took her by the elbow and steered her outside.

With the weather turning bad and the snow piling up, Aretha had taken a chance and left the Volkswagen parked behind some boulders close to the trailer. The little car actually handled better in the snow and ice than the two-wheel drive truck. Because we seldom went to town, the snow had obliterated most traces of its tire marks. If William hadn't been in a hurry, though, he could've found it. I pushed that speculation away as we drew near its hiding place.

Its rounded shape hunched under a layer of crunchy snow. I opened the passenger door and helped Aretha in then ran to the driver's side. The engine started right away. While the car warmed up, I laid the camera on the back seat then jumped out and scraped the ice off the windows and knocked the largest amount of snow off the hood and the top of the car. Done, I climbed in. The Volkswagen's heat exchangers, never great at pumping out heat, left the windshield fogged. I used the end of my shirt sleeve to wipe a spot clear enough to see then I steered from behind the boulders and down the slope to the gate. The little car plowed bravely through the crusted snow. Once we got to the gate, I followed the ruts made by William's Jeep. The steering wheel jerked in my hands as the car bounced from side to side.

As the car slithered around Buzzard Peak, I hit the steering wheel with the heel of my hand. "We can't do this!" I jammed on the brakes. The vehicle slid. I wrestled the wheel as the car tried to swap ends. Finally I got the front end pointed down the center of the snow-shrouded road. Carefully, I found a wide spot and turned around.

Aretha stared blankly out at the night, not even speaking when I headed the car back toward the farm. "Aretha?" No response. Not even a slight movement of her head. I reached over, grasped her upper arm and shook hard. "Aretha!"

In slow motion, her head swiveled toward me, the look in her eyes the blank gaze of a victim of war. "Are we going back so we can take him to the hospital?" She spoke slowly, as if she had to find each word and then had to decide on how to enunciate it.

"He's dead, Aretha," I told her bluntly, hoping to shock her back to reality.

Stubbornly, she shook her head. "He can't be. He's just a boy, Jaz." She responded as if Ralph's age made him invincible, or maybe immortal.

"Snap out of it!" I growled. "He was a man. He came up here with William and that other man to destroy whatever he could and to kill us. Now, he's dead. Beaten to death by his so-called friend."

Aretha stared at me, the kind of look you give a lunatic talking to God in a roll of toilet paper.

"Aretha! Get yourself together. We have to decide what we're going to do." I hadn't shut the gate, so without slowing I swung onto the icy ruts leading up the slope to the trailer.

After an eternity, she blinked then rubbed her hands down her face. Voice dull, she spoke. "You said we have to go to the sheriff."

"I wasn't thinking clearly. If we go to Sheriff Daly, we'll be accused of killing Ralph." The V-dub slid as I parked. I stared out at the snow drifting from the harsh black sky. Not a star in sight.

"What else can we do?" With an unblinking gaze, she stared out of the windshield.

A sigh leaked out as I rubbed the back of my neck. "Bury him. Like we did the chickens and the goats."

Her head snapped around, her dark eyes finally alive. "We can't...his parents..."

"We have to. If his parents had kept him home, they could bury him themselves," I snarled. Head resting against the driver's door window, I closed my eyes.

"We can't, Jaz."

Not wanting to see the pain I heard in her voice, I kept my eyes shut. "Why not? No one's going to tell that he was up here tonight. If they did they would have to admit to being here, too. William certainly isn't going to want to draw attention to himself. Neither is that other guy." I turned my head so I faced her and opened my eyes. "No way either one of them is going to say one word since it would put them right in the middle of it. I'm sure not going to say anything."

"It isn't about getting blamed for his death..." I heard a hitch in her voice. "We just can't bury him like...like that."

I shot up in the seat and slammed my hand against the steering wheel. "If we go to Daly it's a toss-up whether we'll be believed or whether we'll be tossed in jail."

She chewed her lower lip, attention locked on the trailer. "What about the pictures? That'll prove we didn't do it."

A dim stirring of hope slithered through me. I twisted and reached behind to snatch the camera off the back seat. A few button pokes and that hope died like a snake smashed by a car.

I ran a hand down my face. "They aren't the greatest." I handed her the camera. "If you know who you're looking at you can identify William and Ralph coming up to the trailer. The other guy's just a dark blob. Of course, there aren't any photos of what they were doing inside, and the last photos only show two large people jumping out of the trailer and running away. I couldn't see either man's face clearly in those shots." Hands gripping the steering wheel, I peered blankly at the small area illuminated by the headlights. "Even if we can use a computer to enhance those photos, it will only prove that William, Ralph, and that other guy were here, but not that they did anything."

"Oh." Aretha switched off the camera. "Jaz," the pleading in her voice dragged my gaze to her face. "We can't simply dump his body in a hole and let his family wonder what happened to him. It isn't right."

"What isn't right is what those men have been doing and how no one is going to believe a queer and a black woman over those homegrown, white men." I flung the door open, snatched my jacket from the back seat, and bailed out. Flashlight beam bouncing off the stark white snow, I plowed through the new powder accumulated on top of the icy crust. I bulled a path all the way down to Boulder Creek.

Flashlight clicked off, hands jammed in my jacket pockets, I stood hunched up at the ice-encrusted edge of the creek and listened to the dark waters moving swiftly past. "This is all so messed up," I whispered to the night. By the time I climbed back up the hill, snow soaked the legs of my jeans all the way up to my knees; however, the chill I felt had nothing to do with the weather.

In my absence, Aretha had stirred up a campfire. The cheerful sound of coffee perking seemed macabre. She flicked a look my way then ducked her gaze back to the fire. "I didn't know how long you'd be gone and I couldn't stand to go in the trailer. I went down to the cave and got the coffee and..." She waved her hand at the cups and pot. "I'm glad we left extra stuff down there. The coffee just finished perking. Pour yourself a cup. We need to talk."

The strong coffee scalded a path down my throat and hit my stomach like a fireball. I rubbed my eyes with my fingers, but the burning didn't lessen. "So talk."

She sipped her coffee, letting the silence of the winter night settle around us. "I can't help thinking about Ralph's parents..."

Aya Walksfar

I slammed my blue enamel cup onto the flat rock next to my feet. Hot liquid splashed out, burning my hand. I yanked my hand up and leaped to my feet, spilling more coffee, thankfully on the ground instead of on me. The cup dropped from my hand as I stomped around in a circle, slinging my hand in the cold air. Curse words boiled behind my clenched teeth. Finally the heat of the burn died down enough that I could sit still again.

Hunched over, forearms braced on my thighs, I said, "Ralph's parents didn't care enough to keep him from harassing us. Why should we care about them?"

When I lifted my head and forced my eyes up from the ground, her dark eyes caught mine. "Jaz, it isn't about what they've done to deserve our caring."

I jerked upright. "Then what *is* it about?"

She set her cup on the ground then linked her hands together. "It's about doing what's right."

Glowering, I said, "What's *right* is taking care of ourselves, and going to jail for something we didn't do is definitely not taking care of ourselves."

She cocked her head and studied me. I felt like a bug under a microscope, and wondered about her thoughts. At that moment, I didn't see Aretha at all. Just Alicia. "Taking care of ourselves is doing the right thing, so we can look in the mirror. Letting Ralph's parents forever wonder where he is, and what happened to him, why he never came home, isn't doing the right thing. You know that, Jaz." With a grace reminiscent of Alicia, she stood, picked up the coffeepot, found my cup where I'd thrown it, and refilled both of our cups. She handed mine to me before she resumed her seat on the damp log.

I pinched the bridge of my nose, took a deep gulp of coffee, welcomed the heat that trailed fire through my body. I was arguing with Alicia again, and I'd never won a single argument with her. "All I know is that Ralph was a grown man. He made his choices. Now he's dead because of those choices."

"Still..."

I bent forward, scrutinized her face as if I could read the magic words on the planes of her cheeks, words that would make her understand. "Aretha, we didn't kill Ralph, but there isn't anybody out there who is going to believe us. We didn't force him to run with William, or to come up here and to try to kill us while we slept, yet we're the ones who will pay for it if anyone finds out he died here."

She closed her eyes, rubbing her forehead with her fingers, like Mom used to do when she felt one of her migraines coming on. "Ralph made a lethal mistake. He paid for it." She lowered her hand and continued in an unnaturally subdued tone. "His parents shouldn't have to pay for it, too, with sleepless nights, always wondering if he'll come home."

Agitated, I carefully set my cup in the snow next to the log and slowly climbed to my feet, afraid that sudden movement would unleash the tidal wave of rage inside of me and drown us both. Hands clenched at my sides, I spat, "Well, I'm not willing to pay for their enhanced sleep abilities with my life!"

I unclenched my fists and it was as if I had breached the dam holding back the anxiety doing butterfly dances in my stomach. I wrapped my arms around myself and looked down at her. "Look, I have to tell you: I'm terrified of winding up looking at life in prison for a killing I didn't do. I don't know how to *not* let that happen."

Aretha stretched her legs out in front of her, leaned back on her hands, and regarded me. She sighed, a defeated sound that I hadn't heard before. "I don't want either one of us in prison."

I turned to face the east where gray crept through the black of the waning night, my back to her. "My mom used to tell me that there's nothing free in life. Everything has a price tag. Love, hate, the right to be left alone." I swiveled toward her. "The only thing we have any control over is what price we're willing to pay."

Speaking softly, she said, "Maybe that's the bottom line, Jaz. This isn't a price I'm willing to pay." Her mouth firmed into a determined slash. Her next words trashed any hope of derailing her course. "Letting Ralph's people wonder what happened to him, if he's ever coming home, is he hurt and needing them, that's not a price I'm willing to pay. I'll share something with you that most people don't know, Jaz. Down in the south, one of the Klan's favorite methods of torture is to make people disappear. The friends and family of that person have to live the rest of their lives never knowing what happened to someone they loved."

I didn't ask if a friend of hers might have disappeared in such a manner.

Her eyes dipped away. A brush swipe of pale pink lightened the sky, tinted the snow. "I thought I hated whites." There was a distant quality to her voice. "They murdered my auntie, and that drunk white man murdered my sister when he hit her car head-on. All he got out of it was a few years in prison and a broken arm. In some ways, maybe I do hate whites, but when I think of Ralph's poor momma..." She shook her head, slid her gaze to me. "It has to end, Jaz. All this pain, all this killing. It has to end."

My heart rocketed into super-drive. My mouth became so dry it felt like my lips were glued together. I licked at them with an equally dry tongue. "Listen, Aretha, we aren't responsible for that boy's mother. We didn't kill him." I begged her to remember that; to value our lives more than Ralph's parents. I knew I'd lost the argument before I ever opened my mouth, but desperation seized me. "What are we supposed to do? Sacrifice our lives so William can go around terrorizing other people while we're locked up in jail?" I shook my head, more in resignation than denial. "It won't change anything, Aretha. The more you give in to people like that, the more they take from you until they take your life. When we go to Daly, if he arrests us, William wins. He wanted us gone, and we'll be gone. By the time we pay attorney fees and bail, everything both of us have financially will be used up."

We had torn down the goat house. One of the first things we did after we buried Little Kid. Now Aretha's face pivoted toward that empty spot. Quietly, she said, "Regardless of how it turns out for me, whether I'm accused of Ralph's death, or not, the boy's mother has a right to know what happened to her son. To me, Jaz, that peace of mind is more important than whether I continue to live here." She stood and brushed at the damp seat of her jeans.

The muscles of my jaw clenched so tightly they ached. I forced myself to speak in a normal volume instead of yelling my frustration to the heavens. "This is crazy. They'll stick us in jail and throw away the key!"

Calmly, she watched me. "Not us, Jaz. Me."

"What?!" My brows crowded low over my eyes. I gave a short, angry shake of my head. "No way! *This* is not negotiable. If one of us cops, we both cop."

Eyes steady on mine, she quietly insisted. "Just me. I have to do this. You have to stay out of it."

Hands held at chest height, palms facing her in a classic stop-right-there gesture, I said, "Uh-uh. We've had this discussion before. I don't split and leave my friends holding the bag."

She pursed her lips and arched her brows as she considered her next words. "You were out hiking around because you were restless..."

"Hiking? In the snow and the cold? In the middle of the night? Are you out of your mind, or just delusional? No cop's going to accept that load of bull."

"Daly won't have a choice, not with both of us saying the same thing." When I started to argue, she held up her hand. "You got back just as I ran out of the trailer. I told you what happened, that Ralph was dead. We both went back into the trailer. You could see that Ralph was dead. You picked the camera up off the floor because I told you I'd taken photos of the men when they'd arrived. You thought the sheriff might want to see the photos. You drove me to the sheriff's office. End of your involvement."

I crossed my arms and belligerently tilted my chin up. "Come on. You cannot possibly believe that that's going to fly."

"Why would I lie? Why would I take all the blame, if it wasn't true?" Her eyes kept a calm focus on me.

I threw my hands up. "Sheriff Daly is not going to buy this. You just watch."

"He doesn't have any choice," she reiterated. "I am confessing to being here alone when William and his friends arrived and when Ralph was killed."

"Look, I can admit to being here, too, that way it's my word and yours against William and that other guy."

Eyes downcast, she murmured, "Unless I miss my guess, those men will have alibis placing them far away from this hill tonight."

A frown creased vertical lines between my eyes. "You're doing what? Putting your head in the noose to spare me?"

She closed the distance between us. "No, I am keeping you free so you can find some way to prove I didn't do this. Someone has to make sure I have a good attorney, and that the investigation moves forward and doesn't get hung up on me as the only suspect." Hand on my forearm she locked her gaze on me. "I'm depending on you, Jaz, to make certain that the sheriff doesn't close the case before he finds the real killers."

Chapter 9

The early morning's promise of clearing skies got smothered by solid gray overcast. Snow showered down fitfully as I drove us into town in her Volkswagen. Silently, I swore that I would find a way to prove her innocent, even if I had to choke a confession out of William.

Deputy Jones' big belly pushed against the desk edge as he studiously refused to look up or acknowledge us in any way. Sick of his bullshit, I lunged across the desk, yanked the graphic novel out of his hands, and flung it across the room. It bounced off the wall as he shot to his feet, one hand on the butt of his pistol.

Instead of backing up like anyone with any sense would do, I jutted my chin out and leaned further over the desk. "Go ahead, pull it. Either pull your gun or go get Sheriff Daly. Or I'll go get Daly. Your choice, big man." The frost in my voice made the weather outside seem warm.

Hate flared in his eyes, but cunning drowned it out. Like other bullies I'd met, my aggression caused him to wonder what I had in my pocket, so to speak. He spun on his heel and slammed through the hall door.

Thunder clouds followed Sheriff Daly into the lobby. Jones walked a step behind the sheriff, a smirk plastered across his blubbery lips. Daly stopped a few inches from my face, definitely in my personal space. "My deputy has lodged a complaint that you threatened him."

Eyes never wavering from Daly's, I kept my voice low, controlled. "No, I didn't threaten the deputy. What I did was throw his graphic novel across the room when he refused to look up or speak. Then he jumped to his feet and made like he was going to pull a gun on an unarmed citizen. I told him he could go get you, or I would."

Daly swung halfway around, kept Aretha and me in his peripheral vision as he faced Deputy Jones. Jones' red face told the truth better than a confession. "I'll see you in my office after I'm done with these ladies. Meanwhile, I suggest you sit down and try to do your job." He turned his back on Jones and moved out of my body space. "If you ladies would follow me."

Daly's office surprised me. I'd expected dull, bland, messy. A jumbled bookshelf sat against one wall. The spines of the texts ran jagged lines along the shelves. A couple of books lay face down on top of the shelf unit, like someone had been interrupted in the middle of reading. Two chairs, well-padded, but not so soft a person couldn't escape them, sat in front of a dark wood desk. The wood gleamed between the stacks of journals, file folders, and loose papers. The seat of the comfortable-looking desk chair held a sunken impression. A framed photograph of a beautiful waterfall, enlarged to an eight-by-ten, graced the wall opposite the sheriff's desk.

Daly waved us into the chairs then rounded the desk and resumed his seat. "How can I help you ladies?"

A few minutes into the telling, Daly halted Aretha's story. He locked up his desk, stuffed the paperwork in the file cabinets, then locked them. "You need to wait here until I'm done talking with Ms. Hopewell then I'll need to ask you a few questions."

Forty-five minutes later, he retrieved me and left Aretha in his office. It didn't take long for me to pretend ignorance.

On the way out, Daly ordered Jones to stay put until he returned. As I pushed out the door behind him and Aretha, I glanced over my shoulder. If eyes could shoot real daggers, I would've resembled a porcupine. The sheriff made Aretha ride in his truck and ordered me to follow in the V-dub.

From the gate area, the white crime scene van and the black corpse wagon were plainly visible, hunched in the snow next to the trailer. Daly stopped at the gate and let Aretha out before he drove on up.

She climbed into the passenger seat of the car, her face a blank mask.

"Why did he want you to ride with him?"

She blinked and the haze seemed to clear from her eyes. "Just more questions, more details. Probably trying to catch me in some lies."

Neither of us spoke again as we watched and waited.

Run or Die

Late morning light spilled across the snow. The tire tracks looked like some giant with dirty skies had cut a swath from the trailer to the gate. I wished desperately for a cup of hot coffee, then wondered if we'd covered the fact that we had sat drinking coffee before we came to town. Directly on the heels of that thought, I wondered if it really mattered.

It seemed like forever before Daly's truck chugged down the slope. When he came over to the car and rapped on the window, I rolled it all the way down. The freezing air rushed in while the meager warmth took flight. A chill ran up my spine and I shivered.

"You ladies should go on down to Willits and get a room. It'll be a while before we're finished here. We'll have to impound the trailer until it can be processed, so you'll need to consider where you're going to stay. Don't know how long it'll take before you can have the trailer back."

"We usually stay at the Sleepy Hollow Motel when we're in Willits." I twisted my head around to look at Aretha.

She nodded.

"Well, don't be going much further away than Willits. I'll need to talk to you again." He stood up and stepped back.

I turned the car and drove slowly away. Glancing in the rearview mirror as I topped the hill, I could see him still standing in the same place, watching us leave.

Fatigue hit me with a sledgehammer by the time we checked in and made our way up to our room. Even though it was only noon, I stretched out on top of the bed closest to the window with nothing removed but my boots, and fell gratefully into the blackness of dreamless sleep.

The drizzling snow had stopped. Weak winter sun creeping through the window woke me. Groggily, I sat up on the edge of the mattress with my hands braced on either side of me and stared blankly around the quiet room. Somewhere beyond the door, footsteps thundered down the hall before the quiet resettled like a cat temporarily disturbed. The demon red digits of the bedside clock blared two o'clock.

On the other bed a couple of feet from me, Aretha lay rolled up in the blankets like a burrito. I wondered what time she'd gone to sleep. It had been a while since either of us had had a decent night's rest. Not wanting to wake her, I slid off the bed, picked up my boots, and slipped out the door.

I walked the five blocks to Mother Earth's Bounty where I ordered a double cheeseburger, large fries, and coffee. A dish of apple pie ala mode had just been placed in front of me when Aretha staggered in and sat on the chair across the table.

"You should've woke me up," she said then yawned.

I shrugged, holding a forkful of pie halfway to my mouth. "Why?"

She sucked her lower lip between her teeth then gave a small shake of her head. "No reason, I suppose."

With nowhere to go and no time to be there, I finished dessert and tanked up on coffee while she ate. When she ordered pecan pie, she asked the waitress to tell Ms. Winters that Aretha would like to speak with her.

Ms. Winters carried her coffee cup in one hand and Aretha's pecan pie in her other hand as she made her way to our table. She smiled as she set the pie in front of Aretha then gracefully sank into a chair. "I heard there was some doin's up at your place last night." She sipped her coffee while her dark eyes darted between Aretha and me.

Aretha washed down a bite of pie with a long drink of coffee then nodded. "Ralph Henley was killed in my trailer."

Ms. Winters raised one elegant brow. "Any idea who did it?"

"Oh, yes. William Radley and some other young man. Most likely one of the ones who came up the first time."

"A bad business." Her lips turned down and her eyebrows lowered over her troubled gaze.

Aretha laid her fork aside and shoved the rest of the pie toward the middle of the table. "A bad business doesn't begin to describe it. I think I'm going to need a good criminal defense attorney."

The restaurant owner scowled. "In a righteous world you wouldn't need an attorney, even if you'd killed that boy. Not after what him and those others have been up to."

Run or Die

A sad smile touched her lips. "This isn't a righteous world, and I don't have any way to prove that William and his friend killed Ralph. I suspect they will both have alibis for the time surrounding Ralph's murder."

With a brusque nod, she rose to her feet. "I'll have Charles Edison contact you. Are you staying at the Sleepy Hollow?"

"Yes."

Two days later, on Sunday, still stuck in town and playing Blackjack 21 in our motel room, I heard the heavy tread of a man's footsteps coming up the hall and halting at our door. I laid my cards face down and answered the door before he could knock.

"Hey, Sheriff," I pulled the door wider. "Come on in and give us the skinny on what you know."

He walked over to where Aretha sat with the tread of a man going to the execution chamber. "Ms. Hopewell, you are under arrest for the murder of Ralph Henley." In a deep, steady voice, he Mirandized her.

When he finished, she stood and walked over to the closet. She removed her jacket from its hanger and slid into it. On the way to the door, she detoured to the desk by the window and picked up her purse then put it back down. Face carefully blank, she led the way to the door. Before she stepped out, she twisted toward me. "Be sure to let Mr. Edison know."

Standing in the middle of the motel room floor, I tried to project a confidence I didn't feel. "Don't worry about anything, Aretha. I'll get a hold of him ASAP and we'll get you out of there."

The tiny smile she forced trembled and faded.

When the door closed, I pulled on my heated jacket, outer pants, and gloves, glad that Sheriff Daly had allowed me to retrieve my bike and gear. The freedom of the bike meant more to me than the questionable comfort of Aretha's Volkswagen, or the increased risk inherent in using a motorcycle when ice and snow dotted the roadways.

By the time I made it to the sheriff's office in Andersville, Daly had already taken Aretha to the back. I slumped in one of the reception area's hard chairs and flipped open my cell phone.

Mr. Charles Edison, black as a moonless midnight, had heavy lips and sleepy eyes so deeply brown they were nearly black, and a charisma that helped make him one of the most respected attorneys in California, according to the internet. I hauled myself to my feet when he stepped into the reception area of the sheriff's office, fresh from visiting with Aretha. I bit my tongue to keep my questions behind my teeth until we walked outside.

As he strode across the parking lot, he said in his smooth baritone, "We have our work cut out for us."

"What do they think they have on her?" I asked as I lengthened my stride to match his, quite a feat since at six-foot-one he stood a good half-foot taller than me.

He pressed his key fob and a silver Mercedes blinked its lights. With a smooth movement he pulled open the back door and tossed in the black leather briefcase then pivoted to face me. "Most of it is fairly circumstantial, and probably would not have merited her arrest, except for the fact that Ms. Hopewell had motive, opportunity, and means."

"Okay, I get the motive part. Those guys tried to kill her and burned her out twice. I'll even buy into opportunity. Ralph was on her farm and she was there. But means? Does the sheriff really think Aretha beat that man to death without a scratch on her?"

"Ms. Hopewell had a gash across the knuckles of one hand."

Dismissively, I waved my hand in front of myself as if I dispersed a cloud of gnats. "Even when Daly took that picture of her hand, we told him how she injured it. We were taking out some dead trees for firewood when she slipped and fell into a tree. Scraped her hand when she fell."

"Yes, Ms. Hopewell explained that to me in detail; however, when Sheriff Daly adds the injury to the fact that Mr. Henley's blood was on Ms. Hopewell's clothes and her finger and hand prints were on Mr. Henley's face and neck, this creates a certain body of evidence that is difficult to ignore. Motive, opportunity, and the evidence allude to the means.

"According to statements given to Sheriff Daly, Mr. Radley and Mr. Evers alleged that Mr. Henley told them on the day of his death that he felt bad about harassing Ms. Hopewell and was going to go up to her farm and apologize."

Run or Die

Rage flushed my face red. "Daly believed that line of bull?"

Mr. Edison stared at me from beneath half-lidded eyes. "Mr. Radley made it a point to say that he tried to talk Mr. Henley out of apologizing to a...quote, 'nigger.' Mr. Radley and Mr. Evers have also provided two people who confirm their presence in Elmsworth for the entire day and night in question."

My stomach cramped and I felt like throwing up. "Jesus! *You* don't believe Aretha did it, do you?"

A bare lifting at the corners of his full lips hinted at a smile. "That, Ms. Wheeler, is not a question a defense attorney ever answers. It is not our place to believe, or disbelieve. It is our duty to defend our client to the best of our abilities." He seemed to consider his next words for a long moment. "However, in the case of Ms. Hopewell, I truly believe she is innocent of any wrongdoing."

His sincerity sounded clearly in his words. I wanted to ask him why he believed in her innocence, but I had no right to. It was enough that he believed.

He opened the driver's door and stepped into the wedge between door and car. "We need one of those men to break, to give us something that we can take to the sheriff." He paused and stared at me. "If I were a betting man, and taking into account the extent of damage done to Mr. Henley, I would assume that some of Henley's blood inadvertently got transferred to William Radley's vehicle. The sheriff needs a good reason, however, to impound the vehicle and to search it for evidence. As Aretha's attorney there is only so much I can do." He held my gaze for a long moment then said, "I don't think it'll be enough. From what I've learned of these men, they know how to play the legal system quite well. Do you understand me?"

Lips pinched together, I contemplated what he said. His face gave nothing away. The man could have played poker with the best of them. Finally, I gave a bob of my chin. "Yeah, I hear you."

Exhausted, I fell into bed that night. My mind kept running in circles on a hamster wheel, but I barely hit the pillow before I dropped into a nightmare-ridden sleep. The next morning my eyes snapped open. I lay there listening as I stared up at the faded watermark crawling across the ceiling above my bed. Someone walked past my door, shushing a fretful youngster.

I hauled myself out of bed when what I really wanted to do was crawl under the bed for an indefinite period of time, however long it took for this bad dream to dissipate. However, unlike my nightmares, this bad dream was reality. Headed for the shower, I peeled off my sweat-soaked t-shirt and the baggy shorts that I'd slept in. The hot water didn't do much to loosen my muscles, but I didn't have all day to stand under the pounding stream. Quickly dried off, I ran a comb through my mess of hair and jerked on jeans and a long-sleeve, flannel shirt. Boots and jacket on, I hustled out the door.

Winter isn't the best time to ride a bike, but some things are worth a bit of risk. Besides, I needed to feel the freedom that I never felt inside of a car. First stop: Bank of America. I withdrew enough money to pick up some necessities for Aretha and me since I didn't know when Daly might let me in the trailer to get our own stuff. At the sheriff's office, a female deputy manned the front desk.

"I'm Jaz Wheeler. I brought some stuff for Aretha Hopewell."

She tipped her head toward the desk in front of her. "Set the bag there so I can go through it." After she inspected the toothbrush for bombs and the toothpaste for a hidden file, she placed everything in a basket. "I'll take it to her when I take her lunch in. Are you aware that visiting hours are every evening from four to six?"

"Yeah, the sheriff told me. So what does the S stand for, Deputy Hardy?"

She grinned. "Shirley."

With a chuckle, I shook my head. "You don't look like a Shirley to me. By the way, where's Deputy Jones?"

I don't think I imagined that her nostrils flared like she'd smelled something especially nasty. "Deputy Jones decided to take some leave time to spend with his family."

Inside I breathed a sigh of relief. "Why now?" I pressed, curious without any real reason. It was enough that Aretha wouldn't have to deal with the pig.

Run or Die

She glanced around like she expected a crowd of newspaper reporters to jump out of the woodwork. "You didn't hear this from me, but Sheriff Daly felt that Jones had a conflict of interest with this case. May have had something to do with the fact that Nick is his second cousin." Her incredibly blue eyes met mine.

For the first time since Alicia died, I felt the distant stirring of interest in another woman. I swatted it away, and bent close. "I'd say he had a conflict of interest with any case that dealt with any minority. You don't need to worry. I'm not one to whisper and tell."

Chapter 10

The remainder of the day I found myself incredibly busy as I prepared to assume the responsibilities that Mr. Edison had outlined.

Two in the morning I crept back into the hotel. The girl behind the counter, who worked nights so she could attend college during the day, snored in her chair with an open text book in her lap. Careful not to wake her, I edged past the reception counter and down the hall. In my own room, I didn't bother with a shower, just slapped a wet washcloth over my face. My grungy teeth got a quick run over with the toothbrush before I peeled out of my clothes, dropping them on the floor as I staggered across the room. I fell asleep almost before my head hit the pillow.

The godawful racket of someone pounding on my door woke me. I groaned, rolled over, and yanked a pillow over my head. Didn't help. The pounding got louder, and now he stood in the hallway shouting at me.

Men! My eyes eased open. I peeked from under the pillow. Sunlight blasted across the not-new carpet. *Crap! Isn't he going to go away?* Obviously not, so I wrapped the terry cloth robe that I'd purchased the day before around me and grumbled my way to the door. As I swung it open, I mumbled, "You had better have brought coffee." Without waiting for a reply, I led the way to the small table by the window. Slumped in one chair, I glared up at him. "Sit."

Sheriff Daly perched on the edge of the plastic chair. "No coffee, questions. Where were you last night?"

Lazily, I lifted my eyes to him. "Why?"

Face set in tense lines, he snapped, "Answer the question."

I gave him an insolent grin. "Uh-uh. I know my rights. You tell me why you want to know and I *might* tell you where I was. Otherwise, there's the door." I nodded with my chin in the general direction. "Unless you intend to arrest me for something. Either way, I believe you have an *obligation* to answer *my* question: why do you want to know?"

Run or Die

"Think you're a tough one, don't you?" He gave me a squint-eyed glare, the muscles in his jaw bunching and releasing.

I slouched further down in my chair, stretched out my legs and crossed my ankles. Hands clasped over my stomach, I gave him a lidded gaze. "Naw, I just don't think I'll answer police questions until I know what you're after. In this town, innocent people wind up in jail. Tell me, Sheriff, why could you never once touch William and his posse, but you seemed to have no problem arresting Aretha?" I taunted him.

If the man had been a tea kettle, he'd have been screaming. I could almost see steam rising off him. "Mr. Edison is aware of the evidence that forced me to arrest Ms. Hopewell. Without evidence, I *cannot* arrest people, no matter what I suspect them of doing."

I tilted my head and leveled a hard stare at him. "Instead of hassling citizens, what are you doing to find evidence that William murdered Ralph? Or are you simply waiting for the judge to find an innocent woman guilty because she's black?"

Daly's face tightened up like a plaster bust. In a flat voice, he answered. "The investigation is open."

"Yeah, like the investigation into the arson of Aretha's cabin not once, but twice." Restless and angry, I jolted to my feet and wandered over to the window. Two stories below, the parking lot lay empty, except for my bike, a beat up car, and a tiny mound of blackened snow. Felt a lot like me. "Why are you here?"

"William Radley lodged a complaint at eight this morning. Someone vandalized his Jeep." I heard him get to his feet and cross the room to stand next to me.

"I'm heartbroken," I said without shifting my gaze from the parking lot.

"He claims he woke up and when he went to his bedroom window, he saw someone who fits your description running from beside his vehicle." He leaned one shoulder against the edge of the window frame.

"So?" From the corner of my eye, I checked him out. The man looked troubled, but not really hostile. "Lots of people fit my description: average height, average build."

Aya Walksfar

In spite of everything, I like the man. I whirled away from the window and him. Stomped over to the closet and yanked a clean pair of jeans and a blue plaid, flannel shirt off their hangers then headed over to the small dresser for clean underwear and socks. "I was here all night. From around nine until you woke me up. I read for a while then sacked out." I stormed over to the nightstand and picked up a paperback novel. I tossed it at him and he caught it without effort. "You ever read about Jane Yellowrock?"

He shifted and rested his lean hips against the windowsill. Paperback hanging from one hand, he propped the other hand beside him on the sill. The stormy sky outside, a mere reflection of his face, he said, "No."

"Real kick butt character. Vampire story, but good reading." Clothes gathered in my arms, I stopped in the bathroom doorway. "You can stay or go. I'm taking a shower."

"I may want to discuss this further with you." He laid the book on the table and moved toward the door.

"Whatever. Lock the door on your way out."

Three hours later, Daly found me eating an Organic Veggie Delight Omelette at Mother Earth's Bounty. He slid into the chair across from me, brushed a dusting of snow from his shoulders. "Thought you might like to know William's going to need a new engine."

I set my fork on the edge of my plate and stared at him. "Seriously? Give me one good reason that I should care? Aretha needs a new cabin and everything else, including her freedom."

Axel, face pinched in anger, arrived bearing a cup of coffee for Daly. The young waiter slammed it down. Coffee splashed out on the saucer. Lip curled, he asked in a hard voice, "Anything else, *Sheriff?*"

Sheriff Daly stuck a couple of paper napkins under the cup. He looked up, his eyes dark with...sadness? "No, thanks, Axel."

The young man swung around and marched away.

Daly murmured as he watched Axel leave, "I've known that young man for four years, always had a smile and a hello for me. Seems like there's a lot of folks who are downright ticked off."

I snorted. "Seriously? Surprised much? There *are* some people around this area who *really* know Aretha. Do you expect them to be happy that she's locked up and William's still running around? Anyone with a half a brain knows how messed up that is."

He shifted his focus to me. "I know you don't believe this, but arresting Ms. Hopewell was one of the most difficult decisions I've ever made. What you, and everyone else, need to understand is that when it comes to the law, I am a sheriff first, and a person second."

I squinched my eyes as I bent across the table. "How you order your priorities doesn't matter one bit to me. Doesn't change the facts. For months now, Aretha has been William's victim repeatedly, and the man's never been arrested for it. William beats a man to death in Aretha's trailer, and Aretha is arrested. Seems like justice and the law aren't even distant cousins in this town."

The sheriff ducked his eyes to his cup and stirred cream into his coffee. When he lifted his face, he changed the topic. "Whoever vandalized William's Jeep did a good job of it." He waited.

I resumed eating.

"Brake lines cut, tires gouged, sugar in the gas tank, seat slashed. Even his fancy paint job was done in. Of course, I had to impound the vehicle to collect evidence."

My fork continued to my mouth. I chewed, keeping my eyes on my plate. *Mr. Edison sure called that one right. Hopefully, the truck will testify to William's actions and the truth about Ralph's murder.*

I laid my fork aside and picked up my coffee cup, my face carefully blank. "What do you want? Why, exactly, are you telling me all this? Hope I'll slip and tell you how his fancy paint job was messed up?"

He matched the neutrality of my own face and spoke. "Did you realize that the seats in William's Jeep are cloth-covered? It's a woven kind of cloth, heavy, almost like one of those imitation Navajo rugs they sell at Rainbow Grocers. Tiny particles of blood would be difficult to get out of cloth like that." He picked up his hat and stood, leaving his barely-touched coffee. "I'm a cop. I care about the law, but I also care about right and wrong."

I watched as he walked out the door. "Yeah, seriously," I murmured then wondered if he really did.

At four o'clock I visited Aretha in the two-cell jail, in the back half of the sheriff's building. Daly opened the door and hauled a folding chair into the cell. "Give me a yell when you're ready to leave."

Aretha perched on the edge of the cot screwed to the jailhouse floor. "Mr. Edison just left." She brushed at her jeans, but didn't look up.

I dragged the chair closer and settled on its hard metal seat. "Hmph. Visiting hours obviously don't apply to lawyers," I grumbled in a teasing voice. My attempt at levity fell as flat as a deflated balloon.

She glanced up then lowered her eyes back down. "He said he'd have me bailed out by Friday."

"Hey, that's good." My words injected with forced cheer sounded hollow as they bounced off the blank cell walls.

Aretha lifted her face and caught my eyes. "Jaz, you're not doing anything to get into trouble, are you?"

"Me? Getting into trouble?" I raised my brows way high and made my eyes big as I jabbed a thumb against my chest, trying for comical denial. If Aretha's response to my act was anything to judge by, I'd never make a living as a comedienne.

She studied me for a long moment. "I got worried after Sheriff Daly told me about William's Jeep. Jaz, listen, don't take too many chances. I don't want you in jail, or hurt. Mr. Edison will figure out a way to prove my innocence."

She took my hands in hers. "I take back what I said up at the farm. You don't need to try to prove someone else killed Ralph. Let Sheriff Daly and Mr. Edison do that job. You really aren't qualified for it. Please? Promise me?"

My gaze drifted around the drab gray, barren cell. Gently, I extracted my hands and caught her eyes. "Aretha, don't get worked up about something you have no control over." I held her gaze for the longest time before I got to my feet and made my way over to the barred door.

Run or Die

At six o'clock that evening I headed south. Aretha and I had gone to Ukiah, twenty-five miles away, a couple times over the months. As the county seat and largest city in Mendocino County with over fifteen thousand people, some of them college students, the city hosted every convenience I needed: anonymity and car rentals. Avoiding the three major car rental places, I headed for one too small to be noticed. Cash kept the paperwork to a minimum.

At nine-thirty that evening, I parked the non-descript compact car in the deeper shadows of an abandoned auto parts store. From there I could watch the parking lot of The Redlight Tavern. For being in a Podunk town like Elmsworth, its parking lot was hopping. Of course, not everyone wandered inside. With binoculars I'd bought that day, I watched money and drugs change hands. Recreational opportunities in this entertainment dead-zone: getting stoned, getting drunk, harassing women, and beating your friends to death.

My watch read ten o'clock when Jimmy drove into the lot and parked under the only security light there. Obviously, he didn't have the money that William did. His truck sported gray bondo patches on the front fenders and interesting globs of rust over the rest of it. The back window was starred from an old impact, lines like spider legs radiating out from the center of where something had hit it. Didn't matter. His truck didn't figure in my plans. Having confirmed his arrival, I drove slowly out of the potholed parking lot.

People are the most vulnerable when they are in their own homes. It's a fact. No one wants to believe they can be attacked in their own house, in their own bed. That's the real terror of it: to find out you aren't safe anywhere at all. According to Aretha, the Klan has successfully used that terror tactic for decades. William and his posse had been way less successful with it, mostly due to Aretha's incredible courage. From what I'd seen of Jimmy, courage wouldn't be a dominant trait.

The young man lived alone in an older, and not too well-kept, two-story house on the back half of his parents' sprawling farm. Far enough away from the main house for the privacy I needed. Ears alert, I listened for dogs as I crept through the skeletal trees. Hunkered in the shadow of a sickly pine, I watched and waited. Jimmy staggered home a few minutes before midnight.

A light came on in a second floor room. His skinny shadow flickered against the thin drapes. Within minutes, he extinguished the light.

Watch held close to my eyes, I could barely read the time in the darkness. Ten minutes after midnight. I blew on my gloved hands, shoved them deeper into my jacket pockets. Wished that I could've worn my heated gloves, but couldn't take the risk of getting blood on them.

At precisely twelve-thirty AM, I crept across the shaggy lawn to the living room window. Good. He hadn't latched it. Earlier that night I'd worked on the old window to insure it opened smoothly and silently. I knew the stairs would creak; I'd found the weak spots when I entered the house the first time while Jimmy tanked up at the bar. Flattened against the wall, I sidled up to the second floor.

Three doors opened onto the second floor hall. An extra room, empty, its door closed. A bathroom with its door standing wide open. Jimmy's bedroom. Darkness leaked from the partially open door of his bedroom. Snores filtered into the hallway. My feet shushed over the worn carpet, stirring up a musty smell.

In and out in less than ten minutes. I carefully shut the first floor window. The dirt road where I'd hidden the rented car showed no signs of anyone passing through. One set of tire tracks in and now another set out as I maneuvered between the ruts. No other cars passed me all the way through Elmsworth then south.

Had to love these rural areas where the streets rolled up when the bars closed. By using the back streets, I avoided Highway 101 that ran through the main part of Willits. I parked the rental near the rental place's shop door and tossed the key through the mail slot. A quick jog to the mall parking lot where I'd hidden my bike behind some dumpsters, and I idled out of Ukiah.

My watch read three o'clock when I rolled off the highway and onto a spit of sand ten miles south of Eureka. I could have snuck into my motel room for the second night or found some place a lot closer to Willits to toss a sleeping bag, but I needed to

Run or Die

be close to the ocean. Waves dashed joyously against immovable black boulders, timeless sentinels guarding the sands. I parked behind a jumble of surf-tossed logs and flipped my sleeping bag out flat. Seated cross-legged, I bent my head back and stared up at the frozen chips of ice glittering against the black endless sky.

A rubber chicken and pig blood. It would've all seemed like a high school prank if the situation hadn't been deadly serious. I could imagine the panic he would feel when he woke to a room splattered with blood, a headless chicken on the pillow next to him, the pillow case stiff with more dried blood.

Even the soothing sound of the ocean didn't chase away the bad feeling in the pit of my stomach. I hated bullies; and now I was one. I dozed for a bit over two hours before I headed for Willits and my motel room.

At eleven o'clock that Thursday morning, Daly pounded on my motel room door. Again. I recognized him by the way he went at it.

Glad that I'd set my watch alarm and had snuck back into the motel unnoticed during shift change, I stumbled out of bed and pulled my robe around me. Taking my own sweet time, I ambled over and opened the door wide enough to give an unspoken invitation to enter. "One of these days someone is going to call the cops on you for disturbing the peace, Daly." I didn't bother to glance back as I made my way to the bed. His heavy size-twelves slapped against the carpet.

Squirming, I pulled and tugged on pillows and blankets until I made myself comfortable on the bed, back against the scarred headboard. "What is it this time?" I stretched out my legs and crossed them at the ankles, fussed with my robe until I was certain it covered everything I wanted covered. My unpainted toenails wiggled.

Alicia had tried hard to get me to paint my finger and toe nails. That woman loved bright colors and wanted to decorate me, like she did herself, in them. The pang of missing her didn't feel quite as sharp as it had. I pushed that realization away and forced my mind to concentrate on the present.

Daly strode across the room, picked up one of the plastic chairs at the small table, and hauled it close to the bed. He swung it backward and plopped down on it, his arms crossed over the back.

"Is this an official visit, or do you just enjoy waking me up so you can stare at me? If that's it, let me remind you that I'm queer. No interest in the male of the species. While we're getting things cleared up, why aren't you in uniform, or are jeans and faded denim shirts an acceptable substitute? And where's your gun? Don't cops have to wear a weapon all the time?" I snarked.

"I am not in uniform because I was dragged out of bed at five o'clock this morning," he said, ignoring the major part of my rant.

I arched one eyebrow. "I'm supposed to care, why?"

"You should."

"Seriously?" I picked at the lint balls forming on the cuff of my new robe's sleeve.

Neither of us spoke for the longest time. His eyes drilled into me and if I'd believed in that psychic stuff, I would've been worried about him reading my mind. Instead, I pretended to ignore him. Abruptly, he stood and snatched the chair up. Chair in hand, he marched over to the table and shoved it under. "Get dressed."

My heart accelerated. Not in a good way. Thankfully, my voice remained steady. "Are you arresting me? If you aren't then I don't have to take orders from you."

With exaggerated patience, he said, "I am not arresting you. I am taking you out for breakfast and coffee, unless you're different than us common folks and don't need to eat."

Both of my eyebrows shot up to my hairline. "Breakfast? *You're* buying me breakfast?"

He propped his hands on his hips. "Yes. Didn't I just say that?"

Giddy with relief, I teased as I slid off the bed. "This some sort of newfangled cop torture? A sneaky way to make people confess to crimes they didn't commit?"

For the first time since I'd met Daly, his smile reached his sky-blue eyes. Not a big smile, but the real deal. Hands spread in surrender, he confessed. "Busted. To think that I even patented that particular torture process."

Run or Die

What is it with this guy? I certainly don't trust his motivation in taking me to breakfast, yet here I am feeling a pleasant anticipation at the thought of sharing a meal with him. If I was straight, I'd suspect myself of having developed a crush on the sheriff. But that kind of attraction isn't what I'm feeling. This is a complication I certainly don't need in my life. Cops and I have never been friendly. Still... Curious about my own reaction to Daly, I dressed quickly. Maybe I'd get a handle on my feelings while we ate; if not, at least I'd get a meal out of it.

Overnight, what few minor mounds of snow there had been had melted off. Except for the icy nip in the air, the sun shone bright enough for a summer's day. The warmth felt good on my tired shoulders. The air in Daly's pickup truck felt stuffy enough to roll the window partway down.

The only place Aretha and I had eaten in Willits was at Mother Earth's Bounty. Daly turned his pickup in the opposite direction. With the reception he'd been getting, I couldn't blame him. South of Willits and north of Ukiah a square box of a café sat in the center of an asphalt and gravel lot. A huge gnarled maple towered over the flat roof, the sole tree within a hundred yards of the small restaurant. The only thing that came close to the same height as the tree was a garish pink and blue neon sign that blared "Mom's Café" in three-foot high letters, then right below it: Truckers Welcome.

Those eighteen-wheeler jockeys must've felt pretty welcome. The parking lot had precious little room even for Daly's pickup. An aluminum screen door hung open and catty-wompus on a broken hinge. Dirty windows on either side of the door permitted only the vaguest of views of the well-lit interior. The place appeared to be packed with grizzly-size forms.

He swung open the door and held it for me to enter first. I stepped into a solid wall of sound: shouted words, bellowing laughter, the clanking of pots and pans in the unseen kitchen. No caterwauling and guitar banging, thankfully.

He wove his way through burly truckers and between chairs, dodged hustling waitresses with plate-lined arms. I stayed close enough behind him to smell the spiciness of his aftershave. Red vinyl seats on gray-painted pedestals bolted to the floor ran along the counter from one end of the diner to the other end. Hefty butts hung over the seats. Truckers bumped elbows as they shoveled in the food. Other truckers stuffed into the wood-backed booths with padded seats of the same red vinyl, laughed and hollered, whistled and banged coffee cups on the Formica tabletops. Daly dodged a ham-sized arm and headed for a two-fer booth at the very back, next to the swinging kitchen door.

A blonde waitress in faded jeans, a tight blue t-shirt, and iridescent orange running shoes busted out of the kitchen and barely missed slamming into Daly's shoulder as he folded onto the bench seat. She gracefully darted around him, not one plate out of the four lining her arms so much as wobbled. "Hey, my favorite copper!" She called gaily as she zipped past.

Still hustling when she breezed back through, she had managed to snatch a pot of coffee and two mugs from somewhere. She stopped long enough to slam the mugs on the table and fill them with a delicious-smelling, black brew then she trotted off again.

"We don't get menus?" I asked as I sipped the midnight brew tentatively then took a longer pull.

"Good coffee, isn't it?" Daly commented.

"Yeah, with it so black I thought it'd be battery acid."

"Back to your original question. You can have a menu, if you insist on one." He settled against the booth.

I glanced around and realized no one seemed to have a menu. "If I get a menu I'm like stamped with a big, red T on my forehead for Tourist, right?"

Daly laughed, a surprisingly deep, warm laugh. "Right."

I pooched my lips out in a pout. "I'm starving. How do I order food?"

"This is breakfast time. Order whatever you want for breakfast." He took a gulp of his coffee.

I relaxed, let my shoulders sink against the back pad of the bench seat. "What if they don't serve it?"

He grinned. "Unless it's something really fancy, or exotic like maybe python barbecue, they serve it."

"Hash browns, eggs, and bacon. And plenty of it," I mock growled.

Run or Die

"That's their specialty, and when you're feeding truckers you'd better make sure the portions are...generous."

Daly ate like me. Mom used to say I ate like I'd just been rescued from starvation. Alicia told me I ate with intensity, but she said I lived that way, too. Glancing across the table I recognized my own style of eating.

I guess we're always trying to find things in other people that are like us. The way they talk or walk, dress, or even eat. Alicia told me people connected that way. It made us feel not so alone. Like a lot of things, until Alicia brought it up, I hadn't thought much about it. Afterward, I thought of such things at the strangest times.

Now while those thoughts drifted through my mind, I remembered what else Alicia said: she said I was so busy bulling through life that I didn't take the time to think about it. She gave me that gift, thinking about life. Not one I always appreciated.

On this morning, as I watched Daly eat, I recognized at least a small part of what we had in common. It made him seem more human. It made me wish for...for what? Not love. I didn't pick from that tree. No, not love, but maybe friendship? It also made the sneaking and lying, made the adversarial position feel like an itchy wool sweater.

I suspected that once Daly befriended a person, he'd go through all nine circles of Dante's hell for them. Too bad he'd made it clear that the law came first, right or wrong. That made us adversaries because, in my book, Aretha and proving her innocence came first. No, Daly and I didn't bat for the same team in any sense of the word. Ignoring that could prove bad, real bad for me and for Aretha.

Breakfast consumed at a breakneck pace, Dee, our bottle-blonde waitress, whisked the dirty dishes away while we sucked up our third cup of coffee. Daly waited until she was out of earshot to speak. He traced the rim of his cup with his forefinger, maybe an abbreviated version of someone rubbing Aladdin's lamp, hoping a magic genie popped out of the black, liquid depths. "I was born and raised in Elmsworth. My mom died right after I was born, so Dad retired from the military to raise me. He was pretty much a by-the-book man." He glanced up at me. "Maybe that's why I've always been uncomfortable around people who break the rules?"

I eyed Daly. *True confessions? Seriously? What kind of game is he playing?*

He squirmed around on the booth seat until he wound up leaning on his forearms halfway across the table. I fought the instinct to rear back; held my position, my eyes never leaving his face. Tension around his eyes and mouth spelled out the internal struggle with whatever he needed to say, the conflict written across his face and as easily read as a page in a book. I wanted to tell him to spit it out, yet I'd learned to hold my tongue the hard way. Like most of the lessons in my life.

He stared at the table like he was trying to levitate the blob of ketchup congealing on the scratched Formica. Finally, he cleared his throat, but still didn't look at me. In a voice so low that I strained to hear his words, he said, "The blood in William's truck was Ralph's."

He ran a hand through his shaggy hair, wagged his head slowly from side to side. "I shouldn't be telling you this. You aren't Aretha's attorney and this is an ongoing homicide investigation." The other sounds in the restaurant faded as he drew in a deep breath and let it out slowly, along with whatever reservations he might've held.

"William claims Ralph cut himself earlier in the summer and bled all over the truck seat. He said he thought he'd gotten all that blood out. He's too cocky, too smooth. Has an answer for everything. His alibi for the night of Ralph's murder comes from his father and uncle. They claim William was home all evening, shooting pool with Nick Evers in the rec room downstairs." After scanning the restaurant, like some kind of covert agent, he slipped two high school photos from an inside pocket and slid them over to me. In a way his discomfort, and obvious unfamiliarity with this whole breaking rules scene, was cute, but the man seriously needed to chill. No one cared about our meeting.

"Which one is Nick?"

Daly tapped the photo of a man with a heavy face, probably seventeen or eighteen at the time of the photo. Football tucked under one beefy arm, he smirked up at me. I fought to keep my face bland. I wanted to smash the smirk off his face. Daly's eyes bored into the top of my head until I raised my face. With one finger I flicked the photo across the table to him. "Nick's one of the men Aretha took pictures of the night Ralph died? The big guy that she saw with William? Could you get the photos on her camera enhanced enough to recognize him?"

He cocked his head, studied me. "No. The photographer was too far away and the lighting too dim. Even the face she claims is William is too blurred to use as evidence."

With as much nonchalance as I could muster, I said, "Is he one of the guys who might've been with William the night they burned her cabin?" The struggle in Daly's eyes had me holding my breath. Would he continue to give me information or would he decide he'd already said too much?

Daly steadied his gaze on me and spoke in a slow, deliberate manner. "He probably was. Just like the guy in the other photo, Sam Haden. William, Nick, and Sam go back all the way to kindergarten. I'm not sure which one is the biggest bully." Without waiting for a response, he continued. "There is another young man besides Sam, Nick, Jimmy, and Ralph who's been hanging out with William. I interviewed him, too, after Aretha's cabin burned." His voice faded out and a troubled look settled on his even features. He wiped a hand down his face. "Johnny Fadden. I don't know how Johnny became involved with these guys. Even when the four of them were on the football team, Johnny didn't hang with Nick, Sam, or William.

"The rest of this is confidential; came from juvenile court records. In ninth grade, a girl claimed that William, Nick, and Sam raped her. Before the case went very far, she withdrew her complaint, said she'd had too much to drink and she couldn't positively recall what her assailants looked like. The girl's family was Hispanic."

"Is she around?"

"No, they moved not long after that."

We didn't say anything more as Dee zipped past, pausing long enough to top off our coffee. When she buzzed out of earshot, he continued. "Law enforcement officers are supposed to be objective." He made a loose fist and tapped it against his lips. "Yet, even when we're studying physical evidence we have to listen to that...that sixth cop sense, the one that tells us we're barking up the wrong tree, or that we're getting close. There's a feeling about people, a..." His eyebrows drew together as his hands spread in an open gesture, waiting to grasp the right word if it flew past.

"An aura?" It was a new word I'd discovered in my paranormal fiction reading recently. Why I threw it out at Daly, I have no idea.

He cocked his head like he listened to a voice nobody else could hear, and gave a brief nod. "Yes, an aura. That's as good a word as any to describe it. Not that I mean I can see something that isn't there. It's an instinct that seems to pick up on people's inner feelings, and intentions, more than normal people do. Maybe I'm simply seeing some body language that most people ignore. Whatever it is, that's what tells me when a person is lying."

"What're you trying to say?" I laid my forearms on the table and crouched over them.

"I've never believed that Aretha Hopewell would hurt another human being, much less kill Ralph Henley."

My brows rose and my eyes widened. "You have some kind of theory about what happened, I mean besides what Aretha said?"

He made a slight movement of his shoulders, perhaps adjusting the weight of his new confession. "Not really. Nothing of any value as far as the *official* investigation goes. Essentially, I believe Aretha's story, with a few minor changes that we won't talk about. It's all speculation anyhow." He eyed me. "There's gentleness in Aretha. You don't have to know her well to feel it. I don't believe she has it in her to harm another person. There are some folks, though, that I can feel the violence in them. Know what I mean?"

When I nodded, he went on. "I feel that in you."

"If you're accusing me of something, come right out and say it," I bristled.

He held up one hand and patted the air in a settle-down gesture. "You can put your hackles down. I don't think you killed Ralph, but I don't buy this idea that you were out wandering the hills that night, either." He bent over the table as if by being closer to me his very presence could force honest answers out. "Were you there when Ralph was murdered?"

I drew back. "You took our statements." Voice steady, but my hands trembled around the coffee cup.

"I don't think you killed Ralph, but I wouldn't put it past you to do a bit of breaking and entering." He drew back, too. With his head tipped a bit to the side, he observed me, a new species of bug that he debated whether he should stomp on or pick up and set it outside. "You put that headless rubber chicken on Jimmy's pillow and poured pig's blood all over his bedroom."

Not a question, and even if it had been, I saw no reason to answer.

"The lab ran a sample of that blood. Pig blood," he grunted.

I sipped my coffee and watched him over the rim of the cup.

He waited. When I remained silent, he continued. "What was that about? Revenge? Pretty petty, if you ask me."

I peered over at him. "I don't do revenge. It always tastes more bitter than sweet."

He rubbed his cheek with the palm of his hand. Even this early in the morning, I could hear a raspy sound. The man's beard must grow like hair on steroids. "Then why?"

I shrugged. "*If,* and that is a very big if, *if* I'd put that chicken there it would've been for a better reason than some high schooler's idea of revenge."

"It scared him pretty good." He studied me. I maintained a blank face that clearly frustrated him. "You ever play poker?"

I gave a slight frown. "No, I don't gamble. Life's enough of a gamble."

"I should've known. You're all about control." He set the cup down. Eyes locked on my face, he said, "You do know Jimmy's a little slow, don't you?"

I'd already figured that out, but the verbal barb stung. I dipped my head sideways in a parody of a shrug while my stomach tied itself into knots. "I should feel sorry for him? After everything he's participated in, all the harassment, all the violence he was part of against both Aretha and me?"

The longer I thought about Jimmy, the angrier I got. My teeth ground together as every bit of sympathy I'd felt for him melted in the hot fire of a building rage. "Don't you recall what Little Kid looked like? How that little animal suffered?" I slammed back against the seat. "Being slow is no excuse to be cruel."

He took a long swallow of his coffee, set the cup on the table. "One of the duties of a sheriff is to obtain information, and sometimes the way we do it feels...distasteful.

"I had this case one time." Voice thoughtful, he gazed at his hand, turning the cup in circles. "A homicide. I was young and anxious to break the case; be the man of the hour." He pushed the cup aside, drew circles on the tabletop with a finger. "The suspect had a friend who was...slow. I pulled the boy in. I won't go over all the details, but I made him so afraid he wound up wetting himself." Restlessly, he shrugged his broad shoulders. "All I cared about was forcing him to tell me what he knew, any way I could. I never stopped to count the cost to him."

He fell silent for so long that I cleared my throat. "Did you close the case?"

He gave a derisive snort. "Oh, yeah, I cleared that case. Cleared the case, but that boy..." A haunted look passed through his eyes.

"Was the suspect the killer?"

"Yes."

I held up a hand as if to say 'sounds cool to me.'

When Daly locked his gaze onto me, I gasped at the pain I saw etched in the lines of his face. "That boy, that slow boy? He committed suicide. I used him, and he died for it."

In a harsh rasp, I said, "This isn't the same. Jimmy was right there with William, part of the posse, when they burned down Aretha's home."

"This is the same, Jazmine. That other boy, he was there the night the suspect killed the other kid. But," he shook his head, "he was a victim as surely as the dead kid. What I did made him a victim yet again. There's always another way." He gulped the rest of his coffee then got to his feet. "Have to get to work. Come on, I'll give you a lift back to your room."

Run or Die

Seriously? Always another way? Fine for him to say. It's not him sitting and wondering if he's going to rot in jail. It wasn't his house they burned to the ground! He didn't know Little Kid, didn't love him. Too bad if Jimmy's scared. He should be scared!

Daly slipped his pickup in the spot between Aretha's Volkswagen and my bike. He stared out through the windshield. "Sometimes, people aren't able to stand up to other people. Sometimes, they're not able to get out of a bad situation."

"Look, if you want me to cry over Jimmy being spooked, you're so far from reality you need to see a psych doc. If he wants to play nasty, he shouldn't cry when he gets a sip of his own medicine." I slid out of the truck.

"He isn't a mean guy. He wound up involved with the wrong people. He hasn't come out of this whole mess unscathed. Ralph and Jimmy were best friends, closer than brothers, from the time they both attended preschool."

I shook my head. "We all make choices, Sheriff. We all pay the price for the choices we make. Thanks for breakfast." Standing in the gray morning, I watched until he turned the corner and disappeared from sight.

***

Mr. Edison missed his guess. Aretha got released on bail late Thursday afternoon, instead of Friday. Since the police hadn't cleared the farm, she had no home to return to. The three of us—Aretha, Mr. Edison, and I—discussed the issue over lunch at Mother Earth's Bounty. Relief at Aretha's being free warred with worries that she'd cramp my nightly activities.

Ms. Winters brought a cup of coffee over and slid into the remaining empty chair. She reached over and patted Aretha's hand. "Honey, why don't you stay with me for a few days?" With a glance my way, she added in an almost warm voice, "You're welcome to stay, too."

I gave her a quick smile. "Thanks, but I have a room at the motel. Aretha could stay there, but...," I slowly gave each one of them a measured look, "there isn't any telling what the local yokels are going to do now that she's out of jail."

Aretha shot me a look as if to ask "what're you really up to?" I gave her my best innocent eyes. I don't think she bought it.

Exhaustion bruised the skin around Aretha's eyes. She rubbed fingertips across her forehead before she dropped her hand to her lap. "That's a wonderful offer, but I can't pull you into this mess. I don't want anyone else endangered."

Ms. Winters' face fell into stern lines. "I'm black, too." She let that pronouncement sit on the warm air. "I am well aware of the risk. My offer stands."

Mr. Edison studied me for a long moment before clearing his throat. He gave Aretha a considering gaze. "Well, hmm. Yes, there is the possibility of reprisals to consider, but it really is up to you, Ms. Hopewell, to decide where you desire to reside, even temporarily. However, I must urge you to consider Ms. Winters' generous offer."

She glanced over at the other woman. "I appreciate your offer, Folami." She levered a hard stare at me.

Uncomfortable with the intensity of Aretha's focus, I scooted off the chair. "Sheriff Daly escorted me over to JR's Junkers where he impounded the trailer. They have a section fenced off just for police impounds. I picked up some of your personal stuff and a few changes of clothes. I'll stick your stuff in your car over at the motel until you decide where you're staying. I can use my bike."

The little trailer had squatted behind a chain link fence topped with five strands of evil-looking barbed wire. With Daly blocking the trailer doorway and watching my every move, I had stuffed Aretha's personal items and clothes into a new backpack purchased in Ukiah the day before.

"Jaz, you can't do that. It's too dangerous with snow and ice on the roads. Use my car." She turned her attention to Ms. Winters. "I...I guess, I'll take you up on the invitation, Folami."

Ms. Winters handed Aretha a set of keys. "Mine's the black Mercedes. Set your stuff on the backseat."

I forced a yawn and stretched. "Hey, if it's all the same to you guys, I'm headed over to the motel. I haven't been sleeping real well. Need to catch a few hours zonked out."

Run or Die

Aretha followed close on my heels as I hustled out to my bike and unstrapped the backpack. When I headed toward the Mercedes, she stepped in front of me and hissed, "What are you up to, girl?"

"Up to?" My eyebrows jolted upward. "What do you mean, up to?" I shifted the backpack into a more comfortable position.

"Why are you so happy for me to stay with Folami?" For one breathless moment, I saw Alicia the day that I met her; saw her hot eyes and tense shoulders.

"You guys made the decision for you to stay with her. Not me." I tried to thrust indignation into my voice and stance.

"Oh, can that righteous act!" She straightened rigidly tall, hands on her hips, her face close enough that I smelled the sage from the meatloaf she'd eaten. "I know you're up to something. What is it?"

Backpack swung to the side away from her, I hiked it further up on my shoulder. I stepped around her, tried to avoid a mud puddle, yet still managed to splash myself. "Hey, how about unlocking the car?"

The lights blinked as I reached for the back door handle. It opened easily and I plopped the pack on the rear seat. The black lump looked out of place in the middle of the luxurious leather. I heard her come up behind me. Without turning, I said, "All you need to worry about right now is this legal stuff. Whatever I'm up to, as you so elegantly put it, I can handle. Okay?"

I closed the door. Aretha's long-fingered hand clamped my shoulder in a grip that would've made a wrestler proud. She tugged until I faced her. "No, it isn't okay. I don't want you putting yourself into dangerous situations. You hear me, Jaz?" Worry furrows creased the area between her brows.

"Life is a dangerous situation, or haven't you realized that yet?" Lips firmed into an unyielding line, I gently removed her hand and stepped away from her. "It's cold out here. Go back inside, so I can head over to the motel and warm up in a hot tub of water."

Chapter 11

The half-moon did wonders for deepening the shadows around Jimmy's house. No fresh snow on the driveway and walkway to tattle on me either. The front porch wasn't much wider than the two chrome and plastic chairs sitting on either side of the door. Sheltered by the porch roof, the light by the door didn't have a glass around it.

He stumbled on the bottom step of the three wooden stairs that led up to the porch. "I know I left that stupid light on. Probably burned out again." He stopped and muttered as he flipped through his keys, trying to use the moon's light to see the house key. He found it and climbed the rest of the steps. Intent on fitting the key into the un-seeable lock, he never realized I stood within a few feet of him until I jacked a shell into the rifle's chamber and flicked on my flashlight. He froze with his hand on the key in the door lock. He barely seemed to breathe.

"Go ahead and open the door. No use standing out here. I didn't invite anyone else to our party." As he twisted the key, I added, "Don't even consider doing anything stupid. Hear me?"

His eyes flicked my way as he stiffly nodded. The door screeched when he pushed it open. I prodded him with the rifle barrel, not the smartest thing to do, but it seemed my life destined me to live in the fast and stupid lane. "Switch on the lights then head on into the kitchen. Here's a word to the wise: don't try to play Super Hero. I know *exactly* where the light switches are." He jerked his head around. A sharp nudge with the rifle muzzle moved him forward.

A few slaps on the wall and the dim ceiling fixture came on. We stood at the edge of his living room. A ratty couch and two ratty, overstuffed chairs sat in a half-circle facing a huge flat-screen television. Beer cans graced the flat surfaces of the end tables and the coffee table. The color of the carpet defied recognition beneath the grunge. "Not much of a housekeeper, huh?" I commented as we walked through to the kitchen.

"I'm not always this much of a slob," he mumbled as he flipped the light switch on the kitchen wall. "Now what?"

Run or Die

"Go over there and sit on the left side of the table." Once he slumped into the chair, I wandered around the kitchen, opening and shutting cupboards and drawers.

"If...if you tell me what you wa...want, I could tell...tell you where it is. I...I don't have much, except the TV and a laptop. The laptop's upstairs. On my...my dresser." His hands wrung together in his lap.

I swiveled my head enough to arch an eyebrow at him then continued my exploration.

When I didn't say anything, he stuttered, "It'd be like...like giving you back some of what...what we took. You can have them. I...I won't tell the sheriff or nothing."

I watched him in my peripheral vision while I opened the refrigerator. Empty shelves except for a six-pack of beer and a six-pack of Pepsi. Ugh! Not diet. I hated the overly sweet taste of regular Pepsi. I snagged a can anyhow, closed the fridge, and turned to face him. He flinched when I popped the top. "Why so jumpy, Jimmy boy?"

Eyes cast down toward the dirty linoleum between his feet, he mumbled. "You got a g...gun and you're in my...my house." His eyes darted up then skittered away when they met mine. "You p...put that put that rubber chicken on my pillow?"

Hip wedged against the countertop, I took a long swallow of the syrupy concoction. I didn't really want it, but long ago I'd learned that casually taking and using something that belongs to someone else establishes a type of dominance over them; like you're entitled. "Tell me, Jimmy boy, how fun was that to wake up to?"

The color in his face washed out to a gratifying paleness.

"A rubber chicken and pig's blood is nowhere near as bad as the carnage we found in the chicken house. You can wash your sheets, but the sheets in Aretha's house burned up. Nothing to wash. Nothing to salvage. If you guys had had your way, we would've burned up with the cabin."

"I...I didn't know...know you guys might be there." He shook his head, his colorless eyes wider than a bunny about to be a Red-tailed Hawk's lunch. "Bill said...said we'd just mess up your...your house, that's all. You...you guys wouldn't be there. Just...just wanted to...to tell you to le...leave."

"Oh, well, man, that makes it all copacetic. You *only* meant to burn down the cabin, right?" I cocked a skeptical eyebrow at him.

His eyebrows crunched down. "What'd you say? Co...cosetik...? What's that mean?"

"The word is copacetic. It means you think just because you *only* meant to burn down the cabin that that's okay. To burn a person out. To leave them nothing, not their clothes, not their books, not their keepsakes that can't ever be replaced. Everything gone. Did you know Aretha had a handmade quilt that her sister made? Her sister is dead. She can't replace the quilt you helped to destroy."

His eyes zoomed around like they were on meth. "That wa...wasn't 'posed to...to happen neither."

"What exactly was supposed to happen? Don't lie to me, Jimmy boy." I jiggled the barrel of the rifle at him.

"No...nothing." He sulled up, his face taking on a sour look.

I bounced the nearly-full Pepsi can off his chest. The brown liquid splashed down the front of his shirt.

"Hey!" He yelled as he sprang to his feet.

My voice dropped low and dangerous. "Sit your skinny butt back down." When he flopped down on the chair, I glared at him. "I told you: don't lie, man. Ain't nobody around here, but me and you. And, this." I patted the rifle stock. "I was there that night. We barely got out of the cabin ahead of you guys. You, Ralph, William, Nick, Johnny, and Sam."

Steaming now, I kept on a'rolling. "Don't tell me you didn't mean to cook us. I heard what you guys were yelling. And the chickens. Remember those poor chickens? You punks blew their heads off, plastered the walls with their guts, but some of them didn't die right away."

Rage clawed my chest with sharp nails, threatening to burst out and rend anything within reach. I stepped forward, stepped close, and pushed the muzzle against his skinny chest. "No, they didn't die right away. The poor things flopped around, wings broken, bodies mutilated, in pain." My upper lip curled away from my teeth as I fought to keep my finger off the trigger.

Face paper white, he pressed hard against the kitchen chair's back. He looked like he might pass out or puke at any moment.

The rage had scrambled up my throat, choking me. I couldn't talk; couldn't look at him any longer. With a hard prod with the rifle barrel against his chest, I spun away from him and paced over to the kitchen window.

Thin rays of silvery light leaked from the crescent moon. The overgrown grass and weeds of the backyard sucked it in so that not one shimmer lay on the ground. "Those poor chickens." Not turning to face him, I spoke in a quiet, even tone, yet every word carved a hole inside of me with a dull knife. "Those poor chickens never did anybody any harm. Cinders loved to follow me around then she'd stop and squat down in front of me, asking to be petted. What was the deal?"

The lump in my chest turned to concrete. Ragged breaths rattled past the congestion of sorrow. "You guys get off on hurting things that can't fight back?" The dam broke. I whirled around and in two strides stood in front of him, rifle barrel jammed under his chin, forcing his head painfully backward. "Answer me!"

He looked like he might cry, or piss his pants. For one crazy moment, I felt my finger tighten on the trigger. Slowly, I backed away from my insanity and the table. Fatigue from deep inside hit me like a freight train. Slammed into me and I slumped against the edge of the kitchen sink. Rust stains that a nuclear explosion couldn't lift painted the bottom of the old-fashioned enameled cast iron a dull red.

Mouth wide open, he gasped like he'd run a marathon, and he looked worse than a heart attack victim I once saw. Too tired to keep the rifle pointed at him, I lowered the barrel. That action relieved his breathing. Shaking my head, I told him, "It doesn't matter what you say. I was there. I was there that night. Just like I was with Aretha when we found those goats. I nursed Little Kid after his momma died giving birth to him, did you know that?"

He shook his head, his hands quivered in his lap like the hands of a palsy-stricken old man.

"I did. Every night for almost six weeks. Every two hours, then every four hours. I was so glad when he could be fed three times a day. You bastards didn't slaughter him; you tortured him. A baby goat! What kind of sick motherfuckers are you?"

For a moment, he lifted his chin and rebellion flared in his eyes. "We ain't the...the sickos. B...Bill says...says you and that nig...nigger woman are perverts. That this town never had no per...perverts in it till you came here. He...he says it's up to us to...to run you out. That our folks got too much to...to lose, so they can't do...do it and the Law won't."

Comprehension drove a spear of truth into my guts. I heaved a deep breath and let it sough out. *What the hell am I doing? Terrorizing a boy as slow on the draw as him? What kind of person does that make me?* Suddenly, Daly's words rang in my head, and I understood what he'd tried to tell me.

In a soft tone, I asked, "Who's the pervert, Jimmy? Somebody who sticks with their friend, tries to help them build a farm and do something worthwhile? Or is a pervert somebody who calls you his friend then beats you to death because the people he meant to beat to death aren't home that day?"

He crossed his arms around his thin chest and his chin dropped. "What...what're you ta...talking about?"

"I honestly didn't come here planning to hurt you. Not if I don't have to."

"You...you must want to hurt me. You...you put that...that chicken on...on my bed and...and when I saw...saw it, I almost had a...a heart attack! And, now you...you got that gun...gun on me. And, you hur...hurt me with it." He didn't raise his eyes, but jerked his head toward the gun.

I rolled my shoulders, trying to release some of the tension that ran grasping fingers down my spine. "I am not going to lie to you, Jimmy. I do *want* to hurt you. I want you to suffer like Aretha did when her cabin burned; like she did when we opened the chicken house door; like we both did while we held Little Kid and watched him take his last breath.

"I could've hurt you bad the night I put that chicken on your pillow. You were passed out drunk. I had a knife." I patted the knife sheathed on my belt. "But I didn't hurt you. I scared you,

Run or Die

but nowhere near the way you and William and your friends scared Aretha and me. I wanted you to feel a little bit of what we've lived with all these months." I shifted my feet and stood up straight. "Tonight, though, I didn't come to hurt you; I came to tell you something important. William murdered Ralph."

His head shot up. Eyes wide in denial, he vigorously shook his head. "Uh-uh! No...no way. Bill would...wouldn't do that. He...he wa...wasn't even there that night. Him and...and Nick were playing pool with his dad and his uncle. You're lying! You're a lying lesbo!" Red suffused his face as he shouted the last accusation.

I waited until he fell silent. Tears stood in his eyes. "I wouldn't lie about that." I fished three photographs out of the inside pocket of my jacket. With a quick step toward the table, I tossed the pictures in front of him then returned to lean against the counter.

A tear wended its way down his cheek when he finally looked up at me. In a choked voice, he accused me, "You...you photoshopped these."

I wagged my head slowly back and forth. "You know better. Aretha and I heard William's Jeep that night as it topped the hill, so we hid in the woods with the rifle and the camera. The camera has a night-action lens. That's what Aretha used to take those. Unfortunately, the faces aren't clear enough to use as evidence, but you recognize them, don't you, Jimmy?" I didn't wait for him to admit it. "We can prove three people were there, but not definitively who two of the three were. Of course, we can readily prove Ralph was there since that's clearly where he was murdered.

"Three men entered Aretha's trailer; two came out."

Tears streamed down Jimmy's cheeks as he stared at me. He sniffled and wiped his nose on the sleeve of his shirt. "Why? Why wou...would Bill do that?"

"Aretha and I heard them arguing in the trailer. William shouted that it was Ralph's fault we got away again."

He straightened up in his chair, mopped his face with the tail of his shirt. "Ralph and me..." A sob choked out. He stopped and his eyes briefly touched mine before darting around the room like a trapped bird. "Ralph...he...he always took up for me. In school. Ev...even told Bill not to...not to be so hard on me a coupla times."

I pushed away from the sink edge, left the rifle muzzle pointed at the floor. "You know if I were you, I'd be careful around my friends. A man could get dead having friends like William and Nick." Backing toward the kitchen doorway, I added, "There isn't any use telling people about our little chat. I have an alibi for tonight. Besides, that'd make me mad enough to maybe pay you another little visit, you know? Heard a story once about a guy who made his girlfriend so mad that while he was asleep she cut off his dick."

His eyes popped wide and his mouth gaped.

"No need to see me out. I know the way. Probably be best if you stayed in your chair for a few minutes. Don't want to make me nervous." He was probably still in that kitchen chair when I dragged into my motel room.

Chapter 12

It snowed that night and all the next day, but I couldn't stomach staying in town any longer. I needed to get away, get somewhere to let my head clear before I did something stupid.

On the way out of town, I silently blessed Aretha for insisting that I drive her Volkswagen and park my bike in Ms. Winters' garage. By the time I reached Buzzard Peak, the highest point on the hill, I couldn't see the road under the snow. I stopped in the middle of the road, climbed out, and leaned against the front of the car. Cell phone flipped open, I looked down. Three bars! Woo-hoo! I hit the speed dial.

On the second ring, Aretha answered. She didn't even say hello. "You're going to be really careful?" Her concern vibrated over the phone.

Her voice, so much like Alicia's, plunged a knife into my heart and twisted. There had been times lately when I thought I might be healing, when the thought of Alicia didn't rip holes in my gut, and then there were times, like now, when I wondered if the sharp edge of missing Alicia would ever dull.

"Jaz? You promised." Aretha's voice rose a notch, out of the range of Alicia's, and I could breathe again.

"I'll be careful, Aretha. I told you I'll sleep in the cave and I'll park behind the boulders. Hey, listen, I have to get on down there and get set up before dark. Don't worry if I don't call you every day, okay?"

After she reluctantly agreed and hung up, I shut off the phone to save the battery and tucked it in my jacket pocket. Hips resting against the front end of the car, I contemplated the sharp slope of the hillside. There's something eternal about the land, a truth I'd only discovered up here, on the hill. Long after my body is moldering bones or ashes spread to the four winds, the land will still be here. Even when people tear down all the trees and murder every living thing, the land will continue to endure, a silent witness to human insanity and greed. I climbed into the car. Seconds later, I continued down to Aretha's farm.

Aya Walksfar

Bright yellow crime scene tape, strung across the opening of the gate, fluttered in the light breeze. It felt good to drive through it. I idled past the lumpy snow near the spot where the trailer had sat. Beneath those clean mounds lay churned mud, frozen in unforgiving clumps. The V-dub, in spite of its small size, maneuvered well in the snow. Having the engine right above the rear wheels gave it traction when larger vehicles did an S and S, sit and spin. Close to the back of the boulders in that protected spot, the black of the ground peeked through. With the way the snow kept coming down, the V-dub's tracks would soon be hidden. Engine off, I got out and listened.

A hawk circled overhead, her occasional scree pulling my eyes to the charcoal gray sky. Somewhere close by, smaller birds chirped and twittered. I had never felt so alone since those weeks after Alicia died. Determined to rid myself of the melancholy, I snatched up the plastic bags of groceries and the rifle then made my way to the cold campfire pit. Fire started, I headed into the tree line and, being careful about where I stepped, wandered down to the cave. With very little snow beneath the trees, only an observant person could track me to the cave.

I dropped off my groceries and picked up the coffeepot and a water jug to fill at the creek. I worked my way down the creek, moving within the shallow water at the edge, glad that I'd spent the extra bucks for truly waterproofed boots. When I was far enough from the cave, I started up the hill with my water jug and coffee fixings.

A doe stepped out of the shadows of the trees on the far side of the meadow. Each footstep a delicate dance with the earth. Even the wind with its piercing teeth, picking up and gusting past me now and again, blew in harmony with the earth. Bare tree limbs danced in a waltz with the deer against the backdrop of the lowering winter sky.

Doe paid me no heed as I passed on the opposite side of the meadow and made my way up the slope to the fire pit. The fire burned nicely, so I tossed on a couple of bigger pieces of wood then brushed the snow off my favorite log round and sat. The cold burgers and fries—a good standby for a quick meal—barely

Run or Die

registered on my tongue. If it hadn't been for the protein, I would've been just as well off eating the paper bag.

Hot and black, the coffee's slight acidic bitterness felt tangy on my tongue. Paper garbage went into the fire before I banked it for the night. The embers hissed and crackled as I poured the dregs of the coffee on them. Empty pot in hand, I made my way down the hill. Inside the cave, I checked the escape tunnel then rigged up some simple tin can alarms across the entry. A heavy, blue wool blanket over the entrance to the room kept the heat from the propane camp stove inside.

Aretha had found that blanket for three dollars at Jason's Secondhand Everything in Ukiah and had spent a good fifteen minutes crowing over her bargain. So like Alicia. To me it didn't matter what type of cloth or how tight the weave of a blanket, long as it did its job. Once when I confessed such sentiments to Alicia, she'd laughed and told me I was a barbarian. I wondered if Aretha would say the same thing.

Night fell like someone tripped her, fast and hard. Sleep had proven elusive over the past weeks, so I'd laid in a supply of books. I leafed through the book on raptors featuring the Red-tailed Hawk and the one on Birds of Northern California. Then I waffled between reading Patricia Briggs' werewolf novel, *Frostbitten,* and Kay Hooper's latest book about the psychic FBI agent, Noah Bishop. The werewolves won.

Late that night I blew out the lantern and laid there listening to the quiet. My mind spun like a manic toy top. There had to be some way to force the truth out into the open. There had to be!

I don't know what time I fell asleep, but Aretha ran through my dreams. Aretha surrounded by a ring of white men. They kept pushing her from one to the other of them, laughing as she stumbled, nearly falling. I yelled for them to stop, but it was like I didn't exist. Desperate, I pounded on one man's back until he turned around. George, my last foster father, stared back at me, his nasty, old-beer breath blowing in my face.

I woke with a sour taste in my mouth and my heart jarring my ribs. It took a long time to fall asleep again. The next time I woke, a thin strip of daylight inched beneath the blanket door and probed the floor of the cave with a long, crooked finger. I crawled out of my sleeping bag and started the propane camp stove. Shivers racked me while I put together a pot of coffee in the icy air. After I got that on the stove, I dressed in jeans and a flannel shirt, heavy socks, and my work boots.

They don't want niggers and queers in their lily-white town. That thought ran in an infinite loop through my brain. Well, it was time to stir the pot. They needed to know that we won't run. And they can't chase us out.

I'd seen Johnny Fadden in the grocery store nearly every time Aretha and I had stopped. He must not have had video games at home since he looked like super glue had connected him to the game machine to the right of the checkout counter. Before Daly had fed me the information, I'd had no idea as to the identity of the gamer or his connection to William.

As soon as I stepped into the store that afternoon I heard Johnny talking to the video game. I've never figured out why people talk to video games and television sets.

I grabbed a quart of milk and a loaf of Oatnut bread then hurried to the checkout counter. As Russell rang up my purchases, I chatted loudly at him. He glowered back as if he wanted to yell at me to shut up. *Chicken shit man!*

"Yeah, I'm going to start building another cabin for Aretha and me. I figure I'll have enough of it done in a week that I'll have a place to sleep."

He growled, "That'll be seven dollars and thirty-five cents."

I slowly counted out the amount as I continued to talk. "Aretha and I, we don't run. Trouble comes, it comes. Even if Aretha gets convicted, she said I can stay on at the farm." I forced a grin and picked up my bag. "Have a nice day, Mr. Russell." I added the last to poke Russell's buttons since Johnny quite obviously listened in; probably committing every word to memory so he could regurgitate it to William.

As I shoved the store door open with my hip, I flicked a glance at the young man. When he caught me looking, I locked eyes with him. A nasty parody of a grin stretched my lips. Johnny didn't know it, but he and I had a date for later tonight.

Run or Die
***

Night crashed against the retreating day and the waxing moon rode a clear, cold sky. I hid the Volkswagen behind some leafless bushes along an abandoned dirt track branching off Washboard Road. I hoped if anyone noticed the tire tracks in the muddy snow they wouldn't give it two seconds thought.

The years I'd spent tromping all over Seattle, up and down hills, made hiking the couple of miles to Johnny's house not exactly easy but far from hard even with the snow. Cold wormed its way in against my skin and I wished for my heated gear. Too bad I needed the greater flexibility of the down jacket and the denim jeans. Shoulders hunched, I strode along, rifle held low against my leg.

In spite of the moonlight, the absence of street lights left plenty of shadows to shield me as I snuck over to Johnny's car parked next to a couple of hefty-trunked, bare deciduous trees. Like a lot of people in the area, Johnny neglected to lock up. I settled into the back floor with the rifle nestled next to me. The sheath knife whispered out of its leather holder, the wood and metal handle familiar to my hand.

At nine-fifteen, by my watch, Johnny's footsteps crunched over the gravel drive. Always on time, as if he punched a strange time clock, the man had never deviated during the nights that I'd followed him. Five minutes after he got on Highway 101 headed to town, I rose silently off the floor and pressed the knife tip lightly against his thick neck. The fool nearly wiped us out in a ditch. After he straightened out the car, I pressed a little more firmly. "Easy does it, Johnny boy. Don't want to die in a wreck, do you?"

The car began slowing.

I prodded him with the knife. "Don't try it. Take her back up to speed, nice and smooth. Don't try to signal anyone with any high beam-low beam crap. That only works in the movies. When you get to Sanders Road, pull a u-y and drive back this way." We passed a station wagon heading north. His eyes jumped from the car, to the rearview mirror, then back to the oncoming car. I could see him weighing the risk, but the car zipped past without incident before he could screw up his courage. "Good boy."

As we neared Sanders Road, I instructed him. "Nice and easy, Johnny boy, unless you want a slit throat." Back on the highway and heading north, I said, "Now, you're going to drive out to Bell Road. When we get there, you will turn onto it and go until I say stop. Got it?"

When he didn't respond quickly enough, I pricked the skin of his neck enough to be painful, but with less bleeding than a paper cut.

"Okay." His voice hit a high note and squeaked. "Just don't go cuttin' me no more."

"How often and how deeply you get cut is entirely up to you."

Long ago I learned people get antsy when no one's talking. It's like they have to have the air clogged up with all these words or they can't stand it. Maybe it's their own thoughts they can't stand. Johnny was no different.

"Hey, what's this all about?"

I remained silent.

He licked his lips and, unwilling to turn his head into the knife, he risked a glance in the rearview mirror. "Come on, I didn't never do nothing to you."

Silence answered him.

"Look, I don't have nothing against you and that nig...that black lady. I sometimes hang out with Bill, but he's the one who has the real problem with the two of you. My family's lived in this area all our lives. My grandparents bought the farm we live on and..."

"And I don't give a flying fuck. Now shut up."

His shoulders locked up tight with the tension of not speaking, of enduring the extra ten miles I'd tacked on this drive by waiting to have him turn at Sanders Road. I grinned to myself. We hung right onto Bell Road, another one-and-a-half lane gravel road much like Washboard Road. The road twisted as it climbed. By the time we stopped on a dirt track that branched off Bell Road, Johnny unfolded from the driver's seat with all the stiffness of a ninety-year-old man. The rifle pointed at him didn't help loosen him up at all.

"You were hoping I only had a knife, weren't you? Thought a big football player like you could get a knife away from a woman. No such luck, Johnny boy. Where I grew up those kinds of mistakes cost you, big time. Step around to the back of the car." I tipped my head in the general direction.

I kept a discreet distance as I followed him around the car. With a tilt of my chin I had him stand a few feet away from the rear of the car. Leaning against the car trunk, I said, "Take your clothes off."

"What?" His mouth gaped.

"Take. Your. Clothes. Off."

"All of them?"

I made a yuck face. "You can keep your jockeys on."

"I'll freeze to death!" His voice rose and cracked, sounded like a preteen boy.

I cocked my head and put a quizzical look on my face. "How do you think it felt to Aretha and me to not have a house, to have no place to sit down and eat a meal, to have no bed to sleep in? You want me to feel sorry for you? Seriously? Get real, man." I moved the rifle muzzle up until it pointed at his chest. "Enough yammering. Clothes. Off. Now. No more jackin' around."

"You're crazy as a loon, you know that?" He hurriedly stripped jacket, shirt, t-shirt, shoes, socks, and jeans off.

"Toss them over there." I tipped my head to one side. After he tossed his clothes, I said, "Let's talk."

Arms clutched around himself, he rubbed his hands on his naked skin. "Yeah, sure, but can we hurry up? I'm freezing."

I returned to my spot against the car trunk. "Wuss. Try sleeping out in this weather. Now shut up with the whining. I really hate whiners. Matter of fact, don't say a word until I tell you to." With sideways glances at my watch, I let him chill for two minutes. It must have felt like two hours to him. At last, I spoke in a level voice. "Tell you what, Johnny boy, you tell the truth and maybe I'll give you some clothes to put back on. How's that for generous?"

"Yeah, yeah, whatever it takes."

"That's the spirit of cooperation. Whose idea was it to burn the cabin, both times?"

"Bill's. He's like far out there crazy. Wasn't supposed to be no one home. Either time."

"Yeah, seriously." Disbelief dripped from each word.

"I swear to God! That's the truth." He stared at my face. "Bill swore nobody was home; nobody was supposed to get hurt."

"Okay, let's pretend I believe you. At least about the first time, but you saw what happened. Why'd you come back with him the second time? You knew then that he meant to hurt Aretha and me."

He dropped his head. His voice lowered to a mumble. "You gotta understand. Bill...he's like crazy, for real. You don't say 'no' to him."

"What the... You saying you're so afraid of this guy that you're willing to be party to killing someone?"

"Honest to God," he raised his head and met my gaze. "I never thought he would go that far."

A headache blossomed behind my eyes. I rubbed my fingers across my forehead. "Who decided to kill the animals?"

The words rushed out of him. "Bill and Nick. It was Nick's idea, though. He's got this thing."

I dropped my hand to my side. "What do you mean, he has this thing?"

Johnny bowed his shoulders inward, half turned his head. "Nick nearly wrecked his old man's truck one night trying to run over a cat. That kind of thing. He's crazier and meaner than Bill."

I thought I might get sick. "He tortured the baby goat." It wasn't a question.

He jerkily nodded. "I tried to tell him it wasn't right. To just go ahead and kill it." A quaver rattled his voice as he went on in a near-whisper. "But then him and Bill started saying things."

"So, you shut up and backed off. Big, brave man. Such big, brave men live in this town. Your parents must be real proud of you, Johnny boy."

"They don't know," he mumbled.

Run or Die

"They don't know. What exactly don't they know?" When he didn't answer, I threatened. "It's a cold walk to town in nothing, except your jockey shorts."

"They don't know none of it. When they heard about what happened, my dad wanted to know where I'd been that night. I lied and told him me and Jimmy'd been watching movies all night. Dad would've killed me if he knew." His voice sounded miserable.

"Why don't you do the right thing? Tell your father, or go to Sheriff Daly and tell him what happened?"

The moon crested the tree line and threw ghostly light over the dirt track where we stood. In the light, I saw fear swamp his face, widen his eyes as he vigorously shook his head. He held his hands up as if to ward away the suggestion. "No way, man, no fucking way."

Softly, I asked, "You know what happened to Ralph, don't you?"

"All I know is Ralph is dead, and he died on *her* farm." He ran a hand over his mouth.

"*Her* name is Ms. Hopewell," I snapped.

He ducked his head and wrapped his arms around his muscular chest. "Ralph died on Ms. Hopewell's farm."

"Yeah, he died all right. William beat him to death." I made it a statement, but he answered it.

"Yeah, I...kinda thought that."

"Doesn't it bother you? A young man you hung out with was beaten to death by the same guy you're still hanging out with." I squinted at him, wondering how he'd gotten tangled up with William.

He shrugged, head hanging.

"What made you think William beat him to death?"

He never raised his head. "The next day Jimmy called me. Said Ralph got killed up on that nig...up on Ms. Hopewell's place."

"And?"

He blew on his hands, picked up one foot then the other and wiggled his toes. "I called Bill. Asked him what happened to Ralph."

I stomped over to where his shoes lay, snatched them from the ground and bounced them off his chest. "Put these on before you lose your toes to frostbite."

"Thanks." He scrambled to get his feet into the shoes. "Really, thanks."

"Yeah, yeah. What happened when you asked him about Ralph?"

Johnny sucked in a noisy breath and rubbed his hands briskly up and down his arms. "He said Ralph had always been a pussy and he didn't want to ever hear his name again then he hung up on me."

"What's the rest of it?" I prodded quietly.

A tear glittered on his cheek, the moonlight reflecting off it. "It could have been me dead." He whispered barely loud enough for me to hear. "It could have been me. Bill had stopped by my house and wanted me to go riding with him and Nick that night. I live with my parents. When I asked my old man if I could go, he set his foot down. Said I had to stay home and spend the night with the family." He pawed at his face with one hand, wiping away the moisture on his cheeks. "My dad doesn't like Bill; doesn't like me hanging out with him. He doesn't understand."

"Understand what?"

"I *have* to." He caught his lower lip between his teeth and when he let it go, he said, "If I don't do what Bill says I could get hurt. Bad, real bad. And…and, it's not just me. I have a baby sister. Bill don't let you just walk away."

I stared at the hunched up young man. I couldn't see an enemy anymore, just this confused early-twenties guy who'd gotten in with the wrong people and didn't know how to get out. Like the gangs in the city, you have to have some real cojones to walk away. I used to despise people like that until I found myself in a similar situation. The fear and worry made me crazy then Mom died and with nothing left to lose, I walked away. Years later the memory still flooded me with shame.

I let the barrel of the rifle drift downward. "Get your clothes on," I spoke softly, suddenly sick at my own actions. What made me any better than William?

Run or Die

As Johnny dressed, I said, "Let me tell you something. If you don't come out and tell Sheriff Daly what you know, an innocent woman could wind up in jail. For a very long time for something that she didn't do."

His head whipped around and his mouth opened. I held up my hand like a traffic cop. "You're scared. I get that. Really, I do. I get that you're William's victim as much as Ralph; as much as Aretha and me. Sooner or later, you're going to cross some invisible line, or maybe it'll just be one of those nights when William's ticked off about something, and he's going to hurt you. You'll be lucky if that's all he does to you."

As he pulled on his boots, I tossed his keys at him, hit him in the chest with them. "You've got a clock on your stereo in the car. Don't even start the engine of that car for ten minutes. Don't fuck with me on this. You hear?"

He nodded. "Yeah, okay."

A jog over the hill took me to the V-dub. I tossed the rifle onto the backseat and cranked up the car. With the end of one sleeve, I wiped a small circle on the windshield clear and started up Washboard Road. Once I made it to the cave, I removed from my jacket pocket the mini tape player that I'd purchased in Ukiah. It went into the bottom of my backpack. Cuddled down in my sleeping bag, I fell asleep wondering how I could use that tape without winding up in jail for kidnapping or illegal detention or some crap.

Chapter 13

Christmas loomed two days away. Snow fell, melted then fell again, making a mucky mess of Washboard Road. I climbed into the Volkswagen and slithered my way up Buzzard Peak to phone Aretha at Ms. Winters' house. Since she'd been released from jail, she hadn't returned to the farm.

Her voice sounded as depressed as I felt. "Folami put up a tree. A beautiful Grand Fir. We wanted to know if you'd like to come down and help us decorate it."

The last tree I had helped to decorate Alicia and I had dragged home to Grandma Pearl's house. Since Alicia died, I had no desire to see a Christmas tree, and certainly no desire to help decorate one. "I have things I want to get done up here. Tell Ms. Winters I appreciate the offer, though."

"Are you coming down for Christmas dinner?"

I cleared my throat and dug through my list of possible excuses. None sounded plausible, so maybe the truth would have to do. "I don't do Christmas, Aretha. Not since Alicia died."

Sympathy wove through her words. "I discovered after my husband died that you can't stop living because someone you loved has died. When are you going to start living again, Jaz?"

The words rankled. "Maybe I'll think about it when you do the same. Ralph wasn't a friend; far from it, yet you're acting like his death is this great big tragedy. You won't even come up here to your own farm!"

The silence on the line hurt, but I refused to apologize for the truth. Aretha needed to face the facts. When she didn't reply, I said, "Hey, look, I'll phone you on Christmas Day. Take care." I didn't wait for a response; just shut the phone off and snapped it closed.

On Christmas Eve I heard someone working a good-sized tractor somewhere up the road. For a moment, I entertained the thought of trying to hire whoever it was to plow a path for the V-dub, but I didn't like asking anyone for anything. I poured myself another cup of coffee as the light snow dusted the shoulders of my jacket.

Run or Die

Christmas Day dawned bitterly cold. Grateful that Alicia had convinced me to buy gear powered by a battery as well as bike-powered, I slipped on the black motorcycle jacket and outer pants once I'd scrunched through the tight entryway.

In spite of the cold, the Volkswagen started right up and plowed through the powdery snow. When I topped the rise that overlooked Aretha's place, the roadway had been cleared. Piles of muddy snow lined the shoulders. Guess someone expected Christmas company.

The drive to Buzzard Peak afforded me enough time to clear my mind and admonish myself to act, as Alicia would say with a grin, civilized. Grandma Pearl picked up on the second ring. A lump formed in my throat. Aretha had phoned her mother and explained that there had been a fire at the cabin, so dancing around the truth wasn't as bad as I expected. Besides Grandma Pearl knew I would rather campout than stay at someone's house.

Actually, the call to Aretha presented more awkward silences than the call to Grandma Pearl. What was there to say after I told her 'no, thanks' to Ms. Winters' Christmas dinner invitation? After a rather lengthy silence, I told her I needed to go and hung up.

I drove back to the farm, stirred up the smoldering campfire, and put a pot of coffee on to perk. While the coffee made, I slapped together a peanut butter and jelly sandwich and ripped open a bag of Lay's Salt 'n Vinegar potato chips. The first gulp of coffee scalded my mouth so bad I spit it on the ground. While I waited for it to cool, I ate the sandwich and let my eyes roam over the land.

Puffball clouds scattered across the brilliant blue sky. The brightness of the day only made me feel worse. From where I sat next to the fire pit I couldn't avoid seeing the chicken house. Since I already felt, in my mom's words, lower than a snake's belly, I decided to work on it.

Sun bounced off the snow, forcing me to squint as I trudged towards the chicken coop. When I got close my feet shuffled to a halt. Mesmerized by the shotgun holes in the plywood walls, I stood there. I wanted to curse, I wanted to scream, I wanted to cry, but mostly I wanted to beat the living hell out of William and Nick. After a while, I forced myself to move, to walk into the chicken yard, to skirt the mound that marked the grave, to open the flimsy door.

The rust splatters of blood made my stomach churn and my sandwich threatened to erupt. I swallowed it down. My eyes burned like salt had been flung into them. Tears I refused to shed clogged my nose. I clenched my hand on the brand new hammer and crowbar I'd picked up in Ukiah. The work dragged. The weight of memories made my arms feel leaden and made my shoulders ache.

By the edge of dark not a lot of progress had been made. All I could think about was how we had so very carefully closed the chicken yard gate every night. How one night when neither of us could recall doing so, Aretha had crawled out of bed, pulled her boots on, and walked down to check.

I whirled away from the splintered wood scattered around the chicken yard and stomped up the hill.

The next morning cold splatters of wet snow soaked my jacket as I worked on destroying the chicken house. This time the work proceeded a bit faster, but not fast enough for me. I hauled the busted plywood up to the cabin's original site and piled it to create a burn pile for later. I got the outer wall ripped off before the feeling of loss wrapped an iron band around my chest.

Standing outside of the chicken yard I stared at the stripped bones of the chicken house. Tears streamed down my face. How could I blame Aretha for not wanting to return? I'd only known Albert and Cinders a short while. She'd raised them from tiny chicks.

The following morning ushered in another bitterly cold day and achingly bright sky. After a quick breakfast of scrambled eggs and coffee, I trudged down to the chicken yard determined to finish dismantling the chicken house. I hacked into campfire wood the two-by-fours without blood splatters and stacked all of it close to the fire pit. By late afternoon, the burn pile blazed and I slung the nest boxes and roosts on it.

Only the grave mound and the wire enclosure with its slatted wood gate gave evidence of what had been lost. The gate hung open. Anger smashed into me like a tidal wave. I staggered from the sad site, my hands balled into fists.

Get away! Got to get away!

Not caring where I went, I plunged down the hill. The boundary of the rushing creek stopped me. Bent over with my hands on my knees, I sucked in the cold air. It scoured my lungs and I had to pull my sleeve across my mouth to reduce the ache. At least the cold dampened the bitter taste of failure that wiggled up the back of my throat. By the time I returned to my campfire, the nearby burn pile had died down to glowing embers. With snow on the ground and no wind, I left it to burn out.

That night in the cave as I attempted to eat a bologna sandwich, it turned to bloody wings in my mouth. I gagged and spit it out then gulped hot coffee. Shivering, I crawled into my sleeping bag and blew out the lantern.

The last weekend in December, I caved and visited Aretha at Ms. Winters' house. When I had worked at house painting for Alicia's Aunt Sylvia, I had painted in a few houses as nice as Ms. Winters, but not many. I slipped my Avia running shoes off at the door under the sharp gaze of the black maid. Real oil paintings hung along the hall. I could see the thick streaks of paint on the canvas. By the time I arrived in the kitchen with its marble-topped counters, I felt like a poor cousin come to hang with the rich cousin. It didn't help my level of comfort that Aretha appeared right at home.

Settled in with a cup of coffee and fresh scones, we quickly exhausted the weather as a topic. Quiet descended, a stiff, scratchy rope choking me. Unable to come up with another topic, I announced that I'd be leaving her car and taking my bike.

"Are you insane?" Aretha screeched.

"I can keep the shiny side up. It's not like I'll be driving it once I get back to the farm. I'll use your truck. That way you'll have your own car here in town." I didn't add that she'd have no excuse not to come to the farm then.

"You need that car. My old two-wheel drive truck can't handle the snow and ice like the Volkswagen does, unless you bottom her out." I could see her struggling to maintain reasonable.

I wasn't feeling very reasonable right then. "The snow stopped and I told you someone plowed the road almost all the way to the farm. Admit it, Aretha, no car is simply another excuse to stay away. If that's what you want, then fine! I'll take the car and leave you your excuse." I surged up from the table under a glare from Ms. Winters. Aretha refused to meet my eyes.

From the hall, I heard the maid talking to someone. I shoved my chair up to the table and headed for the front door. Sheriff Daly waltzed in.

Hat in his hands, the perfect picture of a gentleman caller, he nodded to Ms. Winters and me then focused on Aretha. "I thought I'd drop by and see how you were doing. Find out if you've experienced any further incidents."

I rolled my eyes. Seriously? All the anger that had built up came snarling out at him. "Why aren't you out trying to catch the real killer instead of coming around here to spy on Aretha?"

"Jaz!"

I snapped my gaze over to Aretha. "Don't tell me you're going to defend this. It's damn near harassment."

"I don't believe Sheriff Daly..." she began in a quiet tone.

I cut her off. "Oh, come on, Aretha. Don't tell me you buy into his so-called concern for you."

"That's enough!" At Ms. Winters' command my head whipped around toward her. She'd risen to her feet and towered regally beside the table. "This is *my* house, Ms. Wheeler. I will say who enters and when."

"Fine!" I whirled toward Aretha. "You keep on playing footsie with the enemy right up until he buries you in a prison cell. I'm outta here." Deliberately, and childishly, I whacked into Daly's shoulder on my way past him. Quite a bit better than slamming my fist in his face.

What is wrong with Aretha and Ms. Winters? Can't they recognize the sheriff's nonsense for the ploy it is? I felt their eyes on my back as I stormed out.

On the drive to the farm the feeling of abandonment gripped me in an iron fist. Everyone I cared about left me in one way or the other. I wrenched the band of loss from around my chest, thrust it into a mental box then slammed the lid on it. Tired, just tired, that's all.

January blew in, dumping piles of snow from depressing gray skies. Where snowdrifts didn't cover the road, sheets of ice did. For a couple of weeks, I didn't dare drive to town, afraid Aretha's V-dub would slide over the hill or wind up ploughed so deeply into a snow bank that I wouldn't get it out before spring thaw. The snow that blocked me in kept William and his posse out. Since I wasn't fit company for a sewer rat, I flung my head back and shouted, "Let it snow!" For the first time in weeks, I slept deeply and woke up rested in spite of the damp cold of the cave.

The second week of January rolled around and I still hadn't had the heart to dismantle the chicken enclosure and leave the dirt mound where Cinders and Albert lay buried unprotected. Somehow, it felt important to protect their grave mound even though I had failed to keep the chickens safe.

My whole life had spun from one failure to the next one. The drugs killed Mom because I couldn't get an ambulance in time. George beat Miriam to death because I couldn't find the words to make her leave the bastard. Cancer stole Alicia. Hell, I couldn't even protect Little Kid. I'd been so wrapped up in my yearly pity-party that I'd left him to William's nonexistent mercy.

It'd been a long time since I'd wanted to drink. Now, I could almost taste the whiskey sliding down my throat. I knew just how it would burn going down and how it would explode into a fiery ball in my gut. Maybe it was serendipitous that the snow was too deep for the V-dub to handle a trip to town.

The next morning, I ripped a small sheet of plywood off the woodshed and gouged a couple of holes in one end. The rope Aretha had purchased weeks ago made an adequate pull for the makeshift sled. After I broke a path through the snow going to Boulder Creek, it wasn't too bad. The sled skidded across the frozen crust even loaded with rocks. My feet slipped and the rope-pull wrenched my shoulders. I bowed my head and dug my boots into the frozen earth.

It required two days of hard labor to haul enough rocks up to the chicken enclosure. On the third day, I covered the dirt mound with a cairn of rocks. Snow fell in lazy, fat flakes. The flakes melted as they hit my face, mingling with the tears I didn't try to stop. It was after dark before I finished.

Mid-week the sky quit spitting snow though dark clouds loomed on the horizon in a silent threat. The sound of a truck engine rolled down the hill ahead of the vehicle. I looked up and watched as it topped the rise and started toward the farm gate. I hooked my hammer and crowbar on part of the fence that remained. By the time the four-wheel drive pickup crunched up the frozen snow of the drive and parked next to the site of the burned cabin, I had blended into the shadows beneath the trees a hundred feet away. I held the rifle loosely in my hand and observed.

Cynthia McKenna stepped out of the Chevy Avalanche and moved toward the campfire that blazed merrily in the crisp air. From where I stood, I noted that she'd at least had sense enough to wear proper clothing this time. Ordinary blue jeans, construction boots that appeared to be new, and a Carhartt work jacket that looked like the ones at the outdoor store in Willits. When no one else popped out of the truck, I emerged from the trees and walked over to her. What did she want this time? A couple of feet from her, I waved my hand up and down to indicate her entire ensemble. "What's with this costume?"

She blushed; the rosy red on her cheeks looked attractive. "Granddad told me it wasn't any wonder you thought I was some kind of nut or something the last time. Dressed like I was going to the mall, I mean. He told me if I wanted to help, I had to look like I could be of some use." She shoved her naked hands into her jacket pockets.

A puzzled frown drew my brows tight over my eyes. "How, exactly, do you think you can help?"

She studied me, maybe wondering why I hadn't chased her off yet. "Look, I admit I don't know much about...well, about farming or building, but if there's something you need taken apart, I'm pretty good at that. You can ask Granddad. And, I'm a fast learner." Her tentative smile trembled, unsure of its welcome.

I flapped a hand to indicate her jacket pockets. "You don't have gloves."

Run or Die

A smile rushed across her face. "In the truck. Lined work gloves. Granddad helped me pick them out."

I relented and let my face relax a bit. Why? I don't know. Maybe I was tired of my own company, or tired of always being alone. "Happens that I'm taking stuff apart this week. I have an extra hammer."

Cynthia should have bragged about her de-constructing skills. She took things apart without destroying them, most of the time. Better than me. Sometimes, I'm not sure I have any virtues, but if I do patience isn't one of them.

Unlike either Alicia or Aretha, Cynthia chattered like a Stellar Jay; a cheerful, and cheering, noise. Out of talking range, she sang. That young woman couldn't be quiet. Her voice was a sweet tenor and sometimes I caught myself humming along.

We knocked off early Friday afternoon. All evidence of the chicken coop gone. Monday I'd start on the woodshed. After that I'd tackle the barn that we hadn't finished before shotgun shells had riddled the sides. I couldn't stand to see any part of what had been tainted by violence. Undoubtedly, the structures would evoke horrible memories for Aretha, too. Not even a nail would be salvaged.

Over a pot of coffee, I told Cynthia we'd knock off until Monday. Provided Mother Nature didn't dump a blizzard on us, we'd start work dismantling the woodshed. The kid left so excited you would've thought I'd given her a belated Christmas gift.

Saturday evening I had stretched out on my sleeping bag to read when the sound of a car engine echoed through the quiet. Hurrying into my boots and dark blue down jacket, I grabbed the rifle and slipped out of the cave entrance. Swallowed by the blackness cast by the boulders, I watched headlights sweep up the drive and stop next to the cleared spot where the trailer had set. A single person, small enough to be a woman, exited the vehicle. The luminance of the headlights prevented me from seeing whether anyone else occupied the car. I waited.

Since the snow had mostly stopped and therefore no longer hid tire tracks, I'd given up hiding the Volkswagen. The thin figure walked up to Aretha's car. "Ms. Wheeler?" A call almost too weak to hear. "Jaz Wheeler?"

No way I'd show myself. I hadn't fallen out of a Stupid Tree and hit every branch on the way down.

"Ms. Wheeler, Ms. Hopewell sent me." The voice wavered.

Yeah. Seriously? Stupid much?

"Please. She said you'd help me." A sob rode ragged on the light breeze.

She cried, her forehead resting against the top of the Volkswagen. Not the show kind of crying with huge racking sobs, but the real, deep down crying where sobs wretched themselves from the bottom of a person's soul. That had been the only kind of crying I'd ever heard my mother engage in, and that was the day I'd asked her about my dad. It hurt to hear it.

On silent feet, I crept to within a few feet of the front end of the car. "What do you want?"

She jerked upright and whirled around so fast that she banged her elbow into the driver's side window. Scrubbing at her face, she said, "I didn't hear you comin'."

Rifle dangling from my hands, I said, "Didn't mean for you to."

"I need that medicine Ms. Hopewell give me last time."

"Medicine?" My head swiveled, searching for any unwelcome visitors sneaking around.

She lowered her face to stare at the frozen earth. "For the change. You know, the change o' life. I...I get real down and I can't take care of my family or nothin'. Please. She said you'd help me."

"When did you talk to Aretha?" Suspicion wrapped around each word, making them barbed-wire sharp.

"This afternoon." She lifted her face. "Saw her down at that nig...hippie restaurant in Willits. I...I been outta medicine for nigh on two weeks and everything seems to be fallin' apart." The pale moon illuminated her wan face enough to see the tears gathered in her eyes.

"I'm not an herbal doctor."

"She said to tell you some of it's already mixed up. She said it's in the blue bag, where she stashed the medicines. Said to scoop some out—it's a powder, kind of brownish. I...I already know how to mix it up." Hope trembled between her words.

Run or Die

My upper lip curled with a dislike so strong for this skinny white woman that her simply standing there made me want to strike her. Instead, I verbally lashed out. "Where were you when Aretha and I walked into that town meeting with our goat, Little Kid?" I didn't give her time to lie. "You were right there. I saw you. Second row from the back with some red-faced guy that sneered at us as we walked out. I remember you. You had a couple of snotty-nosed kids sitting on the other side of you. Now look at you, up here wanting us to help you. Why should I?"

"I know...I know I got no right to ask. But...Ms. Hopewell's medicine's the only thing ever helped me. Doctor can't help me. I tried. Doc Randal's medicine makes me so tired I can't take care of the kids and Ben. Sometimes, it gets so bad I cry for days on end." In the glow of the headlights, her gaze skittered everywhere, except to my face. "Ben gets so mad at me sometimes. Not that I blame him. A woman a'weepin' and a'wailin' all day long's enough to get on a man's nerves after a hard day's work."

"He hits you." Sometimes the truth is so loud you don't need to ask the question.

"No." Her eyes darted to my face then away. "Not really. He slaps me a little, but he don't hit me. He's just tryin' to get me back to my senses."

Yeah, I'd heard that excuse before. "Right." I stared down the night-shrouded drive. "Where's your old man think you are right now?"

"Home. He's down to the Redlight Tavern with some fellas from work. Won't be home till late. My sister, Elsie, she's mindin' the kids for me."

I wanted to walk away, leave her standing there begging. A breeze gusted past, running icy fingers through my hair. "Crippled Christ! Okay. It's Aretha's medicine and I suppose she has the right to give it to anyone she pleases. You drive on up around Buzzard Peak and wait."

When the taillights of her car rounded the curve, I darted a crooked path through the woods to the cave. Within fifteen minutes I stepped out of the Volkswagen and shoved a jar of the powder in through her car window to her waiting hands. "Now get out of my sight. You make me sick!"

Aya Walksfar

Cold-numb fingers stuffed in my jacket pockets, I watched her old clunker slip-slide along the slick road then I cautiously turned the car and idled back home. I wanted to keep hating that woman, yet when I got to the cave and poured a cup of lukewarm coffee from the thermos, I found myself pitying her instead. If I wasn't careful, I'd be trying to understand these spineless idiots.

Time to apply the thumbscrews before I got soft in the head. I couldn't recall which novel I'd read about thumbscrews in, but it had certainly sounded satisfying. "Well, Nicky boy, it is time for you to feel the love."

***

When people dream of tormenting their enemies they usually come up with things like staking them out naked on a red anthill in the hot noonday sun. Or something equally boring, like whacking off pieces of their fingers. If you intend to murder them in the end, that's an okay way to go; otherwise, you have to be more creative.

I intended to use something simple. A goat carcass given to me by a farmer south of Ukiah on my last trip to town before Christmas. I'd seen the dead animal in the field and turned up the drive to the ramshackle farmhouse. I don't know if the poor thing starved to death, or dropped dead of something else. Didn't matter. I buried it in a shallow grave, just deep enough to keep it from freezing hard as granite.

Earlier that day I'd dug up the goat, laid a plastic tarp out in the cave, and placed the frozen carcass on it. The heavy blanket, stretched across the cave entrance, held the heat of the propane camp stove in the cave, so it only took a couple of hours to completely defrost the goat. Once I slit the goat open, I held my breath against the sweet rotten odor of decomposing entrails. Latex gloves on, the entrails slimed in my hands as I placed them in plastic Ziploc bags. I wanted to ensure that I'd be able to spread them out on Nicky's truck seat quick and easy.

The quart Mason jar of pig blood had a skim of ice on top. It melted by the time the goat defrosted. The farmer, south of Willits, who sold me the pig blood had given me one of *those* looks. I could almost hear him telling his wife he's sold blood to a witch for some kind of dark ceremony. He wouldn't have been too far off.

At three o'clock on a freezing Sunday morning, no one stood witness to my visit. Nicky's truck sat parked in the asphalt driveway of his parents' house. Not a light on in any of the residences to either side of their place.

Back in the cave, I set the windup alarm clock for eleven o'clock. I timed it to arrive at Hamburger Haven around noon, its busiest time.

The buzz of conversations solidified into a molasses-thick wall of silence as I strolled through the glass door. I waded through it, listening to burgers sizzling on the grill and the rustle of clothes as people shifted in their seats to watch me walk up to the counter.

A matronly woman served me, though she refused to look at me, and spoke only enough to take my money. A brown paper bag with two cheeseburgers deluxe and a large fry in one hand and a strawberry shake in the other hand, I chose a corner and settled into the booth. Back to the wall, I stretched my legs out under the cheap table and soaked up the sunshine magnified through the dirty plate glass window. Ten minutes into my burger everyone seemed to forget my presence and tongues started flapping again. Fortunately, my mother's accusation that I had the hearing of a good dog had proven true. I listened as I ate. It helped that no one tried to keep their comments especially quiet.

"Poor Nick," one slender redheaded girl began. "I heard that all that slime and stink probably won't ever wash out of his seat."

"Yeah." A boy fighting a losing battle with acne added, "Nick says when he catches the S.O.B. that did this, he's gonna kill 'em."

Ineffectively blocking her mouth with her hand, the redhead said, "Well, you know who it has to be." She nudged her head ever so slightly in my direction. "It being a goat carcass and all."

Since the rest of the young people pretty much repeated that general train of thought, I finished up my dinner and walked out, whistling. Feeling the best I'd felt in a long time, I drove down to Willits. Ms. Winters didn't welcome me like long lost family, but she must've forgiven my outburst the last time because she invited me in for coffee.

Like the first time I'd walked into her house, I almost feared to step off the flagstone entry, afraid I'd mar the spit shine on the hardwood floor. This time I took a better look around. A large antique clock hung on the wall to my left, its slick cherry wood carved with vines and some kind of flower. A toilette sat against the opposite wall—a beautiful white ceramic pitcher sitting in the middle of a large bowl with the same pink flower pattern. I recognized the antiques because I'd seen pictures of similar ones in a book in the library back home.

Alicia had been looking for something to read, and since I had my selections, I browsed while I waited. A big, heavy book with a real leather cover caught my attention. Beauty from The Past, the embossed title read. The awesomeness of the photographs of the furniture and other antiques mesmerized me as I leafed through its pages. Sunk in an overstuffed chair, I remained hypnotized by the grace and beauty in those photos until Alicia slid onto the arm of the chair and looked over my shoulder.

She would've loved Ms. Winters' stuff. This time instead of a hot lance of pain, a soft shawl of sadness cloaked my heart. Ms. Winters led me into the living room and I felt like I'd stepped into one of the pages of that book. I must've gasped. She looked at me and smiled. It reached up and crinkled the skin around her eyes in happy wrinkles.

It was the first time she'd ever smiled at me. "You're impressed."

"You might say that." I tried to regain my cool, not very successfully.

She waved an elegant hand to include not only the room we walked into, but the entire house. "Every time I look around my house, I think how lucky I am, yet I can't help remembering how much of what I have is built on the broken dreams and broken bodies of my ancestors, and how much my people still suffer."

Run or Die

"Least you got people," I muttered, not expecting her to hear.

She slung a sharp look my way. "Everybody got people, girl."

I shoved my hands deeper into my jacket pockets. "Yeah, right."

"Don't give me that," she snapped. "You're white. Your people are everywhere you look." She focused hard eyes on me.

My good mood morphed into a lava flow of hot anger. Guess I wasn't in the mood to be somebody's doormat even while I stood in their fancy house. "*Don't* tell me who my people are. I have fewer people than you. I'm queer. Lesbian. Lesbo. Bull dyke, or whatever else you want to call it. Black or white or purple, people don't want queers.

"Oh, yeah, it's better than it used to be, at least in some areas, but it's far from the land of the free for lesbians. Seventeen states allow lesbians to legally marry, but thirty-three states have banned lesbian and gay marriages.

"And get this: it wasn't just Aretha them punks tried to kill. Don't go telling me who my people are!" By the time I finished the veins in my neck bulged with the anger pumping through them.

Ms. Winters stared at me for a minute then quietly said, "Aretha will be down momentarily. Have a seat. I'll get some coffee for all of us."

The rest of the visit went well enough. The three of us lounged around the living room. Aretha gave me the lowdown on her legal situation. My news dealt with Helen Dooley's visit for herbs and with the land. I told her about Cynthia coming over and helping to clean things up. No need to discuss the gossip about Nick's truck. She'd hear it soon enough.

Ms. Winters threw in a question now and then. All very civilized. She extended an invitation for me to have dinner with them. They expected Mr. Edison at any moment. I declined. Made some excuse about needing to get back up on the hill before it got too late. I could only be civilized for a finite period of time.

Daly tromped up the sidewalk as I walked out the door. He halted, his bulk occupying the entire center of the walk, blocking my way unless I wanted to squish through the lawn. "Where were you early this morning?" He demanded in an unyielding voice.

I narrowed my eyes at him. "Where do *you* think I was, Sheriff?"

"Stop playing games, Jaz. This is serious. Where were you?"

Lips pressed together, I gave an abbreviated shake of my head. "I know it's serious, Sheriff. Better than you do, but that doesn't mean I'm going to stand here and answer your questions. If you have something, arrest me. Otherwise..."

"Otherwise step aside, Sheriff, and let the young woman proceed along her way." Mr. Edison's melodic voice interrupted.

I'd seen Mr. Edison coming, but the sheriff hadn't. He flinched and moved aside.

Of course, I didn't head up the hill. Instead I practiced some of the skills I'd learned in various foster homes.

I should've been a second story woman. That's what my roommate, Angela, a kid at one of my foster homes called herself. A second story woman. Sure learned a lot from that girl. If she'd been giving out degrees, I'm certain I earned at least a Bachelor of Nefarious Methodology and Spy Skills.

It helped that Nicky's parents vegged in front of the boob tube every night while he caroused. Without so much as a cat to give me away, I climbed the trellis and entered through the guest bedroom's window. Prepared to try out my skills with jimmying, disappointment rushed through me when the vinyl-framed window soundlessly opened. Really, what was it with the people around Elmsworth and Andersville? Did *no one* lock up anything?

From what I'd seen, Nicky loved his clothes. Rummaging through his closet, I rubbed the cloth of his shirts between my fingers: silk and a few everyday cottons. Dress pants that must've cost more than my entire wardrobe I'd left behind in Seattle. His parents had to be wallowing in the green.

I laid out a silk shirt, dress pants, and a suit jacket in such a way on the king size bed as to look remarkably like a headless body in the dim light. Within five minutes, the clothes had suffered the same types of wounds I'd found on Little Kid. Holes and rips in painful areas of the anatomy. Pig's blood spattered

Run or Die

over the clothes. In and out in twelve minutes. I pumped my fist. *Yes! I'm good!*

Around noon the next day, Monday, Sheriff Daly arrived and parked next to the truck Cynthia drove. Big eyed, she watched him walk across the crunchy, frozen mud to join us at the fire pit. A pot of coffee perked on the hot rocks set close to the campfire. I got up and poured another cup and held it out as he sat on the end of Cynthia's log. I flashed him a wry grin. "You must've smelled it perking." Yummilicious to look at, with the earmarks of a real gentleman, too bad Daly was a cop or I'd be trying to fix him up with Aretha.

He accepted the cup and sipped. "I don't know where you learned to make coffee, but it's good."

"Thanks." I refilled my cup and settled on my log. "This must be an official visit, what with you in your official uniform and all."

He stretched his legs out toward the fire. "Has to be, I guess."

I cocked an eyebrow. "What is it that you *officially* want?"

"Some of the men in town have accused you of harassment."

Both of my eyebrows booked for my hairline. "You don't say? Wow, those big, strong men being harassed by one little ole queer. I must be pretty scary."

"They're pretty uptight about it," he replied in a conversational voice.

Mimicking him, I stretched my legs out. "Any evidence against me?"

He shook his head. "Nope."

I sipped my coffee, watching him over the rim of the cup. "Who's accusing me of what?"

"William and Nick." He blew into his cup and took a longer drink this time.

"They the only ones?"

"Should there be anyone else?" He countered.

I shot him a sassy grin. "Unless I'm guilty of harassment, there's no way for me to know the answer to that question."

With peripheral vision, I watched Cynthia. Jaw hanging open, her head bobbed back and forth as she followed the verbal volleys.

He gazed around the empty land and asked, "Where do you spend your nights?"

A rough laugh bubbled out. "I crawl under a rock."

He studied me. "I imagine it gets pretty cold."

I rolled a shoulder in a half-shrug. "Can't be helped. The trailer's still in the impound yard. Besides, I wouldn't be able to sleep in it with any feeling of safety, anyhow."

He stood and tossed the dregs in his cup off to one side then set the cup on a rock by the log. "Make sure your rock isn't anywhere easy to spot. Those guys are riled up."

I inclined my head toward him. "I'll remember that, Sheriff."

Chapter 14

Another week rolled by with the weather alternating between light snow and icy rain. With Cynthia's help, I got the woodshed and the barn torn down and most of the lumber burned. Friday, when we laid down our hammers, I asked Cynthia if her granddad would mind her driving me into town on Monday to pick up some building supplies. Aretha's two-wheel drive truck would do what Mom used to call a 'sit and spin' on the icy road and I didn't want to pay a hefty delivery charge. She grinned like I'd given her a prize. "Oh, no, he wouldn't mind at all."

I frowned and held her gaze. "Be sure to tell him what we're doing, okay? I'd like to be double sure he doesn't mind you using his new truck for hauling lumber and whatnot."

On Monday, Cynthia maneuvered down the slick road to the highway without once skidding. The four-wheel drive on her granddad's Avalanche rocked.

"Swing by Hamburger Haven and I'll buy lunch."

Cynthia flicked a glance at me. "Are you sure you want to stop there? We could stop in Willits and get something to eat."

I rolled my eyes. "Okay, I confess. I want to eavesdrop on whatever gossip's going around."

The look she gave me clearly said "it's your funeral."

Unfortunately, the hamburger joint was empty, except for a young man and a young woman, both of whom looked to be in their late teens.

"Hey, Rosalind," Cynthia spoke as she strolled up to the counter.

"Whatcha doin' hangin' with her?" Rosalind snapped her gum and nodded toward me.

A blush reddened Cynthia's neck, but she answered in a calm voice. "I'm helping her rebuild Ms. Hopewell's cabin that burned down."

Rosalind wagged her head sorrowfully. "You shouldn' be hangin' with people like *that*."

Cynthia's back stiffened. "Why shouldn't I?"

"Bill said..."

Cynthia slapped the counter. The crack startled the other young woman and she jerked back several steps. "I don't give two cents what Bill says. When are you going to start thinking for yourself, Rosalind? Bill is a racist bigot, and you didn't used to be that kind of person."

Rosalind's face blazed red while anger and embarrassment warred in her light brown eyes. "Maybe I am thinkin' for myself, Miss Know-It-All! Maybe *I* don' want that kinda folks livin' here neither." She huffed off to the back and disappeared through a doorway.

"Well, Ted," Cynthia focused on the young man wiping down the refrigerator. "What do you have to say? Are you thick with Bill, too?"

The lanky young man slouched over to the counter. "You know me better than that, Cynthia." He ducked his head. "I don't have anything to do with Bill. He's bad news." He cleared his throat and glanced my way. "Mr. Connors told us we aren't to serve troublemakers, though."

Cynthia frowned. "Do you think I'm a troublemaker?"

Ted blushed and mumbled, "No way, but Mr. Connors specifically mentioned Ms. Hopewell and her...friend."

Tired of being ignored, I bellied up to the counter. "Look, Ted, I'm the lesbian; not Ms. Hopewell."

"I didn't mean...I mean...," he stuttered.

"Good. You really meant that Aretha and I are friends, *without* benefits. Great. Now for the second issue. Are you calling me a troublemaker?" I scrunched my face, the picture of total puzzlement.

Anticipating that he would either back away from the subject or puff up like an angry adder, he surprised me. "No, ma'am, I didn't. Mr. Connors did."

I gave him a wolfish grin. "Troublemakers," I repeated with satisfaction in my voice. "Fair enough. Let's you and me talk about this, Ted. Tell me, would you consider a person who beats his friend to death a troublemaker?"

He folded and refolded the dish rag he held then laid it to one side on the counter before he met my gaze. "Is that a trick question, ma'am?"

Run or Die

With a short shake of my head, I reassured him. "Nope. Straight up question, no tricks."

"If you want a straight answer then yes, a person who hurts his friend is a troublemaker, and worse. Someone who kills another person goes beyond being a troublemaker, ma'am."

"Very good. Now for the next part of this quiz. Where do you live?"

"You ain't gotta talk to her, Ted." Rosalind had reappeared from the back and propped herself against the far wall, her red painted lips pooched out in a pout.

Not gracing her with a look, I snarled. "Shut up!" I repeated my question in a conversational tone. "Ted, where do you live?"

He cocked his head, took his time thinking about whether or not to answer me. In the end, I think curiosity got the better of him. "456 Elm Street. Over by the high school."

"Good. This next part of the quiz is real simple, but I want you to think about it before you answer. Okay?"

Suspiciously, he gave a slow nod.

"Here it is: what if some night, simply because you're different than me, I snuck over to your house with some of my friends and poured gas all over your porch and all on the walls of your house while believing that you were in there and then set it on fire? *And,* once it was burning, I took a gun and started shooting into your house. Would you call me a troublemaker?"

While I spoke his face blanched. I could almost hear him regretting that he'd told me where he lived. His wide eyes broadcast "OMG, she's really crazy!" Before he could drop dead of a heart attack, I said, "Well, what do you think, Ted? Would that be the actions of a real troublemaker?"

He opened his thin lips to answer. Nothing came out. He closed his mouth then reopened it. Out of the corner of my eye, I saw the color completely drain from Rosalind's face. Cynthia stood next to me, silent; I could feel her studying me like a high school chemistry project.

He swallowed hard, lifted his chin and looked me in the eyes. "Yes, ma'am." It came out a croak. He cleared his throat. "Yes, ma'am," he said in a strong, pleasant voice, "that would certainly be a troublemaker and then some."

I smiled at him. "Well, Ted, you and I think alike. Anyone who would kill someone from meanness, and anyone who would burn down someone's house because they don't like people who are different from them, those folks are troublemakers, and like you said, way beyond just troublemakers. But," I held up a finger. "Aretha Hopewell did not kill Ralph, no more than I burned down your house." My smile stretched wider and I hoped it wasn't too wolfish. "Mr. Connors must be mistaken about Aretha and me. As you can see, we aren't troublemakers."

A smile inched across his face and sparkled in his eyes. "You didn't used to practice law up where you come from, did you?"

My own smile reflected his good humor. "No. Just a house painter, and now I'm a farmer."

Cynthia and I ate in the truck on the way to the lumberyard in Willits. "It would've been easier to get the burgers in Willits," she wryly commented.

I swallowed a mouthful. "Yeah, I know. I think it might've been worth the hassle, though."

"Ted's a nice guy. I had him in my senior year Honors English class." She washed down some burger and fries with a long draw of milkshake.

"The problem with people like Ted is that they don't always stop and think for themselves. They take rumors, or allegations, and never ask for the other side of the story."

"Yeah, I know." A few miles passed before she grinned. "Bet Ted does his own thinking from now on."

I told Cynthia to take Tuesday off so I could study the book, *House Building Made Simple,* which I'd bought at the lumberyard. Grateful for the sunshine, even if the temperature felt as cold as the backside of a polar bear, I sat on the log by the fire pit.

Why did I think I could do this? I've never built anything bigger than a little greenhouse by myself. I slapped the book shut and tossed it on the frozen ground. Legs kicked out in front of me, I gulped my coffee as I stared across the clearing.

The sound of an unfamiliar vehicle rolled down the hillside. I set my cup next to the log round, snatched up the rifle next to my feet, and stood. It fleetingly occurred to me that maybe

Run or Die

I should make myself scarce. Irritated at the thought, I moved my shoulders as if to dislodge it. Tired of playing rabbit, I waited.

A battered pickup sputtered to a stop next to the Volkswagen. As soon as he unfolded from behind the steering wheel, I recognized the lanky form of Ted from Hamburger Haven. He spotted me immediately and raised a hand in greeting.

I didn't respond; just waited.

He halted on the opposite side of the fire pit. "Hey," he said.

In a flat voice, I asked, "What do you want?"

Hands in his jacket pockets, he tilted his chin toward his truck. "It's around lunch time. Thought you might like something to eat."

"Who knows you're up here?" I shifted the rifle to a more comfortable position.

His eyebrows shot up. "Nobody. Nobody, except my dad."

"You didn't drive all the way up this icy hillside simply to bring me lunch."

Elbows sticking out from his sides like chicken wings, he shrugged and stared at the scuffed toes of his boots. "Thought maybe we could talk."

He looked so forlorn, I huffed a sigh. "Go get our lunches."

He scrambled for his truck and in moments came hustling back holding two bags and a drink tray. When he got to the campfire, he grinned and held up the bags. "Two cheeseburgers with the works for each of us, large fries, and..." With a flourish he lifted the drink tray. "And, strawberry shake for you and a root beer shake for me."

I waved the rifle barrel toward the log on his side. "Sit." Once he sat, I said, "Put your lunch on the ground on your right side and my lunch on your left side." When he did that, I made shooing motions with one hand. "Leave the food and scoot down to the end of the log."

When he was far enough away to satisfy my paranoia, I picked up his bag of food and his milkshake. I walked to the far side of the fire, sat on my log seat, laid the rifle across my knees and opened the bag. "Go ahead and get your lunch. Just be sure to stay seated over there."

He nodded toward my milkshake. "You do realize that is my shake, right? It's root beer."

"I think I'll drink this one." I watched him with half-lidded eyes.

He frowned. "It's root beer. I brought you strawberry. It's what you usually ask for."

"Root beer's fine. Matter of fact, I got a sudden thirst for a root beer shake. You drink the strawberry one."

He moved his shoulders a fraction as if to say *whatever*. "I like strawberry."

We ate without speaking. When I balled up the last wrapper and tossed it on the fire, Ted took a drink of his milkshake then said, "I talked to my dad about what you said."

"Yeah?"

"We talked for hours." He grinned. "Dad and I do that sometimes. Get started and don't know when to stop, I guess. Anyway, he said he never thought Ms. Hopewell hurt Ralph, not unless it was in self-defense. Said he'd heard too much good about her." A light blush pinked his cheeks. He inhaled and let it out slow. His eyes steady on mine, he said, "I had, too, but I guess I didn't really stop and think. I'm sorry about that."

I waved a dismissive hand. "Next time, stop and think." One brow raised, I asked, "Is that the reason you hustled up here? To apologize?"

"Not the only reason." He shifted on the log. "I was wondering if you could maybe use some help. Rebuilding. I phoned Cynthia last night and she said you're letting her help out, and I thought..." As his words drifted to silence, he ducked his eyes.

"You want to help?" I stared at him. A thread of steel in my words, I said, "Aretha and I don't need your pity, or your charity."

His attention refocused on me. "It isn't like that!"

"Then explain to me why you want to help."

"When Dad and I were talking I told him it wasn't right what happened to Ms. Hopewell's cabin. He told me that talk is cheap; that a man's actions define him. I want my actions to be the right kind, and that means I have to do what I feel is right." He squared his thin shoulders. "I think it's right to help a neighbor when they've had bad things happen. That is, if you'll let me?"

Narrowing my eyes suspiciously, I dropped my voice low. "None of this has anything whatsoever to do with Cynthia working with me, right?"

Ted's face blazed red. "What do you mean?"

I chuckled. "I saw you eyeing her yesterday."

Indignantly, he frowned at me. "I would offer to help even if Cynthia wasn't going to be around."

"Smooth out your feathers, Ted. I'm just messing with you. To tell the truth, I may not be able to continue this project."

"Why not?"

I pointed an accusing finger at the book on the ground. "I'm handy with my hands and can build stuff, but I've never built a house and that...that book is *not* helpful!"

A grin split Ted's face. "Oh, are you ever in luck. My dad's a contractor. He built houses until he hurt his back a couple of years ago. And, I," he puffed out his chest and poked himself with a thumb, "worked every summer with him. Before Dad hurt himself, he was going to start a second crew after I graduated and let me ramrod it."

I scrunched my face in mock severity. "I pay in cups of coffee and meals."

"As long as the coffee is hot, you've got a deal."

Chapter 15

Cynthia drove in a few minutes after Ted showed up Wednesday morning. Within moments, my quiet had been invaded by a chattering horde of monkeys, complete with the screeching, which was solely Cynthia's doing. In fact, I'm not sure Ted got in two words. Finally, Cynthia came down to where I stood next to the fire and poured a cup of coffee. "What are we doing today, Jaz?"

Before I could answer, Ted blurted out with a huge grin, "We're going to start rebuilding Ms. Hopewell's cabin."

"We are?" She swung around beaming at him then turned all of that unfathomable good cheer on me.

I grunted and kept drinking my coffee.

"Yeah, we really are." Ted's smile reached up and lit his eyes. "Come on, I'll show you where we're building it. This is so awesome."

Feeling beyond old, I sat there, but turned around so I could watch the two of them. Ted's voice carried on the clear air, his hands waving as he explained where the door would eventually go, how many windows there would be, and where we'd place them. The young man had listened to, and remembered, everything we had discussed.

Wistfulness wrapped around me like a familiar blanket. Had I ever been so young?

I tossed the dregs of my coffee in the fire, set the cup next to the log, and headed over to the work site. For a young man who'd been fired from his job for serving me, he was certainly gung-ho. A chill of foreboding slithered over me. *I don't know if I can stand the guilt if William hurts or kills one of them.* Right then and there, if I hadn't needed the help, I would have chased them off.

A heavy weight settled on my shoulders as I stopped on the far side of the potential cabin site. "Hey, you two, we've got to talk." The seriousness in my voice flooded over their smiles and enthusiasms, washing both away. They looked at me, slight frowns tugged at their eyebrows and pulled their lips tight.

Run or Die

"William and his friends aren't playing checkers with Aretha and me. Have you considered that hanging out with me could make you a target?"

They glanced at each other like they had a secret language that didn't require words. Maybe they did. The language of young people who hadn't grown up in the poor part of a big city, or with the Klan appearing in the dead of night.

Ted shrugged. Cynthia, of course, vocalized. "Granddad and I talked about that possibility before I showed up the first time."

"And?" I arched a brow at her, the one with the silver ring through it.

"Granddad said if something's worth doing, it's worth taking a risk."

When she didn't say anything else, I focused my attention on Ted. "What about you?"

He kicked at a lump of mud. "My dad says a man has to stand up for what he thinks is right, no matter what happens."

In a grim voice, I said, "Dead could be what happens. William didn't mind murdering one of his own posse."

Cynthia's mouth turned down at the corners. A bit of the color leached out of Ted's face.

I swiveled my eyes to her. "Well?" I demanded. "Did you and your grandfather factor that possibility into the equation?" I hooked a clump of wayward hair behind one ear. "Listen, you guys, there isn't any shame in leaving before you get sucked into something dangerous. This *really* isn't your fight."

He locked eyes with me, but once again it was Cynthia who spoke. "You won't need to find a third hammer. Ted brought his own." She turned and started for the truck and the supplies.

The next day, when Cynthia stepped out of her granddad's truck lugging a JVC RV NB70 Kaboom, I could feel myself drooling. "Hope you brought some decent music." I yelled from beside the fire pit.

She snagged a piece of scrap lumber and headed my way. Board placed on the ground, she set the portable music player on it to keep it out of the slush. "I brought one of my USB keys, the one that has a lot of different kinds of music. Granddad said he's never seen anyone who loved music, any music, like I do."

Ted pulled up and parked his raggedy truck next to the Avalanche, hopped out, and rushed over to the fire pit. "Girl, that's some music box! I've wanted one of those JVCs for months. Haven't quite saved up the three hundred plus, though." He grabbed a cup from the makeshift table, a piece of plywood set on a couple of log rounds. "Can I bring some music tomorrow? I have a USB with Hunter Hayes and Josh Turner."

Cynthia rolled her eyes. "Oh, puhleeze. Josh Turner?" She filled a cup and sat next to me on another alder round.

"What've you got?" Ted stayed standing as he took a drink of coffee.

"Good songs. Things like 'Stronger' by Kelly Clarkson and 'Blown Away' by Adele."

"Girly stuff." He snorted.

"Okay, you two." I tossed the grounds in the bottom of my cup on the fire where they sizzled. "I don't care what we listen to as long as it doesn't slam women. Be nice, and take turns. Let's get to work."

By the end of the week, we'd framed in a one-room cabin while listening to everything from a piano concerto to Spanish Guitar to Faith Hill to Justin Moore to "Jumpin' Jack Flash" by the Rolling Stones. That one had surprised me. I guess I didn't expect someone like Cynthia to like the old music. Apparently, I was less immune to thinking in stereotype than I thought.

Ted's dad had taught his son well. I learned a lot. When we knocked off Friday, I handed Ted some money. "We need tin for the roof."

His eyes lit up. "You want me to pick it up? Have you phoned in your order?"

"You know what you're doing, heck of a lot more than I do. Why don't you choose it?" I wrote down the length and width of the area to be covered. "Maybe you and your dad could figure out how many sheets we'll need. That is if you don't mind getting it and hauling it up here next Monday?"

A smile split his face. He straightened his shoulders, going for the more mature look.

I nearly laughed out loud, but turned it into a cough at the last second.

Run or Die

"There's a whole range of colors. You'll need to tell me which one you want. There's the standard red, blue, beige, browns. I'd suggest staying away from the dark ones since there aren't any trees shading the cabin and dark colors absorb heat. In the summer that could make the cabin pretty warm."

"Something neutral and not hugely expensive."

The weekend flew past. Monday sported pale blue skies and a golden sun warming the air. I hoped it stayed that way until we got the roof on.

Ted's truck chugged in with Cynthia's Avalanche close behind. Dove gray tin hung out over the top of Ted's tailgate. He parked and got out with brown paper bags in hand. He lifted his arm, grinning. "Breakfast is served."

With a chin tilt towards the logs around the campfire, I said, "Coffee's on. Might as well take time to eat."

He set the bags on our makeshift table then turned and handed me an invoice and change. Frowning, I said, "Hey, I think you gave me back too much."

He wagged his head. "Nope, Mr. Oldson called Dad and asked if he could put the tin under Dad's account. Dad said sure."

"How's that translate to money in my hand?"

Cynthia reached into a bag and pulled out a breakfast sandwich. Perched on an alder round, she listened.

Ted grabbed a sandwich for himself before handing me the bag. He poured coffee into Cynthia's usual cup, handed it to her, then poured himself a cup. Settled on the log next to her, he unwrapped his sandwich. "Contractor's discount."

"Oldson know it was for Aretha and me?"

"Yep. I told him."

"Why'd he do it then?" My words escaped sharper than I'd intended.

He washed the bite of sandwich down with a swallow of coffee before he looked at me. "Not everyone around here is a butt hole, just because some folks are. And not everyone is out to get you."

His words woke up a memory of something very similar that I had said to Aretha. "Sorry. Guess I'm stuffing everyone into the same shoebox."

"'S okay."

Cynthia twisted so she could flick a switch on the boom box behind her.

As I unwrapped my sandwich, I asked, "What kind of music do you call that?"

Cynthia smiled. "Jazz organ."

"Never heard of it." I took a big bite and washed it down with hot coffee.

She giggled. "I don't believe it. I actually know about something that you don't."

Tugging at my eyebrow ring, I said, "I'm sure you know lots of stuff that I don't. Like Miriam used to tell me, don't sell yourself short."

"Who's Miriam? Your sister?" Ted asked around a mouthful of bacon and egg on pretzel bread.

"Miriam was my foster mother." It felt natural to share memories of her with these two. "Eat up. We've got enough work for four women to do."

"Yeah, and Dad said the forecast is more snow heading our way on Wednesday." Ted brushed his hands off and headed for the building site.

The tin slipped onto the roof beams like a new skin, all tight and perfect. By late Tuesday afternoon, we had the skeleton of the cabin roofed. "Hey, guys, this looks like a good stopping point to me."

"Same time tomorrow?" Cynthia asked as she helped put away the tools.

I shook my head. "Not with the snow that's being predicted, and," I pointed a finger up at the gathering clouds, "real likely to happen. Besides, I need to have Ted bring in some plywood sheets for the sides. Take tomorrow off, and, if we don't get hit with a blizzard, we'll resume Thursday, snow or shine."

Ted handed Cynthia the last hammer. As she put it in the toolbox in the back of the Avalanche, he asked, "Hey, want to have dinner with me and my dad then hit a movie in town?"

"I can't go to town looking like this." Cynthia's voice reflected her horror at the thought.

Run or Die

"I could follow you up to your granddad's and wait for you. Don't need to dress up."

I never heard the conclusion since they headed for their vehicles. I found myself smiling, though, remembering the times I had followed Alicia home and waited for her to get dressed. I hoped Ted was a patient young man.

An hour and a half later, restless and hungry for something more substantial than a sandwich, I dressed in clean jeans and shirt. A night in a motel with all the hot water I wanted sounded like heaven to me. I tossed my backpack with clean clothes and essentials on the back seat of the Volkswagen then laid the rifle on top, within easy reach.

Headed down the hill, I tapped the steering wheel to the rhythm in my head and bellowed out the lyrics to a song my mother used to sing as I rounded the last curve in Washboard Road before getting onto the main two-lane highway. That's when I saw them. What they ultimately meant to do, I will never know. Did William and his posse intend to beat Ted to death then rape Cynthia? Whatever they had planned, it couldn't have been good, not with how Nick pinned Ted up against the front fender of his own truck. William planted himself and hauled back his fist. Sam Haden had one of Cynthia's arms cranked up between her shoulders, but that didn't stop her from kicking him in the knee.

The V-dub barely stopped before I jumped the clutch and bailed out, rifle in hand. At the same time, Cynthia broke loose and leaped on William's back.

I love rifles. When you jack a shell in the chamber, if you're close enough, everyone hears it. "Stop!"

Cynthia yanked William's greasy hair and kicked his leg before she backed off, keeping herself clear of the line of fire.

"Let him go." I swung the muzzle toward Nick.

"You can't shoot. You'll hit him," Nick smirked.

"Want to bet your life on that, Nicky boy? Better check my line of fire before you hand over your money."

His smirk faded, replaced by an ugly look, lip curled away from his teeth like some kind of rabid animal. "You ain't got the balls to shoot me."

Aya Walksfar

"No, I don't have the balls to shoot you, but I certainly have the tits to do it."

William wiped his hands on his pants and backed toward his Jeep. "Let 'im go, Nick."

Nick stepped away. Ted slid down the truck's side, and landed on his butt in the muddy slush. Cynthia hurried over to him.

William sneered as they climbed into his Jeep. "We ain't done with you and your little friends, bitch. Ya'll better be looking over your shoulders from now on."

"Yeah, well, *boys,*" I waved a dismissive hand at them. "Next time you gang up on somebody make sure it's me and not some guy who isn't even a part of this feud. That is, if you've got the *balls* to face me."

William slammed his door and gunned his Jeep, fishtailing from the loose gravel road to the asphalt, two-lane highway. Mud and slush spit up from his knobby tires and rattled against the front of Ted's truck. I watched the Jeep, kept the rifle ready until his taillights disappeared into the early evening dusk before I strode over to Ted.

Hunkered on my heels, I examined Ted's battered face in the fading light. "Anything broken?"

"Not...sure. Help...me up."

I got one of his arms over my shoulder while Cynthia draped his other arm over her shoulder. We eased to our feet on the count of three. Ted's face paled and a pained grunt tore from behind clenched teeth. "Bet you have a couple of cracked ribs." I wanted to chase down those guys and stomp them!

He spit a gob of red mucus on the ground. "Naw...probably just...bruised. Help me...in and...I'll drive home."

"Seriously!" Cynthia snapped. "We'll help you in all right, in the passenger seat, and I'll drive you to the hospital in Willits."

On the way to Willits, I phoned Ted's father. Ted hadn't yet come out of x-ray when his father arrived. Stan Sullivan stood about five-ten, not physically a big man, yet his presence filled the emergency room, though he entered it clinging to a walker. When Ted said his father had hurt his back, I'd thought a back brace, a

Run or Die

doctor's order not to lift anything over ten pounds, that kind of situation. I had not envisioned a walker and one leg that dragged.

Stan thump-stepped across the gray tile floor and the sound reminded me of Grandma Pearl with her walker. I briefly wondered what she'd have to say about all of this then I released the speculation in favor of concentrating on the present situation.

Stan held out a callused hand. "You must be Jaz. Ted's talked a lot about you."

I grabbed his hand like a life preserver. I hoped he hadn't noticed my staring. Heat climbed up my neck.

He gave me a tired smile. "Don't worry. Everyone stares at first. I've gotten used to it." Then in a brisk tone, he asked, "How is Ted? Tell me what happened."

"Don't you want to wait until your wife gets in here?" I glanced over his shoulder toward the door.

"She won't be coming. She died a year and a half ago from a stroke."

"I'm batting a hundred tonight, aren't I? I'm sorry, but Ted never talked about his mom. I just thought...well, that it was a guy thing."

"Reasonable assumption. No need to apologize."

I motioned to Cynthia on the far side of the room. She tossed the magazine she'd been leafing through on a table full of old magazines then headed over. I waited until she got there.

"Mr. Sullivan, I'm sorry about Ted." Tears puddled in her eyes.

He patted her shoulder, but didn't offer any empty platitudes. "Tell me what happened."

In spite of her usual verbosity, Cynthia gave a concise report of the attack, concluding with, "If Jaz hadn't come along I don't know what would've happened."

In my peripheral vision, I noticed the double doors labeled "No Admittance" swing open. A doctor in a white lab coat stepped out and headed our way. "Stan," he reached a hand out when he drew close.

Stan shook his hand. "Roy, how's the wife and baby?"

I searched Stan's face. Unlike so many people, the question felt sincere as he waited quietly for the answer.

Dr. Roy Ingersol beamed a smile. "That little rug rat's already pulling herself up and toddling a couple of steps. Lorelei is so thrilled you'd think she personally invented babies."

Briefly, good humor sparkled in Stan's eyes. "Well, she did have a lot to do with the creation of that one. That's really great news. You two waited long enough."

"Thanks." The smile dropped from the doctor's face. "First let me say Ted's not badly injured, nothing permanent."

Relief flooded Stan's face as tension whooshed out of his body. "That's...," he paused then started again. "That's real good to hear, Roy."

I waited until the doctor completed his report. "He's asleep right now, Stan. I gave him a good dose of painkillers. Sometimes I think bruised ribs hurt worse than cracked ones. We'll see how he does tonight then re-evaluate his case tomorrow. We should know by morning rounds when he'll likely be able to go home."

Report delivered, Dr. Ingersol hustled through the swinging doors. I turned to Stan. "I know you're anxious to see Ted even if he is asleep, so I won't take long to say this. Don't let Ted come back up on the hill. It's too dangerous." I pivoted to face Cynthia. "That goes for you, too, young lady. Stay away from Aretha's place, and don't go anywhere by yourself for a while. Next time William catches up with you could end a lot worse."

Defiance lit her blue eyes as she lifted her chin. "I'm no quitter, Jaz. Neither is Ted." With her back ramrod straight she marched away.

A gentle smile spread across Stan's face. "Jaz, you can't assume responsibility for everyone. Only for yourself. I'm proud of the decision those two kids made, and will obviously continue to make. They know the score. You have to give them the respect of accepting their decision." He laid a fatherly hand on my shoulder. My eyes burned and I blinked rapidly. "We'll talk some more later. Right now I need to look in on my son."

I watched as he shuffled past me and down the beige hall.

Chapter 16

Sheriff Daly caught up with me at Mother Earth's Bounty. I finished mopping up gravy with a bite of homemade sourdough bread. He slid into the other side of the booth and two seconds later Axel materialized wielding a pot, a cup, and a menu. He'd dialed his hostility down several notches. Daly waved away the menu while I wondered what had modified Axel's feelings toward the sheriff. He hadn't cut Aretha lose.

Daly sipped the black brew while he studied me. "Stan Sullivan filed a complaint an hour ago. Said William and Nick beat up his son."

I forked up the last bit of meatloaf before I bothered to look up from my plate.

"I just came from talking to William and Nick. They claim they saw Ted leaning against his truck, and stopped to make sure he was okay. They saw he was beat up and were going to offer to take him to the hospital when you arrived and started waving a rifle at them." His mouth flattened in a grim line. "What's your story, Jaz?"

Lounging on the booth seat, one hand wrapped around my coffee cup, lips pursed, I met Daly's eyes. "Why ask me? So you can disregard everything I say like you did with Aretha? If you want to arrest me, go for it."

Daly rubbed his eyes. "I am trying to do a tough job here. How about cutting me some slack?"

I lunged forward, and nearly spilled my coffee. "Cut you some slack?" I whispered furiously. "Give me a break, Sheriff! I'm sleeping outside in freezing weather, and Aretha faces a possible prison sentence! Don't look for sympathy from me." Nostrils flared, my face twisted into an angry mask.

He ran a hand along his jaw, eyes lowered to the tabletop. When he looked at me again, I noticed how bloodshot his eyes appeared, like he'd been getting as much sleep as me. "Damn it, Jaz," his voice held a bone weariness I recognized from my days after Alicia's death. "I believe in Aretha's innocence, but the law has my hands tied!" Frustration creased lines around his mouth and furrowed his forehead. He held my eyes and braced his arms on the table. "Listen, I don't want your sympathy. I simply want the truth about what happened."

Deliberately, I relaxed my fisted hands and moved away from him. I drank the rest of my coffee and set the cup down harder than necessary. The crack against the saucer attracted the attention of several other customers. "Okay, you want the truth. Here it is, for whatever it's worth." Succinctly, I recounted the events.

"Pretty much what Cynthia McKenna said. I haven't talked with Ted yet. He's out on painkillers until tomorrow morning." He shoved his nearly-full cup of coffee aside and got up. "Guess I'll pick up those men and charge them. Be aware, though, that they'll be out on bond within the next day or so. Both of their folks have money."

That evening I visited Aretha at Ms. Winters' place then headed for the farm as dusky dark edged the horizon. A mile north of Willits, I glanced in my rearview mirror. A vehicle trailed along behind me a few car lengths back. From the height of the headlights, it had to be a truck. With no other cars on the highway, his hanging back rang all my alarms. I slowed to ten miles under the speed limit, but he maintained the distance between us. A car passed us heading toward Willits. In the flash of their headlights, I recognized the truck. Jacked up a ridiculous amount and with antennae sprouted across the top of the cab, I couldn't mistake it. "Great, just great! Deputy Dumbass." Headed in the same direction or tailing me? I picked my speed up to the posted fifty-five.

The closer I got to Washboard Road, the closer the truck came until he rode my bumper. When I slowed to turn off the highway, the Ford blasted past, narrowly missing the Volkswagen's rear quarter panel. The deputy's beefy hand shot out of his window in the one-finger salute.

Even with my string of cans alarm rigged across the cave entrance and the loaded rifle next to my bedroll, I woke up at every change in the sound of the wind moaning through the crooked entry.

Run or Die

Sleeping in the cave necessitated using an alarm clock. Monday morning when it screeched in my ear, I reached out and slapped it silent then burrowed deeper in my sleeping bag. I might've stayed there except my ears picked up every little sound and kept my body tense. I gave up and crawled out of the warm covers, shivering in the brisk air. My teeth chattered from the cold, so I jogged up the hill to the banked campfire.

By the time I downed my second cup of coffee, the sun streaked the canvas of the eastern sky with fingers of gold and pink, a big kid playing with finger paints. The shadows of the passing night grasped the piles of melting snow in defiance of the approaching day.

The diesel engine of the truck idling down the road sounded too smooth to be Ted's, and Cynthia's Avalanche was gas-powered. Déjà vu hit me as I set the cup on the ground, snatched up the rifle, and stood. I was so done with running and hiding.

The rising sun reflected off the windshield, obscuring everything except that there were two of them. When they stepped out of the truck, I recognized the body shapes and the distinctive limp. Ted and Stan walked around the back of their rig and lifted out a toolbox. I propped the rifle against the log and headed their way to talk sense into those two fools.

"What are you guys doing up here?"

Startled, Stan nearly dropped his end of the toolbox. Ted, having more experience with my sudden appearances, didn't flinch. "Hey, Jaz, the plywood's in the back. Check it out. I think it's what you told me to get."

I waved away Ted's concern with one hand. "I'm sure it's fine. What are you guys doing up here? I could've arranged someone to deliver the lumber. I told your father at the hospital to keep you away from here. What about your ribs? I don't think the doctor would approve of you working construction yet."

"Let's set it here for a minute, Son." Stan twisted his arms around, loosening his shoulders as he faced me. "The Sullivans don't start things unless they intend to finish them, but to set your mind at ease, Dr. Ingersol said Ted could work, just to take it easy and if he got too sore to let the doctor know."

I spread my arms out in exasperation. "You're painting targets on your backs."

He shrugged. "That may be so, but a man has to do what he feels is right. I'll be coming with Ted, cut down some of the risk from William and his gang." He bent and grasped the toolbox handle. "Come on, let's haul this closer to the job."

Tagging behind them, I tried again. "This isn't your fight."

They set the toolbox down. Stan tilted his head at me. "Where's the coffee? An employee on a job has the right to expect decent coffee to be brewing at all times. Ted assured me that you met that employer requirement." A grin crinkled the corners of his sky-blue eyes. In his face I could see Ted twenty years down the line. I only hoped he didn't get killed before he got there.

I jerked my chin toward the percolator I'd set on a flat rock close to the campfire. "Made a fresh pot a little while ago." As I picked my way to the campfire, I tried again. "Look, I appreciate what you're trying to do, but this isn't your fight, Stan. Get out of the middle before either you or your son get badly hurt, or maybe dead."

Stan limped to the fire pit. "Hey, Son, bring those cups out of the truck, please." He turned back to face me. "Do you think I'm not taking your warning, or the danger, seriously?"

I shrugged, uncomfortable under his steady gaze. "I'm worried that you aren't. These men have come up here in an attempt to kill Aretha and me, not once but twice."

He pursed his lips then said, "I am now aware of the severity of the attacks on you and Ms. Hopewell. To be honest, I don't attend the monthly joint town meeting and I'm a bit of a hermit. It wasn't until Ted talked to me that I realized how badly things had escalated." He paused. "The risk does scare me, Jaz, but not taking that risk would scare me more. Do you understand?"

"Crazy as it sounds, yeah, I understand that."

By the time I'd poured coffee for the men and refilled my cup, Cynthia's Avalanche eased in next to Stan's truck. "Crap! Another hard head!"

Run or Die

A grin stretched Ted's mouth and he jogged over to meet her.

Stan eased down on an alder round and stretched out his bad leg.

"Where's your walker?"

"In the truck. I don't always need it. Later today, when my leg starts getting tired, I'll need to use it." He sipped his coffee, his big hands cradling the cup. "Listen, Jaz, I really do understand that you're trying to protect us, to keep us out of harm's way. I appreciate that.

"You know, since the accident I read a lot. Not long ago I read an account of the Holocaust by a minister from the Warsaw Ghetto. I don't remember what he said, word-for-word, but this is the gist of it. He said that when the Nazis came for the Jews, he stood aside and said nothing. He wasn't Jewish. When the Nazis came for the blacks, again he stood aside and said nothing. He was white. When they came for the Catholics and the Gypsies, again he stood silently aside. When they put pink triangles on the homosexuals, he never protested." Stan looked at me as he finished.

"He said that when the Nazi came for him, there was no one left to protest." His gaze drifted toward the meadow. In a thoughtful voice he said, "There are some fights, Jaz, in which there can be no fence-sitters." He swung his gaze toward me. "Even if I were inclined to be one." In a soft voice that I could barely hear, he added, "I'm just sorry it took so long for me to show up."

By Friday, the cabin had plywood siding. As Stan and Ted packed up their tools, Stan caught my attention. "How about you ladies spending the weekend with us? I have a couple of guest rooms and a big screen television. We can pick up some movies on the way home. And I cook a real mean breakfast omelet."

I wagged my head in disbelief at him. "Are you *trying* to get killed?"

Ted turned pleading eyes on me. "Come on, Jaz. Please? "

"I stay some weekends at the Sleepy Hollow Motel in Willits. It's close to where Aretha's staying, so I can check in with her. There's really no need to put you guys to any trouble."

Cynthia's eyes sparkled as she joined in. "If you stay then Granddad won't object to me staying." She put her hands together in the classic prayer position then tucked them under her chin. "Say you will. Please, please, please?"

Mischief glittered in Ted's eyes. "I'll make the popcorn."

With everything that's been going on, how in creation did Ted remember me mentioning how much I liked popcorn? I threw my hands up, surrendering. "That does it! Can't resist movies and popcorn. It would be un-American!"

The Sullivan house was as comfortable and unassuming as Stan Sullivan. Friday and Saturday passed in a pleasant blur. I slept without once waking.

Sunday dawned clear and cold. Before heading home, I swung by Ms. Winters' to check in with Aretha. Sheriff Daly's truck sat next to the black Mercedes. I slipped the V-dub in on the other side of the Beemer. Someone must've heard me coming because the maid, Tisha, swung the door open before I pressed the doorbell.

In a proper maid's uniform of crisp black and white, she inclined her head. "Nice to see you again, Ms. Wheeler. Ms. Hopewell is in the kitchen with Ms. Winters and Sheriff Daly."

"Thanks." Uncomfortable with the idea of servants, I quickly slipped past her before she could offer to show me in.

A large pot of something cooked on the stove while Ms. Winters stirred it. Aretha and Daly sat close together at the kitchen table, drinking coffee. The sheriff said something I couldn't hear. Aretha threw her head back and laughed. That golden laughter rippled out from the space between them and filled the room. They both looked up as I stepped through the doorway.

A smile creased Daly's cheeks, dark with a five o'clock shadow. Aretha's eyes sparkled, the warm caramel skin of her face flushed, one hand rested lightly on his forearm.

A big bucket of mad dumped all over me. The nights of freezing my butt off, the lack of restful sleep, the constant looking over my shoulder, it all crashed over me in a huge wave. I strode over to the table. "What're you doing sitting here sucking up coffee and telling jokes when you should be out there," I pointed a hand that trembled with anger, "investigating Ralph's murder?"

"Jaz!" Aretha rose partway off her seat, her shocked voice censored my tone.

Never taking my eyes off of Daly, I growled, "He needs to be gathering evidence on Ralph's real killer, not sitting here cuddling up with the woman he arrested for Ralph's murder." I swiveled my eyes to her. "What is *wrong* with you? This...this *sheriff*," I imbued the title with as much contempt as I could squeeze from my anger, "hasn't done anything to help you, yet here you are acting like he's your best friend! Do you *want* to spend the rest of your life behind bars?"

Before she could speak, Ms. Winters walked over and stood in front of me. Chin lifted, she gazed down her nose at me. "*That* is enough. This is *my* house and you *will* respect folks who are sitting at *my* table, or *you* can leave."

I whirled to face her. "I'm leaving all right. At least, *I* know what my priorities need to be." The weight of the heavy oak front door made slamming it impossible. I gave it a good try anyhow.

Fuming, I failed to watch my back trail on the road between Willits and Elmsworth, and didn't even notice Deputy Dumbass' pickup truck until I was a few miles from Washboard Road. I floor-boarded the V-dub, glad that the sanding trucks had made a recent pass along the highway. The little car topped out at sixty-five, engine screaming. The pickup rode my bumper, probably not even grunting. Two big silhouettes took up the cab of the truck.

If I'd been thinking clearly, I would have shot past Washboard Road. Would have tried to make it to some populated, public spot, but like any hunted animal I headed for my burrow.

The driver played cat and mouse all the way up the hill, closing in on me then falling back. *Herding me to a particular spot?* A shiver ran over me, and raised goose bumps on my arms. Adrenaline dried out my mouth. My heart pounded a frantic rhythm. *Can't stop and try to get to the rifle. They'll be on top of me before I can grab it. What possessed me to put the rifle on the back seat?*

Aya Walksfar

The higher we raced up the hill, the worse the road became. The tires shuddered with the washboard effect of the ripples that ran across the pitted dirt surface. The front of the little car jigged. I fought as the steering wheel vibrated and wretched back and forth beneath my iron-tight grip. We entered the curve of Buzzard's Peak. The pickup popped into the Volkswagen's bumper.

The car skidded. I turned into the skid and let off the gas, then punched the accelerator to straighten back out. My forearm ached from my hand clenching the steering wheel. I glanced into the rearview mirror. The truck closed in again. *Who's riding shotgun?* The thought flashed through my mind as the peak of the curve loomed.

Cynthia had shown me the turn off for her granddad's place. *If I can make it five more miles I'll head for the McKenna place.*

The pickup slammed into the V-dub as I entered the outside curve where the mountain dropped away. Even under that punishing assault, I might have maintained control if the rear tire hadn't blown. The small car fishtailed wildly then careened over the soft edge.

The car flew for a moment that stretched to eternity then slammed to the ground. My head whipped forward, smacked the steering wheel then back, banging into the seat's headrest. Tops of tall brown grass poked up from the snow and whipped past the windshield as I wrestled the wheel.

I spotted the rock jutting sharply up on the right side. Desperately, I wretched the wheel to the left. I don't think I altered my course one iota. I was on a ski slope without any ski poles.

The right front tire popped up and over the rock. The car tilted sharply. When the back wheel hit the rock, what little grip the car might have had on the snowy hillside skidded away. The V-dub flipped onto the driver's side and continued rocketing down the hill. Held in by the seatbelt, I watched as the car raced toward a black boulder. I don't recall smashing into it.

***

Cold, so cold. Can't see! Panic surged through my chest, lashing my heart into a thundering gallop. I struggled to get free. Something bound my left arm against my side. I couldn't feel my legs. A hand touched my cheek. I flailed with my right hand and smacked into flesh.

A deep grunt sounded. The hand retreated. "Now, lassie, I mean ye no harm."

There was a soothing quality about the voice. "I...I can't...can't see." My lungs refused to pull in a full breath. I panted, short and hard like a dog run too far in the heat of the day.

"Easy there, lassie. Take a deep breath and hold it for a minute."

I yanked at my left arm, squirming.

"Now there, ye need to be still. Ye've gotten yerself a nasty gash on the forehead."

I heard the distinctive click of a flashlight. "It's night and the blood's stuck yer eyes shut, that's why ye can't see. If ye will hold still, I will run up and get some water and mayhap I can unstick yer eyes. Will ye hold still while I am gone, lassie?"

"Yes," I gasped out.

It seemed like forever before I heard the crunch of frozen snow as my rescuer slid back down to me. The gurgle of water pouring from a bottle sounded loud. At the touch of a soft cloth against my eyes, it hurt so bad that I jerked my face to the side.

"Be still, lassie. I will try to be gentle."

I fought not to move. At last, I could open one eye a slit. A dark figure hulked in front of the Volkswagen. The missing windshield allowed an arm to reach toward me.

I cringed away. "Who...who are you?" A buzzing in my ears nearly drowned out the soft voice. A black hole sucked at my consciousness. The hulk faded in and out. I caught a few words.

"Fergus McKenna. I've...the ambulance... And..."

Losing the fight, I slid into the black hole.

***

Aya Walksfar

Vision restricted to a tiny slit, I peered up at fluorescent ceiling fixtures flashing past. Distantly, I felt vibrations tingle along my back, but it didn't feel connected to me. The clack of wheels sounded like they echoed up from a tunnel. Pain radiated through my body and a groan worked its way free.

A voice floated over me, making sense in an abstracted way. "Ye in the ER at Willits Hospital. Ye going to be all right, lassie."

The next thing I saw was a man with wild, curly red hair and green eyes standing beside me and staring down. I licked my lips. "Where am I?"

A woman in a white uniform appeared beside the man. "What did she say?"

I tried to repeat my question, but the words tangled, became trapped in my chest.

The woman's lips moved while bushy, ginger-colored caterpillars crawled across the man's forehead.

Shadowy forms drifted in and out. Sounds blared then faded. I tried to move my arms. Nothing moved. Panic closed my throat. The black reached up and mercifully swallowed me.

***

Lips parched, head full of cotton, I woke up to the flashing screen of a television hovering above my feet. After a moment, in spite of the dimness of the room, I made out the wall shelf on which the television perched. Images chased silently across the screen. The low murmur I associated with hospitals shushed past the open door. Pale white light leaked in from the hall.

Tentatively, I turned my head. Slumped in a chair next to my narrow bed was a red-headed man. His full, flowing beard rested against his barrel chest. Work-roughened hands held a paperback book propped up on his flat stomach. Blue-jeaned legs stretched out of sight.

I know him. At least, I think I know him, but I can't remember his name. Frustrated, I blew out a breath.

Run or Die

His eyes flicked up as he dog-eared the page and laid the book on the bedside table. Incredibly green eyes studied me as he stood and moved closer. "I see ye've finally decided to wake up."

I nibbled at peeling lips. He wheeled a moveable hospital table closer then nudged a few melting ice chips into a plastic glass. Bent over, he spooned the refreshing, cold moisture into my mouth, one ice chip at a time until I finally croaked, "Enough."

"How..." My voice came out like a frog with a bad cold. I cleared my throat and tried again. "How long...?"

"Ye came in on Sunday evening and today is Monday morn."

I struggled to push myself up on the bed. He picked up a control switch and with a hum the bed slowly rose. When it was upright enough, he positioned a pillow behind my back, hiked his chair closer.

"Who are you?"

"Fergus McKenna, Cynthia's granddad." He must have noticed me licking my lips again because he spooned another sliver of ice into my mouth then returned the cup to the table. "Ye got awfie banged up."

I let my head drop against the bed. The ice melted in my mouth and the cold liquid trickled down my scratchy throat. "The pickup?"

He shook his shaggy head. "I saw the truck, lassie, but I was too far away to get a good look. Sheriff Daly asked me aboot that, too." He pressed the buzzer tied to the bed rail.

A young woman in a white uniform and with her long brown hair fixed in a high, bouncy ponytail whizzed in. Fergus stepped aside. She slapped a blood pressure cuff on one arm and a thermometer strip against my forehead. "Doctor's going to be pleased to see you awake, Ms. Wheeler." Blood pressure and temperature devices removed, she scribbled notes in the chart that hung off the foot of the bed. With a kindly look, she lowered the bed. "You should try to rest. Doctor will be in later for rounds. He'll answer any questions you have."

As soon as the nurse disappeared, Fergus returned to his chair. "Ye heard her, lassie. Go on to sleep. I'll be right here."

His assurance that he would be right there draped a blanket of comfort over my achy body. I closed my eyes.

When I opened my eyes again night had wrapped darkness around the world. The door to the corridor, halfway open, redirected the light so none of it shone on my bed. I heard voices in the hall, but couldn't make out their words. Someone had placed a hand towel over the shade of the bedside lamp to block its light from me. I shifted my eyes to the side and saw Fergus sitting in the chair, reading like he'd never moved. Maybe he hadn't.

"Could I have a sip of water, please?" My throat burned, but I could actually talk.

He dog-eared the page, laid the book aside and got up. The glass he brought over looked tiny in his big hand. I suspected that a lot of things appeared small next to him. The man must have stood over six feet tall and built like the proverbial brick outhouse. After a couple of sips of water, I turned my head. When he took the glass away, I asked, "What are you still doing here?"

"My turn to watch." With a slight shrug, he set the glass on the hospital table then slouched in the chair, legs spread.

Brows furrowed, I stared at him. "Your turn?"

He nodded. "Aye, the others, they took turns sitting with ye most of the day. I told them to go on home and get some rest. I'd watch over ye."

My eyes burned. I blinked hard several times then tried to swallow the lump in my throat. "I appreciate all of you watching out for me, but I'm okay now. You can go on home, or whatever."

The corners of his mouth turned up, the smile apparent in the tangle of a thick, full beard and mustache, as red as the wild curls on his head. "Dinnae work like that. Friends give a wee hand to each other."

"How can we be friends? I don't even know you. You're a stranger." I yawned and skooshed down in the bed, pulling the sheet up under my chin.

He chuckled, a warm chicken soup sound. "Strangers are friends that we have yet to meet. Now we've met, so we are friends."

Run or Die

Tuesday morning I woke up fully alert and feeling well-rested. Still had a banged-up body, but the pain was manageable. Sheriff Daly came in right before Doctor Randal. I told him Deputy Jones ran me off the road. He assured me that he'd look into it, but I didn't expect it to go anywhere. If he couldn't arrest William for burning Aretha's cabin, there wasn't any hope of him caging Deputy Dumbass.

Doctor Randal discharged me with a list of instructions that boiled down to: don't do anything strenuous for seven to ten days, don't fall, don't hit your head again, and call immediately if you experience vision problems, headaches, nausea, dizziness, loss of consciousness, or anything that worries you.

I nodded and obediently climbed into the wheelchair for the ride downstairs and outside to Ms. Winters' car. Aretha opened the front passenger door and steadied me as I climbed in, careful not to bang my bandaged ankle.

On the way to Ms. Winters' house, I stared out at the bright sunlight that poured over the shops and houses that flashed past. A concussion, a sprained ankle, two black eyes, and eight stitches in my forehead. I'd been lucky.

My good fortune did not appease Aretha's worry. Once I settled on the plush blue couch in Ms. Winters' spacious living room, Aretha paced like an agitated lioness. "You are not going back to the farm. I'll have someone trailer your bike to Willits then we'll find a way to ship it to you since, even if you weren't recovering from a concussion, it's the wrong season to undertake a long ride, especially headed north."

I held up one hand like a stop sign. "Whoa! Who said I was leaving?"

She whirled and faced me. "I did. I've talked it over with Folami and she's agreed to drive you to the airport tomorrow morning. We can purchase an online ticket for you. I'll contact Momma and have her meet you at the Sea-Tac airport."

"What are you going to tell Grandma Pearl about me coming back?"

"I'll say that I haven't rebuilt yet from the fire and since I'm staying with a friend it would be best if you returned to Seattle."

"Slick, Aretha. Everything you just said was true, up to a point. What makes you think I'll go along with this plan?" I rested against the softness, one arm flung along the back of the couch.

Hands propped on her hips, so much like Alicia when she was mad, Aretha stopped on the far side of the wood and glass coffee table. "You don't have a choice, Jaz. I don't want you back up on the farm."

I rolled one shoulder in a half shrug. "So I won't stay on the farm."

She pressed her lips so tightly together that vertical lines surrounded her mouth. "I won't lend you a vehicle and you can't ride the bike. Even if the weather was riding weather, you're in no shape to handle that bike on slick mud and ice."

I slid to the edge of the couch cushion, laid my hands on my knees, and looked up at her. "I have money, Aretha. You pay well and I never had any need to spend much of my wages or the money I carried down here with me. I can rent a car, or a truck for that matter. I can rent a motel room. I don't need your permission to be on the hill. You only own forty acres of it."

Her face crumpled and her lower lip quivered. "Why, Jaz? Why are you insisting on...on being stubborn? It's going to get you killed and..." A tear broke loose and slipped down her cheek. "It's going to get you killed. I don't want to attend your funeral." She spun and ran from the room. From somewhere deep in the house, a door slammed.

"Guess I messed that up." My shoulders slumped and I felt drained. Hardly enough energy to slide down on the couch cushion so I could drop my head back and close my eyes.

In a quiet voice, Ms. Winters asked, "Why *do* you insist on staying, Jaz?" It didn't sound like it mattered all that much to her one way or the other. Maybe that's why I pushed myself upright and scooted around to face her.

"Truthfully, Ms. Winters?"

She dipped her chin down once.

"Lots of reasons, I guess. I don't like being bullied, or chased off. I'm not the kind to run from trouble. Pride, that's part of it, but not the biggest part. Aretha's part of Alicia's family, and I know Alicia would want me to help her aunt. I guess that's the deal breaker."

"What's the third part, Jaz?"

"Why would you think there's a third part?" I eyed her warily.

She stared at me from under her brows like Grandma Pearl sometimes did to call my b.s.

I sighed and glanced away then back. "I care about her. I look at her and I see Alicia, but more than that, I see Aretha. I love her. Not sexually. She's an attractive woman, and almost a clone of Alicia in looks, but she's not Alicia. I love her because she's Aretha. I can't explain it any better than that." I climbed to my feet and grabbed the crutch propped against the couch arm. "If you don't mind, I think I'll go to bed."

The next morning rain splatted against the kitchen window and meandered down its face. The outside looked like I felt: washed out, gray, depressed and depressing. I hobbled into the kitchen tugged by the smell of coffee with chicory. As soon as I sat at the table, the maid hustled around getting my coffee and asking what I wanted for breakfast. "Nothing, thanks," I mumbled, hunched over my cup, inhaling the flavorful steam.

"She'll have the same as I do: eggs over easy, bacon crisp, and hashbrowns, Tisha." Ms. Winters said as she swept into the room.

"I thought she was your maid, not your cook." I nodded at the young black woman, scurrying around the kitchen.

Ms. Winters smiled as she poured herself a cup of coffee and settled at the head of the dining table. "Tisha is neither my maid nor my cook. She is not anybody's servant."

I lifted both brows and pointedly gazed at the young woman.

She laughed. "Tisha and I are participating in the oldest institution known to humankind."

I made a get-real face. "Prostitution? I didn't think you swung that way."

They both swayed their heads back and forth, obviously commiserating over the ignorance of this white woman as they laughed. Tisha's light, crystalline laughter mingled with the deep peals of Ms. Winters' laugh.

"Barter, Jaz. Tisha and I have arranged a satisfying barter. She attends college, all expenses paid by me; and I get to enjoy her wonderful household talents, which include excellent cooking skills."

Tisha turned partway from the stove and shot me a smile that reached all the way up to her golden brown eyes. "When I graduate, I'll attend medical school at Cornell University, thanks to Ms. Winters."

The older woman waved a hand as if shooing away an annoying gnat. "Judith owed me a favor, and you'll do her a favor by attending Cornell."

Tisha returned to her culinary duties as Aretha walked in. She bestowed a sour look on me before she sat next to her friend. "I suppose you haven't changed your mind?"

"'Fraid not." I eyed her as I sipped my coffee.

The sharp sound of fear lay like razor blades in her words, cutting her. "You could've been killed. I won't allow it!"

The calm, even voice didn't sound like mine as I said, "Unless you're a whole lot more powerful than I realize, I don't think your vote counts, Aretha. At least, not when it comes time for me to die."

She slapped the table and focused snapping eyes on me. "Don't joke about this!"

I heaved a breath and huffed it out. "I'm not joking, Aretha. I get that this is serious, but if it's my time to die, then I'll die." I shrugged. "I don't think it's my time. However, whether it is, or it isn't, I'm not running away. We've gone through this scenario before, remember? Well, let me assure you that I haven't changed my mind. *Especially* after being run over a hillside."

"What should have scared you into running, just angered you, didn't it?"

I dipped my head in agreement.

Aretha slumped, hands lying on the table, clasped so tight that the bones of her knuckles stood out. "You're going to get your fool self killed, girl."

Run or Die

    I rolled my head around on my shoulders, trying to roll out the ache of the accident. "Like I said, it's not my time. However, whether it is or isn't, I'm not going to spend a lot of energy thinking about the possibility of dying. I am not going to find a rabbit hole and sit quivering in it, either, waiting for someone to pull me out and slit my throat." I pinned her with my gaze. "Just get used to it. I'm here and I'm staying."

Chapter 17

Blackness. So dark I can't see the potholes along the road. Running, my foot plunges into one filled with icy water. I smash down, my hands scraped raw on the road, my knees jarred and aching.

A truck engine growls, low and dangerous, from close behind me. I can't see it! The sound bears down on me. Heart pounding, I scramble to my feet. Pain shoots up my leg. No time to rest. No time. I try to run, but can't put weight on my one leg. Hobbling, I glance over my shoulder. Why can't I see them?

Suddenly their voices split the darkness. "Burn, bitch, burn!"

I jerked up in bed, eyes wide, breath heaving.

Shouts blasted through the bedroom window. "Burn, bitch, burn!"

I leaped to my bare feet as yellow flames whooshed toward the night sky beyond the guest room window. For precious seconds, my night vision was stolen.

"Nooooo!" Aretha's tormented voice ricocheted up the stairs and along the hall.

I snatched the crutch leaning against the headboard of the bed and hobbled as fast as I could down the carpeted stairs. Flames from outside lit the living room in jagged tongues of gold and fiery red. Immobilized in front of the big window that opened out on the front lawn, Ms. Winters held a trembling Aretha wrapped in her arms. On the other side of Aretha, Tisha stood with a deer in the headlights look on her face. I froze on the bottom step.

Ms. Winters glanced my way. In an incredibly calm voice, she said, "Would you be so kind as to call the fire department and then notify the sheriff's office, Jazmine?"

The older woman's demeanor jolted me into action. I surveyed the scene outside of the window as I hopped-ran across the room and lunged for the phone beside Ms. Winters' favorite chair. A twenty-foot tall cross towered above the lawn. Yellow and blue flames swarmed it. I quickly made the call then hung up while the dispatcher still talked.

Run or Die

Anger engulfed me as hot as the flames devouring that obscene cross. Mouth a grim, hard line I thumped over to the coat closet. I yanked open the polished, maple burl door and snatched Aretha's rifle from the corner, thankful that Fergus had retrieved it from the wrecked Volkswagen. I checked the loads then hurried in a hobbling run to the front door.

Five bulky shadows stood behind the blazing cross. I racked a shell, doubting that they could hear it over the roar of the flames and their own vicious yells. With careful aim, I pulled the trigger. Since Aretha had left the farm, I had diligently practiced my shooting. The truck's left headlight shattered.

"What the fuck!" William yelled.

I racked a second shell, aimed and fired. This one drove through the driver's side door. The men scattered like cockroaches when a light switched on.

I racked a third shell, but by that time they had piled into the truck. The engine revved and tires squealed as they hauled out of there. Not wanting to chance the bullet penetrating the truck and killing one of them, I held my fire. When the evil, red eyes of their taillights disappeared down the street, I locked the front door and with pain shooting through my ankle, I gimped over to the couch.

Sheriff Daly arrived moments behind the first fire truck. Firemen efficiently doused the burning cross, blessing the night with normal darkness. After the firemen left, the five of us gathered around the kitchen table.

Daly carefully placed his hat on his knee then looked up, his eyes going from one face to the other. "Is there any way I can convince you ladies to leave town for a few days?"

Ms. Winters' dark eyes sparked. "This is my home, Sheriff Daly. I will not be run from my home simply because you cannot apprehend the perpetrators."

He leaned forward and folded his hands on the table. "Sometimes, retreat is the better part of valor. I am doing everything I can, but this situation is escalating too fast. I've contacted the FBI for assistance, but they can't send out an agent for at least two more days. They're stretched thin right now." He rubbed a hand on the back of his neck then dropped it to his lap. "Will you at least consider leaving until I get some assistance?"

"Sheriff Daly," Aretha perched rigidly on the edge of her chair, "if we leave it will only validate that what they are doing may not be right, but it certainly worked." Bags big enough to hold all my possessions perched beneath her bloodshot eyes. The fatigue in her face scared me. Running on empty, I didn't know how much longer Aretha could hold on before something inside her broke.

"Are we back to formality?" he asked softly.

"I think that might be best for now." She squared her shoulders.

"You can't think I had anything to do with that cross out there?" Hurt wove through his words like a cat weaving through a picket fence. Even I could hear it.

"I don't know what to think any more. But...no, I don't think you knew anything about the cross." Aretha rubbed fingertips back and forth across her forehead.

"Then why?"

She dropped her hand in her lap. "Jaz is right. I am a suspect in a murder you are investigating. We, Jaz and I, and now Ms. Winters, are being attacked with impunity. You are investigating our accusations. Meanwhile, accusations are being lodged against Jaz and me. This is a tangled web. You need to concentrate on your job, and I can't deal with...with anything else at this time. Please, if you have any questions ask them then leave." A chill distance crouched next to her words.

He held her eyes for a long moment then shifted his gaze to me. "You said you shot out the driver's side headlight and hit the door?"

"Yeah."

He shoved himself away from the table and slapped his hat on. "I'll run over to William's place and see if his truck is in plain sight. If it isn't, I'll ask Judge Connor to give me a search warrant." He lowered his eyes to his feet before lifting them to my face. "I am doing the best I can. If William's truck has a bullet-shattered headlight that should be enough to impound it and see if we can physically connect it to this latest crime and to the vehicular assault on you last week."

I rose, using a hand on the table to keep weight off my throbbing ankle. "Do you really think you'll be able to keep his truck impounded this time? I mean, even with Ralph's blood on his seat it only took two days and an expensive lawyer to get his truck back," I snarled.

He rubbed his forehead like all the troubles had gathered in an aching mass behind his eyes. "We have the evidence that we took from his truck, Jaz. But, no, I wasn't able to hang onto it that time. His attorney convinced the prosecuting attorney that the evidence was too circumstantial to warrant the impound."

I rammed a hand through my bedhead hair. "What's happening with the assault charges Stan and Ted lodged?"

"As you can see from tonight, William and Nick bailed out. Matter of fact, they got bailed out this morning. It might be a while before anything happens with the case. Criminal investigations take time."

I shoved my long hair away from my face, hooked it behind my ears. "Well, I hope we can get something to stick before him and his friends wind up killing someone else." I shuffled my feet, trying to find a comfortable way to stand. No such luck. "What's happening with the digital photos Aretha took?"

He propped his hand on his gun holster. "The local lab hasn't been able to enhance the photographs enough to do any good. I've sent them to the FBI lab to see if their people can pull something out. I'm hoping this cross burning will get us at the top of the list for assistance from the Bureau. The cross makes this a hate crime and that's really their territory."

"I've always heard that the local cops hated the FBI coming in and taking over." I cocked my head and studied him.

Daly barked a harsh laugh. "I'm not so proud that I would turn away help in getting a killer off the street. Be careful, ladies. I'll let you know as soon as I know anything."

We didn't speak until we heard the soft whoomp of the front door closing. I pivoted around to face Aretha. "Well, that was fun. What do you think we should do for an encore?"

Chapter 18

Friday afternoon Fergus McKenna hauled me up the hill since the V-dub was totaled. I felt bad about that. It'd been Aretha's car and she'd lent it to me. I shoved the guilt into my treasure chest of regrets and guilts and might-have-beens, determined to beat them off until some future time when staying alive didn't require my full attention.

He parked the Avalanche close to the partially finished cabin. The fact that the cabin still stood surprised me. Its bones rising up out of the gravesite of the original cabin made me think of the story of the phoenix, rising from the ashes. It wasn't even charred. Guess William and his posse were too busy getting things organized for the cross burning. After I slid out of the passenger seat, I poked my head back in. "Thanks for the lift, Fergus."

"Ah, lassie, it was nae trouble to lend ye a wee hand, but I dinnae think ye should be here alone."

"I'll be okay. I have Aretha's truck if I need to go somewhere. Remember to tell Cynthia and Ted that I'm taking a couple of weeks off. Going to hang out around here and just veg."

He shot me a suspicious look. "Ye widnae be thinking ye friends should stay away, now would ye, lassie?"

I made a production of rolling my eyes. "No. I just need some alone time. I'll give them a ring."

He gave me a brusque nod as I shut the truck door.

I watched his truck top the rise and disappear. My ankle throbbed a bit, but the heavy ace bandaging had met Dr. Randal's requirements for getting rid of the crutch. I made my slow way down the mushy hillside and ducked into the cave. Stretched out on my bedroll, I stared at the gray rock ceiling.

When I told Aretha I needed some alone time and she agreed to stay with Ms. Winters a huge weight fell off my chest. It was simply too dangerous for her to come back to the farm right now.

I wondered what would happen next, and if we would all survive it. Sleep overtook me while I wondered about that.

Run or Die

The next morning I woke to sunshine pouring into the cave. I'd forgotten the blanket door, and even the tin can alarm system. With a lot of grunting, I wiggled out of the sleeping bag. Once free of its confines, I stretched, happily surprised that the weather had warmed enough that my teeth didn't chatter. Maybe spring would show up someday soon.

Hope and the promise of hope, part of Step Two of the Alcoholic's Anonymous 12-Step Program. I felt a grin spill across my face. I hadn't thought of those words in years. Before the meth, and during one of Mom's longer-running attempts to sober up, she'd gone to AA meetings. She'd dropped me off at Al-Anon. The condition of sobriety hadn't stuck to Mom, but some of the AA/Al-Anon sayings had lodged in my brain. They popped out at the oddest moments.

My injuries had taken a lot out of me. Simply getting up the slope from the cave required several rest stops. I finally made it, rested on my log seat, then hobbled to my feet and stirred up the banked embers of the campfire. Birds twittered "loud enough to deafen a dead man," as my mother used to say. That thought stopped me in my footsteps.

These sayings, gifts from my mother, like many of my insights into myself. Gifts. All gifts from her. It had been a long time since I'd given thought to what my mother gave me, those intangibles like tenacity and pride. Maybe I'd been too involved in tallying up her offenses.

She'd been a kid of sixteen when she gave birth, uneducated, unskilled. She told me once that she couldn't find legitimate work, at least nothing that would take care of her and me. Since then I'd had reason to understand what she said.

She'd told me her story one night when she'd been too drunk to evade my questions. When she turned twenty-one, she'd thought she had it made, she could quit the streets and get a real job, a legit job. After a week of being turned down for no experience and no skills, she made one last stop: a bar. The bartender, a big burly man, laughed in her face, told her he had no use for inexperienced children. A man two stools down from where she sat with her head bowed in defeat ordered a burger, fries, and a coke for her then scooted his drink along the bar to the empty stool beside her.

After she ate and they'd talked a little, he led her out to his car. Parked in a dirty, garbage-strewn alley, he'd taken her in the back seat of his Lincoln. He dropped her off three streets from the cramped, basement room where we lived with a full stomach and enough money for rent and food.

That's when she accepted life on life's terms. Men liked the young girl who stood on the corner of Broadway and Denny. But, they weren't all kind. And certainly all of them were not gentle. I recalled too many times when she crawled home beaten up, stabbed in the side once, jaw broken another time, a dislocated shoulder when she'd fought a man who thought he could take by violence what other men paid for.

I stared down the hill as the small herd of two does, three fawns, and a buck strutted from the trees. Once I asked my mother why she hadn't put me up for adoption.

She ruffled my hair. "You're not a puppy to be given away." She looked away and added, "I...I wanted to do right, by you." In a whisper, she mumbled, "But I guess I failed."

It had been a long time since I'd recalled that conversation with my mother. Now, I carefully built the fire and put the aluminum coffeepot on the edge of it. It rested on some flat rocks I'd placed there for that purpose. Eyes on the wet ground, I sat on the damp alder round that I favored for my seat.

Yes, my mother had been a drunk and a drug addict; yes, she sometimes lost it and beat the crap out of me; those other times, the good memories, I had shoved to one side and denigrated as if only the bad times counted. As the strengthening March sun wrapped loving arms around my back, I open the closet where I had hidden the good times.

Times Mom sat up all night telling me stories she made up because I had a nightmare and didn't want to go back to sleep; times she refused to dine with her john until she'd brought food home for me; times she'd sung and played the guitar and I had lost myself in her voice.

Run or Die

Memories rushed over me like a gentle creek, washing away some of the bitterness I had hoarded against my mother. Tears ran freely down my cheeks and for once, I refused to brush them away, refused to stem them, to swallow them down. Maybe the time had come to grieve the loss of the woman who had given me birth, taught me what she could, shared all she had, and had loved me the best she knew how.

Finally, my tears ceased. With my stuffed-up nose, I poured myself a cup of coffee as I hummed one of my mother's favorite songs, "Look to Your Soul" by Johnny Rivers. How clearly I recalled the one line: "...look to your soul for the answer..." Funny what I remembered.

All that day I found myself remembering—remembering my mother, remembering Miriam, remembering Alicia. Tears dripped from my chin as I pounded nails and dug a new latrine. By evening, exhaustion rode me hard. I guess grief can do that to a person, grab them tight and wring them dry.

After the tears stopped, that big, empty hole inside my chest began filling up. It filled up with remembered love, with recalled laughter. It filled up with the dreams I'd once shared with Alicia. Love and laughter and dreams that had been locked away, caged by my own fear, caged by my reluctance to feel my own pain, to feel my losses, and to move beyond them. *Is this what it means to grow up?* I snorted a laugh through my clogged nose.

That evening as I stared into the campfire, the chugging of Ted's truck jarred me out of my thoughts and shot me to my feet. His headlights bounced crazily as he drove way too fast. My heart pounded against my ribs. Ted wasn't a reckless driver.

When he skidded into the parking area, I waited there. He jumped the clutch as he leaped from behind the wheel. His feet hit the muck and he slipped, nearly landed on his butt. "Jaz!" He yelled as he rounded the front end of the pickup. "Jaz." He slid to a halt in front of me, his pale face paper white, hands shaking. "Jaz, you gotta come."

Brows crunched in puzzlement, I said, "I need to come where, Ted?"

He sucked in a breath. I could see him fighting to control the anxiety chasing across his strong, young face. "To town. To Willits, I mean. They burned down Ms. Winters' restaurant."

"Shit!" I scrambled to the fire pit and dumped the rest of the coffee on the fire then kicked some loose clumps of mud over the embers. Snatching up the rifle and my jacket, I hobbled to his truck. I'd barely shut the door when he goosed it and whipped around.

"Is...is..."

He swung on the wheel as the tires hit the ruts of Washboard Road at an unsafe speed and yanked the truck toward the hillside. "Ms. Hopewell and Ms. Winters are okay. I think the restaurant was closed and nobody was in it."

The rest of the ride was a blur until we got within two blocks of Mother Earth's Bounty. Traffic, both vehicular and pedestrian, had ground to little more than a crawl. Ted parked on the sidewalk. We leaped out of the truck. He grasped my hand as he bulled a pathway through the crowd.

People are pyromaniacs, lovers of fire. Candles, campfires, bonfires, burning buildings. These are magnets for people. Mouths gaping, eyes wide and staring, tongues clucking, I wondered if they knew how truly idiotic they appeared. I fought the urge to slap them. Might as well sell popcorn and soda pop, and charge extra for the front-of-the-tape-seats.

Arms laced around each other's waist, Aretha and Ms. Winters stood mesmerized by the flames. I shoved my way to them. A loud crash as firemen broke out one of the large-paned windows drew my attention. Hungry yellow, orange, and blue flames licked avid tongues up the outside wall of the wood structure. Pulsating snakes spewed powerful streams of water over the hungry flames. I turned to face the conflagration and felt Aretha place a hand on my shoulder. I reached up and patted her hand. Ted stood on the other side of me, still clutching my other hand. We stood there, the four of us in mute witness to the death of a dream.

It had been an old building, its wood tinderbox dry, except for the flammable cooking grease it had soaked up over the years. The fire fighters contained the hungry beast to its single victim, saving the house behind and the hardware store on the north side.

Sheriff Daly appeared and spoke quietly with Ms. Winters. Captain Elder of the firefighters spoke briefly with her, too. The words "arson investigator" were the only ones I caught.

Icy rain drizzled from swollen, lazy clouds. Our clothes drenched, still we stood there in silence. The last slithering tongue of flame died a hissing death. Firefighters rolled up their hoses and stowed their pickaxes. The crowd drifted off to their own homes, murmurs of gossip drifting like a cloud of gnats around them. Still, we stood there in silence.

Finally, Ms. Winters drew in a shaky breath, let it sigh from her. "Cowards." Slumped shoulders squared, bent back straightened, she spoke in a no-nonsense tone. "No sense standing here getting soaked, and maybe catching pneumonia. Let's head home."

We somberly trooped into the kitchen where Tisha waited with hot coffee and warm scones. We sipped the coffee and crumbled the scones on the delicate, blue-flowered dessert plates.

Aretha lifted her head, tears swimming in her dark eyes. "I am so, so sorry, Folami." She used a finger to brush away the ones that escaped down her cheeks. "I never should have come here. I brought trouble to your doorstep."

"Nonsense!" Ms. Winters' head snapped up. Her gaze pinned Aretha to the chair. "You did not burn down my restaurant. You cannot accept responsibility for someone else's evil actions. I'll hear no more such nonsense talk!"

"But...," Aretha began.

"No buts." She reached across the table and squeezed Aretha's hand. "Don't worry. I was thinking I needed to change my image, anyhow. Since I have a very healthy insurance policy, this is the perfect time to rebuild and to recreate."

Aretha turned her hand up so the two women were palm to palm. She tightened her grip on Ms. Winters' hand. A game smile trembled on her lips then faded. "When life hands you lemons—"

Ms. Winters' smile bloomed slowly, shifting her features from stern to soft, inviting, like you could tell her your heart's deepest secret. "You make lemonade. And, girlfriend, when I make lemonade, *everyone* wants a glass!" She threw her head back and deep, rich laughter poured out. Aretha's warm musical laugh blended seamlessly.

For a crazy moment, I wanted to laugh with Aretha and Ms. Winters, but my knotted-up insides forbade it. I cleared my throat and lifted my eyes. "It's all well and good, as my mother used to say, to make plans, but you'd better watch out for reality. The reality is that things are getting worse. The violence is spreading a wider net and escalating. What are we going to do about it?"

Aretha's laughter trickled to a stop. For a moment, I hated that my words had sucked her laughter into a bottomless hole. She sank further into her chair, her fingers rubbing across her eyes. "I don't know. I just don't know."

I shoved to my feet, my chair scraped across the floor like fingernails on a chalkboard. "Well, I can't sit here waiting." I snatched my down jacket from the chair back and slipped it on. Determined to ignore the pain in my ankle, I gritted my teeth as I strode toward the kitchen doorway and the hall beyond.

"Where are you going, Jaz?" Worry, a chill frost, coated Aretha's words.

I stopped with my hand on the doorjamb and peered over my shoulder. "I'm not sure. I just can't stay here is all I know."

Chapter 19

Sunday I woke up to sunlight puddled on the motel's carpet. My clothes smelled of smoke and the sweat of despair. A quick shower later, I stood along Highway 101 a few feet from the "Welcome to Willits" sign, thumb held high.

An eighteen-wheeler screeched to a halt on the shoulder and I ran-hopped to the tall step. I grabbed the handhold and swung up into the cab. A grizzled white man held the wheel in big hands. As soon as my door shut, he flicked on his turn signal, shifted gears, and entered the light flow of early morning traffic. "Hey, thanks for the lift."

"Where you headed, girl?" He slanted me a quick look, more like an assessment than a check-out-the-chick.

"Ukiah."

"You hungry?" He grunted.

I shrugged. "Sure, maybe."

He laughed, a good laugh, a clean laugh. I breathed a little easier.

"Now that's what I'd call hedgin' your bet. I'm getting ready to stop down at Mom's Café. Good food. If you don't have the money, I can stand you breakfast."

"I have a bit of cash. I'll pay for yours since you're giving me a lift."

He eyeballed me for a moment then nodded. "Don't like charity, do you, girl?" Before I could answer, he grinned. "Me, neither. I'll take you up on your offer and thank you for it."

After breakfast, the trucker dumped me off on the edge of Ukiah four blocks from the car rental place. Tired of cars that depended on how many chipmunks raced each other under the hood, I laid out extra cash for a four-wheel drive SUV that had a monster engine. It guzzled gas, but it booked when you punched it.

After a quick shopping spree, I found a Bed &Breakfast place that looked out over a small, private lake. That night I slept in a cute room with frilly curtains. As soon as my head touched the pillow I was asleep.

The next afternoon when I arrived at Ms. Winters' house, Tisha opened the door, her usual smile absent. In fact, stepping into the kitchen reminded me of stepping into a funeral home. Only thing missing was the dead body. At the table, Aretha hunched over her coffee cup. Shoulder propped against the kitchen window frame, Ms. Winters stared out, the grim set of her mouth making my head shift into overdrive. Sunlight beamed through the glass, but inside the house fear gripped the women with an icy clasp.

Slowly, I eased into a chair and searched Aretha's face. "What's happened?"

She raised haunted eyes to my face. "Cynthia and Ted are missing."

The fear that I'd seen wrapped around them embraced me and I shuddered. Heavy footsteps coming up the hall drew my eyes to the kitchen doorway. Daly strode in. The snarky comment that rushed to my mouth never made it from behind my lips. The man carried suitcases beneath his bloodshot eyes, and an invisible weight bowed his shoulders. Black stubble peppered his cheeks. The last time he shaved must've been the night of the fire. Charcoal streaks marred his beige uniform shirt; his uniform pants had lost any semblance of presentable. He slumped into the chair next to Aretha, head drooping.

Silently, Tisha set a cup of coffee in front of him. He stared at it as if he couldn't quite identify it. For the first time since I'd met him, Sheriff Abe Daly looked lost, and scared.

"Anything, Abe?" Aretha laid her fingers on his arm and gazed hopefully into his face.

His eyes slanted toward her as he gave a slight shake of his head. "Nothing." The heaviness in his voice reflected his general demeanor. "No one saw anything, no one heard anything. Not in the theater; and not on the street."

Fear and rage warred within me and I snapped. "When were they snatched?"

Every eye in the kitchen focused on me. Daly said, "They aren't officially kidnapped. They're missing."

"What the hell?"

Run or Die

He caught my gaze and held it steadily. "Yesterday afternoon, Stan Sullivan dropped Cynthia and Ted off in front of Livingston Theater so they could attend a matinee. When they asked to go, he thought it would get their minds off the trouble and since it was daylight and in the middle of Willits, he saw no reason to worry. He cautioned them to be careful then he watched the kids go inside. He went about doing the shopping he'd come to Willits to do then went to their meet-up place, Books and Coffee Café. It's only three blocks away from the theater. They were to meet him there at three. They never arrived."

"Do you know if they were snatched from inside the theater and brought out; or, when they came out of the theater after the movie?"

He shook his head. "We don't know."

"What about William and his posse?" I asked.

"According to William's father and his uncle, Robert Radley, William and several of his friends took off for a cross-country jaunt to somewhere around Lake Tahoe and haven't been home in a couple of days."

I threw my hands up in the air and let them slap against my thighs in frustration. "Seriously? Gone after the cross burning, but before the restaurant arson? Right." I glared at him. "Did you ever see William's Jeep after I shot out the headlight?"

Daly had the good grace to blush and look away. "No. By the time I got a warrant to search Radley's garage, it was empty except for Mr. Radley's Corvette."

"What *have* you done?"

He toyed with his coffee cup, twirling it around and around on its matching saucer. "I've alerted the state police and adjoining jurisdictions that William Radley and Nick Evers are wanted for questioning. I've issued a BOLO—be on the lookout—for both of them and their vehicles."

Elbows propped on the table, I buried my face in my hands. The truth burned a hole in my chest, scorched my heart. "This is my fault. I should never have allowed them to help."

The sound of the front door closing jerked my head up. Daly shifted so his hand rested on the butt of his gun as he watched the hall. Fergus strode into the kitchen with Stan Sullivan close behind. Stan's leg dragged as it did when he got overly tired. I stood up and motioned him into my seat. Too worried and fatigued to protest, he accepted without a murmur.

"Any news of my granddaughter?" Fergus asked.

Daly shook his head. "I've got a call into the FBI. Maybe they can lend some manpower. I have Deputy Shirley Hardy re-canvassing that entire area with a couple of off-duty borrowed uniforms and a couple of suits from Ukiah. Deputy Jones is handling calls at the office. I take it you men came up empty, too?"

Fergus McKenna accepted a cup of coffee from Tisha then rested his lean hips against the counter edge. "We didnae find anythin'. Their friends havnae heard from them." Fergus' thick brogue testified to the intensity of his worry.

Ms. Winters shoved away from the window, walked over to the table. "We have to do more, Sheriff Daly. We know who's behind their disappearance. There has to be something we can do with that information."

He climbed wearily to his feet. "I'm doing everything I can think to do, Ms. Winters. If you come up with any ideas, you tell me and, if it's legal, I'll try it." He clapped his hat on his head and the other men followed him out.

Ms. Winters slumped into Daly's chair. Tisha braced her hips against the kitchen counter, weariness apparent in the slouched posture.

"Do we know who's with William?"

"Johnny's parents, the Faddens, claim that their son is with his grandfather in Oregon. So far, however, no one has been able to contact the grandfather. When the local police checked, no one was home. Jimmy is missing and his parents appear to be genuinely concerned. William, Nick, and Sam are together, according to Radley." Aretha listed the core group. "If there's anyone else involved, we don't know it."

"Do you think the father and uncle are involved, or simply covering for William?" I ventured as I glanced around at the others.

Ms. Winters gave me a thoughtful look. "Without a doubt they are involved, but proving it will be a challenge, I'm afraid.

Meanwhile, the real concern is finding those children before something happens to them."

Dread filled my chest like lead. Cynthia and Ted had been gone nearly twenty-four hours; way too much time to be in the hands of sadistic men like William and his posse.

"Okay," I drummed my fingers on the table as I considered what we knew. "Come on, ladies, think! With road conditions as they are, with a limited amount of time, and with no results on the BOLO, they can't have gone very far."

Tisha's eyes rounded. "You think they're right around here?"

I gave a decisive nod. "They have to be. They haven't had time to disappear this completely otherwise. They're holed up somewhere. All we have to do is figure out where."

That afternoon the sky opened and a deluge fell. Streets flooded, causing traffic to grind to a near-halt. A light gray Lexus and a modest Ford sedan sat in the driveway of Johnny Fadden's house. I pulled up behind the Ford, shut off the SUV, and watched the rain thunder down the windshield as I gazed at the tape player, loaded it with the audiotape then stuck it in my jacket pocket.

By the time Mrs. Fadden answered the doorbell, my jacket was a sodden mess. She pulled the door wider. "Come in out of the downpour, dear." Door closed, she clasped her hands in front of herself and waited as if sopping wet people arrived all the time.

"Mrs. Fadden, your son is in a lot of trouble. He's with William Radley, Nick Evers, Sam Hadden, and Jimmy Donaldson. Those men kidnapped two young people, Cynthia McKenna and Ted Sullivan. A few weeks ago, William and Nick beat Ted pretty badly, and might have killed him if I hadn't intervened." I took a deep breath and exhaled slowly. "Johnny and I had a...talk one night. If what he told me is true, he's in a lot of danger. I know you may not believe it, but Aretha Hopewell didn't murder Ralph. William murdered Ralph."

"Johnny isn't with those men. He hasn't been hanging out with them lately." She glowered down her nose at me.

I didn't know the woman personally, but I heard the lie in her voice. I struggled to keep my tone level. "You told Sheriff Daly that Johnny took his car and went up to Coos Bay, Oregon to visit his grandfather. He isn't there, Mrs. Fadden. Sheriff Daly had the Coos Bay police check." I motioned with my head over my shoulder, toward the entry door and the driveway where two cars sat out in the rain. "Johnny's car is in that garage, and as soon as Sheriff Daly gets a chance, he'll get a search warrant and find it there. Meanwhile, your son is in serious danger."

    I shoved the small tape player with the audiocassette already in it into her hands. "Listen to this tape then call me. Here's my number." I thrust a piece of paper at her. Automatically, she reached out and accepted it. I wheeled around and marched out to the SUV.

Chapter 20

I can't think of any place more depressing than a sheriff's office at eight o'clock at night. The interview room held a long table. Elbow propped up, head braced against her open palm, Aretha sat with her eyes closed. Everything from the bowed shoulders to the lifelessness of her usually bouncy hair shouted defeat. She walked, talked, and acted like a friend of mine in high school…right before she committed suicide.

My stomach clenched at the thought. I couldn't lose Aretha! I slid onto the folding metal chair next to her and put a hand on her shoulder. "Hey, you okay?" As soon as I said the words, I realized how stupid they sounded. No, she wasn't okay. None of us were.

She opened her eyes and forced herself up straight. "I'll be alright, Jaz. Just worried about Cynthia and Ted."

Deputy Jones straddled a chair against the far wall, as far away from us as he could sit. I slanted a look at him and caught a smirk on his mouth as he stared our way. No sense in confronting the man, but his presence made me uneasy. Briefly, I wondered why Daly had pulled Jones in from his leave of absence, especially after I told him the deputy was the one who'd run me off the road. One more person searching *couldn't* be that important.

Deputy Hardy and the four law enforcement personnel on loan from other jurisdictions gathered next to Sheriff Daly, studying the map pinned on the wall. Two German Shepherd search and rescue dogs lay next to a couple of chairs at the table. The only thing moving on either one of them were their eyes, ever alert to their surroundings. Their K-9 handlers, both female cops from nearby jurisdictions, stood behind the other law enforcement people and listened as Daly pointed out different areas on the map.

Stan limped in and as he passed Jones, he shot the man a look that dared the deputy to speak to him. Another Deputy Jones fan. Fergus followed close behind and didn't design to glance at Jones.

Ms. Winters bustled in bearing boxes of doughnuts and several large pizzas. Tisha followed closely behind with a grocery sack swinging from her arm and a huge coffee urn in her hands. They hurried over to the card tables someone had set up along one wall.

As soon as the red light on the pot went out, signaling that the coffee was ready, I wandered over. Fergus fell into line behind me. I scooped the only bear claw pastry out of the box and put it on a paper plate with a slice of vegetarian pizza. Cup of coffee in the other hand, I hauled it over to Aretha. She shook her head, but I gave her my "you-eat-it-or-I-feed-it-to-you" look. With one finger, she poked at the bear claw, dislodging one of the almond slivers. It never made it to her mouth.

I understood her all too well, so I left to fix myself some coffee and a plate.

Deputy Jones may have disliked blacks, but that dislike didn't extend to the food Ms. Winters brought. He loaded up a plate with several pastries and three slices of pizza, and filled his huge to-go mug with coffee, then resumed his seat by the door.

A white-haired man with a craggy face and dark eyes entered the room and strode over to Daly. Daly shook his hand. "Is the room all right?"

"It's fine. Thanks for arranging it."

Daly faced the table. "People," he called out.

The low buzz of conversations died and all eyes focused on the sheriff. "I'd like you to meet Special Agent Lou Sheffield. San Francisco's current crisis with a number of bomb threats has drained the Bureau's resources for the time being. Agent Sheffield was kind enough to voluntarily cut his vacation short to assist us."

The man cleared his throat and ran his gaze around the table. "I met with Sheriff Daly earlier this evening when I arrived in town. From what I see, the sheriff has covered all the bases, and has done a good job of it. At this moment, what I can offer to this search is lab access, database access, and computer expertise. I will coordinate the use of those services with Sheriff Daly."

Daly tilted his head at the tables along the wall. "Help yourself to the food and coffee, Agent Sheffield. It's courtesy of Ms. Winters."

Run or Die

The agent wandered over, plucked up a paper plate, and loaded it. He filled a cup and settled in an empty chair at the table.

Sheriff Daly quickly ate, dumped his trash, and strode to the front of the room. "I'll get started while everyone finishes eating. The news from the bordering jurisdictions and the state police isn't good. No one has spotted either the Jeep or the truck; and no one has seen Ted, Cynthia, or any of William's group."

He surveyed the room then let his eyes linger on Deputy Jones. "According to Deputy Jones, no one has called in any sightings of the involved young people." Daly's eyes flicked toward the FBI agent before he continued.

"Deputy Hardy confirmed that Ted and Cynthia purchased tickets for the double feature at noon yesterday. During intermission, the counter help sold Cynthia a box of popcorn and a diet Pepsi. She thinks she saw her speaking with a girl with long brown hair, but they were off to one side and the counter help couldn't identify the girl."

With a stick pointer, he tapped the map on the wall behind him. "The areas outlined in black are the ones we've searched. The other areas are labeled by number. I'll assign teams to each numbered area.

"A friend of Stan's has arranged for their company helicopter to participate in the search tomorrow."

A tall, lanky woman in a red flannel shirt lifted a finger to get Daly's attention. He nodded toward her. "Our dogs will need something from each of the young people they'll be searching for, and we'll need a starting point."

"Agent Sheffield." Daly gave the man a nod.

Sheffield stood up. "Before this meeting, Sheriff Daly asked me to do a database search for hunting cabins, resort cabins, that sort of thing, owned by the Radleys or the Evers. I located two such cabins in the first search. They are located in areas 11 and 9. Sheriff Daly has maps of those areas."

Not long after that the meeting broke up. Outside the rain had slackened from downpour to steady-but-not-so-hard. "I'll see you guys in the morning. I'm heading up to the farm."

Aretha put her hand on my shoulder. "Why not stay with us at Folami's place?"

"Can't. I...need some room to breathe." I stepped out from under her hand. "Catch you in the morning."

All the way up the hill, I kept thinking about how William had looked at Cynthia that day he and Nick had beaten Ted. A sick feeling churned in my gut.

With rain slapping the ground, I grabbed the rifle, my duffle bag with a couple of changes of clothes in it, and the grocery bag, and headed into the shell of the cabin. As I moved inside every step reminded me of Cynthia's chatter and Ted's seriousness. Those two kids had helped lay every board on the floor, nail every piece of tin on the roof, and set every bit of plywood on the outside of this one-room house.

They have to be safe! They just have to be. If I had believed in any gods or goddesses, at that moment I would have prostrated myself on the ground at their feet. I tossed my duffle bag on the floor to one side of the rough frame where the door would hang. The rain hadn't reached its icy fingers in that far yet. Cross-legged on the floor, I uncapped the thermos and poured a cup of black coffee into the insulated cup. No good thoughts occupied my mind as I stared out at the darkness. The headlights of a truck topped the rise and dipped down the hill toward Aretha's gate. It jarred me from that dark space in my head.

Run or stand? *No more running!* A quick slide of the bolt jacked a live round in the rifle's chamber. Rifle safety off, I waited in the deeper shadows of that thin plywood, cabin wall.

As the vehicle idled up the slope I thought I recognized the sound of its engine, but still I waited. The headlights shut off. A door opened then closed. "Jaz?"

I walked out of the shadows and called over to him. "Fergus, over here at the cabin."

He flicked on a flashlight and the beam illuminated the muddy path as he picked his way to the cabin.

Inside the cabin, I lit a kerosene lantern and set it away from us to preserve our night vision. Handing him a cup, I poured some coffee in it then dug the box of doughnuts from my grocery bag and handed the box to him. Settled on the floor with coffee and doughnuts, I chewed on a sugary pastry and waited.

Run or Die

He glanced at the pastry and coffee in his hands. "I couldnae sleep. I thought I might drive down to town and have a wee drink." He shook his shaggy head. "It has been many a night I havnae done that, and I think my granddaughter widnae be happy if I did it noo. The drink does bring the devil out in me."

"Yeah, it's not exactly my best friend, either." We ate the six-pack of doughnuts and emptied the thermos while we watched the rain. I don't know when I dozed off.

The rain had stopped and the grayness of dawn lightened the sky as I rolled to my feet. Fergus stood in the cabin's doorway and stared out.

"I can see why Ms. Hopewell loves this place. Tis a pretty piece of land," he said without turning.

"Yeah, I think so, too." I brushed past him. "I'll get some coffee started then scramble up a few eggs."

"I would ask ye to my house, but I dinnae think ye would come." He followed me to the fire pit.

"Not today. Maybe...when things...settle down one of these days."

After breakfast, I rode into Andersville to the sheriff's office with Fergus. Daly teamed Fergus and me up. At the end of that third day of Ted and Cynthia being gone, the searchers met at the sheriff's office and reported nothing except dismal failure, frustration, and frayed nerves.

Each hour that ticked away brought more horrid images to my mind. When Fergus dropped me off at the farm, I wanted to scream. The topography kicked our asses. With so many ravines and cutbanks, stands of trees and caves created by boulders, and streams that had cut holes through the hillsides, we'd never find those men if they didn't want to be found.

Ordered by Daly to catch some sleep before we headed out again in the morning, I drank cold coffee and watched the moon sneak out from behind a cloud bank. We needed answers and I was tired of passively waiting for them.

***

Aya Walksfar

The clock read ten p.m. as I slid out of the SUV and marched over to the Fadden's door. I held my finger on the doorbell until Mr. Fadden opened the door then I bulled my way inside. As soon as he closed the door, I charged into him, my forearm against his throat and my knife out where he could see it.

"Wh-what do...do you wa-want?"

At that moment, he reminded me so much of Johnny that I nearly backed off. Until the pictures in my head reminded me of how Ted had looked after he'd been beaten. "What I want is the truth. I am sick and tired of lies and evasions. Where are they?"

"I...I don't...know."

"From what Johnny said, I had the impression you were pretty on top of things. You wouldn't let him go with William the night Ralph was murdered."

"Leave us alone, or I'll phone the sheriff!" Mrs. Fadden shrilled from the end of the hallway.

"Go ahead. Phone the sheriff. I'll be glad to hand the original of that tape over to him. It implicates your son in enough crimes to get him sent up for years. How long do you think he'd last in prison?" I bluffed.

"Please...don't do this." A sob broke on the end of her words.

"Tell me where they are! There is a young woman who has probably been repeatedly raped by now and a young man who may not have survived the beatings I know they've given him. I don't have any more time to play around with you."

"Deborah, show...show her the...the note."

I heard the rustle of her clothes as she moved away then moments later she returned holding a piece of computer paper up toward me. I flicked a glance at it. "Read it to me."

From the corner of my eye I could see her hands tremble as she unfolded the page. "Dear M...Mom and Dad, I'm so...sorry to disappoint you...both." She inhaled and held her breath then slowly exhaled. Her voice steadied as she read on. "Jimmy and me took Cynthia McKenna and Ted Sullivan. We were sick of the perverts and niggers taking over the town. You have to understand they brought this on themselves. I can't come back

Run or Die

home anymore so whenever you think of me think of the summer we camped out and how happy we were. Love, Johnny."

Tears streamed down Fadden's face. I dropped my arm and stepped back. He crumpled down the wall; knees jackknifed, he buried his face. Keeping an eye on him, I held out my hand. Mrs. Fadden handed me the paper as she went to kneel next to her husband. I reread the page as she stroked his thinning hair.

"I take it you don't think Johnny wrote this." I waved the unsigned, undated, computer-printed note.

"Oh, he might have written it, but not because he wanted to." Deborah Fadden looked up at me, a steely glint in her faded blue eyes. "My son has never used the word nigger, and how would a boy who doesn't have the heart to kill a deer during hunting season kidnap and harm another person? Even if he and Jimmy could physically subdue them both."

"You're telling me he may be a victim, too."

"That is exactly what I am saying."

"Help us find them!"

"If you catch up to these young men, I have no doubt that they will kill our son."

"What makes you think he's not in this with them?"

"Our son told us about your...talk with him. He also told us about what's been happening. He said he was afraid. Don and I were arranging for him to...disappear for a while. I don't know what happened, but the next morning when I went to wake him, Johnny was gone and this note was on his pillow."

"Do you have any idea where they might be hiding?"

Mr. Fadden lifted his face and brushed his sleeve across his eyes. "I've been thinking and..."

"What?"

"I couldn't figure out why he would mention that summer. He *hated* that we went camping nearly every weekend. It was my...my attempt to introduce him to nature." He forced a dry chuckle that choked him. He cleared his throat. "Johnny wanted to...to go to ball games and to a dude ranch to ride horses."

"Why do you think he mentioned that summer?"

"We went to the Grand Canyon and camped at Yosemite National Park, but I...I thought it'd be good for him to experience the wonders of nature at his own backdoor. We...we went camping at a different spot around Northern California every weekend for two months—July and August."

"You think he was trying to give you a hint as to where he thought they were hiding?"

"It's possible, isn't it?" Mr. Fadden's face held so much hope that I had a hard time injecting reality.

"Possibility? Maybe. Probability?" I shook my head. "I don't know. If he was trying to leave a clue, where was he talking about? Northern California is a big place."

"Let me get up and go into the den. I...I've been giving this a lot of thought."

Chapter 21

I bolted awake at the sound of a truck coming down the hill and snatched up the rifle lying on the floor next to my bedroll. Hidden in the shadows inside the cabin, I watched the vehicle approach.

The first blush of daylight rimmed the horizon when Fergus blasted his horn and shouted for me.

Heart pounding, I sprinted to the truck. "What's happening?"

He waited until I got there then lowered his voice as if he thought trees had ears and might divulge secrets. "Abe wants us to meet at Ms. Winters' place. Get your stuff and come on."

Tisha met us at the door and led the way to the spacious living room. I frowned as I realized that only part of the group sat scattered on the couches and overstuffed chairs. Surely, the rest of them hadn't given up the hunt yet.

Rifle propped in a corner against the wall, I walked over to Daly and handed him the list Fadden had compiled. I snagged an ottoman and set it against the wall to one side of the fireplace. The position made a good observation post. After a quick survey of the room I noted the absence of the out-of-town law enforcement people, both dog handlers, and Deputy Jones. Not sad to be missing Jones, I wondered if the others had been called back to their own jurisdictions. Surely, they could be spared for more than four days.

When I caught Aretha's attention, I raised my eyebrows. From her place on the couch, she shrugged and spread her hands, palms up. Apparently, she didn't know any more than I did.

Tisha and Ms. Winters walked in bearing coffee, tea, hot chocolate, and croissant breakfast sandwiches. After they passed around the food and beverages, they sat on a couple of padded footstools on the other side of the fireplace. Grateful for the food and coffee, especially if we faced another super long day of hiking rough terrain, I started eating.

Daly levered himself off the kitchen chair and set his cup on the occasional table he shared with Ms. Winters. He walked over and stood in front of the large fireplace. "Agent Sheffield discovered that we had an information leak."

Heads twisted this way and that, shooting looks and questioning frowns around the room. *Jones. No wonder he smirked through the meetings. Wonder how Daly caught him.*

"Agent Sheffield intercepted phone calls between Deputy Jones and William Radley late last night. Jones informed Radley of our search plans."

"Is that why Sheffield was here in the first place?" Stan asked from a chair near Daly.

"Yes. I suspected Jones to be more than a sympathizer with the Radleys. Agent Sheffield removed Jones from his home an hour ago."

"If William's using his cell phone, can't we track him through it?" My heart beat wildly at the prospect of any kind of lead.

"Agent Sheffield has already set that up, but the call last night was too brief to track and apparently William knows enough to remove the battery from his phone when he isn't using it."

"Now what?" Stan shifted and I saw the grimace he quickly hid.

"Jones will be questioned by Agent Sheffield. Anytime a law enforcement officer is involved in this type of illegal activity, the FBI gets involved. Agent Sheffield has assured me that if he discovers any information that might prove helpful in our search, he will immediately inform me."

"Why're the dog handlers and the other cops not here?" I asked.

"We needed to have this meeting without them since I don't personally know those six people, and we can't afford any more leaks. Agent Sheffield is doing deep background checks on all six people, but until I receive those reports I will be assigning them to teams with our own people in charge. They will have only the information they need and only when they need it.

"Ms. Winters has agreed to handle the phones. We've had a number of people who wanted to volunteer to assist in the search. I've turned them down due to the nature of this situation. I can't afford to have a civilian stumble into what I believe to be a kidnapping scenario. The helicopter crew is from Stan's contacts, so I'm not concerned about information leaks from them. They're getting the chopper ready to lift off at first light."

He glanced around. "Jaz obtained the Fadden's cooperation and they've given us a list of places where William might be hiding. I'll assign teams to search those areas."

***

Fergus glanced over at me then reached and took the to-go cup of coffee from the holder in the console of the truck. "I thought we would go to Iron Mountain first then work our way over to Hawk Hill."

I ran a hand over my face, trying to wipe away the tiredness, and took a gulp of coffee. The caffeine didn't seem to be working very well. "I wish I'd never let those two help."

"Aye, lassie, I know ye wish that, and I wish I'd been more vigilant. Stan wishes he'd gone to the movies with those youngsters. But wishing the past different willnae do anythin', except to make our hearts too heavy for us to carry."

A one-lane dirt track led up Iron Mountain, so named due to large deposits of iron ore, and a consequent interference with cell phone reception. Without the means to actually search the entire mountain, we did the only thing possible: we searched dirt tracks to inevitable dead ends. A lot of signs of human trespass blossomed along the way, Styrofoam cups, old television sets, a couple of stripped down hulks of cars, some dead embers of campfires. No sign of our quarry, though.

Night approached in the fast lane as Fergus left the dirt road and hit the asphalt.

By the time we arrived at the sheriff's office, sandwiches and urns of soups lined the card tables. Another card table had sprouted since earlier that day. Coffee and tea, sugar and creamers sprawled across it.

As the rest of us ate, Stan shoved to his feet and reported. "Jaylene and her dog, Maverick, found Cynthia and Ted's scents in a cabin. It was one of the places Mr. Fadden listed. From the unburned wood in the fireplace, I'd guess they left sooner than they had expected to. Aretha discovered a note stuffed under a dirty mattress on the floor. Officer Timmons took control of it to preserve chain of evidence." Stan sank into his chair.

Daly climbed to his feet. I'd never seen a man as haggard as him. "The note was written on a piece of brown paper sack. It simply said: 'William got a call. He knows my parents talked. Planning to kill me. Going to try to escape tonight. Him and Nick talking about moving to Iron Mountain. Whoever finds this tell Mom and Dad I'm sorry, and I love them. It's not their fault. Johnny Fadden.'"

"That makes this an official kidnapping, doesn't it?" Stan asked quietly.

"I've called Agent Sheffield and I'll courier the note to him. He said his boss intends to send out several agents. Sheffield will phone as soon as he knows their ETA and where to meet them."

I absently combed my hand through my tangled hair, yanking my fingers through the knots. "We can't sit here all night! Let's head up to Iron Mountain and start looking for those guys."

Fergus wagged his head slowly side to side. "Can nae do that."

I lunged to my feet. "Why not?"

"There're ravines and gullies, and drop-offs that we wouldnae see until it's too late. William and his people could walk right past us, lassie, and we wouldnae see them."

I threw myself into my chair. "What *is* the plan?" I glared at Daly as if the night and the rugged terrain were somehow his fault.

"At first light, the two search dogs and handlers will go with me, Aretha, Stan, and Officers Smith and Timmons. We'll start a ground search from the cabin on Day Hill."

He glanced around. "The helicopter crew," he nodded at the man and woman seated to one side of the room, "will start a search pattern with the Day Hill area and widen it until it includes all of Iron Mountain and then onto Hawk Hill."

"Detective Edison from Eureka, Officer Mathews from Ukiah, as well as Deputy Hardy will go with Fergus and Jaz to Iron Mountain. Fergus, you've got a feel for the topography, so you'll

Run or Die

lead the crew, but Deputy Hardy retains ultimate authority. What she says, goes. Anyone have an issue with that?" He looked around, his gaze lingered briefly on the out-of-town cops.

Edison gave a nonchalant, one-shoulder shrug and Mathews mumbled "fine with me."

"Agent Sheffield will phone me when he arrives and we'll coordinate his involvement at that point. Any questions? No? Okay, everyone who doesn't live within ten miles of Andersville, head down to Willits and over to Sleepy Hollow Motel. I've arranged rooms for all of us so we can get an early start. Ms. Winters will arrange a buffet breakfast at the motel and have packed lunches for everyone. She'll also handle the phones again."

After yet another day of failure, we gathered in the Sleepy Hollow's conference room that the owner of the motel had offered to Daly for the duration. Discouragement laid as heavy as a wet wool blanket over the gathered searchers. Somehow, Ms. Winters had arranged a hot meat loaf and potatoes dinner for everyone, but I noticed I wasn't the only one pushing the food aimlessly around my plate before dumping it in the trash.

When the others headed for their rooms, I stepped outside. Even here in Willits it was dark enough that the stars blazed overhead. The gauzy swathe of the Milky Way flowed across the void.

Fergus stepped out and looked up.

After a while, without taking my eyes from the sky I said, "What would you say to sleeping up on the farm tonight?"

"Well, lassie, I say that would be a fine thing." He reached into his pocket and tossed me the keys to his Avalanche.

The tires thumped along the ripples of Washboard Road. "I didn't know this hill was called Hawk Hill until Daly explained it."

"Aye, that it is. There is a story aboot it." He fell silent, gazing out the side window.

"Okay, you can't say there's a story and then not tell the story." I flashed him "the look."

He squirmed around on the seat until he found a comfortable spot. "The story goes that before the whites came to this land, there was a very bad winter. The Native People were starving. One of the lassies went to seek a Vision to help her people, vowing nae to return until a Vision came.

"Her family tried to persuade her nae to go. Tried to tell her she was but a bairn, a young one, to let the Medicine Man seek Visions. But, the lassie was adamant.

"It was so cold that tree limbs broke off, fell, and shattered on the ground like glass."

His voice deepened and a melody ran through it. "During the time she was gone, a blizzard hit the hill. Snow drifts higher than a warrior's head piled up. The cold seeped into the tightest lodge. Several of the people died from the bitter cold.

"The lassie's parents lost hope for their bairn, thinking she must surely have died.

"She was gone for four days and four nights. On the fourth night when she was weak from hunger and thirst, a Red-tailed Hawk came to her and told her to follow. She stumbled along, watching the Hawk soaring above her until she came to a small valley. In that valley was a herd of deer. She returned to her people, her feet bloody, so weak she collapsed as she entered the village. But when the Medicine Man came to her and asked about her vision, she rose and led the hunters to the valley.

"They only took a few deer. Once the people had eaten and some strength returned to them, the hunters led the village to the Valley of the Deer. That winter the people lived on the deer and the rabbits, and fished the creek. Every day a pair of Red-tailed Hawks soared above them. The highest point of this hill, what we call Buzzard Peak, is where the lassie sought her Vision and Hawk came to her. So the story is told."

"Whoa! That's some story. Do you think it's real?" I dodged a pothole while I waited for his answer.

"Such stories usually have at least a kernel of truth within and, sometimes, a whole lot of truth."

"Where's this Valley of the Deer?" I topped Buzzard Peak and bumped down the other side. Fergus remained quiet for so long that I thought he wouldn't answer.

I topped the rise above Aretha's farm before he spoke. "Ye are looking at the Valley of the Deer."

Run or Die

Without thinking, I stomped the brakes. The Avalanche slid a little. I eased off the brakes. "You're kidding!"

"Nae. Oft' I have wondered if Ms. Hopewell knows the story for she lets the deer in her valley live in peace."

"Wow. I wonder if the Red-tailed Hawk I see is a descendant of the one that brought the girl here."

"I would nae doubt but that it was so, lassie."

Chapter 22

The three-quarter moon dribbled a mellow whiteness across the sleeping land, like a night light switched to dim. Leaning against the cold, gray boulder, I could see Fergus hunched on a log with his back to the campfire. He had chuckled when I declared that I was sleeping outside. A shiver ran up my arms. I huddled deeper into my jacket. Maybe I was being paranoid, but the thought of being caged in by cabin walls...well, it gave me the heebie-jeebies.

He finally conceded I might have a point, so we'd set up our sleeping bags on the far side of the boulder that hulked behind and to the left of the cabin. I'd been uneasy since shortly after we arrived on the farm, but it was late and going all the way back to town held no appeal to me. I decided I'd hike up to the boulders to star watch. Fergus said he'd be up in a bit, but wanted to enjoy the warmth of the fire a little longer.

I figured he had a lot on his mind with Cynthia missing. I filled our thermos and grabbed a bag of trail mix before walking upslope for a short way. Settled in the darker shadow of the boulder's broad side, I laid the rifle across my lap, a comforting presence.

Something nagged at me. I couldn't force it into the front of my mind. I tried unsuccessfully to brush it away, yet it continued buzzing around in my head, persistent as an annoying mosquito.

I poured a cup of coffee and grabbed a handful of dried fruit and nuts from the open bag on the ground beside me. The moon spilled silver light across the hill, but not so brightly that I couldn't see the stars flung across the heavens. Temperatures hovered in the upper forties, the rain gone for the moment. Beautiful. And quiet.

Too quiet. Earlier the coyotes had serenaded each other down by Boulder Creek. Now not even an owl rustled. Nighttime in the natural world was never so quiet.

I laid aside my snack and coffee; strained my eyes in every direction. Nothing. Could it be that the coyotes finally hushed to go hunting? That the owl had found his dinner early?

Run or Die

As I chastised myself for seeing phantoms, gunshots rang from the cover of the trees just beyond the glow of the campfire. Fergus dove to one side. Dirt kicked up where he'd been seated moments earlier. He dashed behind a flattish boulder barely high enough to afford him cover.

With him out of immediate danger, I held my fire, unsure where Cynthia or Ted might be. I crawled around the side of the boulder where I could watch, yet still have good cover. I wondered if they knew I was there.

"Payback time, old man," William's voice blared across the clearing. He emerged from the trees, Cynthia a living shield in front of him. "Wanna watch me carve up this sweet thang?" He waved a knife in the air, the moonlight glinting on the blade.

"Let the lassie go, William," Fergus yelled.

"Bill! My name is Bill!" He snarled.

Fergus didn't answer.

"Whatcha willin' to give for 'er, old man?" William taunted. "It ain't like she was a virgin when I got 'er."

I marveled that Fergus didn't charge from cover. I certainly fought the urge. Instead his voice shot across the clearing, steady, cold, determined. "If ye know what's best, laddie, ye'll let the lassie go. I will meet you man-to-man, if ye be a man."

"Oh, I'm a man, you ol' bastard." William called over his shoulder, "Hey, Nick, bring Teddie out to join our little party."

Nick strolled from the tree line, a firm grip on Ted's hair and a handgun pressed against the young man's cheek. Ted's face resembled raw hamburger.

William shoved Cynthia so hard she fell then scrambled to her feet. "I'm done with that piece anyhow." He clutched his crotch. "If you try to get away with her, I'll kill you both and him." He jerked a thumb over his shoulder.

The thundering of my heart filled my ears and a coppery taste flooded my mouth. I'd bitten my lip bloody.

Cynthia staggered to the front of the truck. She stopped and stared over at her grandfather. "Go on, lassie. Get yerself in and be gone."

She swayed for a moment, then sliding along the body of the vehicle she got to the driver's door and crawled in. I wanted to pump my fist in the air that Fergus had told me to leave the keys in the ignition. The truck fired up and spit mud as she wheeled it around and shot down the dirt track.

"She gone. Now come on out, ol' man. Time to pay up." The smirk in William's voice made my stomach churn.

"I'll wait until the lassie tops the rise."

As soon as the truck disappeared over the hill, Fergus stood up.

"I know you got a gun, ol' man. Toss it away. Now."

Even from this distance, I could see him hesitate, weigh his chances before he carefully pulled the pistol from the back of his waistband. He tossed it as far behind him as he could.

"Come over here, Pops."

Fergus walked steadily toward William, stopping within arm's length of the younger man.

Sam stepped out from the trees, a rifle held across his body.

I swallowed hard. Did they intend to gun Fergus down right where he stood? I aimed my rifle at Sam, finger on the trigger, and waited. He wouldn't get the rifle into position before I shot him.

William called over his shoulder, "Sam?"

"Yo!"

"Take the short cut an' go get that 'ho."

Sam sprinted for the trees.

My heart slammed my ribs and, for a moment, I couldn't breathe.

"Ye bastid!" Fergus lunged at William. As they grappled, Nick slammed the barrel of his gun into Ted's head. The young man crumpled. Nick snatched up a branch about as big around as a man's forearm, stepped close, and swung it into the back of Fergus' head. The big man folded to the ground.

I watched it all go down within minutes. With the fighters so close together, I hadn't dared chance a shot. Wiggling, I slipped over the hill and ghosted toward the creek. Once I got far enough away, I ran.

I heard Cynthia gunning the Avalanche before I rounded the bend in the trail. When I was still a good hundred feet away

Run or Die

with trees still obscuring my view, I heard a thud then a thump-thump-thump. One time, I'd been riding with a friend when he hit a deer and couldn't stop before running over the body. There was no mistaking the thud of metal against flesh or the thumping sound of a body beneath a vehicle.

By the time I exited the woods all I saw of the Avalanche was its' taillights. In the center of the muddy road, Sam sprawled with his eyes staring at a sky he would never again see. His rifle lay close by him. I left him and the rifle where they laid.

I reentered the woods and flipped open my cell phone. Three bars and the fourth one flickering! I hit speed dial as I jogged. "Aretha, listen. William and his posse are up here on Hawk Hill. They have Ted and Fergus. Ted looks real bad and they clobbered Fergus in the head with a tree branch a little while ago. Cynthia's in Fergus' Avalanche. She ran over Sam down by the shortcut exit. He's dead. Cynthia didn't look like she was in good shape when she got in the truck. Gotta go." I flipped the phone closed and jammed it in my jeans' pocket.

One down and three to go. I hadn't seen Johnny, so that must mean he got away or they murdered him. Briefly, I wondered where Jimmy was. Time to worry about him after Fergus and Ted were safe.

***

It isn't hard to follow a herd of elephants trampling through the woods. I found where the vehicle must've been parked. A large circular area in the grass showed where he'd turned it around. Had to be William's Jeep because I didn't think Nick's fancy truck could run across rough country. Breath rasping in and out, I jogged along the clearly visible path, hoping they weren't going too far.

From the way my breath sawed in and out, I figured I'd jogged a good two, maybe three miles by the time I heard William's big mouth.

"Toldja, Nick, my man, that we'd have a use for Officer Timmons. How lucky was that? Fucked up sheriff invited my fourth cousin to hunt for us."

"Yeah, but he said the bitch would be with McKenna at the farm. He heard them talking after the meeting."

"Who knows? She probably went home with them nigger bitches. We'll get 'er."

I slipped closer. All the times I had sneaked around foster homes and city streets finally paid off. Well, that and trying to creep up close enough to see the new fawns this past spring without spooking them or the does.

Two dome tents sat close together. A few feet away, Nick squatted by a ring of stones. He stirred the glowing embers and fed the fire. Crumpled on the ground not far from the fire ring, lay a long, thin body. When the fire finally flared to life, its golden light danced across the bloody face. Even this close, I barely recognized Ted's features. For a moment, my heart clenched, certain he was dead. Then his chest rose a fraction and I sucked in a silent breath along with him.

Nick's voice whined across the quiet. "You sure that 'ho didn't get away?"

"You questionin' me, Nick?" The danger in William's tone must've registered.

"Nah, man, just asking. Seems like Sam's been gone too long, you know?"

"He'll get the job done. 'Sides, the man has to drive the long way over here, so it'll take him a bit. That Avalanche is a sweet truck, but it's not a Jeep. Chill, my man."

"Do we have to wait for him before we have any fun?"

"Let's have a drink." William stooped and reached into a tent, pulled out a bottle of whiskey. He uncapped it and took a long drink.

Nick walked over. When William handed him the bottle, he swilled the liquor down then wiped his mouth with the back of his hand.

"We could do Jimmy again." Nick took another deep chug of the whiskey.

"You like that boy-snatch?" William sneered and his teeth gleamed in the firelight.

All levity disappeared from Nick's face, his fist balled up. "You calling me queer, Bill?"

Run or Die

"Naw, my man!" William slapped his shoulder and with his other hand relieved Nick of the whiskey bottle. "Just askin'. It was pretty tight, wasn't it?"

"Yeah, tight. Tighter'n that ho's snatch." Nick looked toward Ted. "We going to do him?"

William handed the bottle to Nick. "Once Sam gets back, we'll drink an' fuck 'em all an' when we're done, we'll get rid of the toys."

"We really going to Mexico?"

"Hell yeah, Uncle Bob says it'd be best for us to lay low till things blow over. Besides, he's got this cool pad down there an' there's lots of brown pussy for the takin'. Just have to grease a few palms, Uncle Bob said."

Way too soon, William belched and capped the bottle, set it aside. "Time to check the ol' bastard an' see if he's awake yet."

Boots squished across the soft ground to the far side of the little clearing. William nudged a shape on the ground with his foot. "Hey, Pops, rise an' shine. Time to get a beatin'."

I heard a groan then William reached down and yanked Fergus to his feet. Ropes bound Fergus' hands, but fortunately they hadn't tied his feet. He stumbled along with William holding his upper arm. At the center of the clearing, William let go and backhanded Fergus. "I'm damn tired of your interference, ol' man."

Fergus stumbled, fell. He rolled to his side and looked up. "Bangster." He spit on the ground. "Ye feared to cut the rope around my hands so we can have a real donnybrooker." His brogue had gone thick, so thick I had to concentrate to understand him. "Yer nae a man; just a scared bangster."

William yanked Fergus back up. With a forefinger, he poked him in the chest. "I don't know what the fuck bangster means, but you best shut your trap, ol' man. I'm gonna whip your ass up one side an' down the other."

Fergus' beard twitched and I imagined the smirk on his lips. "Bangster means bully." He spoke slowly like William didn't have enough brains to comprehend words.

William swung wildly. Fergus ducked under the swing and head butted him in the gut. William stumbled, tripped, and fell.

Contempt dripped from Fergus' words as he glared down at the younger man. "Ye have this old man's hands tied and still ye cannae whip my ass."

Nick started toward Fergus.

"No!"

Nick halted and waited as William climbed slowly to his feet, rage written in every tense muscle. "I'm gonna fuckin' kill you."

Fergus ignored the threat and cocked his head at William. "Where are the other bangsters, Johnny Fadden, and Jimmy Donaldson?"

"Johnny ain't around no more," William sneered. "As for Jimmy...hey, Nick, bring Jimmy over here."

Nick walked over to the smaller of the tents and entered. Moments later he returned dragging a body by bound hands. He plopped Jimmy at Fergus' feet.

I wondered if the young man lived then he moaned.

"Ye are a good friend, I see. What did ye do to the laddie?"

"Fucked 'im. He's a pansy ass, so we just helped him live up to his...what do they call it, Nick?" William smiled as he glanced at Nick.

"Potential, Bill. We helped him live up to his potential."

Neither man had been paying attention to Fergus, but now I realized what he was doing. Hurriedly, I crouched against a tree and steadied the rifle.

Fast as a striking rattlesnake, Fergus lashed out at William with one foot, connected, then fell. He rolled to his knees and lunged up onto his feet.

William folded to the ground, clutching his crotch.

I fired high, not wanting to hit anyone accidentally. "Stop where you are!"

Nick tackled Fergus as William jerked to his feet. I raced toward the scene, yet it felt as if my feet dragged through molasses.

William reached behind himself.

"Hands on your head, William! Now!" I screamed.

Only a few more feet to cross then I'd be able to hit him with the rifle barrel.

Run or Die

His hand came around to the front of his body and the pistol came up.

I slid to a stop.

His pistol cracked a millisecond before I pulled the trigger. The rifle bucked against my shoulder then something hot and hard slammed my other shoulder and spun me around. Somehow, I clung to the rifle as I fell to my knees. I threw myself sideways as another shot shattered the night. Dirt flew up where I'd been seconds before.

I whirled to face the threat. Nick held the gun to Fergus' temple. "This is it, bitch!" He shouted in a wild voice. "This is it! You hear me?"

I glanced around until I located William on the ground and unmoving. "Throw it down, Nick. It's all over. I phoned Sheriff Daly. He'll be here any moment now."

"I'm getting out of here and gramps is going with me." He sidled toward the far side of the campfire.

I took a deep breath. One wrong move, one wrong word, and Nick would kill Fergus. "Come on, Nick, make it easier on yourself. We know William was the ringleader."

Nick shuffled closer to Jimmy's body. Backing away from me, he never saw the bloody hands until they grasped his ankle. Frantic, he shook his leg, but Jimmy had clamped on with a death grip. Panic flared across his face then the gun dipped and he shot.

Fergus jerked free, stumbled over the rocks around the campfire, fell, and rolled. Nick turned and his pistol swiveled toward Fergus, who was struggling to get to his feet.

I squeezed the trigger. The first shot hit Nick high, in a shoulder. He jerked, but didn't go down. The gun in his hand kept moving, kept seeking Fergus.

I squeezed the trigger of the rifle for a second time. The shot slammed Nick squarely in the chest. He had a moment to raise his eyes toward me before his body crumpled to the damp ground.

I raced across the campsite as I pulled my knife from my jeans' pocket. I slashed the rope from Fergus' wrists. As he crawled to his feet, the echo of sirens rolled over the hill. I dropped to my knees next to Ted.

Chapter 23

Sheriff Daly called in a cadaver dog from a civilian search and rescue group. They found Johnny's body in a ravine on Iron Mountain. In his hip pocket was a piece of a brown paper bag and a pen whose top had been chewed. On that scrap of paper he'd written about escaping, being lost on the mountain, and realizing he would die. At the end, he asked his parents to forgive him for failing them. The boy might've survived his injuries if it hadn't been so cold that night; or he might've survived the cold, if he hadn't been injured so badly.

I felt like I'd failed Johnny. If only I could've gotten him to go to Sheriff Daly right after we had talked...

The top of Jimmy's head had been blown away. Nick was dead before the EMTs arrived. William lived a few days before succumbing.

All six of the men who'd attacked and harassed Aretha and me were dead. Three by the hands of those who proclaimed friendship; two by my hands; and, one under the wheels of the truck Cynthia drove. I should have felt jubilant, or at least victorious.

I felt exhausted and sad. So sad.

***

I hobbled into the sterile hospital room on crutches, my sprained ankle having graduated to a cracked bone. Stan looked up with swollen, red-rimmed eyes and motioned me to the chair next to him. Machines hissed and beeped; tubes ran in and out of Ted's body. He looked so much like Miriam the last time that I'd seen her, beaten too badly to live.

After a while, Stan stood and motioned toward the door with a tilt of his head. Out in the hallway, he wiped the tears from his eyes and looked at me. "I'm having the machines removed tomorrow morning."

Tears burned my eyes. I turned my head away.

"Jaz." His quiet voice called my attention around. "It's not your fault."

My jaw muscle ticked. I swallowed to force the lump out of my throat, so I could give the man the respect of speaking to him. "If I hadn't let him and Cynthia..."

He laid a work-roughened hand on my forearm. "Look at me," he commanded.

I lifted my eyes to his.

"Give my son the respect he deserves, Jaz. He is a man; and, he made a man's decision. I'm proud of him."

"Pride won't bring him back," I choked out, the bitterness puckering my lips.

"No," he sighed. "Pride won't bring Ted back." He fell silent for a long moment. "Dying isn't the worst thing that can happen to a person, Jaz. I think you know that."

I pressed my mouth shut against the scream that wanted to burst out. *Why? Why did the good ones die?* "I'd...I'd like to be here."

Tears flooded Stan's eyes. He nodded. "Of course. There'll be a few of us here to say good-bye."

The next morning dawned with a bright golden light streaking across the horizon. The curtains in front of the hospital room's bank of windows had been drawn back. Ted's bed sat close to the windows, the head of it facing the sky outside as it transitioned from dove gray to azure.

Stan stood on one side holding Ted's right hand while Cynthia sat in a wheel chair on the other side, clutching Ted's left hand. Each person present walked forward, spoke softly to Ted and in some way touched him—a hand stroking his hair, lips against his forehead.

As the sun broke over tops of the buildings and streamed into the room, a beam bathed Ted. For a moment, it looked like a halo wrapped around him. At that instant, Dr. Roy Ingersol shut off the machines. A tear coursed down his face.

Ted's last breath soughed from him.

Chapter 24

Spring crept onto the land, shy as a girl on her first date. I stapled the insulation to the back wall and wiped sweat from my forehead against my shoulder. A glance at the sun through the salvaged window had my stomach rumbling. Lunch time. I laid the staple gun on the floor and headed outside.

After pouring a cup of warm coffee from the pot on the campfire embers, I settled on the alder round that had been my makeshift chair for so many months. A Red-tailed Hawk soared overhead.

The sound of a truck engine topping the rise pulled my eyes to earth. I watched as it slipped and slid along the muddy tracks. When it reached the parking area next to the cabin, I wondered why Fergus had come.

Instead of him, Cynthia stepped from the truck. Faded jeans, a baggy tee shirt, and work boots couldn't hide the young woman's natural beauty. She moved with slow, deliberate steps toward me and I mourned the loss of the chattering, bouncy girl she'd been.

She reached the fire pit and eased onto the log across from me. "Hey, Jaz."

"Hey. Coffee? I can get another cup from the house."

A slight shake of her head answered me. She peered around, like she'd never been here before. "It's so beautiful. I almost forgot."

I shifted on the log round. "Haven't seen you around. Where've you been?"

"Granddad thought I needed to get away for a few weeks after...after Ted's funeral."

"Go someplace nice?"

"Up to the redwoods. Got a room at a bed and breakfast in Crescent City."

"Sounds nice." I tilted my head. "Why did you come, Cynthia? I can see something's on your mind."

She locked her gaze on mine. "Granddad wants to move."

Carefully, I set my cup on the ground next to my foot. "I can see why he might want to do that."

"He doesn't want me to have to put up with people staring at me and...and whispering."

I crossed my legs and linked my hands over my knee. "He loves you, Cynthia."

"He feels guilty that he couldn't...protect me." She lowered her gaze and picked at the hem of her shirt. "But, we can't run away from what happened, Jaz." She lifted her eyes and met mine. "It'll always be right there, right with us."

"Sometimes," I chose each word carefully. "Sometimes, leaving can be good. It can give us a little bit of distance and time...to get things clear in our own heads. It's not running away to do that."

She worried at her lower lip with her teeth.

"That's how I wound up down here, you know?"

"You never told us why you came here."

"Actually, it was Aretha's mom's idea. Grandma Pearl thought I might heal better if I had some time away from where everything reminded me, day after day, about what I'd lost."

She chewed her lower lip. "I...I think this might be a little different."

"How's that?"

"It'd be like letting Sam and Nick and William win. This is our home. Granddad loves the farm, and so do I. After Mom and Dad died, Granddad came and got me from L.A. I was fifteen." She bent her head back and peered up at the sky. I wondered if she tracked the hawk soaring overhead. "I'm not running, Jaz."

"People will talk for a long time, you do know that, right?" I reached down and retrieved my cold coffee.

She dropped her head down and slanted a glance up at me from beneath her long hair. "Maybe it's good for them to talk, to remember what those men did, to remember that hate can kill." She cocked her head. "It's not like we don't have friends here. And I want to see Ms. Winters' new restaurant open up."

"Remember, Cynthia, you're asking your grandfather to live with the whispering, too."

A smile slowly bloomed across her face. "I think Granddad wants to stay and make everyone who didn't help face him every time we come to town."

"Yeah, but sometimes there are things that are harder for men to handle."

Her smile faded. "Rape. It's better to give it a name, Jaz. The therapist says it takes away the power of the act if we can name it and understand that rape is simply another form of violent assault."

"Yeah, you're right. But what about the rape? It's one thing to know you killed Sam in self-defense and live with that, but rape can be...difficult to...get past."

"Voice of experience?" Her eyes held a world of memories she never should have had.

I nodded. "One of my mother's johns. He kicked in the door when my mom wasn't home."

"I'm sorry."

"Me, too. I never told my mother, but I still hated her for it, for a long time."

"Do you still hate her?"

"No. Not anymore."

***

Aretha returned to the farm a week after Cynthia's visit. Neither one of us mentioned her absence.

The man with the goats, Big Al, pulled in one day, hauling a trailer. Inside two, full-grown Nubian nannies with kids and a mature billy verbalized their displeasure with the trailer. Their long ears flipped back and forth when they shook their heads. He offloaded them then bartered with Aretha for some of her salves and potions.

All summer we poured sweat into the land. Sometimes Fergus or Stan would stop by and lend a day's labor. Cynthia came by now and then, chatted with me and learned about herbs from Aretha.

Sheriff Abe Daly was a constant. Every Saturday he arrived and he didn't leave until Monday morning. Late August I finally

Run or Die

heard Aretha laugh again. I don't know what Abe said, but in my heart I blessed him for saying it.

In September we all gathered for a celebratory dinner at Ms. Winters' new place, The Rainbow Walker's Restaurant.

By late fall, we had completed the cabin, the goat house, and the chicken house; and canned food from Aretha's bountiful garden.

For the first time since Alicia died, no nightmares haunted me around Thanksgiving. The week after Thanksgiving charcoal gray skies dumped half a foot of snow on us.

I stayed on through that winter and helped with spring planting. As May raced into June, I packed my belongings in the saddlebags on my bike and strapped the duffle bag to the sissy bar. The lids of the hard-sided saddlebags barely closed, I had stuffed so much in there.

In addition to my few possessions, Aretha insisted that I take a number of herbal concoctions, poultices and remedies for everything from the common cold to skin rashes. In that moment, she reminded me poignantly of Alicia. My heart lurched, but the sadness morphed into a bittersweet memory.

That sunny, hot June day I leaned my head back and gazed up at the azure sky. A pair of Red-tailed Hawks floated lazily above us, dipping and circling. The day I had arrived on Aretha's farm, a Red-tailed soared above this valley. I wondered if one of those now soaring in the clear sky was the one I'd seen those many months ago. I liked to imagine that one of them was.

Aretha's young hens and the inexperienced Rhode Island Red rooster squawked and flapped, racing this way and that way around the protected chicken yard. The hawks circled a while longer then wove spinning ovals as they drifted further and further away.

"You don't have to leave, you know," Aretha said for the hundredth time.

With a gentle smile, I dropped my head so I could look into her dark eyes. "Yes, I do. I have to get an education like I promised Alicia. Then I have to make something of my life, so Mom's and Miriam's lives are honored."

"Is that what you want as well?"

My smile split into a wide grin. "Yes. Yes, it is."

"You could attend Mendocino College in Ukiah, and I know for a fact that Folami would give you a job and rent you a room in her house. You know she's always asking about you." She raised her eyebrows.

I threw my head back and laughed. "I can see us now, Ms. Winters and me butting heads."

Aretha chuckled. "Well, when you put it that way..." We both turned and looked down the hill. The doe had two spotted fawns at her side. The yearlings from the previous summer jumped and played in the sunshine while the buck grazed, periodically raising his antlered head to gaze around majestically.

"That new restaurant is even better than the old one. Ms. Winters was right. She needed to change." In a soft voice, I added, "And, so do I."

When she turned to face me, I went on. "I miss the mountains of the Pacific Northwest, Aretha. I even miss Seattle's rainy days. Never thought I'd say that. Sylvia said my job on her house painting crew is open."

"House painting is only a stepping stone?" She tilted her head and studied me.

I nodded a confirmation. "Yeah, I've finally allowed myself to dream again, and I have to try to follow where those dreams lead."

She wrapped her arms around me, hugged me close, and whispered in my ear. "Remember, you know your way home now." She pulled away and put her hands on my shoulders. When I met her eyes, she said, "There will always be a place here for you, Jaz, for as long as I live."

"Thanks." I swallowed and blinked hard. "Tell Abe I said to take good care of you."

She smiled. Contentment shone on her face. "He's going to miss you."

I tried to laugh, but the sound faltered to silence. "He really helped me. Pointed me in the right direction."

She let go and stepped back. "I'm not so sure criminology is the safest profession."

Run or Die

"Told you I intend to be a private detective. No running gun battles for me." I hiked a leg over the V-Strom, twisted the key, and pressed the start button. The bike roared to life. "Besides, life isn't a safe proposition."

She chuckled.

I revved the engine and cruised up the hill, afraid to look back, afraid I would turn back.

Epilogue

The envelope crackled in my hand. I laid it on the kitchen table, poured a cup of coffee, and carried it to the north-facing window. I sipped the black brew, remembering how Aretha had finally given in and bought coffee.

White Horse Mountain glistened under a fresh quilt of new-fallen snow.

The dark hoods of Oregon Juncos and the yellow wing bars of Pine Siskins swirled down from the naked branches of the plum tree, settling on the cedar wood feeders. A pair of Northern Flickers glided into the hanging suet, scattering a six-pack of Stellar Jays who had been arguing over the greasy cakes. A doe and her previous spring's fawn unconcernedly pawed at the snowy grass down near the creek bank.

A year earlier, Dawn Samira, an investigative reporter and my then-girlfriend, had shuffled from my living room and poured herself a cup of strong coffee. I'd stood at this very window. She had set her cup on the old wooden pedestal table I'd found at Value Village for fifteen dollars and spent two months refinishing. It reminded me of Aretha's Grandma's table. Its silken dark oak top shined in the light of the hanging chandelier.

"You never said what Aretha wrote about." Dawn nodded at the crumpled envelope clutched in my hand as she slid onto one of the kitchen chairs.

I swallowed hard. "She has cancer."

"That's not always a death warrant nowadays," she said quietly.

"Apparently, she's had it for some time. They've tried everything." The lump in my throat choked me.

"Aretha's an herb doctor, isn't she?"

I nodded.

"I recently wrote an article about an herb doctor and spiritual woman who lives outside of Mount Vernon. She's had some success with cancer victims."

I whirled on her. "What does she do, kill a chicken on the night of a full moon and dance naked under the stars?" I snarled. "Aretha doesn't need a quack taking her money."

"Mrs. Greene is far from a quack. Why don't you give the information I have to Aretha and let her decide?" Dawn's voice remained calm.

Against my better judgment, I sent the information to Abe. He flew up with Aretha the following weekend. Aretha lived with Mrs. Greene for six months. Abe Daly took a leave of absence from his job and stayed at my place, unwilling to return home without his wife.

The cancer, inexplicably, went into remission. Abe and Aretha flew home.

Now, a year later, I had received another letter. E-mails were more our style, hers pounded out on the sheriff's office computer while she waited for him. Or phone calls. She'd drive up to Buzzard Peak where at least three bars lit up on her cell phone. I hated letters. Seemed like they always carried heavy news.

I pulled the single sheet of paper from the envelope and re-read the scrawled lines.

"Dear Jaz,
We wanted you to be one of the first to know. In approximately six months, you will become Auntie Jaz.
Love,
Abe and Aretha."

A warm breeze blew from the past and kissed my face. Once again I heard the scree of the Red-tailed Hawk, and saw it hanging effortlessly between earth and sky.

Run or Die

I opened my eyes and gazed out of the window, across the acres I had reclaimed from beneath the invasive European blackberries, reclaimed inch by painful inch. The neglected, overgrazed farm had been transformed into a wildlife and wild bird habitat.

Clouds scudded across the deepening gray canvas of the sky. The hazy disc of the sun slipped behind the mountains. A late season snow drifted down. Small flakes danced in the light breeze, melting as soon as they touched the earth. My eyes filled with tears. I blinked to clear my vision then stepped over to the kitchen counter and picked up the landline phone.

It rang twice. When she picked it up, I said, "Dawn, I know I haven't been in touch for a while, but I just had to tell you..."

THE END

Old Woman Gone

Prologue

The back door stood open. Slanted rays of sunshine ducked beneath the porch roof, tumbled through the doorway, and spilled across the slightly warped kitchen floor. The dark floorboards shone in the soft light. The house had been old when her husband brought her home to it all those years ago. Now he was gone, but the house still whispered of his love.

Merlie Greene stood right inside the doorway, enjoying the warmth of the early March morning. A gentle breeze wafted the faint, sweet smell of sage from the silvery green bushes guarding the four steps from the porch to the white rock of the garden path. To the left side of the path grew salmonberry bushes. The peeling, papery bark of their brown trunks could be easily seen in the leafless thicket.

She sighed and turned away. Time to go upstairs to her bedroom closet and get her purse. The steps creaked as they were apt to do in older homes and the sound brought another smile to her face. The creaks were like brief conversation from a longtime friend.

A quick check confirmed the presence of her wallet inside her purse. She scooped her key ring from an abalone shell on her dresser then ran a finger lightly along its rounded rim. George gave her that shell. A gift from Water. How well he'd understood her connection to Mother Earth, and the Elements.

What in the world is wrong with me lately? Not one to dwell in the past, the past seemed determined to haunt her for the last few weeks. Dreams stalked her—dreams in which she ran and ran, hearing the calls of the children and never able to reach them. Never before had the anniversary of Chelsea's death drawn her into the past. *The end of this month, March 30th, my sweet girl will have been gone fifteen years. Let my sorrow at her loss be what's happening, Sweet Mother. I don't think I can stand to lose any of my other girls.* Shaking the thoughts from her mind, she went downstairs to wait for Nita and Dawn to arrive.

Run or Die

She placed her handbag in the center of the plank kitchen table, dropped her key ring beside, it then immediately walked over to the cook stove and checked that all the burners were safely turned off. Done, she returned to the doorway and her perusal of the garden.

Not long after, a whisper of cloth sounded behind her. She grinned. Nita, obviously trying to sneak up on her again to convince her to lock her doors even when she was home. *Why does that child persist in thinking age compromises my hearing?*

While her years weighted her steps, Goddess had blessed Merlie with perfect eyesight and acute hearing. She started to turn, a good-humored teasing on her lips. As she shuffled around to face Nita, black hood-covered heads popped into view right behind her. The breath she gasped in caught like a fishbone in her throat, choking back the scream that tried to escape.

She spun around and lurched for the open back door. Her hand touched the screen door as a black-gloved hand clamped on her upper arm and yanked her backward. She stumbled and fell to her knees.

The hand that was clamped on her arm tightened until she thought the man it was attached to would snap the bone. He dragged her to her feet. Jerking her around, her back pinned to his chest, he clamped a hand on either upper arm. The big hands lifted her off her feet. Feet freed, she kicked fast and furious. She felt her soft leather shoes connect with her assailant's legs, but the monster didn't even grunt.

She sucked in a lung-bursting breath then shoved it out in an ear-piercing scream. The stink of dirty leather filled her nostrils as a hand clamped across her mouth, cutting off her scream. Her teeth cut the inside of her lip. The metallic taste of blood flooded her mouth. Her jaw throbbed from the pressure.

Abruptly, her body went limp. The sudden change caught the monster unprepared and his grip slipped. She sank to the floor in an untidy heap at his feet.

He bent over at the waist and reached for her. Grasping her upper arms once again, he hauled her to her feet. With the positions of their bodies slightly changed, she waited until she heard his breathing directly behind her head, close, very close to her ears. She slammed her head backward, felt the impact, the satisfying crunch of cartilage.

The big hands released her so quickly she stumbled. A muffled, "Fuck!" came from behind the cloth mask.

The anger in that one word spurred her as she whirled and darted for the hallway, the blood thundering in her ears. She dodged past the startled second masked man. Breath ragged from fear, she bolted down the hallway. For the first time in her memory, she inwardly cursed her age, the slowness of her run.

A couple of feet from the front door, she reached for the door knob. Her fingers touched the cool brass of the original knob. A flash of hope burned through her as she twisted and yanked. Sunlight streamed in through the narrow portal between door and doorjamb.

Something smashed into the center of her back. Hand jerked loose from the door knob, she flew to the side and forward. The door crashed shut. Panicked, she threw her hands out. Her wrist snapped back. Hot pain shot up her arm. Her cheek cracked against the now-closed door. More pain, this time engulfing her face. Barely staying upright, her fingernails scrabbled against the polished wood.

A hand grabbed a clump of her moderately short, black hair, digging into the soft, tight curls. She flopped like a rag doll. The big hand pulled her head back then slammed it forward. Her forehead bounced against the door. All thought shattered.

Her legs gave way. The grip on her hair released. She slid to the floor. Cheek against the soothing coolness of the gleaming old planks, waves of black washed over her.

The sound of male voices echoed through a tunnel. A rough hand flipped her onto her back. The dull smack of her hand banging into the floor felt disconnected from the rest of her.

A finger peeled back her eyelid. Before the welcoming blackness claimed her, she heard one of her captors say, "She'll live. Long as she's alive, that's all he cares about." Encroaching darkness muffled the harsh laughter.

Made in the USA
San Bernardino, CA
29 September 2014